Ex-National Hunt Champion Jockey John Francome is a broadcaster on racing for Channel 4 and is fast establishing himself as one of the front runners in the racing thriller stakes. He lives in Lambourn, Berkshire.

His previous bestsellers have all been highly praised:

'Francome can spin a darn good yarn'   *Racing Post*

'Thrills, twists and turns on and off the racecourse. Convincing and beguiling'   *Irish Independent*

'Move over Dick Francis, here's competition'
                                    Me magazine

'A thoroughly convincing and entertaining tale'
                                    Daily Mail

'The racing feel is authentic and it's a pacy, entertaining read'   *Evening Standard*

'Irresistibly reminiscent of the master . . . a most readable yarn'   *Mail on Sunday*

'Thrills to the final furlong . . . Francome knows how to write a good racing thriller'   *Daily Express*

'Pacy racing and racy pacing . . . Francome has found his stride as a solo novelist'   *Horse and Hound*

'Mr Francome adeptly teases to the very end and cleverly keeps a few twists up his sleeve until the closing chapters'   *Country Life*

Also by John Francome

High Flyer
False Start
Dead Ringer
Break Neck
Outsider
Rough Ride
Stud Poker
Stone Cold

Also by John Francome and James McGregor

Eavesdropper
Riding High
Declared Dead
Blood Stock

Safe Bet

John Francome

HEADLINE

First published in 1998
by HEADLINE BOOK PUBLISHING

First published in paperback in 1999
by HEADLINE BOOK PUBLISHING

10 9 8 7 6 5 4

ISBN 0 7472 5926 7

Typeset by
Letterpart Limited, Reigate, Surrey

Printed and bound in Great Britain by
Caledonian International Book Manufacturing Ltd, Glasgow

HEADLINE BOOK PUBLISHING
A division of Hodder Headline PLC
338 Euston Road
London NW1 3BH

Safe Bet

Chapter One

January – West Virginia

'Where have you been?' There was hurt and resentment in Dianne Clayton's voice.

George Parker didn't look at her. He walked across the big kitchen where she sat at the table, surrounded by papers and dictionaries; she'd been working on her lap-top, writing her so-called novel, like she always did when she was unhappy. He hung his coat on the back door while he decided how to reply.

That evening he hadn't been anywhere or done anything that he shouldn't have, and he was angry at the note of accusation in her voice. But he was careful not to utter the first, antagonistic words that leaped into his head.

Dianne may have become obsessively jealous of every moment he spent out of her sight, but she was also very rich.

After her father had died two years before, leaving her the mansion, two mines and an enormous estate, Dianne had become the wealthiest woman in the small mountain town of Orange Creek. It had been inevitable that when George heard of her fortune he'd looked her up and moved in. Since then, whenever he'd wanted money, she'd given it to him – until the last month or so, when the handouts had become fewer, and smaller. 'I'm doing it for your own good, George, for your own self-esteem,' she'd said earnestly. 'You need to get a job.'

Well, he'd gone out and got a job all right. He'd made money – and spent it all in New York.

The problem was that, like most of the money he'd ever made, he'd broken the law to get it, and left somebody a whole lot poorer for having met him. Any day now there'd be someone looking for him here. He was going to have to leave Orange Creek for a while, and to do that he needed one last, large loan from Dianne.

He turned to her with an innocent expression on his handsome, boyish face. 'Honey, take it easy, okay? I've just been playing pool with some of the guys.'

He walked over to her, bent down and kissed her lightly on the lips.

'George, you never play pool.'

He straightened up. 'Well, I did tonight – and I won! Ask Jimmy.'

'You must have cheated.'

'Oh, Dianne, lighten up,' he said, disappointment in his voice. He gave her his best crooked, hurt smile and walked from the kitchen. He went upstairs to the top floor of the big, clapboard mansion, to a room he'd made his own – a den where he could be private. Closing the door, he took a deep breath and shut his eyes. He was going to have to be very patient and cautious with Dianne.

George Parker had been a chancer all his thirty-five years. He'd been bright enough to shine at Orange Creek High, even got himself to college and the beginnings of a mining degree.

But he had suffered from the double handicap of being too good-looking, and having just too much charm. For most of his adult life, he'd coasted by on the bare minimum of input. He'd gone out and remorselessly cheated people he had made his friends with such consistent ease it had become a big game to him.

But his latest effort had unintentionally left an old friend penniless with a wife and five kids to raise. It was only a matter of time before that man came looking for him, and George was very sure he didn't want to be there to give any answers. In a list of fifty adjectives describing George Parker, the word 'brave' would not have figured.

With the exception of half a dozen cities where he still owed large sums of money and where his reappearance would arouse violent resentment, he could go anywhere.

Thoughtfully, he walked over to the empty fireplace, took a cigar from a box on the mantelshelf and lit it. From among a pile of old newspapers, he pulled out a copy of *Hello!* magazine which he'd been reading on the plane back from New York two days before. He opened it and gazed for the twentieth time at a photograph on an inner page, nodding with a contented smile.

England.

Nobody would come looking for him there, and he guessed he could lie low and have a very good time in

3

London. Especially as it looked like he'd found himself another little gold-mine to live off.

January – Lexington, Kentucky

'It's crazy! The biggest thing to happen in a horse's life, and it's all over in a couple of minutes.' Bill Corbin's southern drawl blended with the Blue Grass twang all around him in the bar at the Keeneland sale pavilion. There was bitterness fuelled by alcohol in his voice. 'It just ain't fair. That smug bastard in there . . .' Bill nodded towards the ring and the sharp-suited auctioneer hammering through the assortment of lots the winter sale attracted. 'He doesn't give a cuss if the animal he's selling is some poor guy's life's work.' He turned to his right, seeking confirmation from the man standing at the bar beside him.

A slim, fit five foot nine, with the kind of good looks that always prompted a second glance, Mike Powell was in his mid-thirties – a well-known British jockey, who had become more famous still for his eventful 'private' life.

Harebell blue eyes flickered beneath his dark, wavy hair. 'Which poor guy?' Mike grinned artlessly at Bill Corbin. 'Not you, that's for sure. You told me you only bought the animal a couple of months ago. But you're right . . .' He became notably more anxious as he glanced at his watch. His own colt was due to be sold in about twenty minutes. 'You've got to send 'em in groomed like a bride and hope the punters think they're looking at a classic horse – not a total no-hoper. The slightest thing – any rumour that makes them think the horse isn't perfect, even if it's total rubbish – will make them sit on their hands.'

Bill Corbin nodded and Mike laughed sourly. He'd already convinced himself the punters' arms would be paralysed for his lot. 'Two minutes, that's all you've got, and when you come out, you've either had it away in some order or you've done your bollocks.' He glanced at the little man beside him whose animal, Mike guessed, had just cost its owner, if not both testicles, at least the best part of the pair.

Mike had consigned a colt he'd bought cheap the year before. He surveyed the crowd, all of whom looked as if they ate fifty-dollar bills for breakfast, and wondered how he'd let things get to a point where he could only afford horses at the lower end of the market. Cheap horses meant thin margins, unless you were very lucky, and for a while now, Mike hadn't been.

'You've got a good eye,' someone had once said, when he'd been moaning about his finances. 'You should try your hand at pinhooking.'

He'd heard the stories: the men who'd bought backward foals for a couple of thousand quid, kept them for a year, taken them to Tattersall's and watched them make fifty, sixty, even a hundred thousand.

Of course Mike had a good eye. He'd pinhooked two beautiful, under-rated foals the first season he'd tried and cleared a profit of seventy thousand, but hadn't worked out how to keep it. Now the taxman was asking for his cut and nothing else had gone right in his bloodstock dealing since. He'd got stuck with a half share in an American colt which he'd persuaded his best friend Jed Havard to buy with him two years before. It was currently being boarded less than twenty miles from Lexington but he hadn't been to see it since he'd bought it, and didn't want to go now in case he was asked to pay what he owed for its keep. For the last few months he'd even managed to avoid talking about it to Jed even though, until recently, they had been brothers-in-law.

The animal Mike had sent to this January sale in Keeneland was presentable but not outstanding. Its full brother had run a promising second first time out and looked as if it would go on to add substantial value to its siblings, but shortly afterwards it had broken a leg in training and the insurance money had been paid out before it had a chance to confirm its early form and influence its brother's standing.

Mike's colt was well bred, by a good American sire, and despite the disaster with the brother it had grown well. He had been optimistic about a result in the previous October Yearling Sales at Tattersall's in Newmarket, until the animal had thrown a splint a few weeks before. It was then that he had decided to send the colt to America and sell it at the first sale of the year.

The colt had left England looking like a hundred-thousand-dollar yearling, but the flight from Luton and the eighteen-hour road trip down from quarantine in Newburgh, New York, had drained it. It had sweated forty pounds and arrived in Kentucky hat-rack thin, with a coat as flat as a game-keeper's moleskins.

Five minutes before his colt was due in the ring, Mike

Powell slipped away from Bill Corbin and went in to sit on his own. He was a few yards to the left of the auctioneer's rostrum, but couldn't listen to the fast-paced monologue which filled the fevered air as a nervous dark bay covered the sandy circle in long, athletic strides and the figure on the electronic display passed the million-dollar mark.

He barely registered the price or the applause which greeted the unexpected final bid for the colt, now being led from the ring.

Mike's was the next lot, and the odds were already stacked against him.

He'd paid £15,000 for the colt, and since missing his slot at Tattersall's in the autumn had had to bear the cost of keeping it for another four months as well as the £3,000 charge for shipping it to Kentucky. It was a risky strategy, though its sire was more popular in the States than in Europe. But Mike hadn't allowed for the young animal's reaction to travel. Usually, he paid Ev Thomas, a long-time friend from Brecknock, to travel with the horses. Ev was an old hand at reassuring a nervous horse, and would fly the whole journey in the cargo hold with his charges if he had to. This time, Mike had cut corners to conserve his dwindling funds, and had let the shippers handle it.

In three minutes' time, the market would decide whether he'd been clever and bold, or foolish and greedy.

Mike glanced nervously at the man on the rostrum clutching the gavel and did his best to disguise his misgivings. If the auctioneer saw Mike's doubts, he wouldn't waste his own time trying to coax nods from reluctant bidders.

Lot number 263 – the unnamed, unraced two-year-old

chestnut colt by Zilzal – was led through the gleaming double doors into the ring. Feeling weak and breathless, Mike lowered his head and bit hard into the skin around his right forefinger while the auctioneer delivered a seamless eulogy on the breeding, connections and potential of the animal in front of him.

The colt, confused by its journey in a metal box from Luton Airport, hours spent rattling in a transporter and the lights and bustle of the sales, spooked at everything that moved in the crowded circle of seats around him.

He sweated up and broke into an awkward trot, tugging his head away from the gnarled old sales groom who was leading him round.

Mike peered through his fingers and felt his stomach knot up. The colt could look great when it was relaxed and happy; now it looked mean-minded, out of condition and tricky to train. A good buyer might have seen through the horse's nervousness, but once doubt had been cast, only bargain hunters with thick skins and thin wallets would risk looking foolish.

The man on the rostrum paused and swept the ring of faces with his eyes to gauge the mood of the audience.

'All right, ladies and gentlemen, the Zilzal colt with a full brother who looked very impressive first time out in England last year. Where do we start him? Fifty thousand dollars? Who'll bid me fifty thousand dollars?'

The request, so reasonably and confidently made in his soft, southern drawl, was met by rows of blank, unmoving, uninterested faces. Mike lifted his head and gazed around the room and the fist which seemed to be squeezing his guts tightened, and took possession of his lungs as well.

'Come on, gentlemen. We all know we'll be way past this in just a few moments. Let's not waste time. I'll take forty thousand to get us started.'

Mike glanced at the auctioneer and detected on his face an almost invisible spasm of annoyance that he should have been expected to get good money for the gangling, skinny chestnut, twitching round the ring below him.

But the man tried. Mike half heard him through the buzzing in his head and the mist that was gathering in front of his eyes.

The auctioneer used all his powers of persuasion to cajole his audience into an opening bid of ten thousand dollars. Sourly, he accepted a bid for five and, with increasing animosity towards the colt in the ring rather than the reluctant bidders, squeezed the price up in increments of a few hundred dollars. By the time the bidding had reached ten thousand, he knew he wouldn't get further without a struggle and the risk of slowing the momentum of the whole sale. Decisively, he looked around, glanced at his spotters, and knocked Mike's colt down for ten thousand dollars.

'Hell!' the man beside Mike muttered to his other neighbour. 'I wouldn't have given ten thousand dollars for a scrawny little thing like that. He ain't worth a thousand.'

Mike felt himself redden, and turned his head away. After the auctioneers' commission, he would get eight and a half; the colt would have made him a loss of £20,000.

A wave of nausea washed through him, triggered by a deep sense of fear. It was twenty-five years since he'd last experienced anything like it, but the memory came back so clearly, it felt as though it had happened yesterday. He had been ten years old and had just let the family's only tractor roll into the winter-swollen River Wye in Mid-Wales. He'd watched the roaring white water close over it while he trembled at the certain prospect of the vicious thrashing his father would give him. He'd walked home, half a mile, with every muscle quivering, feeling like a disembodied spirit.

Now, absorbing the implications of the huge loss he'd just made and the knock-on consequences for what seemed to be a bottomless pit of debt into which he had sunk, he felt the same overwhelming fear and for a moment wished himself dead.

As with the tractor, there was nobody else to blame. All the decisions had been his, and the consequences of his own lack of judgement stared him in the face.

He left his seat and blundered through the crowds by the door, out into the crisp Kentucky evening air, gasping deep draughts of it to calm his nervous shaking and quell the regrets threatening to choke him.

The wrong sale, he told himself bitterly; the wrong place; the wrong bloody horse. And he'd lavished all that money on it!

He wished he'd shot it.

Two days before Mike's Zilzal colt walked into the ring at Keeneland, Jed Havard arrived in the States.

He shuffled along with the queue for US immigration at JFK, grateful for the small relief this brought to his damaged joints. He'd mangled an ankle at Uttoxeter and smashed a hip at Wincanton in his final year as a professional jockey. Both injuries, though dealt with as competently as medical science allowed, were with him for good. They bothered him most when locked in the same position for endless hours in an airline seat.

In his hand Jed clutched a black UK passport which certified that he was Jeremy Hopton Havard, born Kington, Herefordshire, on 21 June 1960.

The photograph, taken hastily in a slot-machine booth six years before, showed an even-featured and open, smiling face, with wide, dark brown eyes and untidy brown hair.

The queue moved forward a few paces; Jed kicked his soft sports bag along the floor in front of him. He was tall to have been a jockey, nearly five ten, and had put on very few extra pounds since he'd handed his licence back to Portman Square at the end of the previous season. Since then, doing two jobs as well as worrying about his wife Sammy's health hadn't given him much of an opportunity to fatten up.

He looked at the line of people in front of him. Most of them had been on his flight from Heathrow. He guessed he had at least another ten minutes before he reached the bored, overweight immigration official. He bent down, unzipped his bag, pulled out a fat sale catalogue and leafed through its pages, pausing at the ones he had already dog-eared and scribbled on.

It was his first visit to the Keeneland Bloodstock Sales in Lexington, Kentucky. This early sale was a more workaday event than the glamorous July Yearling Sale, but it was here that a good potential brood mare might be found among the fillies and mares still in training. If Jed had been buying just on his own account, Keeneland wouldn't have entered into his calculations, but a small consortium of racehorse-owning businessmen had promised to look seriously at anything he brought back, and he'd been encouraged to cast his net wide.

Once he had been formally admitted to the United States, Jed made his way to the domestic terminal and a shorter flight, via Allegheny Airlines, to Blue Grass Field, Lexington, Kentucky.

There was a distinctly racing flavour to the passengers on this flight; half of them had a racing paper or breeding glossy on their laps. Jed nodded at the few people he knew, and wondered how much competition there would be from the breeders and bloodstock agents he recognised.

'Excuse me – I hope you don't mind my asking, but aren't you Jed Havard?'

Jed had nodded 'hello' to the woman in the window seat beside him; he had noted, in a purely reflex way, that she was young and pretty, and for no particular reason had assumed she was American. If her accent hadn't corrected that assumption, her apologetic English manner would have done so.

'I don't mind your asking, and yes, I'm Jed Havard.'

The girl's eyes shone. 'I knew you were! I won my first bet on you at Worcester when I was still at school.'

'Can't have been long ago.' It was meant as a compliment but not taken as one.

She looked hurt. 'It was six years ago, actually,' she said.

'I've done three years at Durham since then, and another three in PR.' As if this made her a woman of the world.

Jed smiled to make up for the offence caused. 'So what's taking you to Kentucky?'

'I'm covering the Keeneland sales for *BBM*,' she said, sounding pleased with herself.

Jed was impressed, then sceptical. *Bloodstock Breeder's Monthly* wouldn't send a rookie, even to a comparatively unimportant sale like this. 'What? On your own?'

He got the wounded expression again. 'Yes. Why not? I've been breeding horses since I was eight. We put my old 11.2 out one summer on Birtsmorton Common, on the Malverns; she got covered by mistake by one of the stallions and came back in foal.'

'Very well planned.' Jed grinned ironically.

'She dropped a lovely filly foal who turned into a Section B champion and foaled three more winners herself after that.'

'But you don't breed Welsh ponies for quite the same characteristics as thoroughbreds.'

This time the look she gave him was withering. 'My illusions about you are fast being shattered. Just because I'm a) young, and b) female does *not* mean I know nothing about horses. If it helps, I can tell you that my father bred Bazooka and Ariadne.'

Two Classic winners. That meant her father was Geoffrey Thynne, who had also bred Jed's best brood mare, Utopian Dream.

Embarrassed by the new edge this knowledge gave to their conversation, Jed looked at her more closely. 'Oh,' he said remorsefully. 'We've met before then. You're Lucy, aren't you? I don't want to upset you again, but you've changed quite a bit since I last saw you.'

'I was only twelve.' Her eyes sparkled flirtatiously.

'Yes.' And if anyone had suggested to Jed at the time that that chubby, snub-nosed little girl with freckles and ginger hair scraped back under an Alice band was going to grow up into what he now appreciated to be this lovely, leggy, green-eyed creature, he'd happily have offered them very long odds.

But, as he always did on the few occasions when an attractive woman was letting him know she was available, Jed tried subtly to make it plain that he wasn't interested.

He loved his wife deeply and, even though they hadn't made love since she'd become ill nearly a year before, he was sure he would never be unfaithful to her. He had pleaded with Sammy for months now to see her doctor, but she hadn't wanted to confront the problem, terrified of what she might be told, or – Jed reluctantly admitted to himself – of being told that it was all in her imagination.

Recently, though, the pain had appeared so acute, he'd persuaded her to go for tests at their local hospital, so they would soon know, one way or the other, what they were dealing with.

In the meantime, with Lucy Thynne beside him, in a plane on the other side of the Atlantic, Jed knew he would have to be resolute. But that was no reason not to be friendly.

'Didn't you ride in a few races yourself?' he asked, handily remembering that he'd read about her winning a couple of high-profile amateur races.

'Yes,' she said with a pleased, self-conscious grin. 'I was very lucky.'

'I distinctly remember whenever I told anyone I'd been lucky to win, I almost always thought just the opposite! I'm very glad I never had to ride against you, though I suppose we're rivals now. I've been asked to cover the sales, too – for the *Racing Record*.'

'I'd seen you were doing a bit of writing now. You're better at it than most jockeys,' she conceded, 'though that's not saying much.'

'Well, thanks. Now, as I'm stuck with you for the next hour or so, maybe you can tell me what you think of some of these mares and fillies for sale?'

It was the right suggestion and when they landed in Lexington, Jed was genuinely grateful for her views.

'Thanks a lot,' he said as he left her to wait for her luggage. 'See you round the sales.' To himself, he vowed he wouldn't make any move to encourage Lucy. He'd enjoyed her company, but hoped he wouldn't run into her again.

Out in the arrivals hall of the small terminal, he caught sight of a few more faces he knew. It wasn't such a coincidence, given the large number of Europeans who travelled over for the sales. Although the high rollers came in their own jets, almost everyone passed through this building.

But one face did surprise Jed. He hadn't expected to see Mike Powell.

Mike was one of Jed's oldest friends in racing and until a few weeks before, when they'd finally divorced, had been married to Sammy's sister, Tessa Langton. Jed had last seen him at Kempton on Boxing Day, when Mike had finished second in the King George VI Chase. They'd talked for a few minutes about the Kentucky sales. Mike had said then he had no intention of flying over for a comparatively unimportant sale, and, at that stage, Jed wasn't planning to go, either; he'd only decided to at the last minute, two days before.

Typical Mike, Jed thought, always unpredictable. For one thing, at the height of the season, a jump-jockey who wanted to go out with a bang in his final year, as Mike had publicly announced he intended to, should have been back in England, clocking up the winners. But Jed wasn't as up-to-date as he should have been, and it was possible – likely, even – that Mike had a suspension to get through. If that was the case, perhaps it wasn't so surprising to see him here. Jed knew Mike had been pinhooking foals in recent years to supplement his dwindling income and reduce his dependence on his much richer wife; and Keeneland, out of sight of prying English eyes, was a good place to do it.

Mike was fifty yards from Jed across the crowded concourse. He jostled his way through until he guessed he was within hailing distance, then dropped his bag and waved his arm. 'Hi, Mike,' he called.

Mike didn't react at once. He glanced around a few seconds later, saw Jed, but let his eyes pass right on by. The next moment he had turned back to be greeted by a woman Jed had never seen before. Together, Mike and she pushed his trolley out through the sliding doors towards a waiting Jeep.

Jed watched thoughtfully. While he'd managed to stand aside from most of the unpleasant aspects of Mike's divorce from Tessa, he'd inevitably been sucked in and – thanks to Sammy's influence – usually on Tessa's side. Mike hadn't shown any great animosity over this. He seemed to accept it as inevitable and hadn't let it muddy the waters between them. At the same time, he obviously wasn't quite ready to introduce Jed to his new girlfriend; Jed assumed that was who had come to meet Mike, though she was nothing like any of the other women his friend had ever fancied. She was well enough dressed and groomed, but plainer and, at first glance, more dour-looking than Mike's usual type. Whoever she was, though, it looked as if he was making an effort for her. His hair was neatly cut and was shorter than Jed had seen it for years, and he was wearing a new, light tweed sports-coat which Jed didn't recognise. When Mike had been married to Tessa, she'd always complained that she could never get him to wear anything other than his old American buckskin jacket.

Jed felt mildly amused by the change in Mike's appearance. He waited while his old friend was driven away from the terminal building before picking up his bag and going to get a taxi for himself.

Over the next three days, Jed planned to spend half his time at the sales and the rest of it visiting some of the great stud farms in the Blue Grass country of Kentucky.

Reluctant though the English and the Irish were to admit it, the sheer buying power of the American breeders over the last half century had brought many significant stallions across the Atlantic, enhancing the quality of their stock to the point where it had eclipsed the Europeans' and was now the fount of the most prominent thoroughbred bloodlines.

This was visible in the calibre of the surrounding buildings and landscape, as well as the mares and young-stock gambolling in the paddocks. Jed couldn't help admiring the lush rolling pastures, and envying the grand, colonial mansions that stood among them.

He saw a lot of people he knew, in and around the sales, and made several helpful new contacts as he drifted among the local breeders, gathering material for the pieces he was hoping to write.

Unlike Lucy Thynne, who had booked into the Hyatt, he was staying outside Lexington on one of the minor studs which made his own in England look like a small-holding.

Jim Halliday, a Kentucky native tamed by three years in Lambourn, was the same age as Jed and an old friend. He had married an English girl who ran the house, which Jim had recently inherited, like a Sussex manor. This helped soften the culture shock for British visitors to Keeneland, and Jed was glad to be based there.

As it happened, he also had an interest in one of the inmates of the stud.

Two and a half years before, Mike and he had bought a mare in foal to Northern Baby, a stallion Mike had always liked. They had bought the mare surprisingly cheaply from a small breeder in Idaho and left her to board in the States, although neither of them could realistically afford to keep her or the colt she produced. But nor had they been prepared to face the loss which was all they'd been offered so far, on top of the ten thousand or so dollars they'd run up in boarding charges.

If anything was going to kill off the twenty-year friendship between Jed and Mike, it would be this colt. At this stage in his career as a breeder, Jed could ill afford losses on this scale. He'd already borrowed as much as he could on the security of the house he and Sammy lived in, which she had bought with money left to her by her father.

He'd hated having to ask her, and it was clear that she hadn't wanted to risk losing the place. But she had agreed, seeing that it was the only way he was ever going to get started in what was a highly capital intensive business. Since then, a week hadn't passed without Jed's having at least one fretful night, plagued by money worries. He was only too well aware he was in a risky business, ruled by a fickle market. There were few breeders who hadn't been through the same financial nightmares at some stage or another, but Sammy's obvious anxiety made it even harder for him to keep an optimistic outlook.

The foal at the Hallidays' had also posed Jed and Mike another dilemma that was hard to call. It had turned out to be an over-leggy animal which looked very unpromising as a yearling but could well have grown into a useful two year old.

The previous autumn, they'd managed to sell the mare and recoup half their loss, but their yearling had been coughing badly and had missed his slot in the sale. Mike had insisted that they leave it in the States where they would get the best price. Now it had turned two and, when Jed went to see it soon after he'd arrived at the Hallidays', it was clear that it hadn't improved. He was already mentally preparing himself to give the animal away.

The hard part was going to be breaking the news to Mike. Contact between them had inevitably been strained since the divorce; Jed knew that asking his partner to take a couple of thousand dollars for something that had so far cost him twenty-five thousand wasn't going to help.

He set off for the sales next morning feeling gloomy but ready to throw himself into the job of studying the sale. It was the second day, and towards the end of the afternoon, a few early two year olds were due to be put through the ring. Jed had no particular interest in any of them. He relaxed, leaned back and stretched, letting his gaze sweep the room. He was always fascinated by the crowds at the bloodstock sales – so many different types, so many different aspirations and angles. These were occasions where through some unplanned, unforeseen juxtaposition of lots in the catalogue, the poorest, most struggling bloodstock agent could find himself rubbing shoulders with some of the world's richest men.

He looked at the catalogue and decided that there was nothing here for him. It was time to go. He was making his way from his seat to the gangway when he found himself squeezing in front of Lucy Thynne.

'Hi, Jed,' she said, smiling up at him and patting an empty seat beside her. He wasn't in any hurry and it would have looked rude not to stop for a moment so he sat down beside her.

'How's it going?'

'Brilliant!' She beamed. 'It's all so glamorous, and the

quality of the horses is just fantastic. I had dinner last night in a beautiful house on one of the studs, and everybody was so friendly.'

Jed looked at her shining eyes. He wasn't surprised people had been attentive. 'So why are you still here now?'

'I just wanted to watch a few of these yearlings go through.'

'Two year olds now.'

'Yes, of course. Look at the one that's just been sold. Isn't he pretty?'

Jed, who hadn't been looking at the sale ring, glanced at the prancing chestnut colt being led out and shook his head. 'Not really a trainer's colt,' he said, glancing at the catalogue. 'By Zilzal. Didn't make much of a price. I wonder who sent him?' He looked at the page again and saw that the horse had been consigned by Hugh G. Bullough of Bullough Hill Farm, a small stud which specialised in entering and preparing horses for third parties. 'I don't know, but he'll have lost them money.'

Suddenly, among the crowd thronging the gate, Jed caught a glimpse of Mike's distinctive buckskin jacket, with its long crimson leather tassels. He had a momentary view of Mike's face, too, in clear profile, before he lost sight of him as a small crowd gathered to get a last look at the animal in the ring. Jed scanned the crowd which seethed around the exit for a few more minutes, but without another sighting.

He sat where he was with Lucy for a while to watch a few more lots being sold.

'How much longer are you thinking of staying?' Jed asked.

'Why?' Lucy glanced at him and raised her eyebrows. 'Are you offering alternative amusements?'

Jed felt a sudden racing of his pulse and a pang of guilt. 'We could have a drink at the bar?' he offered lamely.

That was enough to get Lucy from her seat; half an hour and two vodka martinis later, they were thinking about where they might go for dinner.

Nothing they said to each other over the canned Country music in a rowdy steak bar specifically suggested a physical attraction between them, but they seemed to have a lot of mutual interests and opinions to exchange.

It was afterwards in a taxi, with Lucy sitting close beside him, that Jed was troubled by a sudden mental picture of his beautiful, fragile wife.

As soon as Lucy had suggested that he might as well come to her hotel for a last drink, a vision of Sammy had intruded. He'd realised, to his horror, just how much he wanted to go to bed with the warm, bubbly young woman beside him. If only thoughts of his wife had not left him feeling guilty and miserable.

Sammy would never know, he told himself, and if she didn't know, how could she be hurt? He let his mind wander for a moment, and Lucy saw, and smiled at him.

But even if Sammy never knew, Jed told himself after a few moments' pleasurable speculation, *he* always would, and as he watched her stoically bearing the discomfort which seemed permanently to afflict her, he would hate himself for knowing what she didn't.

He glanced at Lucy. 'One for the road, then I'm off.'

Her smile faltered momentarily, but she had youth and

time on her side. She shrugged her shoulders.

'I'd love to come out and see your stud in Gloucestershire some time,' she said later, as he climbed into the taxi which was going to take him back to Jim Halliday's stud.

'Great! Any time. I know Sammy'd love to meet you.' Jed smiled, wishing he'd meant that.

Chapter Two

February – Sandown Park, England

A big, bay gelding twitched his long ears back and forth as he jogged a stylish half-pass down the laurel walk to the course.

Leading him was Josie Whittle, a heavy, irritable girl who jerked the leading rein, jabbing the horse on the bar of his mouth. 'Stop muckin' about, Ferret,' she grumbled in a testy, rural accent, loud enough to impress the scattered punters.

The six-year-old gelding had been bought as a yearling by a West Country antiques dealer. Despite the advice of most of his friends, Dan Ferguson had named the animal Dan's Ferret. He'd kept the horse at home for a couple of years before he'd sent it to a trainer and watched it win impressively over hurdles for two seasons. Now it was going out as the favourite of ten runners in a two-and-a-half-mile novice chase.

Mike Powell sat lightly into the horse's bouncing walk. He'd known many more glorious mounts than this. He'd been riding professionally over fences for nearly two decades but it was four years now since his best season. His strike rate, and the number of rides he'd been offered, had dwindled sharply in the last two, in inverse proportion to his mounting financial need.

When Mike had first come into racing at the age of sixteen – cunning, instinctive, darkly handsome – people had called him Mickey. Somehow, this light-hearted version of his name no longer fitted the race-roughened, hard-drinking cynic he'd become. Only a few of his oldest and most loyal friends still called him Mickey; like Ev Thomas, Dan Ferguson, or Jimmy Fitzosborn, who trained Dan's Ferret.

But even Jimmy had had a momentary lapse of faith when Mike had arrived in the parade ring that afternoon in Ferguson's colours. 'Jesus, Mickey, you look rough!'

'You probably did too occasionally, when you were my age,' said Mike in his musical Welsh accent, just a hint of sourness evident under his easy grin.

Jogging sideways down to the course on Dan's Ferret, he felt suddenly queasy and was glad Jimmy couldn't see him now.

The stout girl at the other end of the lead-rein didn't turn, and so didn't register that his face was a startling shade of eau-de-Nil, in dire contrast to Dan Ferguson's emerald green silks.

Mike looked up at the low, steel-grey clouds, and winced. A few beads of sweat broke out below the rim of his helmet and dribbled down to sting his eyes. He cursed his own weakness for letting things go on so long the night before.

Three card brag till four in the morning, God knows how many bottles of Black Bush, and it wasn't as if he could afford the losses.

He didn't want to ride this horse, either.

Why was he doing it? Why couldn't he accept, as he got older, that it hurt a little more each time he hit the deck? And he was acutely conscious these days that jump jockeys who hadn't retired by the time they were his age were only there for the money. Though he'd won nearly all of the big races in the calendar at least once in his twenty-year career, he'd never risen higher than third in the championship.

Miserably, he wondered who he'd thought he was kidding when he'd declared that he'd go out at the end of the season with a bang and a hundred winners. Lately, his weight had been edging up towards its natural level, though for most of his career he'd ridden at a comfortable ten stone. Today, he'd struggled to do ten stone nine.

Out on the track, Josie unclipped the lead-rein.

'Good luck, Ferret.' Her harsh voice floated down the course behind Mike as the horse set off at a sharp canter to the start.

Mike hooked the gelding back before he ran away with him and used up too much of his impressive energy. In spite of his earlier discomfort, Mike could still switch into auto-pilot when his jockeying skills were needed and winning the race became his sole objective.

It always amazed his supporters just how much Mike still liked winning. He wasn't aware of it himself; just knew he hated losing. But it was this unquenchable desire to win, and twenty years' experience, which continued to persuade trainers to give him rides, and the public to back his mounts; Dan's Ferret was an odds-on favourite for this race.

Pulling up to a trot in front of the first fence to give his horse a look, Mike was receiving all the signals that he was sitting on a winner.

Jimmy Fitzosborn was demanding of his horses. They tended either to break down or become hard as nails. The animal Mike was on felt like a greyhound on steroids, and he knew it was a natural jumper.

He also knew the course better than his own back garden.

At a well-controlled walk, he rode round behind the start where he grinned and winked at Barney Kane, a twenty-year-old Irishman, only two years in England, who was already heading the winners' table that season.

'Is this your race, then?' Barney asked.

'Who knows?' Mike answered, in a tone that nevertheless implied that if anyone knew, he did. 'Anything that beats him will know it's had a race.' He laughed and nodded towards the starter, who was just beginning to call them up.

The horse didn't deserve such a ridiculous name, Mike thought, as Dan's Ferret cruised past the stands for the first time and he heard the commentator call it out.

As they turned away, down the hill, the pace began to quicken. He squeezed hard with his legs, asking his mount to lengthen his stride to hold his position. They skipped over the next fence before swinging right-handed into the back straight, where the railway line from Waterloo to the South-West ran parallel to the course. From the corner of his eye, Mike noticed a train rattling in to London. But he didn't allow himself to become distracted as he held Dan's Ferret on a long, easy rein, letting him jump freely out of his stride. With a lot of concentration, and years of experience, Mike rode the horse to meet all three railway fences on a perfect stride. The distance between the fences meant that horses only ever met two on the correct stride unless their jockeys had worked hard to change it.

Turning for home, Mike judged it was time to leave the running rail where he was still tucked in behind four leaders. He snatched a glance over his shoulder to check he was clear, but as he looked round, the horse in front of him stumbled. Dan's Ferret couldn't get out of the way in time and careered right into the back of it, clipping its heels. There was a loud clatter as hooves and aluminium plates crashed together. Both horses completely lost their balance and struggled to stay on their feet. Mike was almost jerked over the Ferret's head, thrown forward as if he'd crashed in a car without a safety belt. He'd lost his whip and let go of his reins. The white plastic running rail was level with his chin and for a split second, his hips were higher than his shoulders. By sheer good luck, his feet stayed in the irons and as the horse regained its balance, its head came up and threw Mike back into the saddle.

He knew it was his own fault. There'd been no need to follow so closely, he told himself, cursing as he gathered up his reins. To his pleasant surprise, though, he found that they'd barely lost any ground, but the stumble had allowed the horse behind to move up on his outside and block his way out. Mike cursed again and guessed that Dan Ferguson would be screaming obscenities at him from the stands by now, but until they reached the point where the rails ended, there was nothing he could do but sit and suffer.

He watched helplessly as the leader began to pull away from the pack. It was only when there was no chance of catching him that Mike was finally able to get out and push for home.

Their valiant run from twelve lengths back into a photo for second place, a length behind the winner, did not impress Jimmy Fitzosborn.

'For fuck's sake, Mickey. What the hell were you doing?'

Mike shook his head ruefully as he unbuckled his saddle.

The trainer didn't wait for an explanation. 'Letting yourself get boxed in like that – at your age!' He threw a sweat sheet over the lightly panting horse. 'That's it – that's the last time I ask you to ride any horse for me, and if you see Dan, I'd keep out of his way. He's just done his head.'

Mike reflected that he'd done Jimmy Fitzosborn enough favours in the past not to have to take this. But he sighed, said nothing and hitched the saddle on to his hip to weigh in for his second place, which had just been confirmed over the loudspeakers.

He walked towards the weighing-room, past a handful of journalists waiting to interview the winner.

'Michael? Mike Powell?'

Mike didn't recognise the man's voice, but the American accent detectable in those few words and the insistent tone made him look up. He didn't recognise the speaker, either, though there was something familiar about him. He had unruly dark hair, parted down the centre, glasses with old-fashioned thick black frames, like Buddy Holly's, and he was wearing a big tweed coat and brown brogues.

Mike stopped, instinctively standing back so that nothing could happen to interfere with his weighing in. 'Hello?'

'You don't know me,' the man said in a pleasantly resonant voice, 'but I wanted to talk to you – a personal matter. Here's my address. Give me a call if you've got time.' He stretched out his hand holding a card which, after a moment's hesitation, Mike took.

Two racing fans standing beside the American gaped at this naked transatlantic gall and watched him melt away into the crowd by the entrance to the stands.

Mike carried on until he had reached the clerk of the scales where he waited for the winning jockey to be weighed in. He glanced at the card. 'The Berkeley Hotel' and its address were printed on it, and below, handwritten in neat copper-plate, 'George Sargent Parker'.

George Sargent Parker?

Mike shrugged his shoulders as he stuffed the card into his breeches.

'Would you mind putting that on my desk, Powell?'

Mike gave the racecourse official a glance of withering contempt. Stifling the response bubbling to the surface, he extricated the card and laid it on the clerk's table.

Mike refused all offers of drinks after the last race. He climbed into his dependable old Mercedes in the car-park and looked once more at the card the stranger had passed to him over the rails of the winners' enclosure.

There'd been nothing threatening about the man, and Mike even felt he looked vaguely familiar. Perhaps he'd seen him on the fringes of his Kentucky dealings. He'd met so many people out there in the last two years, and couldn't remember them all.

He drove moodily from the jockeys' car-park, his quick temper fired by frustration and a lurking suspicion that any American wanting to talk to him could either mean good news or very, very bad.

Until his disaster with the Zilzal colt, Mike had regularly sold poor quality horses in the States – a long way from home. It was famously difficult to judge yearlings, and most people were heavily influenced by the 'black print' in the horse's breeding – black print indicating relations and forebears which had won big races.

People didn't usually blame the vendor when a horse turned out to be a dud. But over the last six months, Mike had sold several young horses with crooked feet skilfully disguised by his blacksmith, and had been half-expecting some comebacks for some time. As yet there'd been none; maybe the man in the heavy glasses was the first.

Passing a large, anonymous red-brick pub, set back to the side of the old Portsmouth road, Mike had to fight hard to stop himself from driving into the car-park. He wanted a drink, but knew that what had happened today – the absurd naivety of his riding – was due to the first drink he'd decided to have after racing the day before.

What really stung was the way Jimmy Fitzosborn had

blatantly hinted that Mike had got boxed in deliberately. Guilt had tightened every muscle in his body at the trainer's taunt.

Mike had always prided himself on his principled approach to race-riding – until two weeks before, soon after he'd got back from the States, when he'd been surprised to be approached by a well-known racecourse hustler with an offer of five thousand pounds to stop a strong favourite in a big handicap hurdle. In the aftermath of the loss he'd just suffered at the Keeneland sales, Mike had decided to go through with it.

During the course of his career, he'd been paid to stop probably only a dozen horses without ever having to do less than his best. If people wanted to pay him to get beaten on horses that couldn't win, that was fine by him. Sure, he'd given horses easy rides when they'd been recovering from injury or were too immature to push, but he had never discouraged a horse in prime condition with a good chance of winning.

This time had been different. He'd deliberately stopped a horse from winning a race it should have won. All he'd had to do was go through the motions of pushing the horse without making any real effort.

Mike hated himself for doing it. He'd made up his mind after that, however desperate he was, stopping to order was something he couldn't do again.

But Jimmy Fitzosborn's declaration that he wouldn't give him another ride – though probably, when it came to it, only said in the heat of the moment – had shaken him. In his final season, he didn't want to lose the trust of any trainers. He needed the rides, and he still wanted his hundred winners.

Mike reached the M25 and accelerated with growing impatience through the heavy evening traffic until he was on the M40 and showing the Chilterns his heels.

Forty minutes later, he drove through the gates of Easerswell, Gloucestershire – his share of the carve up during the divorce. It was a classic Cotswold cottage built of the local honey-coloured limestone. It had been extended a hundred years ago and again three years before, so well that the joins didn't show, and what had started life as a small-holder's modest dwelling had become a well-equipped five-bedroomed property. The brook that trickled down the wooded coombe behind the house, the small, skilfully aged stable block and two flat, well-drained paddocks, completed a picture that would have made any estate agent drool.

Mike heaved his kit-bag out of the back of his car and let himself into his house.

His sharp blue eyes fell on the near-empty bottle of Irish whiskey in the middle of his kitchen table. He shook his head, trying to erase the memory of the four slobs with whom he'd sat and played cards for five hours the night before.

He shrugged off his battered buckskin jacket, threw it on a chair and sat down. He took the American's card from his pocket and speculated about the man who had given it to him. George Sargent Parker – what kind of a name was that? Why couldn't he just be called George Parker? Not so memorable, of course, Mike reflected, but then, he didn't look like the kind of guy who'd particularly want to be remembered.

The urge to find out what this was – good news or bad – became unbearable.

Mike picked up the phone and dialled the Berkeley.

George Sargent Parker hadn't been back there all day.

Mike walked through to a room at the front of the house which he used as an office. Since he'd taken up his part-time bloodstock dealing and at first had made money from it, he'd set aside this room as a place to study sales catalogues and search through the records for well-bred horses which had failed to make a price that reflected their production cost. There were always plenty to choose from.

But, as always, he soon found his attention straying. After a while his eyes started to wander around the room.

When Tessa had left him, she'd taken most of her pictures and photographs with her, but a few still hung on the walls. Over the fireplace there was a large Cornish seascape which she'd bought in St Ives. Mike vividly remembered her enthusiasm, seven or eight years ago, when she'd dragged him down to Cornwall where she'd been filming.

They had chosen this picture together, wanting something to remind them of a wonderful, tender, loving week, and she had always cherished it.

He'd grown to like it too, willingly acknowledging Tessa's superior judgement in these things. For a while, he'd wanted to learn, to understand her cultural terms of reference, but she hadn't wanted to change him; had always said that the sexiest thing about him was his complete absence of any aesthetic appreciation.

Mike had ended up both admiring and despising Tessa's constant desire to intellectualise everything. Everything but sex, that is. He'd always been excited when she whispered coarse encouragement at the height of their love-making, yet contrarily he disliked hearing her lower her standards to his.

In the end, it was the differences in their backgrounds that drove them apart. Mike found himself compelled to exaggerate those differences to express his own personality. He had deliberately allowed his drinking, his language and manner to deteriorate to an extent that made Tessa cringe.

When he tried to reverse the process, he shouldn't have been surprised to find that it was too late, and the further she moved away from him, the more he wanted her back. But perversely he persisted in indulging in bad behaviour. In rare moments of detachment – or rarer ones of sobriety – he saw to his own fascination that a man could apparently become addicted to a certain type of behaviour, especially when fuelled by an increasingly out-of-control fondness for alcohol.

Now, sitting in his study in the house he and Tessa had once shared, he gazed at the Cornish landscape and longed to have her back.

The sound of the doorbell dragged him into the present. Few casual callers came to the house, especially since Tessa had moved out, so Mike was automatically on his guard.

The caller had gone to the front door, which was hardly

ever used. The outer light wasn't working and Mike couldn't see anyone through the spy-hole. He left the security chain in place and opened the door six inches, astonished to find himself looking at the same vaguely familiar face he had seen over the rails by the weighing-room at Sandown that afternoon.

'Hello, Mike.' The same pleasant baritone voice with its soft American accent. 'I hope you don't mind? I knew you lived out this way and looked up your address in the racing directory.'

He nodded, noting that the man had known he wouldn't have to remind Mike who he was. He unhooked the chain to open the door. He still couldn't think why his visitor seemed so familiar but, as before, there was nothing outwardly aggressive about him and by now Mike was intrigued to know what had brought him here.

'You'd better come in. Let me take your coat.' He hung it on one of the big wooden hooks in the hall and led his guest towards the kitchen. 'Would you like a drink?'

'Just coffee, thanks.'

In the kitchen, while Mike made a pot of strong coffee, he waved George Parker towards an old church pew set against the wall below a window-ledge cluttered with plants Tessa had left behind.

'What did you want to talk about?'

'I thought you might have guessed.'

Mike looked at him as he poured boiling water into the pot. 'I'm not sure,' he answered cautiously. 'Usually people want to talk about horses.'

Parker shook his head. 'Not me.'

'No. You don't look the type. So,' Mike said with relief and a growing sense of curiosity, 'what is it?'

'I wanted to talk about my mother – Gwynneth Meredith.' He left the name hanging in the air.

Mike said nothing as he finished making the coffee and put the pot on the table. He filled two mugs and pushed one across to his guest, followed by a milk bottle and sugar bowl.

'Who's Gwynneth Meredith?' he asked finally.

'Don't you know? Her sister married a Powell.'

'There must be a few hundred thousand people in Wales with the surname Powell, probably the same again in England, and for all I know in the States too. Like your general. It's a very common name. So's Meredith.' Impatiently, Mike poured a little milk into his mug. 'If you're on a hunt for your roots, you'll need a little more to go on than just your mother's name.'

This wasn't the first time he had come across fans claiming kinship through their shared name, though this man didn't look the usual type and Meredith was his own mother's maiden name.

'Gwynneth Meredith was the younger daughter of Emrys and Margaret Meredith of Cefn Llys in Brecknock.'

Mike halted the coffee mug halfway to his mouth, and slowly returned it to the table. 'What are you talking about? My mother never had a sister.'

George Parker widened his eyes in surprise. 'Didn't they ever tell you? She went off with an American GI. When she wrote to them and said she'd had a baby, they disowned her.'

'Are you serious?'

'Yeah, sure. That's what I'm saying. Your mother and mine were sisters.' He paused, looking quite composed, long accustomed to the knowledge. 'We're first cousins.'

'Good God! Why did they never tell me?'

'My mother was killed in a Greyhound bus crash while running away from my father. I was with her. Fifteen people were killed; one survived.'

'You?'

George nodded. 'I was only five at the time. Must have obliterated the scene from my mind. I have very little recollection of my mother, and just this one picture.'

From an inside pocket of his jacket, he had pulled out a stiff brown envelope from which he extracted a grainy monochrome photograph. He passed it over for Mike to examine, and went on.

'My dad came and got me, and married the woman he'd been running around with for years. She became my mom; no one ever referred to my real mother again. I guess that's maybe why no one ever told you about your Aunt Gwynneth or me.'

Mike was still gazing at the photograph of two teenage girls in simple summer frocks, in front of a banner proclaiming the Royal Welsh Show. It had been taken sometime in the early fifties, he guessed.

'Do you have a birth certificate, that says who your mother was?'

'Not on me.' George shook his head. 'But I guess my dad or my step-mom filed it away somewhere. All I've got is the photograph.'

Mike had seen an almost identical photograph at his parents' home and had been led to believe that the young girl standing beside his mother was a friend, not a sister.

'It's okay. I believe you. It's just going to take a bit of getting used to,' he said, shaking his head. 'Besides my mother, I thought I was the only person left in the family – the end of the line.'

'Is your father dead, then?' George asked.

'Fifteen years ago.'

'And you've got no kids?'

Mike tried to soften the bitterness when he laughed. 'No. The woman I was married to wasn't ready for children, and now she's left me.'

'You might marry again.'

'I doubt it,' he answered gloomily.

'Why not?'

Mike looked at George, a total stranger ten minutes ago but now his only relative besides his mother, whom he hadn't seen in twenty years. And he wanted to talk to him in a way he couldn't have done with anyone else. 'It was my fault she went. I was drinking too much, working too hard. She's a famous actress, my wife.'

'So they told me.'

'Who told you?'

'The porter at my hotel.'

'What's he got to do with it?'

'Relax, Mike. If it hadn't been for him I wouldn't be here now.' George topped up his coffee and, after a moment's thought, tipped a slug of Irish whiskey into it from the bottle on the table. 'I've been over here on a bit of business.'

'What sort of business?'

George gave a quick evasive smile. 'I trade in metals and such. I don't know a lot about racehorses, but I thought I'd like to see some racing while I was here. I asked the porter at the hotel where to go. He turned out to be a fan, and sat down with me to show me what was what in the racing papers. There was a big picture of you with your name underneath. I knew I had Powell relations, though I wasn't planning on looking them up.' George shrugged. 'But, of course, I had to ask where the guy in the photo came from, and he knew all about you – how you used to do some little races back in Wales and so forth. And about your marriage and divorce.'

Mike nodded. 'It was well covered by most of the tabloids.'

'I took the train and went to see you riding at Newbury. I loved it,' George said candidly. 'And I bet on the two races you won.'

'Last Saturday? I hope you had them doubled?' Mike laughed.

'Come on, I'm a novice at the gambling game, but I enjoyed the afternoon a lot. I was sure you were my cousin – my last remaining link with the UK – and I was going to make contact with you then, but I thought maybe there'd be no point. Didn't know if you'd want to hear me out so I went back to London. I finished my business there but I'd decided to stay on for a few more days, so I rented a car and drove to Sandown this morning.'

'I hope you didn't have a bet today?'

'Just a small one. But those other guys . . . it looked to

me like they were deliberately stopping you from getting out.'

'Maybe, but they did it without breaking any of the rules of racing, and I shouldn't have let myself get boxed in like that. I'm supposed to be one of the older guys who knows how to handle himself.'

'So I understand.'

The boost Mike had got from meeting his cousin suddenly ebbed, leaving him feeling drained and tired. 'I wanted to go out with a century – just once more – before I hung up my boots, ' he sighed. 'What happened today won't help. But that's another story. You want to know something? I kept the card you gave me and rang your hotel as soon as I got back here.'

'And I thought maybe you wouldn't mind if I just turned up. So I bought a map, and here I am.'

Mike held out one hand across the table. 'And it's bloody good to meet you, Cousin George.' He grinned. 'You're more than welcome to stay for a bit. I think we could have some fun, you and I.'

George grinned. 'That's exactly what I thought.' His face became more serious. 'But there's something I must ask you first – something important.'

'Sure. Go ahead.'

'I'd prefer it if you didn't tell anyone about me. Or not for a while, at any rate.'

'Okay.' Mike shrugged his shoulders. He liked the idea of keeping his new cousin to himself. 'But why?' he asked.

George looked embarrassed. 'The fact is, I just bust up with my girlfriend and I'm afraid,' he held up his hands in a gesture of modest surprise, 'she's taken it bad. She's kind of jealous, if you know what I mean? That's one of the reasons I thought I'd come to England for a bit. But if she heard I was here – well, that could cause problems.'

'How would she hear?'

'She knows people,' George said vaguely. 'And you're a well-known guy. People are interested in what you do – who you're hanging out with. They might start wondering who the hell I am – and I just don't need that.'

'Don't worry about a thing.' Mike grinned at the irony. 'Your secret's safe with me.'

Chapter Three

Next morning, Mike parked his car in the big open square in the middle of Stow-on-the-Wold. He locked it and shrugged on his buckskin jacket as he walked towards the newsagent's on the far side of the square to collect his racing papers. He'd almost reached the shop when he was drawn up sharply by a familiar voice hailing him.

He stopped and fixed a pleasant but not too approachable smile on his face before turning to greet Nick Thornton-Jones.

'Morning, Nick.' He nodded. 'How's Garry?'

Mike already knew that Nick's stable jockey, Garry O'Driscoll, had broken his thigh, and wasn't going to be much use for at least eight weeks.

'Terrible.' Nick Thornton-Jones was a trainer not given to euphemism. 'It's a disaster, frankly.'

'Anything I can do to help?' Mike asked, knowing there would be plenty of good spare rides to be had.

'Anyone would think you were offering me a favour.'

Mike grinned. 'It's an ill wind turns none to good, and all that.' The musical cadences of his Powys accent gave the

45

hackneyed saying more freshness than it merited. But the trainer knew well enough that a top jockey like Garry leaving the field for a couple of months was always a source of covert jubilation to his colleagues; it meant that a few more slices of the pie were up for grabs.

'If you came over to do some schooling tomorrow, I could see what there is for you,' he said, keen to show who was doing who the favour.

Mike enjoyed schooling. He preferred to sit on a horse over a few obstacles at home before he raced it, rather than just turning up at a course and being told what to expect of his mount by the trainer, who would always be generous to his animal in an effort to boost his jockey's confidence.

Nick's house was only five miles away, and his head-lad was an old drinking mate of Mike's. Trainer and jockey agreed a time, and wished each other a polite farewell.

Mike carried on to the paper shop.

'Morning, Beryl.' He grinned at the plump, tomato-faced woman in a pinafore behind the counter. 'By God, you're looking lovely today.'

Beryl giggled gratefully, as she always did, and passed a bundle of newsprint to the jockey, who was a local celebrity.

'Thanks, love,' Mike said, and leaned forward, dropping his voice to a whisper. 'And if by any chance you're going near the bookie's today, try Amber Light in the last at Worcester.'

The woman grinned. 'Thanks, Mike.'

He seldom issued tips but knew Beryl liked a bet and the horse he had mentioned would give her a good run for her money.

He drove back to his house, three miles from the hill-top town, parked his Mercedes in the garage beside the stables and walked through a garden ready to burst into fresh green buds, letting himself into the house by the back door.

He dumped his papers on the table beside an empty cereal bowl that hadn't been there before he'd gone to Stow.

'George!' he called, and stood and listened for a moment. When he received no answer, he opened one of the antique wall-cupboards and took out a bottle of whiskey. He poured two inches into a stout tumbler and, as he took a gulp, his eye was caught by a note pinned to the cupboard.

'Gone walking. Back about 11. G.'

Mike glanced at his watch. It was ten to. He lifted a lid on the Aga and put a kettle on to make a pot of coffee. While it was coming to the boil, he went through to his office where his answerphone had fielded some calls in his absence.

The first was from Tessa. As soon as he heard her soft voice, he knew she wanted something. He was right; she had a day off filming and was coming down to pick up the last of her pictures. She would arrive about one o'clock.

Mike tried to control a flutter of excitement and cursed his own weakness. But he had to admit that, despite all the squabbling and acrimony of the divorce and their patent inability to live together peacefully, he still wanted Tessa as much as he'd ever done.

There was a second message. It was from Jed Havard who, without a hint of what he wanted, asked Mike to call him back as soon as possible.

Mike sat down, took another slug of whiskey and

thought about Jed, his sensible, talented ex-brother-in-law, who had never put a foot wrong and, despite their very different personalities, was one of his oldest friends. Jed, who had retired from race riding right at the top to start a fresh career as a bloodstock-breeder and journalist. As far as Mike could tell, he was beginning to make a go of it, despite being pathologically incapable of lying or pulling any of the strokes used by so many other people in the business – people so accomplished that when they told a lie, they could almost verify it.

It was through Jed that Mike had first met his ex-wife ten years before. He smiled at the memory.

They'd all been standing around in Thornton-Jones' yard. Sam and Tessa had come with their father, Adrian Langton, and Jed to view a horse.

In those days, Mike rode regular work for Thornton-Jones and when he strolled up to the group in the yard, Jed had introduced him.

It was immediately obvious that Tessa found Mike attractive. She hadn't exactly flirted with him – but almost.

She was already well known by then; she'd played significant parts in two films and had just finished another in America. In England, she'd recently had a long run in a BBC costume drama, and was fresh in everyone's mind. The tabloids, unable to link her romantically with anyone in particular, had predictably got involved in a never-ending guessing game and produced a new suitor for her every few weeks.

A handsome jump-jockey with an army of his own fans

and a reputation for outrageous behaviour made an interesting match for the heroine of an Edwardian costume drama – an angle that appealed to them both too.

Jed had warned Tessa that Mike would be more than a handful. But after a well-documented courtship and two years of cohabitation, Mike and Tessa had married. After that their relationship had gone steadily downhill.

Mike picked up the phone now and dialled Jed's number. Samantha answered.

'Hi, Sammy. Jed left a message.'

'Hello, Mike. I'm afraid he's just popped out but he'll be back in a minute. I know he wanted to talk to you as soon as possible.'

Mike smiled to himself. 'Okay then, I'll be round in twenty minutes.'

Sam Havard put down the phone and looked across the Windrush Valley. She could almost see Mike's house, four miles away, and the thought of it made her sigh. She'd never shared her sister's enthusiasm for Mike, and deeply resented what he'd done to her now. Tessa had always been tougher than Sammy and the years with Mike had hardened her to the point where Sammy couldn't imagine her sister ever being able to love again. She'd wanted to tell Mike exactly what she thought of him, but Jed had persuaded her that to fall out or to have a show-down with him would achieve nothing. Now, she hoped Jed would be back before Mike arrived.

George Parker heaved open the back door of Mike's house,

kicked off a pair of borrowed green wellingtons and hung up his damp Barbour.

Mike heard him come in. 'Hello, boyo! Did you have a good walk?'

'I just love your English rain.'

'Welsh rain's better,' laughed Mike.

'Of course.' George smiled gratefully, taking the mug of coffee Mike handed him as he walked into the kitchen. 'You look a little edgy. What's the problem?'

'Tessa's left a message. She wants to pick up some pictures and she'll be here in a few hours' time.'

George nodded, pulled out a chair and sat down. 'That's okay. I'll keep out of the way until she's gone.'

Mike looked relieved. 'It's just that you haven't met Tess, and there's no way of knowing what kind of mood she'll be in. She can be a real drama queen sometimes, I can tell you. Hardly surprising for an actress, I suppose.'

'But you wish you'd never got rid of her, don't you?'

George's astute observation pulled Mike up for a moment. 'I'm not saying that.'

'Well, if you *do* want her back, what you have to do is treat her real nice – be attractive, witty, considerate. Make it obvious you don't mind how long she stays, you'll be the best possible company so long as she's here.'

'Tessa knows just how to wind me up, though.'

'And that's why she got bored and left.'

'She didn't – it was mutual.'

'Oh, come on, Mike. You just said you want her back – and I know about these things.'

Mike sat down opposite his newfound friend and

relation. He picked up the whiskey bottle to pour himself another shot.

George stretched his hand across the table and put it lightly on Mike's forearm. 'Listen, cuz, you'll do better if you're not drunk when she arrives.' He nodded at the bottle.

Slowly, Mike put it down on the table and smiled, shamefaced. 'Yes,' he nodded. 'You're right.' He glanced at his watch. 'And I've got to go over and see Jed before she gets here.'

Mike set off down the narrow lanes to cross the broad valley of the Windrush to Jed's stud farm at Batscombe Manor. Sunbeams pierced the cloudy sky like distant spotlights and lit the higher hills which rose beyond the ridge on the far side, reminding him of Wales.

For years he'd seldom thought of the mountains of Brecknock which surrounded the farm where he'd grown up. But the recent disasters in his marriage, riding, horse dealing, to say nothing of George Parker's sudden appearance in his life, had rudely jerked his mind back to his lonely childhood in the empty Cambrians.

He had miserable memories of that hard, comfortless existence and the total lack of any warmth or humour in the bleak hill farm which his parents had worked. Even so he might have gone back to see them from time to time, in spite of the depressing memories, if they hadn't thrown him out in disgust the day he'd announced he was going to be a professional jockey.

Ivor and Megan Powell's belief in the Almighty's capacity

for benign intervention was fully vindicated when the teachers at the High School in Llandrindod Wells told them their only child was exceptionally bright. They allowed themselves to nurture fond ambitions and fervent hopes that he would use this ability to go into the law or any other lucrative profession away from farming, so that eventually he'd be able to help his parents out of the poverty trap that gripped them.

But while Mike was scoring top marks in his O' levels, at the weekends and on summer evenings he escaped from his family's farm to join his school friend Ev Thomas down in the valleys, where the grazing was always good and the corn grew high. Here the farmers made money enough to indulge their love of racing ponies and horses, enthusiastically and in their own unregulated way, with no bureaucratic interference from the grandees of the Jockey Club.

With their own association restricted to the border counties of England and Mid-Wales, they held trotting races, ridden and with sulkies, as well as out-and-out flat races over tight little courses.

This was racing in the raw, with no regard for Jockey Club rules. A horse's origins and past form were the owners' private business; punters could only speculate wildly. Many a useful animal had been bought cheaply out of training at Ascot or Doncaster to have its former identity discarded as soon as it arrived in one of the small farms in the valleys of Brecknock or Radnor.

At an early age Mike had shown an innate ability to communicate with horses. He also had a neat, athletic body and rode his first flapper at the age of ten, tipping the scales at seven stone. That same season he discovered the joy of winning, and the ignominy of losing.

He knew his parents disapproved of the wealthier families from the valley floors with their drinking and gambling. He knew they would stop him if they found out what he was doing and so developed an elaborate pretence of becoming a keen angler. After a day's racing he would always take home a few trout, which friends had caught, to prove it.

The idea of riding on real courses as a career first occurred to him when he was fifteen, after one of his owners had taken him to an evening flat meeting at Chepstow. It was one of those rare meetings for Welsh courses when all the big-name jockeys were there, and the farmer who'd taken Mike told him how much money these men earned.

In the five years he'd been spinning round the tight little Welsh flapping tracks, Mike had gained far more race-riding experience than a flat-race apprentice of the same age. There were no camera patrols or stewards, and he'd learned to look after himself as well as his horse, and to anticipate what the other jockeys around him were about to do. His name was soon at the top of every flapping trainer's list when they wanted a jockey for a runner they fancied.

The next time he went to Chepstow, he identified a trainer with a small but busy yard, not far away in Herefordshire. Ron Prichard ran his horses under both codes. He was as much a dairy farmer as a racehorse trainer, with his origins in Mid-Wales. Although his training licence automatically precluded him, under pain of being 'warned off', from having anything to do with the Wales and West Trotting Association and their flapping races, he was still steeped in the culture and knew all about Michael Powell.

A week later, after a blazing row with his father, Michael moved into a tiny room above a cow shed on Prichard's farm. It was full of corn dust, with windows that hadn't been cleaned for twenty years. For the first few mornings he woke painfully and sat on the springless old bed, wondering if this new way of life would ever justify being told never to return to his parents' farm on the hills above Beulah.

But once he'd swung his leg over one of Prichard's wire-muscled, supremely fit horses to ride out from the yard, he'd known it was more than worth the loss of his parents' approval, and that will to succeed hadn't wavered since.

'Jed here yet?' Mike called, seeing Sammy framed in the doorway of the Havards' handsome Georgian house.

'No, but come in and have a drink while you wait.'

He strode over from his carelessly parked car, up the steps to the grand front door, and walked into a dark, flag-stoned hall in which a pleasant musty smell of dried flowers and old timber blended with gusts of wood-smoke from the open fire.

He followed Sammy into a large kitchen where she heaved an iron kettle off the range. 'I'm just making a pot of coffee – want a cup?'

'It's just about midday, I'd rather have a drop of whisky.'

He tried to ignore Sammy's tight expression before she

went off to the drinks cupboard in the drawing-room to fetch a bottle.

While she was out of the room, he glanced at a pile of letters which had been opened and lay face up on the table. Idly he read the top one.

It was from a London hospital, confirming that Sammy would be admitted for unspecified tests in six weeks' time.

Mike shut his eyes and shook his head. He disliked anything to do with medicine and doctors. His only dealings with hospitals so far had been concerned with the simple repair of limbs damaged in the course of his work.

He had guessed long before that there was some problem with Sammy's health. He had noticed that Jed's attitude – always ultra-protective and chivalrous – had lately become even more solicitous towards his delicately beautiful wife. Very occasionally he would see, through a chink in Jed's discretion, a hint of scepticism over Sammy's continual complaints, but he was far too loyal ever to express any suspicion that, just possibly, his wife's problems were more psychological than physical. In Mike's view, Sammy had never looked particularly healthy, but he'd noticed recently that her eyes had become circled with faint dark rings.

She came back into the room carrying a bottle of Famous Grouse. Mike stood up and looked at her with a sympathetic smile. Searching for a reason, she saw the letter on the table. Her face paled and her eyes flashed angrily. She banged the bottle down on the table. 'You've been reading my letters, haven't you?' Her lips trembled. Mike felt his face redden. He went to apologise, but Sammy turned and she rushed from the room.

Cursing himself, Mike found a glass in a cupboard and poured himself a large measure of Scotch.

There was a daily paper lying beside the post. Mike sat down and automatically turned to the inside pages. As he began to read an unflattering piece about his riding the day before, he heard Jed's Range Rover crunch to a halt on the gravel outside.

He read the rest of the paragraph, conscious there was some truth in it and privately conceding the fact that making the weights was costing him a lot more effort than it used to.

Tessa had told him bluntly that it was the booze. Mike looked at his glass and told himself that one more wouldn't make any difference. But before he'd poured it, Jed came through the back door.

He nodded. 'Hello, Mike. I see you've already got a drink.' He glanced at his watch.

Mike looked at his glass and left it where it was.

Jed was carrying a bundle of papers. As he dropped them on the table, he saw the letter from the hospital, picked it up and glanced over at their visitor.

'I suppose you've read this?'

Mike nodded. 'Yes. I'm sorry, I hope it's not too serious?'

'It may not be; we'll just have to wait and see,' Jed said with forced hopefulness, turning the letter face down on the table to close the subject. 'Anyway, thanks for coming round. I hear Peter Robinson's colt has got a leg?'

'That's the first I've heard of it.' The young horse, already a winner as a three year old on the flat, was entered for the juveniles' Triumph Hurdle at the Cheltenham Festival, and was favourite in a largely untried field. Though favourites seldom won the Triumph, this was one of Mike's better chances in the big meeting.

'I spoke to Rupert this morning, and he told me.'

'So you wanted to be the first to pass on the good news that I haven't got a ride for the Triumph?'

'I just wanted to know if you fancied the ride on Panpipe instead?'

Mike did a sharp double take, but tried to cover his surprise. 'Garry was going to ride her, wasn't he?'

Jed nodded.

'I saw Nick in Stow just now,' snorted Mike. 'Pompous bloody windbag! Why did you take Panpipe away from him?'

'So I could keep her at home.'

'Why did you want to do that? Aren't you too busy with other things?'

'Yes, but Panpipe came here as a yearling with a brood mare called Bella. The pair of them became inseparable and Bella fell to pieces when we sent her mate to Nick's; Panpipe never really settled there either but as soon as I brought her back, they were both fine again. So,' Jed shrugged, 'I've got a happy racehorse and a happy young brood mare.'

'But what are you doing about gallops?'

'That's easy. I just box her to Nick's and his lads take her to the races. It's extraordinary but Bella seems to know that Panpipe's only gone for the day and is perfectly settled.'

'Yeah.' Mike nodded. 'I've heard of other horses getting

that close. Anyway, thanks for the ride. I'll take it.' He shrugged his shoulders nonchalantly.

Jed smiled. 'Panpipe needs a strong ride, and frankly, I can't think of anyone better.'

'Or you'd have asked them,' Mike added, half thinking that might be true.

'Come on, Mike, I've nothing against you. How long have we been mates, for God's sake? Anyway, I think the filly will win, especially with Peter's colt out of it. I just want to give her every chance.'

'I know. Thanks.' Mike picked up the whisky glass before slowly putting it down again, still full. He nodded at the letter on the table. 'By the way,' he said in a gentler tone, 'I really do hope Sammy's okay.'

Jed sighed heavily. 'She says she's in quite a lot of pain but we don't know for sure what it is. Nothing's confirmed yet, so please don't tell Tessa. Sammy would rather do it herself, and Tessa said she was coming here later, after she'd been to your place.'

'Bloody hell!' Mike grunted. 'What's the time? I'd better get going – I don't want to be late.' He pushed his chair back and got to his feet.

'There was something else,' Jed said.

His tone warned of bad news.

'Yeah?' asked Mike apprehensively.

'The colt in the States . . .'

'Which one?' he asked, truculently.

'What do you mean, which one? Ours, of course – the one that's munching its way through a few tons of feed at Halliday's in Kentucky because you said: "Don't bring him home. Keep him going through the winter; break him early to sell in the spring." '

Mike sighed. 'If you want more money out of me, it'll have to wait. I'm well stretched at the moment. But we should be able to sell him in the first Breeze-Up sale.'

'I don't think he'll look any better then than he does now, and he looks a complete pig.'

Mike winced. 'He can't be that bad, surely?'

'I don't want to lose money on him any more than you do, but if we don't get rid of him now, I'm telling you, we'll just lose more, especially if we have to keep and prepare him for a sale in April. Even quite decent-looking animals were going for very little when I was over in January.'

Mike glanced at him for a sign of any sub-text. Reassured, he went on, 'Yeah, well, there could have been all sorts of other reasons for that. We might just as well hang on until April now.'

Jed raised his eyebrows. 'I wish to God we'd never seen the bloody animal.'

Tessa Langton drove her BMW through the gates of Jed's house just after two o'clock.

Stacked on the back seat were the half-dozen paintings – landscape and equestrian – she had just recovered from her old home.

People had often tried to identify that special quality in Tessa that had made her stand out so strikingly from the horde of aspiring actresses who had burst out of drama school the same year as she had. She was conventionally good-looking, perhaps pretty rather than beautiful, but there was a piquant sense of danger about her, a kind of feline unpredictability, and real loveliness in her lustrous blue-green eyes, brimming with an unexpected innocence which even fifteen years of acting had failed to eradicate.

Her black hair was cut short and spiky for a part she was filming. It didn't really suit her, but made her look ten years younger and her eyes twice as big.

At five foot seven, she was a little shorter than people expected from her TV appearances, but always walked with the long, lazy stride which she'd learned early on at the Italia Conti School.

Sammy, slightly taller and slimmer, came out of the house to greet her. In contrast to Tessa's colouring, she had long, wispy fair hair, grey eyes and a delicate pale skin.

The sisters hugged warmly and kissed each other on both cheeks.

'How was he?' Sammy asked, expecting to hear of an acrimonious meeting.

'Mike? He was utterly charming, but I pretended not to notice. I hardly looked at him. Not surprisingly, he hadn't taken my pictures down off the walls. Of course, I wouldn't let him help.'

'Was he drunk?'

'Not at all. Why?'

'He came round here earlier this morning, very keen on his whisky.'

'Why was he here?'

'Jed wanted to ask him to ride Panpipe.'

Tessa laughed. 'That's very generous of Jed.'

'Jed's priority is getting Panpipe to win. He thinks she's

the best he's ever bred. After all, she ran well on the flat last year, and seems to love jumping, too.'

'Good old Jed, not letting anything get in the way of his breeding ambitions.'

Sammy laughed with her, then spoke more seriously. 'Did Mike mention he'd seen me?'

'No. Why?'

'When he was here, he saw a letter I'd left lying open. Come in and I'll tell you about it.'

Ten minutes later, Tessa got up from the kitchen table where she and her sister had been sitting. She knew Sammy had always been more frail than her, but recognised now with a painful stab of guilt that, over the years, she'd developed the habit of assuming that most of her sister's ailments were psychosomatic. Sammy had always been more introverted than Tessa, and would often cry off parties or dinners blaming spurious headaches or stomach pains.

Even now, Tessa still couldn't be certain that this new, much more serious suspected condition wasn't imaginary too.

She wondered what Jed thought. 'Sam, would you mind if I got myself a little vodka? This is all a bit of a shock.'

'No, of course not. Sorry, I should have offered you one before. There's a bottle there in the cupboard, and tonic in the fridge.'

Tessa helped herself. 'When did you start thinking it might be . . .' she faltered a moment over the word '. . . cancer?' she asked when she'd taken a sip and sat down again beside Sammy with her arm round her shoulders.

'I've suspected it for ages, but I didn't want it confirmed. Then it got too much, and Jed insisted I tell the doctor.'

'What does he say?'

'He said it could be one of several things and sent me to the local hospital. They did a test, but it was inconclusive so Jed got me to a consultant at the Marsden.'

'How long have you suspected this?'

'Three or four months.'

'And if the tests are positive, will they have caught it in time?'

'I don't know. They say anything's possible. Jed says they're just covering themselves until they're certain what's wrong.'

'I'm sure that's right,' said Tessa quickly. 'So there may not be too much to worry about, even if it is . . . what you think. But take the tests, see what they say, and then why don't you go down to the villa in St Rémy and have a long rest? Build yourself up with some good French food.'

'I'd love to. But I wonder what sort of condition the villa's in since Mum died?'

'I should think it's fine. I told that French lawyer to carry on employing the cleaner and gardener. I quite fancy going down there myself, when I get a chance.'

'In a way, I suppose it's great you haven't got a moment to spare; every other actress is always moaning they haven't any work. But I'd love it if you could come down with me. Maybe once the chemotherapy sessions are over?'

'If you need them – which I hope you don't! Anyway, let's go to France no matter what, at least for a bit,' Tessa declared. 'Those wretched producers don't own my soul. As a matter of fact, they probably wouldn't know what a soul was if they had one presented to them on a silver platter with parsley round it.' She could see that Sammy was already taking heart from her offer, and promised herself that, for once, she'd stick to her word.

'You're a good sister to me, Tess,' said Sammy, throwing her an affectionate glance.

'No, I'm not. I'm useless. I should be telling you the tests will be negative and you won't need any damn' treatment. After all, if the local man thought there was a real problem, he'd have got you there a lot sooner.'

'I'm sure there is, though,' Sammy said wanly. 'But I feel strong enough to take it now, thanks to Jed and you.'

Tessa spent another half an hour with her before she left to drive back to London, praying that her sister's illness was no more than hypochondria.

Chapter Four

The following Monday evening, four days after George had first appeared in his life, Mike arrived home from the races. It had been a moderate day, yielding only a single visit to the second slot from four hard-ridden races.

George had ended up spending most of the weekend at Easerswell; Mike could hardly believe the rapport they seemed to have developed in such a short space of time, but there was no sign of his cousin in the house that evening – just a note on the kitchen table: '*Gone to London. I'll call you soon.*'

Mike didn't want to admit to himself how disappointed he was to find his cousin had left without prior warning. He'd enjoyed having some company and found it a real support to share some of his problems with a person who seemed to understand him so well.

He screwed up the note, threw it in the kitchen bin and walked through to his study where he sat down at the big roll-top desk Tessa had given him and picked up the phone to call his oldest friend, Evan Thomas.

Ev and Mike had spent their first sixteen years growing

up together. They'd both gone off to be jockeys: Ev, who was two stone lighter, to the flat; Mike over the sticks. Ev had returned to Wales under a cloud a few years later, after he'd foolishly let himself be talked into taking money for stopping a horse – a pitifully small bribe that amounted to nothing beside what he'd lost. His relationship with Mike had been altered irredeemably too.

Though Ev knew more about Mike's early life than anyone else alive, by mutual tacit agreement they very seldom discussed their private lives. But Mike had never lost his sense of loyalty to his diminutive boyhood friend. Whenever he could, he gave Ev jobs – these days, travelling his horses and helping out at the sales.

'Hello, Ev. How are you doing?'

'Good and bad,' said the ex-jockey philosophically.

'Tell me the good.'

'My elder girl, Beccy, just got a scholarship to the Cathedral School.'

Mike tried to remember Beccy, to lend some weight to his congratulations, but could only summon up an indistinct picture of the tribe of six small dark-haired children of whom his old friend was so proud, determined they should have every advantage that education could offer.

To that end, Ev was prepared to offer his special skills and knowledge to all comers, and still risked his neck a dozen times a week during the summer on the unregulated flapping tracks of Mid-Wales.

'That's great,' Mike enthused. 'You'll be able to buy her uniform after the little job I've got for you.'

'What is it?'

'I may have a couple of two year olds to sell at the Breeze-Up in Saratoga in April, and I'll need all the help I can get to have them looking better than their best. I'm hoping to buy a nice cheap one next week which will have to go from here. The other's already in Kentucky.'

'Okay, Mickey. You're on. Just let me know a few days ahead, okay?'

'I will. Have you seen my mam?'

'Last week, in the village. You should come up and see her yourself, Mickey. She hardly seems to know who anyone is these days, muttering to herself and all, like some mad old thing.'

'My God, it would only make her worse if she saw me,' he said. 'I just hope she can look after herself.'

'Don't worry about that, look; she's fit as a fiddle in her body.'

'I wish I were,' Mike muttered, wanting to change the subject. He still felt guilty, after twenty years, for never having been back to see her, even when his father had died.

'You haven't been riding so well, I must admit,' Ev said bluntly.

'I'm riding as well as ever, you cheeky sod! Things just haven't been going my way.'

'Well, don't give up. Now, I've got to go but you just tell me when you need me, look.' Ev paused. 'And thanks, Mickey.'

He put the phone down without waiting for a reply. Mike was used to that. He knew Ev hated to talk about his racing and how bitter he still felt that the Jockey Club hadn't considered giving him a second chance after a crime that was little more than a piece of youthful misjudgement.

The following morning, Mike was driving to Towcester where he had four good rides waiting for him. He'd left home early enough to stop off at a small stud in Buckinghamshire to view a yearling colt by Precocious.

The Long Crendon Stud, though small, had big, knowledgeable money behind it and was in the habit of producing six or seven foals a year, all with pedigrees good enough to qualify them – on paper, at least – for Tattersall's premium Highflyer yearling sale each September.

But the auctioneers demanded more than mere breeding to accept an animal for the most prestigious sale in Britain. A yearling had to look right, too, in conformation and movement.

Of the half-dozen foals produced at Long Crendon each year, an average of three qualified for the Highflyer; another two might be accepted for the sale that followed, and there was usually at least one dud amongst the crop.

Even the coupling of the finest mares with the most highly rated stallions didn't always produce progeny of comparable quality.

Henry Danvers, an Old Etonian with the manners and appearance of an eighteen-year-old schoolboy, was the manager of the stud. He didn't attempt to disguise the fact that it pained him to have to consider selling one of their progeny to a middle-ranking jump jockey who was also a notorious hustler.

Danvers asked a groom to bring the colt from his box.

He and Mike stood in the spotless brick and gravel yard and watched while the young horse was trotted up and down a few times.

Henry Danvers could barely bring himself to look at the ungainly animal. It had inherited nothing of its dam's impressive back end or its sire's gait. With relief, Mike saw that it wasn't without short-term possibilities – good enough, anyway, to convince an arrogant man who knew nothing about horses. At least until he saw it run. And that event was so far in the future, Mike didn't let it worry him.

'Hmm,' he said, trying not to gloat. 'Could make a good lady's hunter, if that foot can be corrected.'

Danvers grunted. 'Do you realise how much that colt cost to produce?'

'No,' Mike said, though he had a pretty good idea.

'His dam cost us eighty thousand, that's about five and a half thousand a year in interest; we'll get ten foals out of her if we're lucky – that's eight thousand per foal write-down in capital cost. The fee for the stallion was twenty thousand, which was payable on foaling – plus another fifteen hundred in interest since then.' Mike stifled a yawn; Danvers carried on. 'The mare costs us in feed, keep, bedding, labour, building amortisation and interest. All in all, around four and a half thousand pounds a year. And the colt has cost us about that since he was born. A total of forty-four thousand pounds.'

'If he'd looked right, you might have got a hundred and fifty thousand for him, maybe more.'

Danvers nodded. 'Maybe.'

'And I'm going to offer you two.'

Henry Danvers raised his eyebrows. 'Be serious, Mr Powell.'

'Well, how much do you want for him?'

'You came here to buy; it's up to you to make an offer we can sensibly consider.'

'You've just turned down my offer. I need to know how high I have to go before you start considering. I mean, would you consider twenty grand?'

Danvers glanced at him. 'Yes, we'd consider that.'

'Right. Well, I'll offer you five, and that's more than he's worth.'

'Why are you offering it, then?'

'Because he might just make an eventer,' Mike said as if reluctant to admit he dealt in such things.

'Yes,' Danvers said slowly, 'he might. I'll put your offer to Mr Stewart.'

Inwardly, Mike crowed. 'I can't go a penny more, mind.'

Danvers instructed the groom to put the colt back in its box. 'I'll let you know, then,' he said to Mike. 'Now, if you'll excuse me?'

Mike carried on to the Northamptonshire racecourse, confident that inside a few days he'd have the colt installed in a small yard down the brook from Easerswell. His blacksmith could perform his usual miracles with the colt's slightly unbalanced gait while it was being fattened up for its journey to America where, Mike hoped, it would go some way to easing his desperate cash-flow crisis. Unlike the Zilzal colt, he would send this one ahead early so that, if it didn't travel well, it would have time to recover.

★ ★ ★

Two days later Mike arrived back at his house after riding work for Thornton-Jones to find George Parker's car parked round by the side. He went into the house by the back door and was greeted by the smell of freshly made coffee.

'Hi, Mike.'

George walked into the kitchen, looking completely at home, calm and self-assured.

Mike was glad to see his cousin, but surprised that he should have turned up unannounced like this.

'Hello, George. When did you get here?'

'Twenty minutes ago. I brought some croissants and made some coffee – it's lucky you told me where you leave your key.' He opened Mike's oven and pulled out a tray containing half a dozen fresh, steaming croissants.

'I can't eat those,' said Mike testily.

George put them on a plate on the table and sat down to pour himself a cup of coffee. 'I read that you'd been having a little trouble with weight . . . and with liquor, too.'

'Where did you read that?'

'The last part I didn't read – I heard it in the stands when you didn't win yesterday. Look, sit down, have some coffee, and tell me what the trouble is.'

'Who says there's any trouble?'

'Mike, I know there is. I can see you're wound up. So, tell me. Maybe I can help.'

Mike stared at him for a moment, uncertain how to react. The sudden offer of a calm, confident brain to share the problems besetting him vied with the ignominy of being so obviously unsettled. But finally it was with a sense of relief at being able to unburden himself to a man of such patently cool judgement that he sat down opposite his cousin, poured himself a coffee and picked up one of the flaky pastries.

'Tessa's leaving me . . . was more than just humiliating,' he began hesitantly. 'Before then, what I earned didn't matter much. We lived bloody well.' He paused. 'Mostly on her income.'

George nodded.

'Two or three years ago,' Mike went on, 'when I first thought we might break up, I realised I'd have to start making a lot more money myself if I was to continue living the same sort of lifestyle.'

'But you're a famous jockey,' George said. 'Doesn't that bring in enough?'

'Not over the jumps, not unless you're one of the top two or three – which I'm not,' Mike added with unaccustomed candour. 'No, I had to find some other way, so I decided to concentrate on dealing. There's loads of money to be made in bloodstock, totally legitimately, if you really know horses and do your homework – which most people in the business don't.'

'But you do?'

Mike got up and walked across the kitchen to take a bottle of whisky from a shelf.

'You don't need that!'

He was startled by the sharpness of George's rebuke.

'Listen,' George insisted, 'I want to help. I could see as soon as I got here you were under pressure, and not just from your divorce. I know the signs, I've been there myself and I want to help. I've got experience, I've got time – use these things and get out from under.'

Mike looked into those unblinking dark eyes. They were unfathomable. But this was after all a blood relation, who surely only meant him well?

Mike put the bottle away and nodded. 'All right. So, as I was saying, a couple of years ago, I thought I'd try and pinhook a few foals.'

'What's that?'

'Buying foals cheap, and selling them a year on, when they fetch the kind of money they're really worth.'

'Why's it called pinhooking?'

'Nobody seems to know.'

'But who sells cheap foals when they only have to wait a year to see the right price?'

'Breeders who have more stock than they want to carry, and who think that a foal isn't going to earn out anyway.'

'And they get it wrong?'

'Not usually, just sometimes. That's when you make a real turn – when they reject a foal because they've judged it wrong, and you get there before anyone else spots it.'

'So, how did you make out at this pinhooking?'

'Very well, the first year – too well.'

'Too well?'

'Yeah, I got careless the next, didn't look quite so hard, paid a little more and found myself bidding for yearlings I thought were being sold too cheap and sending them to the States. I had a few results, but suddenly realised the cost of it all had gone over the top and I'd had too many losers. The one colt I reckoned was really going to get me off the hook, I sent to sell in Keeneland last month – it should have made a hundred thousand. But it sweated up in the ring, looked a mess, sold for ten thousand dollars and lost me another twenty thousand pounds. And now I've run out of money.'

'Hmm,' George said. 'Still, all is not lost. You have your house.'

Mike glanced at him, but he couldn't bring himself to tell his cousin that unless something very lucky happened soon, he wouldn't even have that.

'The house is yours, isn't it?' George pressed him.

'Yes. Tessa gave it up as part of the divorce settlement,' Mike admitted grudgingly.

'And it's not hocked?'

'No, there was never a mortgage or anything.'

'So you could always use this as collateral for borrowings?'

As if I didn't know, thought Mike.

'And there's still time to use it to trade out of the mess you're in,' George went on.

'What are you talking about? I don't want to borrow money to buy more horses. Having said that, I did buy one the other day . . .'

'No, no. Not horses. Money – currency. Believe me, it's a much more scientific gamble than thoroughbred horses – and the numbers are a helluva lot bigger.'

'Have you done it?'

'Of course. It's my business. I know everything there is to know about it.'

'But you said you were a mining engineer.'

'I was, when I started, then I got wrapped up in buying and selling mines. After a while, I figured it was easier just to buy and sell the minerals than to dig them out of the earth. In the end, you never get to see an ingot; it's all paperwork – except the money at the end of it.'

'Did you make a lot?'

'Oh, yeah. I got to twenty million ahead.'

Mike noticed a slight pause. 'And then?' he asked.

'And then . . .' George said with an enigmatic smile '. . . let me tell you what most folks think is going to happen to the mighty Japanese yen – then I'll tell you what's *really* going to happen, and how you could make so much money from knowing it that buying and selling a few bits of well-bred livestock will look like a two-bit card game.'

The following Sunday, eleven days before Panpipe was due to run in the Triumph Hurdle, Jed spent most of the morning in the stable yard at Batscombe with his vet. Two of his most expensive mares were causing him problems: one had simply failed to get in foal despite repeated coverings by a highly fertile stallion; the other had spontaneously aborted her foal for the second year running.

When all the costs were taken into account, each failure to produce represented an irrecoverable loss of around fifteen thousand pounds to the stud for that year, and now the vet was advocating that the barren mare should pay a visit to an equine fertility clinic whose rates made the London Clinic look cheap. But the stud was already operating on such a tight budget that there was just no surplus to pay for it.

Jed walked back to the house at the end of the session feeling shell-shocked; his problems were increasingly hard to take. He lingered in the garden, not wanting to face Sammy in this condition.

Jed knew that her sensitivity had, in itself, been one of her attractions for him. During their early courtship, after they'd met at university, he'd been willing to accept a long suspension of their first love-making, due to her nervousness and the significance she attached to the event; when the time had eventually come, Jed acknowledged, it had had a far greater impact on them both as a result.

But along with her nervousness, Sammy had also had tremendous vitality and a vivid imagination, which contrasted with her periods of notable weakness. Above all, in her pale, pre-Raphaelite way, she had been breathtakingly beautiful. Jed had spent the first ten years of their marriage feeling deeply proud of her and confident of the support he gave her; he didn't want to start letting her down now.

After ten minutes dead-heading the roses, he felt ready to go into the house where he found Sammy sitting in the kitchen.

She glanced up as he walked in. 'Jed? Are you all right?'

He forced a grin on to his face. 'Yes, of course. Why?'

'You looked really worried. But you mustn't be.' Her eyes glowed. 'I'm fine. Tessa's here.'

As she said it, her sister came into the room, bringing with her all the infectious warmth of her personality.

'Hello, Jed darling.' She offered him both cheeks in quick succession before sitting down with a large cup of cappuccino.

'Tess, you certainly seem to have put the colour back into Sam's face.' He meant it. He was always grateful for Tessa's talent for lifting his wife's spirits, and on this occasion his own. 'Are you staying for lunch?'

'Yes, please.'

'I'm sure Sammy doesn't feel like cooking. Let's go to the White Horse.'

The pub was like a racing canteen, full of lads and assorted hangers-on from the three local yards. Bertie Winthrop, the vet, was tucked into a corner having a pint with the farrier. He nodded to Jed as he walked in with Sammy and Tess.

Jed asked the landlord if they could eat in a small room at the back where it was quieter. Once they were there, although all three of them wanted to talk about Sammy's condition, they found themselves avoiding the subject and, as they often did, talking about Mike instead.

'It's very strange, you know, Jed,' Tessa said. 'You're one of the few people he seems to respect.'

'I'd say he and I are still pretty good friends, in spite of everything that's happened, and I still rate him as a pilot. But it's not surprising he's been a bit more sensitive than usual recently.'

'He seemed quite touchy when he came round the other morning,' Sammy said, 'as though he had something on his mind.'

'Probably psyching himself up to see me,' Tessa laughed.

'Maybe. It's such a relief it's all over between you, though, and I don't have to worry about you and him.'

'I would go back, though. If I had to.'

Sammy looked indignant. 'Why should you have to?'

'I mean, if Mike got himself into a real mess and needed me, I'd still go back to him.'

Jed looked at her, shaking his head. 'Tessa, I know you mean well and you really think you could help, but believe me, the more you see him, the less chance there is of his getting his act together and standing on his own two feet.'

'What do you mean, getting his act together? He seems to be doing all right without me.'

'Not really. He's having trouble with his weight and nothing is going right for him on the track. People are beginning to notice that he's drunk just a bit too soon after racing. Apart from anything else, he'll lose his driving licence any day now if he's not careful – and that'll really set him back.'

'Why have you asked him to ride your precious filly, then?' Sammy asked.

'Because he's still got a great pair of hands and he's always been good with young horses; he gives them confidence.'

'You're just being kind to him,' Tessa said.

'If Mike thought that, he wouldn't take the ride; and anyway, you're absolutely wrong. I'd never put up a jockey just to be kind.'

'It's time he gave up,' Tessa declared, 'like you. But I suppose he wants to earn more, now I'm not subsidising his little extravagances.'

'I'm surprised,' Jed said thoughtfully. 'I was sure Mike had made a few quid from his bloodstock dealing. He and I had several quite good deals together. He may not

be a sophisticated businessman, but he's very fond of
money and knows enough bullshit never to be short of
punters.'

'So he was always telling me,' Tessa grunted, 'but I never
saw any of it, and nor did my solicitors.'

'Hmm,' Jed grunted. 'I think maybe things haven't been
going too well for him lately on that front either.'

Tessa had driven to the pub in her own car. When they'd
finished lunch, she went straight back to London.

Going home with Jed in the Range Rover, Sammy once
again raised the question of Mike's riding Panpipe.

'I think it's so insensitive of you to ask him,' she said.
'After all, Tessa's my sister.'

'I wasn't asking Mike to ride *her!*' Jed laughed.

'For God's sake, Jed. He put her through hell.'

'Sammy, calm down. Tessa's a big girl. She can look after
herself. Everyone warned her about marrying the hot-
headed bugger in the first place.'

'Jed, if he's such a hot-head, why are you giving him this
ride?'

'I've already told you,' he said patiently. 'Mike's good
with a young horse and he's got an instinctive ability to
read the way a race is being run. And anyway, he and I go
back a long way.'

'But what about Tessa's feelings?'

'Sammy,' he said, barely controlling his impatience, 'if I
really thought Mike's riding Panpipe was going to hurt
Tessa one jot, I wouldn't have asked him. But frankly I
don't think she gives a tuppenny toss about it – she's far

more interested in seeing Panpipe win. For God's sake, you must know you can trust me by now?'

He glanced across at Sammy to see that she was smiling, and nodding faintly. 'I do know it, Jed. You've been good to me, through all my ups and downs. I just don't want Tessa to feel we've betrayed her. She's more sensitive than she looks.'

When they got back, a small silver Peugeot was parked on the gravel circle in front of the house.

Jed didn't recognise the car, but was struck by an irrational sense of guilt when he saw Lucy Thynne, leggier than ever in a tiny jersey mini-skirt, walking round the side of the house to greet them.

'Hi!' she called, beaming at Jed and Sammy as they climbed out of the Range Rover. 'I thought I'd take you up on your offer to show me the stud.'

Jed felt himself redden and quickly turned so that Sammy couldn't see his face. 'Great!' He dithered a moment, wondering why he felt so guilty when he had firmly resisted temptation the last time he'd seen Lucy in Keeneland. 'Come on in.' Without waiting to see Sammy's reaction, he led the way through the front door. 'I'm afraid we've just had lunch, but can I get you a drink?'

Lucy glanced behind at Sammy. 'Jed, is it inconvenient, my turning up here?' she murmured. 'I didn't think it would be a problem. After all—'

'No. No, of course it's okay. It's just that Sammy hasn't been too well recently, and she gets tired very easily.'

'Oh. I'm sorry.' Lucy hesitated. 'I'd never have come if I'd thought for a moment it would upset her.'

'No, I'm sure you wouldn't,' Jed said, kindly. 'Now, what would you like to drink?'

'Look, why don't I go straight over to look at the mares, which is why I came.'

'Yes, that's a good idea. You'll find Catherine in the yard; she'll tell you who's who. I'll be with you in a minute.'

He led Lucy through the back door and showed her how to get to the stable block. As he walked back into the kitchen, Sammy was sitting down at the table. She rested her head in her hands for a moment. 'I don't blame you, Jed,' she said quietly. 'She's lovely, and I haven't been any kind of a wife recently – no kids; no love-life.'

'What are you talking about?'

'You're a man. I know it's been difficult for you.' Sammy looked up at him, grey eyes wide and opaque. 'But why did she have to come here?'

'Who, Lucy? Sammy, you don't think I've slept with her, do you?'

'I just had to see the way she looked at you, the way she smiled.'

Jed tried to control his frustration and the guilty knowledge that the idea had entered his head in Keeneland. 'Oh, Sammy, you're being paranoid. She's just another bloodstock writer. We met at the sales in Kentucky; we talked. That's all.'

'You didn't have dinner with her or anything?'

'No, of course not.'

Jed could see that she didn't believe him. But he couldn't back-track now, or she wouldn't believe anything else he said. 'Look, we had a quick drink at the sale-ring bar. After all, I did get that mare from her father years ago, and we're professional colleagues.'

'But she so obviously wants you. I can't believe it didn't strike you.'

'If she fancies me, so what? It's not the first time I've managed to avoid being seduced by a woman who fancies me.' Jed immediately regretted the defensiveness in his voice.

Sammy looked steadily at him. 'If it's such a sacrifice living with me, maybe we should call it a day.'

Jed sighed and sat down opposite her. He reached across the table to cover her hand with his. 'Sammy angel, of course it's not a sacrifice. I love you and I want to be with you, and no one is going to come between us. I'll be with you as long as you want me to be.'

Her hand lay quite still under his. 'I hope so, Jed,' she said in little more than a whisper. 'I do hope so.'

Chapter Five

The following Wednesday, Jed took Panpipe over to work at Fencote with Nick's horses. On his way back, he decided he had time to drop into Janey Marchant's yard, half a mile down the brook from Mike's house.

Janey was on the fringes of active racing but her skills as a healer and breaker of horses brought her into regular contact with several of its stars. She often learned more than people closer to the centre and Jed always enjoyed a gossip with her.

He had been sitting in her unofficial 'office' in the tack-room for ten minutes or so when Mike's Mercedes nosed into the yard.

Janey leaped up and went out to greet him. 'Hi, Mike. Have you come to see your new colt?'

Jed walked out of the tack-room behind her. 'What colt is this?' he asked. 'You're an optimist, Mike, buying more horses when we haven't sold the dud we've already got.'

'I only bought this one because they said they'd wait for the money,' he blustered, acutely conscious that the cheque he'd written would arrive at his bank next day and would need some skilful persuasion if it was to be paid.

Janey was already leading them to a box at the far end of her row of stone stables.

'He's got a super nature,' she said defensively as she opened the door to let them in.

Mike didn't follow Jed into the box. 'He was very cheap.'

Jed laughed. 'I can see why! What the hell did you buy him for?' he asked as he made the ugly animal stand upright.

'People pay a goodish price for a nice quiet thoroughbred like this for a lady's hunter, and I've already got a punter for it.'

Jed straightened up from where he'd been examining the colt's legs. 'What?' he asked incredulously. 'Since when have you been dealing in ladies' hunters?'

'Well,' Mike said, 'the fact is, like I say, he was cheap – considering his breeding – and I happen to think he'll grow up a hell of a lot better than he looks just now.' He managed to sound convincing but Jed left the box, shaking his head.

'I should think your punter wants it to pull his caravan by the look of it – if it ever learns to move in a straight line. It looks a bit like that one we're already stuck with in the States.'

'It'll be okay,' Mike said defensively, trying to disguise his irritation at Jed's obvious dislike of the horse.

Mike drove the half-mile up the lane to his own house wishing he was as certain of his punter as he'd pretended to Jed. Just thinking of the consequences of not selling the horse filled him with desperation.

With a supreme effort, he turned his attention from the colt and tried to concentrate instead on the deal he hoped to set up with George Parker that day.

Mike hadn't heard from his cousin for a while since they'd talked about the idea of a currency trade the week before. Then George had phoned, the previous night, to say he would be down by twelve; it was already half-past.

When Mike reached his garage beside the house, he saw George's rented Jaguar already parked. George himself was sitting at the desk in the study, with the inevitable cup of coffee, studying prices on Teletext.

Mike sat down beside him.

'So, what's the yen trading at?' he asked eagerly.

'Just under two forty.'

Mike nodded with satisfaction.

When George had suggested that he should get involved in currency trading, Mike had made him explain every aspect of it.

He'd come to the conclusion that, in principle, it wasn't dissimilar to betting on a horse, only it took longer to lose. It was a matter of taking a view on whether the relative value of a particular currency was going to rise or fall over a period of time. Fluctuations in currency values occurred for a whole lot of different underlying reasons, mainly financial and political, but in the end, sheer market forces always prevailed. In that respect, currencies were the same as apples or pork bellies. If everyone wanted them, they went up; if nobody did, they went down.

Usually it was a hike in interest rates coupled with a

strong economy that caused an increase. Common sense dictated that a 7.5% return on capital in US dollars was much more attractive to investors than 6% in German marks, provided the asset value remained constant. If a change of government occurred, however, and the new incumbents were prone to heavy public spending and the incurring of debt, leading to high inflation, 7.5% on an asset that would buy, say, 20% less than it would have done a year earlier, wasn't such a smart move.

George had convinced Mike that the yen, currently dropping in value like a barrel over the Niagara Falls, would shortly undergo a dramatic turnaround. He had told Mike that he had a friend in the US Treasury who had given him a private preview, which ran counter to the prevailing market view, of the outcome of secret negotiations, culminating in talks due to be announced the following month between the two governments.

'So it's still going out, then?' Mike said, eyes fixed on the screen.

'Yeah.'

'Not for much longer, though? Not once people start talking up this April Treasury summit in Washington,' Mike said. He added with a laugh, 'One of the guys in the *FT* was trying to say that the Japs were just going along to show willing, and have got no intention of signing up to any more restrictive trade deals.' He snorted cynically. 'He's got to be punting the other way, hasn't he? To keep the yen going on down until after the meeting.'

'I doubt it. I guess an *FT* journalist would be a little more sophisticated than that,' George murmured. 'Maybe the

Japs will try to trade their way out of recession after all.'

'That's not what you said last week,' Mike said indignantly. 'And I think you were right then – I'm bloody sure of it.'

'Why so?'

'I'll tell you why. If the Americans are offering to come in and prop up the yen, jack it up to where it was at the beginning of the year, they'll save the Tokyo market from total collapse. I mean, the yen would have to slide a hell of a lot further before Japanese production starts to look cheap enough for it to make a real difference to their exports to the States.'

'Wow!' George Parker exclaimed with friendly sarcasm. 'Who's suddenly the international currency expert?'

'Look, George, I understand markets. Buying and selling bloodstock is all about markets, though with yearlings, you're dealing in potential – not actual value – and that's a tricky commodity to read. So, you were right when you said this currency thing is much more scientific.' He stood up to emphasise his commitment. 'I want to go for it.'

'You really want to get into some serious foreign exchange?'

'Yeah.' Mike nodded vigorously. 'Yeah, I do. And I've got the funds to do it with.'

'How much?' George asked quietly.

'I spoke to some mortgage people last week. Their surveyor came round yesterday. He valued this place at four-hundred-and-fifty-thousand pounds, and they rang to say I can have three-hundred-thousand pounds at nine per cent.'

'That's a little high,' George said.

'Yeah, but what the hell? We'll only need the money for a few weeks, won't we?'

'Hang on, Mike. Just hold hard and don't get so excited.'

'I'm only going by what you said. Just tell me how the deal works again?'

'It's not too complicated. First, you need an account at a bank with a first-class forex division.'

'Forex?' Mike asked.

'Foreign exchange.'

'Well, how do I do that?'

'You don't. Any of the serious banks are only interested in opening trading accounts for very substantial individuals – people who count their assets in tens of millions.'

'But . . .' Mike spluttered with disappointment. 'You said I could do this kind of trading.'

'Well, I'm sorry Mike, I thought you were a wealthy man, but you don't have much more than this house, do you?'

'No, but I told you, I can raise three hundred grand cash against it tomorrow.'

'Then why don't you use that for horse trading, which you know already?'

'Because when you buy a currency you don't have to pay someone to look after it and feed it until it's sold. It looks a cleaner deal all round, and it was you who said how much easier and less risky this currency trading is. So how do I get an account?'

'If you really want to do it, I can help. I've a dormant account with Crédit Lyonnais here in London. If I put in your three-hundred-thousand pounds, they'll let me gear up to ten-to-one, and I could trade for you.'

'So I could buy three million quid's worth?'

'On the harder currencies, yes. For softer ones – roubles, HK dollars – they'd probably only go five-to-one.'

'It's the yen I'm interested in. I mean there's bugger all downside; it's hardly going to get much lower than it is now. It's at a seven-year low.'

'You *have* been doing your homework,' George said approvingly. 'Okay, if you want to buy a few hundred million yen, I'll get 'em for you.'

'Great! Are you going into them yourself?'

'Sure. I'm already in there, big. But I'll only use this London account for your trades – so there's no confusion. And, listen, you'll have to sign the supplementary guarantee, so you're liable if it goes too far the wrong way – you understand that?'

'Yes. I thought I'd have to do something like that. Besides, there's no way you'd want to take any of the risk if you were trading on my behalf. Not that there's much of a risk – not like with a horse, when you don't even know if you've got a sound animal to sell until it's actually stepped into the ring. And even then the slightest bloody rumour can turn the punters off.'

'You should know,' warned George, 'financial markets don't like rumours either.'

Mike had to leave to ride in the last two races at Stratford that afternoon. The heavy clouds overhead had decided to lighten their load on the Cotswolds, and now the rain was coming down in torrents.

As Mike prepared to make a dash for his car, George

called after him, 'If you want to play the market, you've got to get in as soon as you can, while it's still heading down. It'll start moving up again soon.'

'What do I do with the deposit?'

'As soon as you've got the money, get a cheque made out to me, and we'll meet up in London to exchange agreements.'

'Okay. I'll call you Tuesday.'

Mike gave George a last nod of thanks and ran to his car.

The currency speculation was a punt, he knew that. For every time money was made, money was lost; there was always that flip side. Mike knew the downside would mean he'd lose everything, and suffered a moment of panic, gripped by the urge to call the whole thing off. But then he thought of the profit and, trying to concentrate only on the job of race-riding, he drove off to Stratford feeling much better. Somehow he just knew this investment was going to be good for him.

Over the next week, Mike followed the price of the yen, hoping that it would not begin to rise before he'd made his investment. It hardly moved and he occupied himself with the few modest horse deals he had going.

He'd already made up his mind to confirm an entry in the Saratoga Breeze-Up sale for the colt he co-owned with Jed. And he still thought he'd find a sucker in the States for the Precocious colt he'd bought from Long Crendon.

When he'd told Jed he already had a customer for this unpromising individual, he'd been talking optimistically. He'd chatted up a few possibles since he'd come back from

Kentucky in January; most of them had since fallen by the wayside, but he still had hopes for one. His problem was that his best route to this potential buyer was through Tessa.

When George had voiced his view that Mike still wanted Tessa, he had been entirely accurate. Mike's regret that he had ever let the divorce happen had not diminished. On the half-dozen occasions he'd seen her since the divorce, he'd sensed that Tessa felt the same.

He was riding in the feature chase at Ascot the following Saturday and Tessa had always enjoyed racing there, because of its associations with the more glamorous summer season, and because it was easy to get to from London.

When he rang her and asked if she would meet him there, she said she'd already arranged to go with Jed and Sammy anyway.

'But I need to talk to you alone,' Mike said. 'It's to do with my bloodstock dealing.'

'Okay,' Tessa agreed. 'I'll be in Max's box, but I dare say we can find somewhere quieter.'

When the day came, and racing was over, they ended up sitting side by side in Tessa's BMW in the car-park.

It was the first time for many months that Mike had sat so close to her, and nothing could detract from the sheer physical excitement her proximity caused him, as much now as it had ten years before.

But he did his best to hide it. Although he wanted to blurt out his feelings of remorse and regret, he sensed she wasn't ready to listen. He would have to concentrate instead on his other purpose in seeing her.

'So,' said Tessa, gazing through the windscreen at the crocodile of damp people heading for the railway station. 'How can I help you in your wheeling and dealing?'

'Are you still in touch with Bernie Capella?'

Tessa turned and looked at him in surprise. 'Bernie? Of course. I may not have been the star of his picture, but I had the most important part.'

'I hear you might be up for some award.'

Tessa shrugged dismissively. 'We'll see. Anyway, what about Bernie?'

'Do you remember once, when you first went to see him in LA and I came with you, we went out to dinner at some crazy Italian restaurant?'

'Yes, of course, I remember it very well.'

'Well, I talked to Bernie about racing then, and he said he'd like to get into it, and I should come and help him buy a few horses.'

'And?' Tessa said, guardedly.

'Well, I've been asking around, and he still hasn't bought anything, and I've got a horse that might suit him very well.'

'What on earth do you mean, might suit him very well? He doesn't know the first thing about horses, so far as I know.' She stopped and gave Mike a fierce look. 'Or is that what you mean by "might suit him very well"? You've got some dog that no one else will touch?'

'It's very well bred. I think it'll grow into a serious animal.'

'Mickey, don't give me your sales spiel, please. I've heard

it all before. But if you want to get to Bernie, you're in luck. He's in London next week to make arrangements for the première of *Tequila Sunset*. He's coming to my house for drinks on Tuesday. Come then, see if he'll listen to you. Okay?' She smiled indulgently, like a generous mother offering her child a treat. 'I should warn you – Bernie may be easy to sell to, but he wouldn't like to be sold a dud. And he considers the due processes of law much too long-winded. So, best of luck.'

Mike grinned. 'Thanks, Tess. I'll see you Tuesday.'

Bernie Capella's ancestors were Jewish and Italian and he vigorously plundered both cultures as it suited him. This provided a combination of attributes ideal for running a small but powerful independent Hollywood studio.

Everyone assumed, though no one could prove, that the Italian connection was the source of his apparently limitless funding while his Jewish connections supplied the creative talent.

But what he had above all else, within his short rotund body, was an enormous and overpowering personality.

The drawing-room of Tessa's house in Margaretta Terrace, Chelsea, was large, light and elegant, but Bernie seemed to fill it with his ebullient presence as soon as he walked in. Mike was impressed.

Tessa did as she had promised and reintroduced them.

'My God!' the producer boomed when Tess had gone to speak to some other guests. 'You're a brave man, coming here. If I'd divorced a woman like Tessa, I wouldn't ever want to remind myself of what I'd lost.'

93

'I didn't see why we shouldn't stay friends,' Mike murmured.

'Hmm,' Bernie grunted disparagingly. 'Never look back, that's what I say. We met before, didn't we? Had dinner in LA.'

'That's right . . .'

'Yeah, I remember. You're a jockey, aren't you? You were going to get me a horse.'

Mike could hardly believe his luck that the topic he had come to discuss had arisen so easily. 'Yes, that's right. You said you wanted to go into racing.'

'So, where's my horse?'

'But I never heard from you again.'

The producer looked at Mike as if he were mad. 'If I say I want something, I don't usually have to ask twice.' He glowered ferociously.

Mike nodded and smiled nervously. 'Yes, but it must have been all of two years ago . . .'

Bernie burst out laughing, slapping his sides like a man in a cartoon.

'Mike, Mike, I'm kiddin'! Tess reminded me on the phone about our conversation back then. It'd gone clean out of my head, but coming here in the limo, I thought: What the heck – a man in my position should have racehorses. So, go ahead. Find me a couple of good ones, and somewhere to keep them where I won't get ripped off. You call my office in California and they'll sort out the details, okay? Just you be sure they're hot enough to win a few races. I want the best!'

Mike had promised Tessa he would leave after his conversation with Bernie Capella. As his taxi rattled up the King's

Road heading for the Berkeley, he was more than grateful to Tessa for priming Bernie; he certainly couldn't complain about the result of their meeting.

Two horses, Bernie had said, but good ones. Even as he'd been talking to the feisty American, Mike had made up his mind that he would have to buy *real* racehorses for this man. But at least he'd have the chance to make a healthy profit from them, and it would give him another reason to go to the spring sales in the States besides making sure he got rid of his two less than perfect colts at the right price.

At the same time, Mike vehemently hoped and prayed that the Japanese-US summit would have been held by then, and that the yen would begin to harden.

The receptionist at the Berkeley was adamant. 'No, there's no Mr George Parker staying here. There was someone of that name here a couple of weeks ago, but we've no forwarding address for him.'

Mike felt a sharp jolt of panic. George had never mentioned that he'd moved out, or given Mike another address. He couldn't remember if his cousin had even told him to come here on Tuesday evening; Mike had just assumed he was still staying at the Knightsbridge hotel.

He was about to press the receptionist again on the date that George had left, when he heard the now familiar, soft Mid-Western voice.

'Hello, Mike. You're looking a little angsty.'

'Thank God you're here! I thought you were still staying in this place.' Mike glanced apologetically at the receptionist. 'When she said you'd checked out, I felt a bit of a fool.'

'Don't worry. I wanted some privacy so I leased a place –
a service apartment in Kensington. Come on, I'll buy you a
drink.' He led Mike to the quiet bar and ordered two large
Scotches.

George leaned back in his chair – a cooler, more relaxed
version of his cousin – and smiled faintly. 'So,' he asked,
'how's it going?'

'I've got the money,' Mike said hoarsely.

George nodded with no great display of emotion. 'You're
sure you want to do this?'

'Bloody hell, man. I wouldn't have gone out and raised
all that cash if I wasn't sure.' Mike patted his pocket in
which there was an envelope containing a cheque made out
to George Sargent Parker for £300,000.

'Okay,' George said mildly. He pulled some folded papers
from his inside pocket, straightened them and laid them on
a table for Mike to read.

There was a simple agreement, in which he granted
authority to George to deal in foreign currency, on his
behalf, through a trading account at Crédit Lyonnais.
Beneath this was a personal guarantee, from Michael Powell to Crédit Lyonnais, for any losses exceeding deposited
funds held to the account.

There was an additional guarantee to George Parker, in
which Mike indemnified him against any losses George
might incur dealing on his behalf.

Mike signed the first two documents. When he picked up
the third, George raised his hand a few inches off the table.
'You don't have to sign that one if you don't want. I didn't
draw it up for me; I brought it because I thought you might

feel more comfortable with it.'

Mike read it again. 'I'm happy with that. After all, I've signed the guarantee to the bank. Besides, let's hope it's all hypothetical.'

As Mike signed the third document, George picked up his glass. 'I'll drink to that. Here's to the rising yen.'

'When will you buy them?'

'As soon as the bank has cleared the deposit – two days.'

'But what if it keeps on going up? We'll have missed out on the maximum profit.'

George shrugged. 'It's a lucky man who gets it spot on both ends of the deal. It's at two forty-five today; if we buy at that, it doesn't matter how much it goes out between now and the Treasury summit, so long as it ends up back around two twenty-five, which would be the most advantageous rate for us Americans.'

'But how can you be so sure the Japs will agree?'

'When the only other option is a complete breakdown of their bank system and financial markets, they'll agree.'

'So we go out with a profit of around seventy million yen – about three hundred grand?'

'That's right, cousin, three hundred grand – half a million dollars. That should solve a few of your problems.'

Mike gritted his teeth. 'I bloody hope so, George, or I'll be living in a tent.'

Chapter Six

When it came to racing at Cheltenham, Nick Thornton-Jones was always glad of the advantage of being one of the small cluster of Cotswold yards. It took the horse-box less than half an hour to get from his stables to the course.

On the third morning of the Festival meeting, Panpipe was the last on to the box at Fencote. She was getting a lift to the races in Nick's lorry, in the care of one of his lads. Nick had already saddled two winners from twelve races of enormous fields, but he didn't have a runner in the Triumph, and was glad to help with Panpipe, though her chances weren't highly rated. The five-pound allowance she got for being a filly wasn't enough when set against three or four horses with better form and more experience. Just one sloppy jump would negate that small advantage.

But Jed had made an early decision not to run her between Christmas and the four-year-old championship, and he'd stuck to it. He had schooled her himself over Nick's hurdles, to the point where she barely noticed them. She'd soon learned that if she tucked her feet up neatly, she'd have a more comfortable run.

Jed had made the filly hard-muscle fit on Nick's all-weather gallop. At one-in-five, this was one of the steepest in the country; a horse didn't have to be moving fast to be working hard, and less speed meant less strain on the tendons.

As Jed watched her being loaded, he turned to the trainer beside him. 'Whatever else, Nick, she'll be the best-looking animal in the parade ring.'

'And the fittest. I've got to hand it to you, you've done a bloody good job.'

The ramp of the lorry was heaved up and three lads leaped into the cab, to shouts of good luck from the others left behind in the yard.

A horse in the stables whinnied to a friend, and had an answer from the lorry as it rumbled out of the yard and on to the narrow Cotswold lane.

Terry, the driver, had worked at Fencote since Nick Thornton-Jones had arrived there fifteen years before and had learned every bump in the road between the yard and Cheltenham. He drove with the deliberate, unhurried control of someone who cared deeply for the cargo in the back of his truck.

The first four or five miles were on narrow lanes. Drivers who used them regularly had trained themselves to be patient. They knew that the only way to travel safely was to travel slowly and vigilantly.

But when a small builder's van from Cheltenham swung round the corner travelling at sixty miles an hour, Terry's first instinct was to minimise the impact. He jerked the steering wheel violently to the left and the lorry lurched on to a narrow grass verge. For a moment, Terry thought he'd kept control, but the verge was soft and though he heaved the wheels back towards the road, the lorry carried straight on until it dropped into the ditch and tipped right on to its side, flattening twenty feet of ancient hedgerow.

Even as Terry fell sideways down the cab, crushing the two lads who'd come with him, his thoughts were for the three precious and terrified animals in the back.

The engine was still engaged but with no traction to contain the spinning wheels, it roared wildly until Terry was able to reach up and turn off the ignition.

Once the sound had died, the frantic banging of flailing hooves and the bellows of three panic-stricken horses reached him. Unconcerned for his own well-being or his mates', Terry clambered up on their backs to reach the door above his head. Wedged between the back of the cab and the steering wheel, he managed to heave it up and scramble out like a soldier emerging from a tank.

He jumped down and ran to the back of the lorry where the noises of battering hooves had grown even louder. The front end of the vehicle had dropped into the ditch, leaving the back a few feet off the ground. Terry fumbled open the catches on the ramp and, without the aid of gravity, summoned supernatural strength to heave the heavy timber door out sideways against its springs. The horses, loaded in a herring-bone arrangement, had their heads tied to the off-side wall of the lorry – now the top. Panpipe had been the last to go on and was nearest the back, dangling by her head collar, crashing her front hooves into the side and scrabbling with her hind legs.

The filly's eyes rolled with terror and white lather covered her neck. Terry risked a lashing hoof to grab her rope and tugged the quick-release knot free from the iron ring. The horse swung her front legs down and out of the lorry with the driver still hanging on to her.

All she wanted was to break loose and get away from this crazy tilted cage. She dropped her front hooves on the tarmac road and bucked her hindquarters, swinging them furiously towards the nuisance who was restraining her.

A hoof caught Terry on his shoulder and sent him reeling back against the ramp while he lost his hold on the rope.

Panpipe knew at once that she was free and clattered off down the lane, putting as much distance as she could between herself and the toppled lorry.

Jed drove his Range Rover out of Nick's yard ten minutes after the lorry. After a few miles, taking a bend into a straight stretch of the narrow lane, he saw a horse, two hundred yards away and cantering towards him over the hard surface.

He knew at once that it was Panpipe.

He didn't stop to think how she was there, only that she must be stopped and saved from any more damage than she might already have done herself.

He swung the big vehicle into three swift turns until it was at right angles across the lane. Then he leaped out and placed himself in front of the bonnet of the Range Rover which he guessed the filly could have jumped if she'd wanted, and waved his arm like a banner across the gap.

The filly saw the blockage, and her step shortened. For a

moment, Jed thought she was going to turn, but she must have remembered the horror of the tilting lorry. A few yards from the Range Rover, she slowed into an uncertain trot. Jed stopped waving and called her name.

Her ears pricked at the sound of his familiar voice and she eased herself into a walk, then stopped six feet from the man she now recognised.

Jed made no attempt to approach her. He carried on speaking her name, reassuring her the way he might have comforted a small child.

Panpipe lowered her neck and stretched out her nose towards him. His familiar scent seemed to calm her and Jed risked taking a few slow steps towards her until, very steadily, he reached out and took hold of the dangling head-collar rope. Still moving cautiously, he put his hand up to stroke the side of her head and fondle her muzzle.

Once he was sure the filly was completely relaxed, he reached inside the Range Rover for his mobile phone, praying that for once it would make a connection down in this dip between the hills.

Mike arrived ten minutes later and pulled in behind Jed's car, now parked off the road in a gateway.

'Do you know what the hell happened?' Jed called over as Mike climbed out.

'Yes. One of the lads got Nick on the mobile. Some little bastard came tearing round the bend by the turning to Naunton and drove them off the road. The lorry was tipped on its side with its nose in the ditch.' Mike nodded at the now docile Panpipe, picking a few mouthfuls of grass at the end of the rope Jed was holding. 'She lashed out and pissed off. It's lucky you were coming behind.'

'She'd already done half a mile then.'

'Is she knackered?'

Jed tugged the filly's head up from the grass verge. 'See what you think.' He led her down the lane at a crisp trot for a few dozen yards.

She moved straight and with her customary fluid bounce. Jed turned her and trotted her back towards Mike.

'It's a bloody miracle,' he laughed. 'She looks sound as a bell to me.'

Jed pulled her up and nodded.

'Will you still let her run, then?' Mike asked, with the sudden unexpected hope that he might get his ride after all.

'She'll need a new set of plates, but she doesn't seem to be feeling sore at all.'

'Great!' Mike nodded. 'I never thought you'd risk her after that. They should be along with another lorry any minute now.'

By the time the second truck rolled into view, the lad who'd been travelling with Panpipe arrived, trudging along the road.

Jed and Mike lowered the ramp, and when the lad brought her round, surprisingly, she let Jed lead her up like a lamb.

The new lorry trundled on to the stricken one, where Terry and the lads, relatively unharmed, had taken off the other horses and were walking them round quietly in the nearest field. One had a cut over the knee, which looked nasty and Terry had a sore shoulder from Panpipe's kick, otherwise they were fine. The road was impassable, but the driver managed to reverse his vehicle in the field, and Jed followed it back round to the next turning and a longer route to Cheltenham.

As he drove, he wondered if he was doing the right thing in letting Panpipe run. It went against all his instincts to expect a horse to go out and race creditably after the trauma and expenditure of energy this one had been through that morning.

But she looked fine. She also had the best part of five hours to recover in before the race was due to be run. And if there was half a chance of winning the premier young hurdlers' race, she should take it; beyond the immediate rewards, it would be a great boost to her reputation as a brood mare.

He had resented Mike's smirk when he'd confirmed he would run the horse – a smirk which suggested Jed had finally joined the real world and the ranks of the greedy, knowing how it would enhance the horse's value to run and win, and prepared to risk her for that. Although, Jed thought, it was obvious that if he'd considered there was any real risk, it would also have meant it was unlikely she would turn in any kind of performance, and that would have done her value more harm than good.

Two flights from the winning post in the Triumph Hurdle, Jed started to fold up his hopes of glory, ready to steal away and nurse his disappointment.

Before the race, despite all the drama of the morning, Panpipe had looked magnificent in the parade ring; every commentator agreed. Now she had only four horses behind her.

The runners had set off on the two-mile trip as if they were going six furlongs at Goodwood. Mike, with no particular instructions other than to pull her up if she didn't feel right, decided the leaders were bound to tire sooner or later. He resisted the urge to go with the early pace, concentrating instead on travelling at a good even gallop from which he knew the filly could jump fluently.

Halfway down the hill, with just a third of a mile to run, some of the field had come back to him, as he'd expected. But there were still eight or so battling it out twenty lengths in front. And however good his filly was, he knew they'd have to tire significantly for him to get even a place.

He pushed the filly hard into the flight at the bottom of the hill and flew it. Panpipe landed running and Mike felt that sudden extraordinary thrill of being on a horse that was going forward when all the others looked like cars running out of fuel.

As they swung round the corner, he asked her for more, and could hardly believe her response. She'd been at the top limit of her cruising speed for almost two miles and now she was straining to give more. She stretched her neck and her legs and, with a tingle of excitement, Mike realised that there was just a chance of getting there.

Jed watched the filly's huge leap over the second last and dug his fingernails into his palms, cursing Mike for holding her up so long in the first mile. In the early stages of the race, he had seen what the jockey was doing and trusted his judgement, but as he gazed forlornly at the leaders battling it out at the bottom of the hill, it was obvious that Mike had underestimated the staying power of the front runners.

Then, with a growing sense of wonder and a germ of hope, he saw that the gap back to Panpipe was rapidly decreasing. As they approached the last, she came within ten lengths of them, and another huge leap clipped off two more. The front runner who had led the whole way was suddenly feeling the hill. His stride shortened drastically and he was passed by the other two, who were also showing signs of serious fatigue.

But Panpipe touched down from the last with her ears pricked and a spring in her stride. Jed held his breath. The filly seemed to bound up the hill, gaining ground with every stride.

She passed all three leaders, fifty yards from the post, and crossed the line going away.

Jed released a pent-up lungful of air with a huge cheer. Half a minute earlier, he'd been certain they'd lost. It took him a moment to adjust to the extraordinary turnaround.

He saw Mike give the filly a pat as he wheeled her round to trot back to the enclosure. There was a huge smile on the jockey's face, and despite Jed's earlier doubts about the way he was riding the race, he couldn't deny now that Mike had produced the filly with perfect timing.

Sammy, who had been beside him leaning weakly on the rail of the balcony of their box, suddenly threw her arms around him.

'Well done!' She beamed ecstatically. 'You're brilliant *and* you were right about Mike.'

Jed acknowledged her admission with a grin. 'For a few minutes even I doubted it. Are you coming down to the winners' enclosure?'

'No. I'm exhausted, but you go.'

Jed took her arm and led her back into the small private box behind them. He left her regretfully, and joined the throng of people streaming down the stairs and out to the paddock to greet the winner. Friends shouted their congratulations as he pushed his way into the ring in time to see Panpipe being led in by Nick's lad, with Mike beaming on her back.

The jockey had started the week some way down the list of likely champions for the meeting. Now he was equal first.

Not bad for a thirty-five year old with a dangerous liking for drink who should have retired two years ago, Jed thought. He reached Panpipe and led her to the winner's slot through a roar of approval. English racegoers were still old-fashioned enough to give extra credit and deference to a filly on account of her gender. And to a trainer who had only two horses.

'Well done, Mike,' Jed shouted up, over the bellow of the crowd.

Mike looked down and winked. 'Well done, yourself.'

When the presentations were over, Jed took his crystal trophy back to the box to show Sammy and their guests.

A private box at Cheltenham wasn't something with which he would ever have indulged himself; it belonged to Tessa and Sammy. Their father, Adrian Langton, had been one of the great theatrical impresarios of the fifties and sixties and an enthusiastic owner of jumping horses for the last thirty years of his life, until he had died six years before, less wealthy than in his prime but still a rich man. In his will, he had made provision for both his daughters to buy substantial properties of their own, and left the rest to their mother, Jean, herself an actress to whom he had been happily married for thirty-five years.

Jean had been buried beside him only two years later and left the remains of her husband's estate equally between the daughters, including the Villa Fleurie, a large beautiful house just outside St Rémy-de-Provence, and a lease on one of the old boxes at Cheltenham racecourse.

Jed had often ridden for Adrian Langton, and became a family friend long before he and Sammy were married. He'd had many a post-race drink in this same box. Now that he was used to having it at his disposal, he enjoyed the advantage of being able to entertain his friends and watch the racing in comfort, especially during the overcrowded March Festival meeting.

Jed had no direct involvement with any of the runners in the rest of the day's Gold Cup card. Although he seldom bet, he loved to watch and judge, now from a long-term, breeder's point of view. Sammy had grown up with National Hunt racing, knew a lot about it and enjoyed it. She loved to see horses out in the fields at home and champions battling bravely up the last furlong at Cheltenham. She used to ride anything and everything until she'd become too ill, but her interest had remained just as strong, and she understood Jed's passion and admired the single-minded dedication he had brought first to his riding, then to his breeding. She was thrilled that at last a big race had turned out so well for him.

During the rest of the afternoon, people were dropping in and out to exchange gossip and congratulations with stories of triumph and tragedy.

It was a few moments after the day's final 'bumper' was over that Geoffrey Thynne walked into the box.

Jed had met the well-known banker and bloodstock breeder a few times; he didn't know him well but knew intimately the bloodlines of most of the mares in his stud. He had also bought Panpipe's dam, Utopian Dream, from him six years before. It had been a major deal for Jed then, risking every halfpenny he could get his hands on. Geoffrey Thynne knew it, and appreciated Jed's confidence in his own judgement. Thynne was delighted to see the grand-daughter of one of his own best mares winning the most prestigious juvenile race in the jumping calendar, even though she'd been bred to win at Royal Ascot, not Cheltenham. He boomed his congratulations at Jed and happily accepted his offer of champagne.

As Jed was pouring it, Mike walked through the door to a ragged cheer from the thirty or so people crammed into the box. He saw Jed and pushed his way through to where he was standing by the drinks table with Geoffrey.

When he reached them, it was obvious that he'd already had a few celebratory glasses on the way and he pounced on the one he was offered now while Jed introduced him to the breeder.

Thynne was well aware that Mike had ridden Jed's winner

that day, but went on talking to Jed as if the jockey weren't there.

'I hear you had dinner with Lucy in Keeneland?'

Sammy, sitting at the table beside them talking to other guests, instantly picked up this information with her sensitive antennae. Jed saw her register the news, and groaned to himself.

'I found myself sitting next to her on the plane from New York,' he said lightly. 'And I saw the piece she wrote for *BBM*.' He turned to Mike. 'More champagne?' he asked, picking up a bottle and pouring the contents into Mike's empty glass.

An hour later, the car-parks outside were less than a quarter full, and there were fewer than a dozen people left in the Langton box.

Geoffrey Thynne had gone and Mike was lounging on a small gilt chair, watching the video of his winning race for the sixth time.

When it was over he tipped the contents of his glass down his throat and brought it back down again on the table with a loud thump.

Jed glanced at him solicitously. 'Mike, take it easy. Maybe we should take you home. You're riding tomorrow, aren't you?'

'No!' he said, apparently sobering up suddenly. 'No, I don't want anyone coming home.'

From the defensiveness in his manner, Jed guessed that maybe he was expecting someone – a new girlfriend, perhaps.

'Okay,' Jed said. 'It's up to you.'

'Bloody right it's up to me,' Mike blustered, getting to his feet. 'Who the hell do you think you are suggesting I can't drive? I drove your bloody horse up that hill all right, didn't I?'

Jed put out a calming hand. 'Relax. You rode a brilliant race. It's been a hell of a day, though, with the crash and everything.'

'Don't patronise me either. I'm not married to your sister-in-law any more, remember. I know what you used to think of me – and still do. I may win races for you, but I'm just a common little Welsh peasant, aren't I?' Mike jerked his chin at Jed aggressively. 'Well, let me tell you, I've got my own family, you know. I don't bloody need *yours*.'

He marched towards the door and out into the corridor. Jed and Sammy stared after him, astonished by the sudden outburst. Jed shrugged his shoulders regretfully, and blamed the champagne.

Chapter Seven

A week after the Triumph, Tessa arrived at Batscombe to have lunch with Sammy. Jed was at the races, the cleaner had gone and there was no one in the yard.

Tessa climbed out of her car into a spring downpour and ran round to the back of the house. She didn't wait to ring the bell but let herself straight into the kitchen. Sammy was sitting at the table with a pile of letters and the telephone in front of her; she glanced up at her sister and forced her lips into a smile.

Tessa noticed the paleness of the drawn features which she knew almost as well as her own and sat down at once opposite Sammy.

'What is it, Sam? What's happened?'

Sammy shook her head. 'Don't ask me now,' she said with a quiet firmness that Tessa had learned long ago to respect. 'I'll make some coffee.' With her jaw set, she got to her feet and gathered up a cafetière and cups. 'How's the film going?'

'Fine. Mel's a neurotic little faggot, but he's turning into a hell of a good director. I think he might have extracted one of my best performances ever,' Tessa said, honestly, not bragging.

'Better than Beth in *Tequila Sunset*?'

Tessa laughed. The rumour that she might be nominated for an Academy Award for best supporting actress in Bernie Capella's film was still being bandied about by the British press though there'd been no confirmation from Los Angeles. 'God knows. That part was so well written it played itself – not something I can say for the angry bitch I'm playing now.'

'I suppose if you can make a success of these older woman parts now, you'll extend your career by a few more decades.'

'Listen,' Tessa said with half a laugh, 'this character may be older, but the men still want her.'

Sammy looked at her for a moment before she spoke. 'How about in real life?'

Tessa took a gulp from the cup of black coffee in front of her. 'Real life? I'm not sure what that is any more. The man who seems to want me most at the moment is the one who fought to get away for most of our marriage.'

'Oh, God! Is Mike still pestering you?'

Tessa nodded. 'He seems to think winning that race for Jed has made him part of the family again. As if all the fighting and hassles of the last two years can just be swept under the carpet.'

'But what does he want?'

'He keeps saying we should see each other again – have dinner together sometimes. And he tries to persuade me to let him come and see me in London. Of course, I still care about Mike, the way you might for a tricky son, but I had to tell him I just wasn't ready to see him on those or any other terms yet.'

Sammy shook her head. 'I've never understood what it was about you that always made you go for bastards.'

'The sort of men you call bastards are often the ones who are most insecure. I suppose that appeals to my maternal instincts.'

'I don't know much about maternal instincts,' Sammy said, 'but I suspect they're the easiest to hurt.'

Tessa looked back at her sister and nodded slowly. 'That's enough about me, though. What's been happening to you?'

Sammy glanced down at the table. 'I know we've never really talked about our sex-lives . . .'

'Oh, Sammy.' Tessa anticipated what her sister was about to say and reached across the table to touch her hand. 'Has it gone wrong for you and Jed?'

Sammy looked up for a second and managed a small grin. 'Not so much gone wrong as disappeared completely.'

'I can't believe he's lost interest in you . . .'

'He hasn't. I have. Since I've guessed what was going on inside me, I just can't bear him to touch me or anything.'

'Are you sure you do know what it is that's giving you all this pain?'

Sammy nodded slowly. 'I've read a lot about it, and even though my consultant isn't sure, I'm prepared for the tests to confirm it.'

'But surely,' Tessa said, 'you shouldn't give in to it, especially before it's even been confirmed?'

'I know what I know,' said Sammy with her customary stubbornness. 'And so does Jed, but he's been so kind and thoughtful. I love him as much as I ever did.'

Tessa nodded. 'He's a good man, there's no doubt about that.'

'Didn't you always think he was *too* good?'

'For my taste, sure,' Tessa admitted. 'But he was right for you, and I'm sure he'll be patient and wait until you've got it all sorted out and can start having babies and things.'

'Oh, Tessa.' Sammy put her head in her hands despairingly. 'I don't blame him, I really don't, but . . .'

'What, Sam? What is it?' Tessa asked with tender concern.

'I think he's been having an affair.'

'What?' Tessa exclaimed, genuinely surprised. 'Jed? Sleeping with another woman?'

Sammy nodded and gulped back tears.

'I can't believe it. Are you sure?'

'Yes. He lied to me and as far as I know, he's never done that before.'

'Just because he lied doesn't mean he's committed adultery. Anyway, who is this other woman?'

Sammy related the story of Lucy Thynne and the conversation she'd overheard at Cheltenham.

'You're mad if you think that confirms he's having an affair.'

'Tessa, I haven't let him make love to me for over a year.'

Tessa looked down at her pale, fragile sister, whose fair hair hung lifelessly around her drawn face.

'Or anything else?'

'No, not really. I don't even want him to touch me.' Sammy glanced down distractedly at her bony hands. 'I'm sorry to come bleating to you, Tess.'

'You bleat as much as you want, girl. That's what big sisters are for.'

'But what do you think I should do?' Sammy pleaded.

'Do nothing. And much more important, say nothing.'

'But I can't!' Sammy wailed.

'You must. I promise you – the minute you bring it out into the open, your relationship with Jed will change for ever. If you say nothing, then knowing Jed he'll be there when you're ready for him. But put any pressure on him and he'll start to pity you. When that happens, knowing you, you'll stop loving him.'

Jed arrived home early the next evening, having driven to London and back through the Friday traffic.

For the last dozen miles, he'd been thinking about Pan-pipe. After her success in the Triumph, he'd felt confident enough to confirm her entry in the big four-year-old hurdle race at the Aintree National meeting.

The filly had come back from Cheltenham looking even better for the day's outing. Jed knew that in some ways the level Aintree course with its sharp turns would neutralise the advantage of her obvious ability to stay, but she deserved to take her chance.

Sitting tensed up in his car for two hours had aggra-vated his battered joints, and he climbed out of the Range Rover with a vicious ache in his hip. Inside, he called for Sammy. When he heard no reply, he guessed she was in the bedroom, as she often was these days. He hobbled upstairs and found her curled up on the bed, obviously in pain.

'Mike's been ringing Tessa again,' she snapped as her husband walked in. 'I knew if you started asking him to ride for you again, he'd use it as an excuse to try to get back with her, and she just can't handle it.'

'Of course she can,' Jed said. 'She can tell him to piss off.'

'You know it's not that simple, not when it's someone she's loved and lived with for years. He may be an arrogant drunk half the time, but there's a vulnerable side to him. And Tessa just isn't as hard as she seems.'

'Well, Garry O'Driscoll's still off, so Mike will still ride Panpipe on Friday. Provided he's in reasonable shape.'

'Jed, please don't give him any more excuses to come back into our lives and cause aggravation.'

'Sammy, I'm a professional bloodstock breeder. It's not a hobby; it matters very much that I'm seen producing winners, and if I think the filly's best chance of winning is to put Mike up, then I've got no choice. I admit that a real professional ought to know better than to bring his personal relations into the job, but it's my decision and he rides. Whether you like it or not, we've been friends for a long time.'

Jed knew he was being hard on Sammy and, reprimanding himself for ignoring her obvious discomfort, forced a smile. 'I promise I'll tell him to stop hassling Tessa when I see him. Now, you're not looking too good. Do you think I ought to get Doctor Gallimore over?'

'I'm okay.' Sammy put on a brave smile. 'I've taken a

couple of painkillers. They should sort me out.'

She was looking more comfortable later, got up and insisted on cooking dinner, but when Tessa phoned, it set her right back.

Jed watched while Sammy answered and stayed quiet while she listened.

'I'll ask Jed,' she said flatly after a few moments. She put her hand over the mouthpiece and turned to him. 'Mike's been on the phone to Tessa – again – drunk and full of self-pity because he missed a winner today.'

Jed nodded. Mike had been too heavy to ride one of his regular mounts and its trainer had booked another jockey. The horse had won easily and now Mike was cross about letting his weight get out of hand.

Sammy went on, 'He's supposed to be one of the guests of honour at the bash at the Dorchester tomorrow. He's told Tessa he's not going because he thinks he doesn't deserve it. She says would you be kind enough to go to Easerswell on the way and make sure he gets there.'

'Why on earth does she care whether he goes or not?' Jed asked.

'She wonders if you could drive him?' Sammy twisted her mouth in a doubtful grimace. 'She'd be very grateful. So would I. The trouble is Mike's got this knack of making Tessa feel responsible for his negative moods.'

'It's absurd! There she is one minute grumbling about him trying to get back together with her, and then she's badgering me to look after him.' Jed sighed, knowing he'd have to do it.

He couldn't bring himself to argue with Sammy just now,

when she was so frail and teetering on the brink of a new crisis.

Sammy had been invited to the dinner too. She didn't want to go but because she knew it was important for his business, she hadn't objected to Jed's going on his own. He'd also made arrangements to spend an hour before it with two French breeders who'd shown an interest in some of his young-stock. He could have seen them afterwards, but had realised a long time ago that talking business late in the evening was generally counter-productive.

Resigned to the disruption of his careful planning of the following evening, Jed nodded, and Sammy told her sister.

The next afternoon, as the wind blustered wetly from the west, Jed drove the few miles across the valley to Easerswell.

He parked beside the high beech hedge which fronted the house and walked over to the chunky stone porch. He tugged the brass handle of an antiquated bell-pull and listened to a tinkling sound at the back of the house, wondering how long it would take to raise Mike.

He was surprised when the front door was opened almost at once. Mike stood in front of him, barefoot but otherwise in full evening dress. Jed saw in his friend's eyes, behind a faint screen of nervousness, some of the genuine charm with which he had arrived in the racing world twenty years before.

'Hello, boyo,' he said in the thick Welsh accent which reminded Jed of the old days.

'Hello, Mike. I got the impression from Tessa I was going to have to shake you out of a stupor.'

'That was yesterday. I'm okay now. Go into the kitchen and get yourself a whisky while I find my shoes.' He padded back up the stairs. Jed ignored the offer of a whisky, and took the opportunity instead to look around the house.

During the years that Mike and Tessa had been married and living at Easerswell, Jed had spent many hours there and had grown fond of the house, but he hadn't been back since his sister-in-law had moved out.

There were no fresh flowers in the vases and Tessa's old dried arrangements and pot-pourris were looking neglected and dusty. There were some pieces of furniture missing and, since her last visit, most of the pictures had gone, leaving sad, pale spaces on the walls. Somehow, though, the cottage still retained most of its charm.

Mike reappeared on the stairs, smartly shod now in gleaming patent leather. 'Sorry to keep you waiting,' he said. 'I think I'll just crash out in the back of the car, if that's okay by you?'

Within a few minutes of leaving the house, Jed glanced in his driving mirror and saw Mike sitting back with his eyes closed and a contented smile on his face.

In fact that contented smile disguised a mixture of feelings, for he was now committed to the largest risk he'd ever taken. George had phoned him three days before to confirm that their deal was up and running, and he had bought three hundred million yen at two forty-seven.

Since then, Mike had checked the price on Ceefax two or three times a day, knowing that every time the yen moved back one point, he gained fifteen thousand pounds.

Once his finances were sorted out, he was certain of

working himself back into favour with the woman he had so foolishly discarded.

So far as that was concerned, staying on good terms with Jed was an important element. It was even more important, George had drummed into him, that he should stay sober. Nearly always, his cousin said, words unspoken worked better than any uttered recklessly.

Mike's eyes fluttered open as Jed slowed the Range Rover, coming off the motorway after the Chiswick flyover.

'Good kip?' he asked over his shoulder.

'Yeah,' Mike laughed. 'Sorry I've been lousy company. But while I think of it, how's that nice little colt of yours with the swollen joints?'

Jed grunted. 'Just the same. If it wasn't for them he'd be one of the best I've produced.'

'Why don't you put him on Bute?'

'I've done that and he's fine when he's on it, but as soon as it wears off he's back to square one again.'

'Well, put him on it for the sales, no one will know.'

Jed glanced at him in his driving mirror under the bright lights of the flyover. 'Mike, I wish you'd keep ideas like that to yourself. I'm not interested in pulling the wool over anyone's eyes. I'm trying to build a reputation, not destroy it at birth.'

'I suppose you're right.' Jed had said exactly what Mike had expected him to. 'If you sold him to me cheap enough, I might take a chance on him.'

'I'll think about it,' Jed replied, implying that he already had and the answer was no.

Mike didn't pursue it. He had enough on his plate with

the colt he'd bought from Long Crendon and besides, he thought to himself with an inward smile, if George was right, these deals with second-rate yearlings would soon be utterly irrelevant.

It was seven o'clock when Jed drew up at the main entrance of the hotel in Park Lane, and an attendant whisked the car away while he accompanied Mike to the American Bar.

Mike went blandly along with it, evidently committed to not causing trouble. He sat down and ordered a mineral water and an *Evening Standard*.

Jed left him and walked across Hyde Park Corner to his meeting at the Lanesborough.

Later, at the dinner, so far as he could tell from across the room, Mike seemed to be in control of himself, chatting politely to the strangers to either side of him. Jed was relieved as much for professional as for personal reasons. Mike's reputation was growing worse by the week, and although Jed knew he could still ride with the best of them on a good day, other trainers, including Mike's old mate Jimmy Fitzosborn, were saying he had lost his edge and blaming his drinking.

When the dinner came to an end, Jed was ready to go home. He wandered over to where Mike sat at the top table, but the Welshman had made other plans so Jed went home without him.

Mike left the Dorchester soon after Jed. He took a taxi to Sumner Place, South Kensington, and climbed out in front of a five-storey stuccoed house in a smart terrace. After pushing a button beside a video entry system by the front door, he was greeted by George's disembodied voice from a small speaker set below the camera.

'Hello, Mike. Take the elevator and press number two.'

The lock on the front door buzzed and Mike pushed it open. He took the lift and stepped out into the small lobby of the smart duplex that occupied the top two floors of the building.

George was waiting to greet him. 'Hello, cuz. Welcome to my new apartment.' He waved Mike through a panelled door into a large drawing-room which appeared to occupy the whole floor. 'Drink?'

Mike nodded with a grin. 'Yeah, please.' Seeing George in these surroundings – clearly rich, obviously successful – did a lot to reinforce his confidence.

'I see you managed to stay sober,' George observed with an approving grin. 'So you'll appreciate the good news.'

Mike glanced sharply at him. 'Yes?'

'The date's been fixed for the Treasury summit in Washington – Thursday third of April.'

'How long do you reckon it'll take?'

'Usually they have these things completed by the weekend, so they can make their announcements before the markets open on Monday morning.'

'Thursday the third.' Mike nodded with a smile. 'First day of Aintree. You should come – I ought to win the big hurdle race.'

'Maybe I will. And I might come and watch you at Kempton Park next week, if you've got anything good to ride.'

'Next Wednesday?' Mike thought. 'Let's see.' He smiled. 'Yes. Come and back Lute Player. If the ground isn't too soft, he'll win.'

By the time Lute Player had confirmed Mike's prediction, the value of the Japanese currency had fallen to a level that made him sick with worry. For the first time in his life, he felt no joy in riding a winner. He could only think how pitiful the purse looked compared to his currency losses.

George had arranged to meet him again that evening at the South Kensington flat, to review the state of their deal. It was only Mike's faith in his cousin's judgement that sustained him. The currency had rallied fractionally after several of the financial pundits had been quoted as saying that the Japanese might, after all, succumb to American pressure to accept the package, even though it would mean the end of the option of exporting their way out of recession on the back of a severely weakened yen.

Later in the evening, sober and more confident about his investment after a long chat with his cousin, Mike drove from London to Easerswell. It was a crisp, clear night. Up on the Cotswolds, away from the polluted night sky of London, the stars seemed closer and brighter, and brought Mike's doubts and dilemmas into perspective. He felt younger, and suddenly better able to handle the new risks he was facing.

As soon as he was back inside his house, he checked the time and realised that people were still at work in California. He picked up the phone and rang Bernie Capella's office in Los Angeles.

One of Capella's aides confirmed his boss's instructions that funds of one million dollars would be available to Mike to make purchases at the mid-April Breeze-Up sale in Saratoga, New York. Mike arranged to finalise the details the week before the sale, and put the phone down feeling that at last things could be swimming in his direction.

He thought of ringing Tessa to tell her how well he was doing. But he didn't touch the phone; there'd be plenty of time for that in a couple of weeks, after Aintree and the US-Japanese summit.

The fine night had left the great Gloucestershire escarpment coated in frost. A warm spring sun was fast burning it off as Jed walked back from his stable block for breakfast but he was too preoccupied to appreciate nature's beauty. Catherine Forbes, his head groom, was with him.

She was a stocky girl in her late-twenties, who'd been at Batscombe since Jed and Sammy had arrived there six years before. She was supremely competent, apparently content with a life uncluttered by men, and passionately loyal to Jed, Batscombe and to the four other girls who worked there.

It was this that was going to make it almost impossible for him to say what he had to over breakfast. He was glad Sammy wasn't down yet; he didn't want to have to explain in front of her, too.

But he didn't prevaricate. As soon as the coffee was made, he filled two cups and sat down opposite his head groom.

'I'm afraid I've got something rather unpleasant to tell

you,' he said. 'We're going to have to lose two of the girls.'

Catherine looked startled, taken by surprise. 'Why?' she asked.

'I'm sorry, Cath. I simply can't afford to pay five people for the next year or so. I think we all know that we haven't got anything at all special to send to the sales this year. It's not our fault. Breeding can be a lottery and our numbers didn't come up this time.'

'There's the grey filly,' she pointed out.

'We might get a halfway decent price for her, if we're lucky. But even if we do, I'm afraid I'm facing a bloody great loss this year, and there's no way I can risk keeping on five full-time staff for the time being.'

Catherine was astounded. 'But, Jed, surely with all the money that goes into producing these foals, the cost of two grooms isn't going to make much difference?'

'I'm afraid it does. If you must know, I've been a little too ambitious and tried to expand too fast. I shouldn't have cranked up the numbers so quickly. That's the point, really. I'll have to get rid of three or four mares, too, including a couple of the good ones. I may even have to consider selling Panpipe.'

'Oh, no!' Catherine moaned. 'She's our flagship horse. And anyway, what would Bella do? You know how much she missed her when she went to board at Fencote. And we've just got everything in order here.'

'I'm sorry. Don't think I don't realise how much you've put in and that you don't want to let your girls down.'

The groom smiled ruefully. 'I'm sure you wouldn't do it if you didn't have to.'

'I'd rather cut back a bit now than lose everything later,' he said, grateful for her sympathy.

'I understand. But couldn't you just go to the banks for more money? After all, this place must be worth a fortune.'

Jed shook his head with a smile. 'I shouldn't be telling you this, but for one thing this house is Sammy's, not mine, and anyway we've borrowed against it up to the hilt already. It was the only way I could buy any serious mares.'

Catherine looked horrified. 'Oh, Jed! I'm sorry I didn't realise.' Then, with a swift change of tone, she became business-like. 'Still, if it's got to happen, we'd better get on with it.'

They discussed the relative merits of the grooms, and the fairest redundancy arrangements. Fortunately, only Catherine lived in at the yard so there weren't any accommodation problems.

Sammy came in wearing her dressing-gown just as Catherine was leaving. She followed her out with her eyes.

'What were you talking about?'

'I've got to let a couple of girls go, I'm afraid.'

'Why's that? I thought you were very pleased with them all.'

'I am, but I'm selling three or four mares.'

'Good heavens! What are you doing that for?'

Jed shrugged his shoulders and sighed. 'I shouldn't have got so many, not until I'd put a bit of fat on the business.'

'You mean, you're short of money again?'

'A little, but it'll get worse if I don't do something about it.'

'Haven't you got some horse in the States that you and

Mike bought and haven't sold yet?'

'There's one. Why?'

'I seem to remember you saying it was pretty well bred. Won't that sell for a good price?'

Jed grunted. 'If it had been any good we'd have sold it last season at the yearling sales. But it looked terrible, and anyway it started coughing and lost its slot so I let Mike persuade me to keep it to sell at a Breeze-Up this spring.'

'I wish you'd never done the deal with him.'

'It was nearly three years ago, and it looked like a bargain at the time.'

'Have you seen him recently?'

'Yesterday at Kempton, briefly. He seemed distracted but it didn't stop him riding a blinder.'

'Tessa says he hasn't been in touch with her since you drove him to London; she wondered if he was okay.'

'There's no satisfying your sister, is there? Either Mike's pestering her, and she's getting pissed off, or he's not, and she's worrying about him.'

'Tessa's never denied she's still fond of him.'

'Hmm,' said Jed tactfully, rather than stating his view that Tessa should stop messing the poor bloke about. 'Anyway,' he went on, changing the subject, 'how are you feeling?'

'I'll tell you after I've had the tests.'

Chapter Eight

Three days before Panpipe was due to run at Aintree, Jed rang Mike and asked him to come over to Nick Thornton-Jones' stables at Fencote the following day to ride her in her final workout.

He drove Panpipe over himself in the lorry next morning and arrived before seven. He found Mike waiting for them in time for first lot, as they'd arranged with Nick, and watched as the horses walked out of the picturesque old yard.

Panpipe was looking relaxed, one of the long string filing out on to the sunken track which wound down to the misty banks of the Windrush, and the start of the gallop. From the top of the ash grove beside the old farmhouse the hollow calls of the crows echoed across the quiet valley, above the shouts of the lads and the clatter of hooves on the stony path.

Jed set off for the top of the gallop with Nick's assistant in the stable pick-up. Nick himself had already left; he liked to ride up on his hack – an old Cheltenham hero.

It was a clear, cold morning up on the crest of the bank.

The grass and hedgerows glittered ice-white in the early light; in a few minutes, the sun would rise like a big red balloon over Stow Ridge and wipe the frost away before their eyes.

Panpipe danced sideways on her toes towards the bottom of the gallop. She was keen to get on with her job and anxious to feel the grass beneath her feet. Mike patted her gently on the neck, spoke soothingly to her and held her in hand just enough to aim her the right way up the gallop. When it was his turn to go, he kept her firmly on the bit at half speed for the first three of the six furlongs.

An experienced two-mile hurdler ran close behind her, also held up by her small, wire-sinewed Irish lad. At the three-furlong marker, where the gallop levelled out at the top of the hill, the two riders got alongside each other, both easing the reins through their fingers as the horses stretched their necks to compete.

In a few strides they were racing hard together, but then Panpipe slowly began to pull away from the gelding and Mike allowed himself half a smile.

Jed stood beside the pick-up, gazing through binoculars at the gallop, more than content with Panpipe's performance, and her rider's.

Nick trotted his hack over to him. 'She looks okay,' he said with characteristic understatement.

Jed knew what he really meant and lowered his glasses to grin at the trainer. 'With that kind of improvement, I suspect even you might fancy her.'

Nick, who was notoriously pessimistic, nodded with a faint smile. 'I might at that.'

★ ★ ★

Jed's quiet confidence in Mike was dampened briefly while they were sitting down to breakfast at Nick's vast kitchen table half an hour later. When he saw Mike's expression, he sensed at once there was a problem.

Mike had come in soon after Jed and leafed through the pile of newspapers that Nick habitually left lying around for general consumption. He had picked out a copy of the *Financial Times*, sat down and buried his head in it to the exclusion of all else.

Jed deliberately didn't pay him much attention until he heard him mutter a couple of obscenities under his breath.

'What's the problem, Mike?'

He looked up without answering and glanced down irritably at his paper again, as if he couldn't quite believe what he'd just read.

The figures on the page seemed to blur in front of Mike's eyes. He had been staring at the exchange rate column, where the yen, at close of business the previous day, was marked at two fifty-six to the pound. Which meant that in the fortnight or so since George had bought the currency on his behalf, he had made a paper loss of £165,000 – which made the loss on the occasional dud foal look like chicken feed.

Then he thought of George's complete equanimity in the face of the yen's fall so far and allowed his own confidence to seep back. There was no other alternative.

Mike looked up at Jed, who was still waiting for a response. He took a deep breath and folded the paper decisively.

'It's nothing,' he said. 'An owner gave me a tip for a share. Turned out he was talking bollocks.'

'I suppose the shares were in his own company? They usually are,' Nick said, joining in the conversation.

'You've got it.' Mike forced a grin.

Jed knew there must be more to it than that. He'd recognised a familiar warning flash of controlled but burning anger behind Mike's bright blue eyes.

'How did the filly feel?' he asked instead.

'Pretty good. Very fit, but she takes a lot of settling,' Mike grumbled, as if this were Jed's fault. 'She really pulls.'

'No, she doesn't.' Jed shook his head impatiently. 'And you know it. Don't forget – I've ridden her myself for the last three months.'

Mike reddened. If he'd forgotten before, he remembered now. 'But you must admit, she *can* pull?'

'Mike,' Jed laughed, trying to defuse a pointless argument, 'you've already got the ride.'

For a moment Mike looked as if he wanted to carry on wrangling but with a palpable effort, he relaxed. Jed was glad when the awkwardness had passed.

The table had filled up with other work riders and Nick's assistants. Jed was surprised but pleased to hear Mike join in the general racing talk without trying to dominate it. He'd noticed that over the last few years, while Mike had been near the top of the jockeys' pecking order, he'd earned a reputation for not bothering to listen to anyone – talking straight over them if he suddenly had something he wanted to say. It was an ugly habit which had neutralised most of the naive charm with which he'd once been blessed.

This morning, with a prompt from Jed, Mike told a few stories Nick hadn't heard before and soon had the whole table laughing.

Later, he turned to Jed. 'I've been thinking about that colt of ours,' he said. 'There's a Breeze-Up sale in Saratoga this month; it should suit him and I'm pretty sure I can get him entered. What do you think?'

'Frankly, the sooner the better. We haven't paid any keep since I was over in Keeneland in January, and I could do with the cash if there's any left for us.'

Soon afterwards, the breakfast table briskly emptied as the people around it got up to carry on with their jobs, and Mike went out to school one of Nick's horses. When Jed and the trainer were left alone together, Nick leaned back in his chair.

'It looks as if Mike is finally accepting the fact that he can't call his own tune all the time. I never thought I'd see the day.'

'How do you mean?'

'I mean,' said Nick with a cynical grin, 'that he's no fool. He likes money, and he's finally got the message that unless he tempers his natural arrogance, people won't bother to do him favours any more or to give him the benefit of any doubts about his competence.'

Jed glanced at the trainer. 'But you're not saying I'm wrong to put him up on Panpipe, are you?'

'No, not at all. I dare say you've noticed I've used him

myself quite a bit recently.' He gave a shrug of his shoulders. 'I wouldn't have done if Garry had been around, but Mike's been fine. He simply isn't my first choice now. I know other trainers are worried about his fitness, too. And his boozing's buggering up his weight.'

'I'm more than happy with the way he rides Panpipe, and he's ridden a few brilliant races recently.'

'He's been lucky, though I suppose you could argue he's made the most of that luck. Anyway, it's your filly and your decision. By the way, I've got a couple of owners coming to lunch tomorrow who might be interested in some of your yearlings – if they're not too dear.'

'God!' Jed laughed. 'I wish they *were* that dear. But if your punters are looking for something they don't want to run for two or three years, I've got a couple that won't break the bank.'

'Then come to lunch,' Nick offered, and added a supplementary reason. 'I'm afraid they're not very scintillating company, and social graces aren't exactly a strong point.'

'What a tempting invitation! But I'm afraid I can't come tomorrow. I'm taking Sammy to London to see a specialist.'

'Oh. Nothing serious, I hope?'

'So do I. It's not always easy to tell with Sammy . . .' Jed reddened at what he realised must have sounded like disloyalty. 'What I'm saying is, I've no idea. I just hope to God it isn't serious.'

Jed had lunch with his accountant at the Carlton Tower next day. At his wife's request, he'd left her at the hospital in

South Kensington. He'd begged her to let him come in with her, but she'd been adamant about going alone.

She was standing outside when he went back at three o'clock, as they had arranged.

He stopped the Range Rover beside her and opened the passenger door.

'How did it go?'

Sammy said nothing. She climbed in and sat beside Jed, staring straight ahead of her.

He didn't press her but glanced briefly at her set pale face and pulled out into the traffic on the Fulham Road. Sammy still hadn't spoken by the time they turned left into the Cromwell Road to head out of London.

Jed took another look at her. 'Sam?' he prompted gently. 'Let's have it. What did they say?'

This time she returned his glance, but said nothing. Her face revealed no more.

'What was it . . .?' he began.

'Jed, I never went into the hospital,' she said flatly.

'You never went for your tests?' he breathed in disbelief.

'No.'

'Why the hell not?' he blurted before he could stop himself, then added remorsefully, 'I'm sorry, Sam.'

'I don't blame you. Of course I should have gone, but I just couldn't face them telling me what it is.'

'But, Sammy angel, until you do, you can't be sure.'

'I'm sure all right.'

'Sam, you've *got* to go. I'll fix another date and this time I'll stay with you. And if it is serious, for God's sake, we will get it treated as soon as possible!'

'I'm terrified of the treatment, too. Being shaved and made to look like a corpse . . . those rays burning into my body . . . I'd almost rather die.'

While she spoke, Jed worked off his frustration by weaving the big vehicle in and out of the traffic, desperate to get out of the urban crawl. 'Please, Sammy. You must be strong. You must fight. We've got a wonderful life in front of us. Look how happy we've been so far.'

'How can you say that, Jed?' she asked bitterly. 'When I haven't even let you make love to me for nearly a year.'

'I've told you,' he protested. 'I can handle that. That's not to say I wouldn't *like* to.' He grinned, trying to lighten the mood. 'But you must go back to the hospital.'

Sammy didn't answer for another few miles, then, as they broke free from the traffic on the flyover heading west at Chiswick, she sighed. 'You're right, Jed. I must face up to it. Just give me a little more time and I'll go again.'

'But what did you do for three hours outside the hospital?'

'I walked around; looked in a few shops. I bought you a watch,' she said, putting her hand in her pocket and pulling out a small gift-wrapped package.

'What on earth have I done to deserve this?' he said, bemused and slightly embarrassed by her gesture. 'What's it for?'

'To let you know I love you,' she said simply.

'Take it out of the box and show me.'

She unwrapped it and leaned across to dangle the gift by its strap, over the steering wheel. The Girard-Perregaux symbol – a rearing black horse – pranced on the yellow face of a handsome chronograph.

Jed sighed and tried to smile. He guessed the watch had cost as much as his best yearling would fetch that year. 'That's fantastic,' he said. 'But you shouldn't have got it. I don't deserve it.'

'I'll be the judge of what you deserve.'

'Well.' Jed shrugged his shoulders and shook his head in bemusement. 'Thank you very, very much. It'll be the best watch I've ever had. But don't try and put it on now,' he added quickly, as she began to undo his cuffs, 'or I won't live long enough to enjoy it.'

When it came to the four-year-old championship hurdle at Aintree, Jed's decision to put Mike on Panpipe was more than justified by the horse's performance. She passed the post at the end of the two-mile race by a margin that emphatically underlined the class she'd shown at Cheltenham four weeks before.

But she was Mike's only winner that week.

Nick Thornton-Jones had been right when he'd said Mike wasn't flavour of the month. And his freelance status, unattached to any particular yard, failed to provide him with a cushion against any falling from fashion.

Most of the commentators agreed that Panpipe's win was due to her own inherent qualities; she had simply required a pilot who wouldn't fall off. Jed couldn't completely reject this line of thought, but as he drove them both back to Gloucestershire after the day's racing, he gave Mike full credit.

Mike himself was barely aware of what had gone on. He'd focused enough to steer his three mounts home, taking every advantage that was presented him, but only Panpipe had had enough natural talent to reap the benefits of his skill. In previous years he would have made his own chances rather than wait for them to arise. Today he'd been too distracted.

Throughout the day, his thoughts had constantly strayed to the deal which, after a meeting of two dozen men on the other side of the Atlantic, would either wipe out his money troubles at a stroke, or plunge him so much deeper into debt that he'd sink for good.

Besides that threat, he was desperate for the boost in confidence he would derive from a successful deal – a confidence which would help him persuade Tessa that he was the changed, or at least the subtly different, man that George Parker had shrewdly proposed he should become.

A few times recently, he'd been sure he was making progress with her; at other times, though, drink seemed to turn him back into the insensitive lout Tessa despised.

Meanwhile, that afternoon as he'd ridden round the famous fences of the Liverpool course, and now, as he and Jed headed south on the M6, the American and Japanese Treasury chiefs were getting down to business in Washington in their efforts to salvage something to their mutual advantage from the wreck of the Oriental economy.

Jed endured half an hour of his passenger's moody silence before he spoke. 'What's the matter with you?'

Mike looked up crossly. 'Nothing.'

'Come on, Mike. I know it's nothing to do with the horses. You had as good a day as anyone.'

'Yeah, sure.'

'Well, what is it?'

'Nothing . . . Just the same as everyone else.'

'If it's money, you're not alone.'

'Well, *you're* all right,' Mike said with a hint of resentment.

'Come on, Mike. It hasn't been easy for me either this year. That's why I want to sell that blasted colt in the States.'

'That reminds me,' Mike said. 'How come I haven't had any more keep bills from your friend Halliday? Have you paid him?'

'As a matter of fact, I have,' Jed admitted. 'He's an old friend. It was getting embarrassing.'

'Why didn't you ask me for my share?'

Jed didn't answer at once. 'I was going to, since you mention it . . .'

'I haven't got it at the moment. Give me a couple of weeks, and you can have the bloody lot.'

'But we may not have sold the colt by then.'

'No, but I've got other deals going on.'

'Like that Precocious colt?'

'No,' Mike said testily. 'Nothing to do with horses.'

'Oh? What then?'

'I'll tell you when it's happened. I'm a bit old to go bullshitting about deals I haven't done yet.'

'Then you've aged very suddenly,' laughed Jed.

'You know that's bollocks, Jed. I've never been one to shout about what I was doing.'

'Yes, I know,' he said apologetically. 'But humility was never one of your strong suits, either. Anyway, you can tell me what this deal is, surely?'

'It's not that I don't trust you, Jed. As a matter of fact,' Mike went on with unusual candour, 'you've been as good a friend to me as anyone, but I want to keep it under wraps for now and that's that.'

Mike knew that George Parker was the only person he could really talk to about his yen deal. He tried several times over the next three days to reach his cousin on the new phone number he'd given him, but to his growing frustration there was never a reply. On the Sunday, he was committed to spending most of the day playing in a charity football match. But as soon as he could get away without looking too unsociable, he drove back to Easerswell and turned on the television for any scraps of news about the financial summit in the States.

But there would be nothing hard to report until the talks broke up, and this wasn't expected to happen until well after midnight, UK time, just before the markets opened in Sydney and Tokyo.

'After nearly four days of continuous crisis talks, repre-sentatives of the US and Japanese Economic ministries have been unable to agree a mutually acceptable policy with regard to the current instability in the Far Eastern markets . . .'

Mike gazed at the White House spokesman on television, and experienced the same kind of sensation he'd had at the Keeneland sale when he'd realised he was going to face a thundering loss on his colt, but – this time – much more violently. He could barely bring himself to breathe as the

Washington official carried on with his dead-pan, earth-shattering statement.

'*The US Treasury made proposals to support the value of the yen on an unprecedented scale, but the Japanese administration felt unable to accept any restraints on their freedom to operate their own fiscal policies . . .*'

The head and shoulders of an earnest young financial journalist appeared on screen. '*So that's it. America's worst fears have now been realised. Japan has effectively announced its intention to trade its way out of recession. This decision will send waves of both panic and relief through the Asian capital markets. The common emotion when the Western markets open tomorrow will be panic. The yen is expected to open at least fifteen points lower against the dollar . . .*'

The reporter's face melted into the mist which had formed in front of Mike's eyes, while his brain grappled reluctantly with the mathematics. His loss on the parcel of yen he had bought now stood at over three hundred thousand pounds – the full value of his deposit. Any further fall, and the bank's margin calls would be triggered.

He opened the Scotch on the table beside him, picked it up and, with his eyes closed, gulped a long slug straight from the bottle.

'Where the hell have you been, man?' Mike shouted at the calm, faintly smiling face in front of him.

George Parker opened the door wider and silently beckoned Mike into his spacious apartment. He showed him into the sumptuous reception room and waved him towards a plump, satin-covered sofa.

'Would you like a drink?' he asked mildly.

'Too bloody right, I would!' Mike snapped, boiling over with frustration. 'But where the hell have you *been*? I've been trying to get hold of you for the last two days, since the arse fell out of the yen.'

George took an unopened bottle of Scotch from a cupboard, broke the seal, half filled a tumbler for his angry cousin and handed it to him. 'Now loosen up, Mike. You're not the first man to find that things don't always go exactly as predicted.'

'Not exactly as predicted? You predicted the yen would go *up* ten per cent – since I bought mine it's gone *down* fifteen.'

'It's come back up a bit since it bottomed out. Everybody says it will get right back up again. Everybody wants it to so it probably will. That's the way markets work.'

'For God's sake, George! You said everybody was wrong before we went into this deal.'

'So?' He shrugged. 'It turned out they were right, so let's go with them.'

'This is bullshit, George – and I haven't got anything to go with anyway.' Mike took a gulp of his whisky. 'The bank will help themselves to my three hundred grand, and then they'll come looking for another hundred and fifty – which I haven't got.'

'Don't worry about that.'

'Of course I'm worried about it! I owe money all over the place already. I haven't even got enough to buy and sell a kid's pony.'

'I said don't worry, Mike. I'll take care of it.' About to

retaliate, Mike closed his mouth while George went on. 'I know the yen will come right back up again – at least to where it was, higher even in the long run, so it's just a matter of sitting it out. I'll get them to hold off their margin call. You can stay on in there – still show a profit.'

George's confidence was infectious. Mike breathed a little easier. 'But how can you hold them off?'

'I told you – don't worry about it. I'm a big player in this field. I got you into it; I'll handle it. Just leave it to me and relax, okay?'

Chapter Nine

Jed didn't have any reason to contact Mike the week after the Aintree victory, but he was surprised not to hear anything from him.

He didn't have to go to the races that week, either, and was glad of the chance to stay at home and be with his wife.

After the abortive visit to hospital, Jed had phoned the clinic to explain what had happened, promising to come back as soon as possible, but Sammy wouldn't agree a fresh date and for the time being refused even to discuss it. She was at least outwardly calmer and said she was in less pain than she'd been for several months. For a few days, he dared to hope that maybe the evil spell had been broken.

The week at home also gave him the chance to set in motion his proposed changes in the running of the yard. His financial problems weren't dire but it was characteristic of Jed to take pre-emptive measures before they became so. Besides, what he wanted to avoid above all else was having to borrow more money, because that would almost certainly involve Sammy. And that was the last thing he wanted to do.

At the same time, he wasn't going to lose sight of the fact that over the next year or so, he would have to be very cautious about his ambitions to produce only top-grade bloodstock.

In bleaker moments, he forced himself to face the reality that he might have to sell Panpipe. In many ways, it was only rational to sell a racehorse while it was performing well, and still improving. Seasoned owners who had learned the hard way knew that there was an optimum moment to part with an animal, and it was nearly always sooner than they wanted.

Jed was painfully conscious that he would probably get as good a price for the filly now, having won the Triumph Hurdle and the race at Aintree, than at any future point in her career.

But every time the idea crept up on him, he did his best to ignore it. He reminded himself that his priority was breeding, not racing, forgetting that the top priority of all breeders – except the out-and-out dilettantes – was to make money. To Jed, though, Panpipe would always be more than a mere horse.

One thing he could do to relieve his cash-flow problems was insist to Mike that their colt was offered without reserve at the Breeze-Up in Saratoga the following week.

But Jed couldn't contact him and didn't hear anything of Mike until Tessa arrived at Batscombe the following Saturday morning. She'd been away in Los Angeles for a week and as soon as she'd got back to London had rung to ask if she could come down for the weekend to restore her sanity.

She roared up the drive in her BMW and skidded to a halt in front of the house. Jed and Sam were sitting in the kitchen, Jed filling in a stack of Weatherbys' forms while Sammy was finishing a tapestry cushion cover depicting a mare and foal. Tessa let herself in at the front and stormed through to the back of the house as Jed was getting up to investigate her noisy entrance.

'Hi there,' Tessa said angrily. 'What a pretty picture of domestic bliss!' She picked up the tapestry which Sammy had dropped on to the table.

'What's the matter with you?' Sammy asked, bridling at her sister's tone.

Tessa was too wrapped up in her own affairs to take any notice of her sister's affronted reaction.

'That *arsehole* I used to be married to – that's what's wrong.'

'What now?' Sammy groaned impatiently.

'He's so infuriating! I told you he's been badgering me for weeks about going out with him sometime? Well, finally I agreed to go to a Variety Club dinner with him last week at the Café Royal, a couple of days before he rode at Liverpool for you, Jed. Did he mention he'd seen me?'

Jed shook his head. 'Nope. But he hardly spoke at all on the way home; seemed miles away.'

'Oh.' Tessa's disappointment showed. 'Anyway, it was a big formal thing and I didn't think I could get into too much trouble, and I could always get a cab home if he started getting pissed and tricky. But he didn't. He was actually charming, thoughtful and good company. I didn't have much chance to speak to him one-to-one, but when I did he talked about things I didn't think he knew anything about.'

'Like what?' Jed asked.

Tessa pulled out a chair, sat down and started to inspect Sammy's tapestry closely. 'My work; movies; even a play. He drove me home really sensibly and behaved himself all evening. Even when he dropped me off at the house he didn't jump on me or kiss me. And he didn't insist on coming in and trying to get into bed with me.'

'Does he still do that?' Sammy asked sympathetically.

'Sometimes, but not this time. He just smiled and said "thanks for coming", and walked back to his car.'

'So, what's the problem?' Jed asked, not disguising his impatience.

'Well, because he'd been so sweet, I dropped in on him at Easerswell on the way here just now, and he came to the door in a filthy mood, looking rough as a tinker's dog – certainly hungover. I suppose he must have piled into the Scotch as usual. Anyway, he was right back to being the charmless bastard I despise.' Tessa shook her head indignantly.

'Can I get you a drink?' Jed asked, understanding her frustration at being taken in by Mike.

'Yes, please.'

He got up to fetch some wine from his cellar.

Sammy looked doubtfully at her sister. 'But, Tessa, even when he's being so nice, like he was that night, you're not saying you still want to be with Mike?'

'I don't know *what* I want any more.'

'Frankly, I think you're crazy to have anything more to

do with him, after all the grief he's caused you.'

'When he's like he was this morning, I entirely agree. But . . .' Tessa paused awkwardly '. . . I caused him a fair bit of grief myself, you know. If he's capable of being civilised – and he's given me brief hints that he can be – then I don't mind seeing him. If only he'd be like that *all* the time.'

Jed walked back into the room carrying a bottle of Burgundy. 'The trouble is,' he said, picking up the conversation again, 'when Mike's being civilised, it's just an act. He's always been a bit of an actor, which is presumably why you like him.'

'He's a typical Gemini, I suppose,' Tessa agreed. 'A split personality with two distinct sides to him.'

Jed tugged the cork from the bottle with a pop. 'We can do without all that astro-babble,' he scoffed.

'Anyway, forget him,' she said mainly to herself. 'I came down here to see you two and your precious foals.'

'Not as precious as I'd like, I'm afraid,' Jed said with exaggerated moroseness.

Tessa phoned Mike twice over the weekend while she was staying with Jed and Sammy at Batscombe. Both times the answerphone was on.

Sitting at home, alone, Mike heard her leave her messages, and resisted the urge to pick up the phone and ask her to come over.

The last thing he wanted from Tessa was pity.

He knew what a good impression he'd made on her when he'd taken her to the Café Royal just before Aintree and, following George's advice, treated her with consideration. But he'd been feeling positive about life then; at that point, the yen hadn't crashed and cost him £450,000.

Late on Sunday morning, Mike had just got back from collecting his papers in Stow when he heard a vehicle draw up outside. Groaning at the thought of having to see anybody, he went upstairs and peered through the bathroom window which overlooked the parking place in front of his garage.

A battered old Land-Rover had drawn up, and Janey Marchant was climbing out. Mike groaned again. He owed her money, which was probably why she had come.

He decided not to answer her loud knocking on the back door. When she opened it anyway, and let herself in, he had to give himself up. He went down and tried to put a smile on his face.

'Hello, Janey! What are you doing here? I didn't hear you come in. I was in the bathroom with the radio on.'

'I knew you couldn't be far away; the bonnet of your car's still warm.'

Mike forced a grin. 'You're a right little Sherlock Holmes, aren't you?' He sighed. 'Would you like a coffee?'

'Oh, yes, please.' She pulled out a chair and sat down at the table. 'Now that poor little colt's gone off, I thought I'd drop your bill round.'

'Ev picked him up all right and everything, then?' Mike asked, filling a cafetière.

'Yeah, sure. He's a good man, your friend Ev, really knows his stuff. He agreed with me, you're crazy to send that colt to the States.'

'Thanks for the advice.' Mike tried to speak lightly, acutely conscious of the fact that she would have been right, in normal circumstances. 'But I know what I'm doing.'

He shoved the plunger down the coffee pot harder than he needed to, but managed to keep up a convincing banter for the twenty minutes that Janey stayed, until he felt he could reasonably make an excuse for getting her to leave.

After that, he saw no one else for the rest of Sunday. He phoned Huey Bullough, his contact in the States, and told him he'd be over for the bloodstock sales starting Tuesday. He phoned his jockey's agent to tell him he'd slipped his cruciate ligament again and had orders to rest it for four days. If he didn't want to decommission his knee completely, he lied, he would have to cancel all his rides until Friday.

He did this without regret. Looking at the rides he would miss, there were only two which might have stood a chance of winning.

At five o'clock on Monday morning, Mike drove to London before the traffic had a chance to build up.

By seven, he was parking on a meter in South Kensington. A few minutes later he was ringing the bell of George's flat.

When his cousin opened the door, he looked as if he'd already been up for several hours. He poured Mike some fresh coffee and waved him to a chair in the drawing-room.

'Okay, buddy,' he said amiably. 'What's the problem?'

Mike pulled an envelope from his pocket and thrust it at George. 'This arrived on Saturday.'

George took the envelope and slowly pulled out the two sheets of paper it contained.

The communication was on headed Crédit Lyonnais paper; addressed to George Parker, and copied to Michael Powell. It was an official demand for a further £143,000 to regularise their position at close of business on Thursday, 10 April.

'Yeah,' George said. 'I got one of these too.'

Mike stared at him. 'For God's sake, you said you'd look after it!'

'And I will, cousin. But I have to free up a few resources over in the States first.'

'How long will that take?'

'A week or so.'

'But these guys want their money in forty-eight hours!'

'That is a little unreasonable, I agree. But like I say, there's no real problem – my money's on its way.' George refolded the bank's letter and put it in his own pocket. 'But maybe to avoid a lot of stupid charges if the process drags on, why don't you get on to those mortgage guys of yours and raise the other hundred and fifty on your property, just to tide things over?'

Mike stared at him. 'You must be crazy. In two hours from now, I'm getting on a plane to the States where I can do a couple of deals that may just pull me out of the shit you've dumped me in – deals I've spent a lot of time and trouble putting together – though I won't see a penny of the profit from them.' Mike drained his glass and stood up. 'I'll see you when I get back. Be here, Friday evening, nine-thirty – or God help you.'

George raised an eyebrow. 'Relax, buddy. Everything will be cool. You just may have picked up a few process costs, but then, the currency's going up all the time.'

Mike didn't bother to answer. The yen had gone up, it was true, enough to reduce his losses by twenty thousand.

But to Mike, twenty thousand was beginning to look like a very small sum.

By Wednesday, Jed was wondering what had happened to Mike. Nobody had seen him for several days now. He'd cancelled all his rides – which was strange, given his need for winners – and wasn't returning messages.

On his way back from Stow that morning, Jed looked in at Easerswell. He saw no sign of Mike or his car, but he did find Dora, Mike's cleaner.

'I ain't seen him since I was here last week,' she said bluntly, 'and by the looks of things, he's been away for a few days.'

'Did he leave a note or anything?' Jed asked.

'No, and he didn't leave me no wages, neither.'

Jed took twenty pounds from his wallet. 'Here's something to be going on with,' he said, handing it to her. 'I'll get it back from him. I'll leave a note for him, and if you hear from him for any reason, could you tell him to get in touch with me?'

Dora agreed gratefully.

Jed thought of the difficulty he was having in getting Mike's share of the cost of keeping the colt in the States and wondered if he would even see his twenty pounds again.

Sitting in his office at Batscombe, he found his mind wandering back to Mike, and the colt which he had confirmed would be sold that week in America.

However, Mike hadn't told him on which of the four days of the sale it was scheduled to be offered. He glanced at his watch to work out the time in Saratoga and was contemplating picking up the phone at his elbow when it rang.

He raised it absently to his ear to hear Mike's throaty Welsh accent crackling down the line.

'Hello, Jed?'

'Mike? Where are you?'

'I'm in Saratoga. Our boyo's just been through the ring, and guess what?'

Jed hated guessing; he liked concrete information. 'What?' he asked impatiently.

'We've sold him!'

Jed could tell from his exuberance, even at this distance, that the colt must have sold well.

'Who bought him?'

'We got four hundred thousand dollars!'

Jed gulped. It was a ludicrous sum for the animal, but his share – £120,000 – was enough to see him comfortably over his own impending crisis.

'That's fantastic! Who bought him?'

'Some bloke with a load of money in the movie business.'

The movie world was a million miles from Jed's. 'He must have money coming out of every orifice to pay that much. Who's buying for him?'

'A chap who liked the look of the colt. He bought another of mine, too, as a matter of fact.'

'Does the guy know who sold ours?'

'It was entered by Bullough Hill Farm, but I guess he could track it back to us easily enough if he wanted to.'

'So where's the money gone?'

'It hasn't gone anywhere yet, but when it does, it'll have to go through the Bullough Hill Farm account, to keep the books straight. I'll sort it out when I get back.'

'When will that be?'

'I've got a few rides Friday, at Sandown, then I'm supposed to be going to a new sportsperson awards ceremony.'

'So am I,' said Jed. 'But I'll see you at the races before that.'

Two days later, Jed met Mike at Sandown Park. He noticed that despite the unexpectedly huge price they'd got for their colt, Mike didn't look happy.

Jed was still amazed by the sum it had made, given his views on the animal. He knew that the buyer must have been misled in some way, but such a large sum would go so far to get him out of the financial hole he was in, he tried to ignore his misgivings. It happened like that with bloodstock sometimes, he told himself. Opinions were subjective, and there was seldom a consensus when assessing a young horse's potential; maybe this colt had looked better in action than they'd expected. Jed had yet to meet anyone who had been in Saratoga for the Breeze-Up who had seen it and could tell him.

He watched Mike force an unwilling partner over the line to win, and then take the novice chase on a mount that looked to be a cut above the average. After the last race he went to find him. Before broaching the subject of the sale, he offered Mike a drink to celebrate his double.

'Yes, I can still do it,' Mike accepted the compliment, 'whatever snotty prats like Fitzosborn and Thornton-Jones might say.'

Jed detected a wildness in his eyes – usually a sign of an imminent binge. 'Calm down, Mike. It's been a good week. I take back everything I said about not hanging on to sell the colt till now. I don't mind telling you, things have been rather tight recently, with not getting anything really outstanding to send to the sales. A hundred and twenty grand is going to come in very handy. What's the story on the money?'

'It's not in Bullough's account yet, but it's coming,' Mike said lightly, as if it wasn't worth discussing. 'I checked before I left last night.'

Jed nodded. The sales company had to clear the purchaser's payment; it always seemed to take a week or so. 'Fair enough,' he said. 'But keep chasing and keep me posted, won't you? There's no reason why the auctioneers should hang on to our funds a day longer than they need to.' Feeling that Mike deserved it, Jed changed the topic. 'Tessa came down last weekend, by the way. She told us you'd taken her to some dinner and she really enjoyed herself. Said you were charming,' he added with an encouraging grin.

Mike's mouth twitched into a quick ambivalent smile.

'She did, did she?' he said, tossing back the two fingers of Scotch still in his glass.

'Listen, Mike,' Jed offered with genuine concern, 'if you're planning to go on to the sportsperson awards ceremony tonight, I'd be careful not to get too plastered between now and then, in case a TV camera decides to zoom in on you.'

'Christ!' Mike hissed. 'I'd forgotten about those bloody awards. I'm not getting one, anyway.'

'Come on, don't be such a miserable bastard. You've had your share of the limelight.'

Mike snorted. 'I suppose I might just turn up and surprise everyone.'

An hour and a half later, Mike climbed out of his car and started to amble along the quiet Chelsea street towards Tessa's house. After a few yards, he stopped to gather his wits.

He'd stayed on at Sandown for half an hour after Jed had left. A couple of big punters who'd backed him well that day were still in the bar, and they'd assuaged his thirst. He could dimly remember the gate-man at the racecourse telling him to go easy on the way home. But he hadn't gone back to Easerswell.

He hadn't forgotten about the awards, but couldn't recall much about his journey up to London. He knew he'd stopped to make a couple of calls on his mobile and when he'd found himself crossing the Thames at Putney, had managed instinctively to find his way to this street off the King's Road.

What he wanted more than anything else right now was Tessa. With this in mind, he persevered up the street until he reached an iron gateway set between well-tended hedges. A short gravel path led to a graceful Georgian portico flanked by a pair of bay trees in old, weathered terracotta pots. He lifted a worn brass knocker and hammered.

Tessa came to the door, already knowing from his phone call that she would find him drunk. From experience she knew that to antagonise him would be self-defeating. Finding him leaning on the door-post, she beckoned him in impatiently.

He smiled benignly and followed her. 'You said you'd always be glad to see me.'

'I meant when you're sober,' said Tessa, closing the door quickly behind him. She wasn't a major Hollywood star, but since she'd started making films, the British tabloids sometimes thought it worth door-stepping her in case a newsworthy lover showed up.

But that evening they must have been after bigger or, at least, other fish – and an ex-husband, even if he was also a half-famous jockey, didn't make much of a story.

'Okay, Mike, what do you want?'

Tessa gestured him into a drawing-room that ran the full forty-foot depth of the house and ended in a pair of magnificent french windows. Beyond them was a broad, flagged terrace and a flight of stone steps down to a densely planted walled garden.

Mike turned to her. 'Like I said, I needed to see you, to put the record straight. Something very strange has happened to me . . .'

'For God's sake, Mike. You're pissed again! I don't know how you got away with driving here.'

'Come on, Tess,' he said, walking over to where she stood in front of a flaming log fire. He put his hands on her hips and grinned slackly at her. 'You liked seeing me the other evening, didn't you? And I had two winners today. Don't you think I deserve a reward?'

'Possibly, but not from me.'

'Why not? Come on, you used to love me . . .'

Tessa wriggled lithely from between his hands and took a few paces away. She stood rigid in the middle of the room, her hands on her hips. 'I *used* to, and there have been the odd moments when you've been so considerate and charming I *might* have been able to contemplate it. But this is clearly not one of those moments, and I see absolutely no point in your staying.'

'All right, all right.' Even through his whisky-dimmed senses, Mike recognised his ex-wife's unyielding tone and started walking towards the door.

'You're not still going to this awards thing, are you?'

He stopped and turned to her with a wide unfocused smile.

'Why not?'

'You must be crazy.'

'Drunk maybe; crazy, definitely not.'

Tessa looked at him, shaking her head. 'I can't let you drive like that. I'll drop you there.'

Mike stood in the doorway, swaying, and leered at her. 'I love the way you never want to lose control of anything. But I don't want to go straight to the studio. I need a shower first.'

'Not here,' she muttered quickly.

'That's okay.' Mike raised his hands in acquiescence. 'I've got other places to go, you know.'

'Whose?' Tessa asked before she could stop herself.

He tapped the side of his nose and grinned.

'I don't care anyway,' Tessa said brusquely. 'But if you want a lift, let's go.'

Outside a light drizzle had started and she quickly persuaded Mike into the BMW parked in front of her house, and with vague instructions from him, set off in the direction of South Kensington.

Towards the end of her road, she saw his car parked on a double yellow line. 'If you give me the keys, I'll put it on a meter for you in the morning. You'll be in no fit state to take it anywhere tonight.'

'You're too kind,' Mike slurred sarcastically. But he fumbled a key from his pocket and passed it over to her.

They reached the stream of traffic swirling round South Kensington, and on their second circuit, Mike recognised where he was. 'That's it – just up there on the left.'

Tessa was about to turn into the road he'd indicated when Mike grabbed the wheel. 'No. Don't bother. I'll walk from here.'

Surprised and suspicious, she pulled up on a double yellow line just beyond the turning and watched him climb out.

'Are you sure you should go to this thing?'

'Oh, yes, I'll be fine.' He blinked owlishly at her. 'I'll show all those bloody cynics who think I'm past it!' He opened the door and heaved himself out of the seat. After he'd closed it he leaned through the window, staring at Tessa. 'I had two winners today. I'll get seventy-five in before the end of the season – just you watch me.'

She sighed. 'Best of luck, Mike.'

He frowned briefly before he turned away, moving unsteadily.

Tessa started to drive off as soon as the road was clear, but kept her eye on her rear-view mirror until she saw Mike walk round the corner.

A sudden pang of jealousy hit her. Abruptly, she drew up, parked and got out of the car. Walking as fast as she could, without drawing attention to herself, she reached the top of Sumner Place in time to see Mike lurch up a flight of stone steps. She glanced at the number of the house on the corner and counted back to the entrance where he had disappeared. Fixing the address in her mind, she went back to her car and drove home, annoyed with herself for behaving like a jilted teenager.

George looked at Mike, slumped on the sofa opposite him, and raised his eyebrows. 'Frankly, cousin, you don't look as if you need another drink – and what are you doing here so early? Nine-thirty, you said.'

'Yeah, but I'd forgotten I was going to a televised awards ceremony. I'm supposed to be at the studios by eight-thirty.' He glanced at his watch and tried to focus. 'Forty-five minutes. I've got to shower and . . .'

'Sober up!' George declared. 'If you're going to be on television.'

Mike shrugged. 'Who cares? Anyway, what's happened about my deal?'

'I've come up with the shortfall – for the time being. Nobody thinks the yen'll sink any lower; we just hang on in there.'

'So I don't have to come across with this hundred and fifty grand?'

'Nope.'

Intensely relieved, Mike gazed at his cousin misty-eyed with gratitude and hope. 'And you really think we'll trade out of it?'

'Just so long as you don't lose your nerve.'

'I've never lost my nerve in twenty years of jumping over the sticks.'

'But you might lose your credibility, if you go on television like that,' George said lightly.

'Bollocks! That's just what all those bastard trainers would like – for me to make a fool of myself. I can handle it.'

'How are you going to get there?'

'They're sending a car. It's coming here at eight.'

'I really don't think you should go, but we'll get you into the shower with a pint of real strong, black coffee and see how you look then.'

Chapter Ten

In the foyer of the Riverbank Studios of UK-ONE TV, Jed handed over his Burberry raincoat and dripping umbrella to a receptionist. He showed his press pass, had his name checked by a commissionaire and was told to make his way to the giant Studio Two, where the invited audience was already filling dozens of tiers of raked seating for the awards ceremony.

The first three rows were empty, ready for the VIPs and journalists currently being entertained in the Green Room. Jed, once a successful jockey in his own right, was encouraged into the reception to mingle.

His eyes immediately swept the room. Although he'd left Mike at Sandown in a deteriorating condition, Jed was hoping that maybe this new resolve which Tessa had described would manifest itself tonight. But there was no sign of him.

Jed found himself being introduced to the commentator who was to present the garish, gilt trophy which was on display centre-stage in the studio. Around him was a crowd of familiar faces, stars – some rising, some falling – from almost every sport imaginable. Among them, wearing their own particular brand of celebrity and influence, mingled the media people.

Jed hadn't expected to see Lucy Thynne. When he did, his first instinct was to turn away. But she'd already seen him, and a smile spread across her face.

'Jed! How are you? How great to see you!'

'Hello, Lucy. What made you brave the torrents outside to get here?'

'I've got a new job,' she said gleefully. 'I'm on the diary page at the *Express* now.'

Jed pulled a face. 'Gossip?'

'Social comment,' she said severely, then laughed. 'And a few one-off racing and sporting events – this sort of thing. Wimbledon . . . Ascot . . .'

'Not exactly the serious side of journalism.'

'Oh, come on, Jed. Don't be so po-faced. Someone has to do it, and frankly it's more fun than writing about how much so-and-so sold his yearlings for.'

'Yeah, I'm sure you're right.'

'And I'm sorry I turned up at your place unannounced.'

'Lucy, I was glad to see you; I'd love to have spent a bit longer with you, but as I said, Sammy hasn't been too well recently. It hasn't been easy.'

Lucy sighed. 'It never is. I'll see you later, okay?'

Jed watched her go. Her long legs brushed lightly together beneath a black leather mini skirt. He wondered what she would be like naked, and hated himself for his disloyalty to Sammy. Still watching, he found himself standing beside Tom Cullen, a wiry little man, just five feet high, and still a top flat-jockey in his late-forties. 'You'd like to be giving her a prize tonight, wouldn't you, Jed?'

He smiled. 'No more than you or any other normal male.'

'Is that former brother-in-law of yours behavin' hisself for once?' the jockey growled.

'I don't know. Have you seen him?'

'Not here. Is he coming?'

'Doesn't look like it now. Probably just as well.'

'Why?' the little jockey asked sharply.

'Nothing,' Jed replied. 'He's just been under a bit of pressure recently.'

'Haven't we all? Anyway, now you're a hack, do you know who's going to take home that naff-looking object out there?' Tom nodded towards the trophy.

He and Jed discussed the various contenders without coming to any conclusion, and soon the floor manager was hustling them all into their seats in the studio.

When Jed saw that he was going to end up sitting next to Lucy, he hesitated a moment, though he realised that backing away now would seem plainly rude. It was in the fervent hope either that Sammy wouldn't turn on the television, or that the cameras wouldn't pan along the second row where they sat, that he squeezed along and took his place beside the woman he'd been trying to keep out of his thoughts for the past three months.

When the event was over, and a procession of embarrassed sports celebrities had culminated in the winner, a monosyllabic boxer, bending over a microphone on the podium to mumble his thanks to his mother and his manager, the cameras stopped running and the more high-profile guests were offered further refreshments.

As they left their seats, Lucy muttered ruefully that she was meeting friends at Kartouche. Disappointed but relieved, Jed gave her a goodbye kiss on the cheek before he turned back to the rest of the gathering and briefly joined a few conversations. It took only a few minutes for him to come to the conclusion that he'd extracted all the enjoyment and professional benefit he could from the event. He left in a gloomy mood, brought on by his worries over Sammy, his concern for Mike's behaviour, and the realisation that he'd have liked to have been going home with Lucy. The rain was still falling steadily as he ran down an empty street to his car, parked three hundred yards from the studio.

Harry Winter was as proud of his unblemished black Daimler as he was of his independence. The car was his own, his life was his own, and he had as much right to his views as any of the famous and influential clients who had sat in the back of his limousine.

Harry was a forthright, honest to God cockney, with a pronounced sense of humour and occasion. He always enjoyed ferrying people to and from the UK-ONE TV studios. As his house and lock-up garage were very close by, in one of the Victorian terraces which still straggled between the monolithic new office blocks of the South Bank, he was regularly booked by the television company.

'It doesn't matter who they are,' he would tell his friends, 'when they're in the back of my car, to my mind, they're the same as you and me. Cabinet ministers, footballers, film stars, even bishops ... underneath the fancy wrapping they're all just ordinary people, so why shouldn't I 'ave a good chat with 'em, same as I would with any of you lot?'

The night he was told to pick up Michael Powell from an address in South Kensington and drive him to the UK-ONE studios, a torrent of rain was lashing down, bouncing off the roads and swirling along the gutters. Harry unfurled his large black umbrella and ushered his passenger beneath it across the wet pavement to the rear door of the low, sleek Daimler.

'Evenin', Mr Powell,' he said with a friendly, deferential smile as he climbed back into the driver's seat. 'It's a real honour to have you in the back of my car.'

To Harry's disappointment, his passenger barely murmured acknowledgement of the compliment, just nodded his head slightly.

But Harry wasn't easily deflected from hobnobbing with the famous. 'D'you think that Olympic rowing geezer deserves to win tonight, then – like everyone says?' he asked as they pulled away from the white stucco building where Mike had changed.

'It's hard to say, really.'

'No, it ain't,' Harry said. 'You're just being – whassaname – diplomatic. I bet you're like me. I bet you think rowing's the most boring sport in the world. Think about it – you'd go mental if you was never in anything more than a two-horse race.'

The man behind him laughed. 'Yes, I suppose I would, but they were racing more than that in the Olympics.'

'Yeah, all right, maybe they was, but that Oxford-Cambridge thing – well, I mean, you can't have a bet on a race like that, can you?' Harry laughed at the recollection of past foolishness which had led him to risk hard-earned money on the outcome of the most famous boat race in the world. 'Mind you,' he went on with easy confidence, 'you and me've been through a lot together. I've won a fair few bob on you, guv – a fair few bob, I can tell you. But not as much as I've lost,' he chuckled.

'I'm sorry to hear that.'

Ponce, thought Harry to himself. He couldn't give a toss. 'I'm sorry to hear that' indeed! All rabbit and bullshit on the telly when he's won a race, but clams up tight when he's talking to an ordinary working man like me.

And Harry remained huffily silent as he negotiated Chelsea Bridge and headed up Nine Elms Lane to the massive gyratory traffic flow at the south end of Vauxhall Bridge.

Five lanes of eastbound traffic waited in the steady downpour. When the lights turned green, the cars to either side jumped off with no concession to the waterlogged surface and sped away in half-a-dozen directions. Harry went with them, to head straight on towards the Albert Embankment.

Looking ahead, watching the traffic slow to a crawl in the rain, he didn't immediately see the forty-foot articulated lorry which had shot through the red lights at the bottom of the bridge.

The massive Volvo unit, painted black, with thirty tons of exotic vegetables from Provence behind it, was already doing 50 k.p.h. and accelerating through close-ratio gears as it crossed the stop line.

Inside the cab, the French driver, on his first assignment to England, was already lost and utterly confused by driving on the left and struggling to interpret incomprehensible road signs. He had been told categorically that he wasn't allowed to stop anywhere in London apart from the fruit market, and under no circumstances should he need to cross the river.

But no sign had told him when he was crossing the Thames. Another French lorry driver had yelled at him helpfully across the street at a stop light, and coming back across Vauxhall Bridge he had stopped to consult a hopelessly inadequate map of the British capital. The double red lines along the side of the road meant nothing to him but other drivers had hooted at him and waved him on so he knew he had to go.

In front of him, a bewildering mass of signs and lights glared through what seemed to be a solid sheet of rain. All he knew was that he must head south, get back across the broad river, and try to follow it until he reached the New Covent Garden buildings.

He crossed the stop line without registering it and was accelerating away when he saw the five lanes of traffic surge out of the carriageway to his right. It took only a second to realise what had happened, and another to respond.

But by the time he pounded the air brakes with his foot, like a mallet on a fence post, it was too late. The whole cab shuddered and hissed and started to stink of hot asbestos as the wheels locked and the rig slithered over the slickly gleaming road. The Frenchman watched in horror as his juggernaut careered out of control towards a sleek black Daimler.

'Oh, Harry!' wailed Beryl Winter, gazing at her husband who lay stretched out on a bed in the Accident and Emergency department of St Thomas's Hospital. His head was wrapped in lint, and his right arm in hardened plaster. 'What happened?'

Harry shook his head and straight away wished he hadn't. 'Gawd knows. They say it was a French lorry. Didn't ought to have been in London at all! There's hundreds of bloody traffic lights down that side of Vauxhall Bridge. Copper said the driver got confused, and came steaming straight across. We had to be in his way, didn't we? Smashed up the Daimler good and proper – total write-off it is.'

'At least *you're* all right, Harry,' she whispered.

Beryl gazed into her husband's anguished eyes and squeezed his hand in hers. Neither of them could bring themselves to talk about the fate of his passenger.

After she had dropped Mike in South Kensington earlier in the evening, Tessa drove straight home. She had invited her agent to come round for a drink and a light supper while they looked at two scripts she'd just been sent.

Tessa's agent, Margot, was a woman not much older than herself who also served as a more like-minded sister than Sammy could ever have been. Tessa relished her company and derived a lot of support from it.

When Margot arrived, the two women shared a bottle of

Chablis and a plate of smoked salmon as they read the first of the two scripts and gleefully tore it to shreds. Tessa had kept her eye on the clock and when the awards ceremony was due on, turned apologetically to her friend. 'I hope you don't mind, but I just want to look at the telly and see how Mike's getting on. He's a guest on some dreary sports programme.'

'How do you mean, "getting on"?'

Tessa had only briefly mentioned her ex-husband's visit earlier in the evening. Now she told her friend about the dinner when he had been so charming and attractive in an entirely new way.

'But, Tessa darling, you can't possibly consider going back to him! He's hardly Richard Burton, and, if you'll forgive me, you're no Liz Taylor either.'

Tessa laughed. 'I don't think I mind that! But anyway, I didn't say anything about going back to him. I told you – he turned up here tonight pissed, I didn't see how he could go to the studios like that, but he said he'd surprise us all.'

She picked up a remote control wand and pressed a button which revealed a television concealed behind some curtains below an occasional table. 'There was something about the way he said it that makes me think he will, and I just want to see what sort of state he's in – purely out of curiosity.'

Margot sighed and sat back. She and Mike had never found much common ground intellectually, but secretly she had always enjoyed his cocky, upfront assertiveness.

Tessa switched on the TV and tuned to UK-ONE. The

awards show had just started and the grinning commentator, every hair on his toupee neatly in place, was presenting the judges and some of the stars who had been invited to witness the event.

The camera swept along the rows of guests and Tessa tried anxiously to spot her ex-husband.

When it was clear that most of the celebrity guests had been shown, she turned to her friend. 'He's not there, is he?' she said, angry despite herself. 'I knew he wouldn't make it!'

'For God's sake, Tessa, the camera can't cover everyone. Anyway, what does it matter? The man was far more of a hindrance than a help so far as your career was concerned, and did nothing but make you miserable for the last few years.'

'Not always,' she said curtly. 'There were good moments too.'

Her agent shrugged. 'I think you're expending too much time and energy on worrying about him.' She nodded at the screen. 'Isn't that your brother-in-law?'

The camera was resting on Jed while he was presented as a previous amateur champion jockey. Tessa saw him sitting beside Lucy Thynne and remembered what Sammy had told her. At the flattering introduction, Jed nodded back with an embarrassed, self-deprecating grin.

'Yes, it is,' Tessa said softly. 'And I bloody well hope my sister doesn't see him sitting so close to that nymphette!'

She laughed and switched off the television.

After Margot had left, Tessa went back down to her

basement dining-room and poured the last of the Chablis into a glass. Taking it upstairs, she switched on the television again.

The ten o'clock news was coming to an end when the editor found time to squeeze in one last item which would be of interest to a sizeable number of viewers.

The newsreader arranged his face into a sombre expression and assumed a tone of regret. '*Top National Hunt jockey Michael Powell has died following a motor accident less than two hours ago. A car bringing him to these studios to appear at a live broadcast was struck by an articulated lorry on the junction at the south end of Vauxhall Bridge. Mr Powell died shortly after he had been taken to St Thomas's Hospital. The driver of the vehicle was also taken to the hospital where his condition is reported to be stable. Michael Powell, one of racing's most colourful characters, was perhaps best known for winning the Grand National in 1990 on Oscar Wilde . . .*'

A clip of the run in at Aintree, when Mike had won on an outsider for a tiny West Country yard, was replaced by a short shot of him taken earlier today, walking in the winner of the handicap chase at Sandown with a weary grin on his face.

'*Michael Powell who died today. And now . . .*'

Tessa stared at the screen in disbelief; that last picture of Mike, grinning from the back of a horse – a grin she'd seen hundreds of times – seemed to be fixed on the back of her retina.

Time froze for her as advertisements and a Clint Eastwood film followed each other on the screen. She didn't move until a violent hammering on her front door, accompanied by a continuous ringing on the bell, forced her from her bewildered trance.

Later – she couldn't judge how much later – she heard knocking again and got up to open her front door to find Jed standing on her doorstep, drenched through by the rain which was still beating down outside.

Without speaking, she opened the door wider and beckoned him in while she reached out to take his sodden jacket. Jed slipped out of it and shook his soaking hair. He stepped towards Tessa and they hugged each other silently for a few moments until he released her and led her into the drawing-room.

'How did you know?' he asked. 'Did the police phone you?'

'No. I saw it on the news.'

'They should have phoned you first,' Jed grunted. 'I heard it on the car radio. I'd nearly got to Oxford, but I turned right round and came back here.'

'Thank God you did! I need someone who . . . understands.'

'I understand all right.'

Tessa began to shake.

'He was here this evening. He came from the races, blind drunk. I dropped him in South Ken, to get changed in somebody's flat. Margot and I turned on the telly later to see him, but when he wasn't there, I just knew something had happened.'

'Is Margot still here?'

'No, she'd gone before the news.'

A telephone on a side table started to trill.

Jed looked at Tessa. She nodded and he picked it up.

'Hello?'

'Miss Langton there, please?'

'Who is it?'

'Christopher Jones, *Daily Mail*.'

'I'm sorry. Miss Langton has no comment at the moment,' Jed said quickly, and put the phone down.

The call turned out to be the first of several which Jed deflected in the same way until the police called to ask if Tessa would mind making a formal identification, since she was still listed as Michael Powell's next-of-kin and there was no way of contacting his mother two hundred miles away in the depths of Wales.

Tessa agreed to go and Jed drove her to St Thomas's.

While he was told to wait outside an anonymous grey cell of a room, a white-coated attendant ushered Tessa to a table over which a plastic sheet was draped.

'I'm afraid the victim's features were a little damaged,' the mortuary assistant said quietly as he prepared to draw the cover from the still figure.

He pulled it back only as far as the chin.

Tessa gazed at the heavily bruised face – eyes closed – looking unexpectedly peaceful, not unhappy in death. She bit her lower lip as she nodded. 'That's him,' she said clearly in her rich husky voice.

'You can confirm that this is Michael Powell?'

Tessa turned to the policeman behind her and, with tears in her eyes, nodded slowly.

The policeman made a note in his book as the cover was pulled back over the still, shuttered face. 'We removed these, madam,' he said, and handed Tessa a pair of gold cuff-links engraved with the intertwined initials 'MP'.

She cupped them in her hand, remembering vividly the day she had given them to Mike – the day before their wedding.

'I can't pretend that Michael was a frequent visitor to this place . . .' The vicar paused and looked around the small congregation who, for the most part, were equally infrequent visitors to this or any other church. 'But I know his heart was with us; parish funds benefited from several good tips he gave us over the years.'

A light ripple of laughter ran through the church. Now the vicar was in territory that his audience understood. Tessa thought to herself that the unctuous cleric had probably made up the story to put this irreligious crowd at their ease.

Sammy had questioned the idea of a full funeral service. She'd felt that few racing people would come on a busy race day. But Tessa had insisted, encouraged by the vicar who looked after the parish church of Easerswell along with seven other similarly under-subscribed local churches. They could have a memorial service in a month or so, she'd told Sammy.

It had fallen to Tessa to organise Mike's funeral because no one else had emerged to claim the responsibility. Mike's only relation, his mother, had made her reluctance very clear when Tessa had contacted her. She would come to her son's funeral, Megan Powell had said, but she wanted no part in the arrangements.

Jed had sent a car to bring her from her cottage above Beulah in the lower Cambrian Mountains. The little Welsh widow, unused to crowds or large churches, huddled in a corner pew, too puzzled to weep, too distant now from a son she had scarcely seen in the last twenty years. His world meant nothing to her, and the wealthy lifestyle it had brought him seemed to her alien, immoral and undeserved.

In the absence of any obvious or accessible family, and despite the heavy publicity over the divorce, Tessa, Sammy and Jed were perceived by most as the grieving relatives. Jed knew that he would have felt great disloyalty to a man who had, after all, been a close friend, if he hadn't been prepared to go along with this.

So he accepted condolences from the people who had come to say farewell to Michael Powell, and listened to several different versions of the more spectacular escapades of his ex-brother-in-law's eventful career.

After the funeral, the noise of loudly expressed views and bursts of suppressed laughter filled the house at Easerswell. A few knots of people deserted the cosy drawing-room and wandered out into the damp air outside.

Despite Sammy's prediction to the contrary, a surprising number of people had found the time to come – a lot from racing and the press, as well as a group of men down from the hills of Radnorshire, small, hard people like Ev Thomas who'd known Mike since his flapping days.

Sammy viewed the throng with dismay and went into the

kitchen to find some respite. There she found Mike's mother sitting alone at the table.

Megan Powell was little more than sixty years old, but a life of continuous toil had bent and shrivelled her. The eyes that peered timidly out of her lined and weathered face had none of the shrewdness and confidence of her dead son's. She was dressed in a dowdy black woollen frock beneath a newly pressed but ancient grey coat and skimpy scarf.

Seeing her, Sammy sensed that she was feeling thoroughly uneasy and out of place among the comfortable furnishings and trophies which adorned her son's house.

With an unexpected urge to reach out to the old woman, Sammy forgot her own problems for a few minutes and sat down opposite her. 'I'm sorry you're on your own, Mrs Powell.'

'I'm used to it. He never came to see me, you know.'

'He was very busy.'

'Hmm. Even when he knew I had no one else.'

'That's a shame, I admit. Have you really no other relations?'

'Both my brothers have gone – they neither of them married. And my sister was killed over thirty years ago.'

'How was that?' Sammy asked. She'd never heard of Mike's aunt.

'Abroad.' Megan annunciated the word as if it were a euphemism for Hell. 'She married a soldier.'

'Didn't she have any children that you could contact?'

Megan nodded and gazed at Sammy through watery eyes. Straight away her gaze swivelled to the cold, unlit

Aga, clean and devoid of the warmth it should have been issuing.

Sammy thought of herself and Tessa, without a child between them and the chances looking slimmer each year. She tried to imagine how important a child of Tessa's might have been to her, and felt that perhaps Megan's obvious hurt was understandable.

'I tried to stay in touch after my sister Gwynneth died, but I never heard anything back. The last letter I sent was returned to me saying "not known at this address".'

'Maybe, if you'd made some enquiries . . .?'

'There's no purpose in chasing after people.'

'Well, even though Mike and Tessa were divorced, they still saw each other; they were still very fond of each other. So,' Sammy spread her hands expressively, '*we're* sort of family to you.'

'What have I to say to the likes of you?' Megan waved a hand towards the window and the lush, expensively land-scaped garden outside where the people who had come to mourn Mike walked, drank and laughed.

Sammy followed her eyes. 'I don't know,' she said honestly. 'But we've got Mike in common, and that makes a sort of bond between us, doesn't it?'

Megan looked her in the eye. 'I doubt it would be a very strong one.'

Later, Sammy wandered back through the other rooms, where Mike's wake was still in progress. She wanted desperately to talk to Jed. They didn't seem to have had a chance since Mike had died.

On the night of the awards ceremony, Jed hadn't come home. And Sammy had seen him clearly on television in the second row of the audience, talking and laughing with Lucy Thynne. Now she clenched her fists, digging her nails into her palms.

Tessa had told her to say nothing to Jed about Lucy, and she hadn't as yet, but now she thought she would burst if she didn't confront him and hear the truth, however much it hurt.

She found Jed talking to a couple of local trainers and tugged the arm of his jacket. He turned to her and smiled.

'Jed, do you think I could talk to you?'

'Yes, sure. I'm all yours. I've had enough horse talk for one day.'

'In private, maybe?'

He felt a chill of apprehension, a fraction of a second too late to stop Sammy spotting it. 'Okay,' he said. 'Let's go into the office.'

The room which Mike had always left in a shambles was now almost empty. Tessa, with Mike's solicitor, had already been through the contents of the desk and filing cabinets and found an envelope addressed to the lawyers, which evidently contained his will. They had taken it away and a formal reading had been arranged for the following day.

Jed led Sammy inside and closed the door behind them. 'Now, what's the trouble, angel?'

'Jed, I haven't really had a chance to talk to you about this yet, but the night Mike died, I saw you on the television. At the awards.'

The anguish in her eyes rang more warning bells for Jed. He stiffened.

She bit her bottom lip and carried on. 'You seemed to be getting on very well with Lucy Thynne.'

'With Lucy?' Jed gave a light laugh. 'Come on, Sam. You're not jealous, are you? After all, I didn't choose to sit there. I was put next to her and I couldn't really ignore her; we're in the same business, and I've known her since she was a kid.'

'No, but you were joking and laughing with her. You hardly ever laugh with me any more.'

'Sammy angel, there hasn't been a lot to laugh about recently, has there? But there will be soon, I'm sure.'

'Jed, where did you stay that night?'

'Please don't worry. I wasn't doing anything I shouldn't, I promise. That was the last thing on my mind. I told you – I heard about Mike's death on the radio as I was driving home, so I turned round and went straight to Tessa's. I thought she'd need our support.'

'I know, but where did you go after you'd seen her? You didn't stay at the Turf?'

Jed looked at her, alarmed that she might have been checking up on him.

'Sammy,' he said, trying not to show his hurt at her suspicions, 'I stayed at Tessa's, of course. She'd been to identify Mike's body; she wasn't feeling up to spending the night in the house alone.'

Sammy screwed up her face in remorse, and blinked away the tears. 'I suppose I knew that really, Jed. It's just that when things have been like they have between us . . . I get paranoid so easily.'

'Listen to me, you've got nothing to get paranoid about. I love you, and everything'll be fine, I promise you. There's absolutely nothing between me and Lucy Thynne, okay?' He put his hands on her shoulders and looked steadily into her eyes. 'Now, don't you think we should get back to the mourners?'

Sammy nodded doubtfully.

Jed crossed the room, opened the door and held it while she slowly walked out into the hall.

Chapter Eleven

It was seldom that Jed was still asleep when his alarm went off, but the morning after Mike's funeral, he woke with it buzzing in his ear, magnifying the pain in his head. The emotional strain Mike's death had placed on the family, and an unaccustomed amount of alcohol, had combined to knock him for six.

He reached out to tap off the alarm and turned anxiously to look at Sammy. Her eyelids fluttered on pale cheeks for a moment, until her breathing resumed its normal steady rate. She would sleep on for another two hours after he'd risen.

Jed slid out of bed, shrugged on a dressing-gown and walked through to the bathroom. Before he'd started to shave, he realised that for the first time in a dozen years he needed a hangover cure. He opened the medicine cupboard over the basin and was confronted with a battery of Sammy's medications and alternative potions. He winced as he shifted aside the plastic bottles of ginseng, vitamin, iron and hay fever pills until he found an old, dusty box of Alka-Seltzer.

He plopped a couple into a glass of water, swallowed down the fizzing liquid, and felt a little better.

Dressed and downstairs in the kitchen, he made himself a pot of coffee and wondered if it was too early to ring Tessa about arrangements for going to the solicitor's.

Jed was becoming increasingly anxious about the resolving of Mike's estate, not because he expected to have been left anything – there was no reason for that – but because he still hadn't had his share of the proceeds of the sale of the colt, though the auction company had confirmed to him over the phone that a cheque had been sent to Bullough Hill Farm, and Huey Bullough had said that, as instructed, he had despatched a cheque direct to Mike's bank in England.

Jed didn't doubt that he could prove his share in the ownership of the horse that had been sold, but the timing was becoming critical.

He'd told two bloodstock agents that he was open to offers on Panpipe and had already had a few exploratory enquiries.

If the unexpected bonus from the Northern Baby colt didn't arrive soon, he'd have to think about accepting an offer.

He was still contemplating this unbearable option when the phone rang. It was Tessa.

'Morning, Jed. Thanks so much for being there yesterday. I don't know what I'd have done without you.'

'You'd have been fine, Tessa, and you know it,' he said affectionately. 'It's a bit early for you to be up and about, isn't it?'

'I've been getting five o'clock wake-up calls for the last week; it takes a while to break the habit. Anyway, I wanted to know if Sammy had decided to come with me to the solicitor's?'

'She's still asleep. I don't really want to wake her yet. What time do you have to be there?'

'Not till ten.'

'Why not just call in here at nine-thirty, on your way? If she's ready, she'll come.'

'Okay. See you then.'

When Tessa arrived at Batscombe, she saw Jed walking down the front steps to greet her.

'Do you mind if I come instead of Sammy?' he asked through the driver's window of her car.

'Not at all – but why can't Sammy?'

'She's feeling lousy. Said if you wanted someone . . .?'

'Yes, please. I'd love some support.'

Michael Powell's solicitors were in Cheltenham. Tessa drove through the narrow lanes to town as if she were on a racetrack.

'Take it easy,' Jed protested, half-serious, 'or they'll be coming to hear *our* wills next.'

'Sorry, Jed. I'm suddenly feeling rather uptight about the whole business. I was still very fond of Mike, you know.'

'Yes, I knew that,' he said quietly. 'Do you think he's left any surprises for you in his will?'

'I've no idea. I don't even know if he had anything much

187

to leave. He certainly didn't according to his lawyers during our divorce settlement.'

Jed nodded. 'I think he was pretty strapped towards the end.'

Tessa frowned and glanced at him. 'Mike was doing a few deals though, wasn't he – buying and selling horses?'

'Yes, though not always successfully, I'm afraid. It's been a pretty tricky market over the last few years.'

'But Mike was a clever guy. He knew a hell of a lot about horses, and though I know as a jockey he wasn't supposed to own any in training, he had dozens of brood mares all over the place and I'm pretty sure he had a few horses running in other people's names.'

'Not that many.' Jed shook his head. 'Though, as it happens, he and I bought a mare a couple of years ago in the States – a night-mare, you might say. She was in foal and then threw a measly-looking little colt. We sold the mare but didn't shift the foal for ages after that.' He stopped; he didn't want to tell Tessa about the money he was still owed for the Northern Baby colt. 'But on the whole,' he went on, 'I didn't encourage Mike. He tried to get me to run a horse for him in my name last year but things weren't going too well between you two, and I didn't want to get caught in the crossfire.'

'Very wise.'

'Anyway,' he asked casually, 'do you know who else is coming to hear the will read?'

'I've no idea. The lawyer didn't say. I suppose, if there is a main beneficiary, it'll be Mike's mother. But you never really knew with Mike.'

★ ★ ★

In the quiet Regency panelled office of an old established firm of solicitors, Geoffrey Tolhurst, the partner who was handling Mike's estate, allowed Jed to sit in on the reading of the will. The only other beneficiary present besides Tessa, as she had predicted, was Megan Powell, whom the solicitors had fetched by car from her inaccessible home.

Had he wanted, Geoffrey Tolhurst could have been a senior partner in one of the big London firms, but he enjoyed the higher proportion of personal business that a practice in a wealthy town like Cheltenham offered. He was in his mid-fifties, handsome, with well-groomed grey hair and a reputation in the firm for never getting ruffled. He loved National Hunt racing, and had made a point of collecting clients who were involved in it. He had acted for Mike since his first contract as a fully licensed jockey.

Once coffee and introductions had been dispensed, Tolhurst drew a legal document from the centre of his desk.

Tessa felt her stomach tighten in trepidation.

'It's really a very simple will,' Tolhurst said, 'which was found when examining the contents of Michael's study. I've made copies which I'll hand round later and you'll be able to read all the small print yourselves, so I'm not going to read the whole thing formally. I'll just run through the principal elements.'

He looked around at each of his audience, before clearing his throat to give an appropriate air of gravitas to the proceedings. 'Apart from the house and contents, the single net asset of the estate is the balance of a sum of money due on a life insurance policy which Michael took out at the time of his marriage to you, Miss Langton. Naturally, your claim on this expired at the time of your divorce. Were it not for this substantial sum of money, the estate would have been insolvent.

'However, we are happily in a position to fulfil all Michael Powell's instructions. First, there are small bequests to various charities: one thousand pounds to the Injured Jockeys Fund, one thousand pounds to the Blue Cross Animal Rescue Centres, and so on – six thousand pounds in all.

'He has also left a sum of one-hundred-thousand pounds in trust to your benefit, Mrs Powell.'

Tolhurst turned and looked at Megan whose face had drained of colour. 'That means that it will be invested by trustees and the income will be paid to you. On your death, the capital, that is the one-hundred-thousand pounds, reverts to the principal estate.'

Old Mrs Powell absorbed the news, puzzled and agitated by its suddenness, overwhelmed by the sum involved.

Tolhurst carried on smoothly, looking now at Tessa, with a faint smile playing round his lips. 'To you, Miss Langton, he has left the house and grounds of Easerswell and all its contents.' He paused. 'On the condition that no further claim on the estate is made.'

Tessa sat up in her chair and stared at him in astonishment.

'The rest of his estate,' the solicitor continued, 'he has left to a George Parker, of Huntington, West Virginia.'

Jed glanced enquiringly at Tessa, who shook her head and gazed back at him blankly. George Parker meant nothing to either of them. Megan still sat rigidly erect, with her jaw set firm, looking at the lawyer. 'How much is it?' Megan asked.

'The precise figure will be published when probate has been granted, but I can tell you that unless anything unforeseen crops up, after the bequests to charity, Miss Langton and yourself, the value should be something in the region of seven-hundred-thousand pounds.'

Tessa gave a surprised, cynical laugh. 'As much as that? That's not what you said when the divorce was going through.'

'As I said, that is substantially made up of the balance of the proceeds of the life-insurance policy which accrues to the general estate after a substantial amount in liabilities has been discharged.'

'But he also owned a lot of thoroughbred horses,' Tessa said.

'Regrettably, Mr Powell did not reveal to us the full extent of his bloodstock holdings, and there appear to be none registered in his name at Weatherbys.'

'But you've been his solicitor for years – you must know.'

'Miss Langton, I'm afraid I don't, but you have received this unexpected, and frankly very generous bequest.'

'Provided I don't contest the will.'

'Provided that you don't even attempt to. And – as you'll see from the terms – sign an irrevocable undertaking that you will not do so at any later date.'

She laughed again. 'I know he had a few mares and yearlings he kept to himself, but why did he take out all this insurance?'

'It wasn't a particularly recent policy,' Tolhurst said. 'I should mention that there was a much more recent one, assigned to a mortgage company; they will receive the bulk of the proceeds of that particular policy to cover a substantial loan Mr Powell had contracted.'

'What for?'

'I've no idea. He didn't tell us anything about it, but I imagine the lender insisted that he took out cover against just these circumstances.'

Tessa turned to Mike's mother, who still sat, silent and motionless, staring out through the large Georgian sash window behind the solicitor's chair.

'Megan,' Tessa said, 'do you know this man Mike's left all his money to?'

'Know him? No.'

'But do you recognise the name?'

Megan gazed unblinking across the desk at Geoffrey Tolhurst.

Jed, Tessa, even the lawyer, expecting a new revelation, waited for her to speak, but Megan offered nothing more.

Tessa couldn't control her impatience any longer. 'Well? Do you know who he is, then? Why's Mike left money to him?'

'I don't know why Michael's done this. But he's done what he's done, and it's none of my business,' Megan declared, shaking her head firmly and fixing her gaze on the window once more.

There was a silence, broken after a quarter of a minute by the solicitor clearing his throat. 'I should add that it's quite possible that Michael Powell made and lodged an entirely separate will under another jurisdiction – the United States, for example. We have no knowledge of any such other will, and no American law firm has been in contact with us. But nevertheless he might have done, and naturally that would be subject to local laws and taxes. If I can be of any further assistance, I am at your disposal.'

Jed and Tessa dropped Mike's mother, still apparently overcome by the terms of her son's will, at Kingham station near Stow. She would catch a train from there to Hereford and, with two more changes, reach the tiny station at Llangamarch Wells, still ten miles from her cottage in the hills.

She had refused the solicitor's offer of a car, and Tessa's offer of a bed for the night at Easerswell. The handling of her unexpected and, in her view, embarrassing legacy, Megan left willingly to Mr Tolhurst, and if she knew any more about George Parker, she resolutely said not another word about him.

Jed and Tessa went on to Batscombe where they found Sammy sitting up in bed, reading the *Daily Telegraph*. Keen to hear about the will, though, she came down and joined them in the conservatory which had warmed up in the spring sunshine.

'Tessa's got Easerswell back,' Jed told her with a satisfied grin.

'Good God!'

'And Mike left a trust fund for his mother – about five grand a year, I should think.'

'How amazing! That doesn't sound like Mike. Megan

must have been astonished. I don't think she'd seen him in the flesh since he left home to go to Ron Prichard's.'

'But the real surprise,' Tessa said, 'was that even after a lot of liabilities, there was almost three quarters of a million from his life insurance and he's left it to a man in America called George Parker, who we've never heard of.'

'Really?' gasped Sammy. 'Who on earth is he?'

'I haven't a clue. When Tolhurst first mentioned his name, I looked at Megan and thought maybe she knew something, but in fact I think she was just as mystified as us.'

'Still,' Jed said, 'it's none of our business. And it was good of him to leave the house to Tessa; he knew how much she loved it.'

Tessa nodded. 'He knew it was the right thing to do. But I must admit, I'm still fascinated by this George Parker.'

'Did Mike never even mention him to you?' Sammy looked at her.

'Not as far as I can remember. He certainly had a few friends he did deals with in the States, but I never really knew any of them.'

'Can't you think of anyone?' Jed asked.

'Well, after I did that picture for Bernie Capella, Bernie said he was interested in buying a few racehorses. Mike was coming over to join me in LA so I introduced them then; they had a brief meeting with a couple of other guys.'

'What were they like? Could either of them have been George Parker?'

'No. So far as I remember, they both had foreign names – you know, Polish or something. What were they like?' Tessa shrugged her shoulders. 'Nondescript, sharp-suited hustlers, like you see all over LA every day of the week; not people you'd trust with their own grannies.'

'But do you think this George Parker is something to do with Bernie Capella?' Jed persisted.

'I've no idea. I was just trying to think of people I met in the States with Mike,' Tessa said, pouring herself a glass of wine from the bottle Jed had opened.

He still couldn't bring himself to tell Tessa or Sammy about his pressing financial reasons for finding George Parker.

'Didn't Tolhurst say that Mike only made this will a few weeks ago?'

'Yes, and he also said that Mike may have made an entirely separate one in the States.'

'But did he own anything in the States?' Sammy asked, looking at Jed.

'Who knows?' he said dismissively.

'Let's look at the copy of the will Tolhurst gave us.' Tessa rummaged in her bag and pulled out four sheets of paper clipped and bound in a folder. 'Yes, look, it's dated March the tenth, only a month or so ago. I suppose you're right, Jed. It does seem rather strange. We ought to find this guy.'

'Why? What's the point?' Sammy asked peevishly. 'As you say, you've got Easerswell.'

Jed took the document from Tessa's hand and leafed through it. There was no mention of the Northern Baby colt, or any agreement with Bullough Hill Farm, or anything to indicate that Mike was due to receive four hundred thousand dollars from them.

'I just don't like not knowing who's getting Mike's money,' Tessa was saying. 'For God's sake, I was part of his life for nearly ten years! I've got a right to know.'

'Really, Tessa,' Sammy persisted, 'you were the one who insisted on a divorce. It's not as though he's left it all to some woman you could feel jealous about. I don't suppose he even got involved with any other women.' A thought suddenly occurred to her. 'Unless George is a girl, that is.'

Tessa dismissed the idea but then recounted dropping Mike off at a flat in South Kensington. 'He certainly had a change of clothes there, and he didn't want me to know where he was going.'

'Maybe he *did* have a girlfriend,' Jed said. 'You can't entirely blame him for that. But I'm afraid there's another reason to look for this George Parker, male or female. I think the police ought to know Mike changed his will in favour of this person – and was killed less than six weeks later.'

Tessa and Sammy stared at him, as they took in what he was saying.

'My God,' Sammy whispered. 'Are you suggesting he was killed deliberately?'

'It's possible,' Jed said, slowly nodding his head. 'And whatever failings he had, Mike didn't deserve to be murdered.'

The wind got up around ten that evening. It didn't ease off until the first pinkness of dawn glimmered across the rolling ridges of the Cotswold hills.

Rain battered the windows of the old stone house at

Batscombe and left the lawn below the cedars soft and soggy as a bath sponge.

Jed didn't sleep. Nor did Sammy, beside him.

He rose with the daylight and went out to check the horses and stables for storm damage.

They all seemed happy enough, despite a few dislodged boards in their stable walls. As usual, Jed spent several minutes talking to Panpipe over her door, while Bella poked her nose from her own adjacent stall and nuzzled his shoulder.

As he looked and noted what needed repairing in the yard, the thought that Mike's death had been no accident never left his mind.

He felt now, as he had before the starts of his earliest races, an overwhelming need for action, for the 'off'. He looked at his watch every few minutes until it was time to catch people in their offices.

Sammy and Tessa were still in bed as he hurtled his Range Rover down the drive from Batscombe soon after eight, on his way to Cheltenham.

Tessa came down to find Rita, Sammy's cleaner, quietly loading a washing-machine in the utility room by the back door.

Rita was a local – a farmer's daughter. She'd married a good-looking oaf whose idea of work was reading the *Sporting Life* and walking to the bookie's shop, and now she was paying the price. She had often met Tessa and was proud of her easy acquaintance with the famous actress. 'Morning, Tessa,' she said brightly. 'Oh, sorry,' she said, more solemnly, embarrassed by her own cheerfulness so soon after the funeral. 'Would you like a cup of tea?'

'Yes, please.' Tessa smiled to put her at her ease. 'And perhaps you could help me make Sammy's breakfast?'

When Tessa took a tray up, Sammy was dozing still, her long dark eyelashes stark against her pale cheeks. At the sounds of Tessa bustling around, her eyelids fluttered open.

'Morning,' she murmured.

'Hi, Sammy. I brought you some breakfast.'

She sat up and winced. 'I only want tea really.'

'You need some proper food. I'm sure that's what's causing a lot of the trouble.'

'I wish it were that simple,' Sammy said wanly. 'But I promise, Tess, I can't eat a thing at this time of day. It was very sweet of you to bring it up, though.'

Tessa sat down on the big bed, on the side that Jed had vacated some three hours earlier.

'Where's Jed?'

'I don't know. He must be outside. Though, come to think of it, I heard the Range Rover leaving some time ago, and he told me he was going to be out and about all day. Knowing him, he's already off looking for George Parker.'

Tessa came to one of her instant decisions. 'If Jed's going to be out all day, why don't you come to London with me? We can have a lovely lunch somewhere, and a nice lazy stroll through the galleries – like we used to.' She turned the full power of her bright, persuasive eyes on Sammy.

And Sammy found the unexpected prospect of having her sister to herself all day surprisingly pleasing. 'Yes!' she said, with an eagerness she hadn't felt for several months. 'Do you know, I'd love that.'

'Great,' Tessa said, already planning the phone calls she would have to make to free herself for the next few hours. 'We'll leave a note for Jed telling him to come up and get you later.'

'I could just ring him on his mobile.'

'No, don't do that. He'll only try to talk you out of it.'

'I don't think he would.'

'I'll write a note, just in case.'

An hour later, the two sisters were strapped into Tessa's car, racing towards London, singing and laughing with each other over an old Neil Diamond tape Sammy had found and put in the cassette deck.

Because Geoffrey Tolhurst's firm in Cheltenham had been handling rich and secretive clients for over a hundred years, partners soon learned techniques for stone-walling inquisitive outsiders, and Geoffrey Tolhurst was no exception.

He sat behind his desk, comfortable in a lightweight charcoal suit, and talked to Jed about racing and breeding, instinctively on his guard to ward off any unwarranted enquiries.

'The reason I came to see you,' Jed said when he felt enough preliminary chat had been exchanged, 'was to find out one or two more details about Mike's will.'

'I see,' Tolhurst said blandly. 'There's very little I can tell you, as you're not a beneficiary – unless, of course, your sister-in-law has granted you power of attorney?'

'No, she hasn't, and it doesn't concern her legacy. So far as I know, Tessa's quite happy about it all.'

'I'm glad to hear it,' Tolhurst murmured, looking disappointed. Disputes over wills could be very long, profitable affairs.

'What we're interested in is the principal beneficiary.'

'George Parker?'

Jed nodded. 'I wondered if you could tell me whether it is a man or a woman and where they can be contacted?'

'Even were I allowed to, I could give you no more than a box number in West Virginia. As it is, my late client made it very clear in his instructions that we were not to reveal any details about the beneficiary. But I can tell you he is definitely male.'

'Have you been in touch with him?'

Tolhurst nodded. 'Indeed. We wrote, informing him that he was a beneficiary under the terms of Michael Powell's will; he telephoned us a few days later and has confirmed that he will be in England next month, when he hopes to be in touch again to hear what we have to say.'

'So you didn't tell him the sum of money involved?'

'It would not be normal practice until we had established positive identity.'

'So he won't get the money until then?'

'No. Besides, it's unlikely that probate will be granted for a month or two.'

'Does Tessa have to wait that long before she gets title to Easerswell?'

'If Miss Langton would like to ring me, I will, of course, tell her all I can about that aspect of the legacy.'

Chapter Twelve

Jed drove out of Cheltenham, frustrated by the crazy traffic system, and the fact that he'd achieved nothing.

If Tolhurst was telling the truth, George Parker didn't even know what he was due.

Or, possibly, knew only too well.

Perhaps Parker was well aware that probate would take some time and was happy to claim a lack of interest; pretend to be in no hurry to rush over from the States to claim his crock of gold.

In the absence of any other clear course of action, what Jed wanted now was some hard evidence to show that Mike's 'accident' hadn't been arranged by a third party. For that he would have to go to London and talk to the people who'd been involved.

As he drove through the winding Cotswold lanes and tried to form a plan, he also found his thoughts turning to his wife and her worsening condition. He was growing more concerned about Sammy and her illness – whatever it was. He still wasn't totally confident that she hadn't chosen to avoid the last appointment at the hospital simply because she didn't want to be told her ailments were all in the mind; although, he had to admit, the pain she suffered seemed real enough.

He returned home to find her note on the kitchen table. A day in London with her sister would do Sammy a lot of good. Jed was only too aware that his own reaction to her crises seemed to encourage rather than dispel them. And he was happy to meet up with her later at Tessa's house, as she had suggested. Perhaps she would feel like staying on for dinner somewhere lively for a change. Anyway, it would suit him to drive up to London and start his own investigation into the events surrounding Mike's death.

He spent the morning in his office, on the phone, discussing the future of some of his best horses. It was becoming painfully clear to him that his best chance of cleanly resolving the financial problems the stud was facing would be to sell Panpipe though as yet there'd been no word from the bloodstock agents he'd approached.

Although he was determined to find the money due to him from Mike, lurking behind that determination was a dawning suspicion he might never see it; it would be sensible to face that now.

He walked out of the house to make a quick tour of the yard. Panpipe, as always, was pleased to see him, and he asked himself for what seemed like the hundredth time why he was allowing fiscal logic to displace his natural affection for a loyal horse. As he wandered listlessly through the rose garden back to the house, he had to chide himself for the tears pricking his eyes.

After a lonely lunch, with only the radio for company, Jed climbed into the Range Rover and headed for London.

The desk sergeant at Lambeth police station had no interest in racing. Neither the name Jeremy Havard nor Jed's face meant anything to him. But he was prepared to be helpful when Jed told him, omitting the detail of the recent divorce, that he was the brother-in-law of the jockey who had been the victim of a fatal road accident in their patch the week before.

After some consultation with his seniors on the sergeant's part and a certain tenacity on Jed's, he was shown to a small interview room. A moment later a large uniformed policeman came in and introduced himself in a strong Yorkshire accent.

'Morning, sir. Mr Havard, isn't it?'

'That's right. Good morning.'

'I'm Constable Pullen,' the officer said, leafing through a brown folder. 'I see you were present with Miss Langton when she identified the body?'

'That's right.'

'Take a seat, sir. How can I help you?'

'I wondered if I could have a look at the accident report?'

'I can certainly go through it with you, sir.'

Twenty minutes later, Jed had learned that Jacques Icart, the driver of the French 38-tonne lorry, had told the police that he had driven into central London illegally without realising it and had panicked, got lost trying to get out of the restricted zone and, in his confusion, failed to see the red traffic light as he came off the south end of Vauxhall Bridge.

The police had held him in custody to face a charge of manslaughter. The magistrates' court hadn't considered this a realistic proposition and reduced the charge to one of causing death by dangerous driving, releasing him on deposit of bail of £1,000 and his passport. The police had also impounded the damaged vehicle and its cargo.

But Jacques Icart had failed to turn up for a committal hearing three days later, and the hotel in Pimlico where he'd been staying told the police two angry Frenchmen had turned up, evidently to take him home, and he'd left with them after being there just one night.

Now the police were candidly doubtful that they would ever see the man again, and were making arrangements to deal with the lorry.

But, in answer to Jed's most crucial enquiry, they were adamant. The event could not have been anything more than an entirely spontaneous accident. It was clear to him that they had approached their questioning only from this point of view, but he didn't press them. There were two more people he wanted to see before he told them about the unexpected elements of Mike's will, and his conclusion that there might be a connection.

He asked the police the name of the chauffeur who had been driving Mike and had escaped with no more than a stiff neck and a broken arm. They gave him Harry Winter's address, and wished him luck.

Harry Winter lived less than a mile from the police station

in Lambeth, in the small, Victorian terraced house which he'd inherited from his aunt twenty years before.

After a few moments' looking in his *A–Z*, Jed drove straight there. Fifteen minutes after leaving the police station, he was knocking on the door of the two-up-two-down cottage in an old, narrow street off the Elephant and Castle.

After his third round of knocking and bell pushing, Jed reluctantly accepted that there was no one in Harry Winter's house. This was confirmed by an old woman shuffling past him on the pavement.

'They're not there,' she said, shaking her head as if Jed were an idiot for thinking they might be. 'They've gorn to the 'ospital.' She carried on and started to let herself into the adjoining house.

'Is Mr Winter ill, then?' Jed asked, alarmed that perhaps he'd already lost access to this witness.

'He were in a crash, weren't 'e?' the neighbour said. 'He won't be back today.'

She evidently didn't think she had anything more to say on the subject, heaved herself through her door and banged it shut behind her.

Jed stared at Harry Winter's front door for a moment, annoyed, considering then rejecting the idea of leaving a note. He knew Sammy wouldn't want to stay up in London for the night, though he would try to persuade her. He'd just have to come back as soon as he could.

Admitting defeat for the moment, he climbed into his car and drove back towards Chelsea, and Tessa's house.

Sunshine poured through the long windows of the Serpentine Gallery.

Sammy and Tessa sat on a bench within the cloistered calm, contemplating and trying to make sense of the starkly presented human waste that formed the centrepiece of the exhibition.

Tessa sighed and picked up her catalogue. 'According to the blurb, this show is designed to shock and provoke its viewers into understanding mankind's state of constant disintegration.'

Sammy made a face. 'I used to go to galleries to cheer myself up,' she said wistfully.

'You still can,' Tessa said decisively, standing up. 'Come on, we'll go to the Courtauld and look at a few proper pictures.'

'Okay,' Sammy said, following her lead. 'And I'll try and ring Jed from your car – just to make sure he got the note.'

They climbed back into Tessa's BMW and wound their way around Hyde Park, baking in the sun.

Sammy picked up the phone and dialled the house at Batscombe. The machine answered so she tried the stud. Catherine told her Jed had already left for London. She cleared the line and punched in his mobile number.

'Poor Jed,' Tessa said when Sammy told her.

'Why do you say "poor Jed"?' she asked sharply, clicking the phone off before pressing 'send' and putting it back in its slot.

'Well, he always takes his duties so seriously – always worrying about me, or looking after you.'

'He wasn't the other night.'

Tessa looked at Sammy quizzically. 'What do you mean? What other night?'

'The night Mike was killed, I saw Jed on the telly, earlier.'

'Did you?' Tessa asked lightly, though she could guess where the conversation was heading.

Sammy was looking out of the window where the sun was drawing a quivering haze from the warm earth. Slowly, she turned her head to look closely at Tessa. 'But what I want to know is, where did he stay that night?'

Knowing what a volatile state of mind her sister was in, Tessa felt alarmed.

It was absurd for Sammy to imply that she and Jed might have slept together, and Tessa had offered him a spare room without even considering such a possible inference. She took a quick sideways glance at her sister, to gauge her mood. 'Oh, Sammy, you don't think he spent the night with *me*, do you?'

She sat forward in her seat and looked straight into Tessa's eyes. 'Why? Didn't he?'

'Of *course* not. After the identification, it was nearly three, so he went off to stay at his club,' Tessa said, hoping that her lie would ease her sister's mind.

'Which club?'

'The Turf, of course.'

'Are you sure?'

'For heaven's sake, Sammy. What do you take me for?'

'I didn't ask if you'd slept with him; I only asked if he'd stayed the night. But you say he went to the Turf, so that's fine.'

Tessa nodded, relieved that Sammy had accepted her

story. 'After all, it was far too late to drive back by then.'

'I wish to God he had, though,' Sammy said quietly.

'Please stop worrying,' said Tessa, stretching out to give her sister's hand a gentle pat. 'Jed would never be unfaithful to you.'

'Do you think we could go back to your house, Tessa? I don't really feel like traipsing round the Courtauld now.'

Tessa stifled a sigh. 'Sure,' she said brightly, and spun her car into a reckless U-turn to head back towards Chelsea.

Once they were in the house in Margaretta Terrace, Sammy said she wanted to lie down, and Tessa led her up to one of her lavishly furnished spare rooms, and sent Pilar, her Spanish maid, to buy an extravagant bunch of flowers which she took up in a large vase and placed on the bed beside Sammy.

'There you are. As lovely as any picture you'd have seen today.'

'Thanks, Tessa. At least *you've* always been loyal to me,' she muttered.

She wondered for a moment what Sammy meant. 'Of course I have,' she said, reassuringly. 'Anyway,' she went on briskly, 'I hope you'll be okay now. I've got to go out later, but I'll ask Pilar to stay here until I get back.'

'Don't worry about me, Tess. I'm going to have a sleep – a good long sleep,' Sammy said dreamily.

When Jed arrived at Tessa's house, Pilar told him Tessa had gone out and Sammy was upstairs in bed.

Disappointed that the day had ended like that for her, Jed went straight up to the room where he himself had stayed on the night Mike had been killed. Slowly, and as quietly as he could so as not to disturb her if she was still sleeping, he opened the door.

The table lamps to either side of the bed were still on, cross-lighting the slight form under the bedclothes. Sammy lay with her head to one side and her pale gold, silky hair splayed out over the pillow.

Jed tiptoed across the room. 'Sammy?' he whispered hoarsely, wondering why he had lowered his voice. Suddenly, he knew that something was wrong and wanted to wake her. 'Sammy?' He spoke the words urgently, at normal pitch. 'Are you okay?'

Her breath came and went, with the languid rhythm of an aspen in a breeze.

'Sammy!' He was almost shouting now. He put his hand on her shoulder and shook it, first gently, then vigorously, with growing panic. Her eyelids stayed firmly shut; he succeeded only in making her breathing more stertorous, in short, rasping chokes.

'Sammy!' he begged with a sob. 'Please, please wake up!' He leaned over the bed and turned her so that she was lying flat on her back. 'Please,' he whispered. Then, from a corner of his eye, he caught sight of the small white plastic tub of painkillers which Sammy's doctor had prescribed. He leaned across his wife, picked it up and shook it.

It was empty.

Desperately he told himself this might not mean a thing, but he didn't believe it.

He turned back to look at her. She was breathing more regularly again. There was still colour in her cheeks. He even thought he detected a faint fluttering of her eyelids.

Abruptly, he knew what he had to do.

He put an arm behind her back and lifted her torso upright. Her head flopped against his shoulder. He stroked her hair for a few moments, listening to her breathing.

Jed pulled back the covers, lifted her from the bed and raced down Tessa's stairs. Pilar was waiting at the bottom, having heard his panicked shouts.

'I help you?' she asked in her halting English.

'Just open the front door and the rear door of my car, please.'

She ran ahead of Jed. He followed, with Sammy lying limp in his arms. She felt to Jed as if she weighed nothing. The adrenalin pumping through him had doubled his strength, and he was able to carry her smoothly out to his car, where Pilar was already holding the door open.

He manoeuvred his wife gently on to the rear seat and got in himself. He drove as fast as he could through the milling Chelsea traffic until he drew up outside the hospital in the Fulham Road, five minutes after leaving Tessa's house.

Jed lifted Sammy out of the car and carried her in his arms, running up the steps into the main lobby of the hospital, where she was rapidly transferred to a stretcher and wheeled away.

She hadn't regained consciousness before he was advised to leave her there, heavily drugged and oblivious. He walked back down the front steps, and drove back to Margaretta Terrace, hardly aware of what he was doing.

Tessa had arrived home moments beforehand and, having just heard from Pilar what had happened, greeted Jed with ready sympathy.

'I'm sorry,' she cried. 'I've only just got back. I must go and see Sammy.'

'There's no point. The nurse said she could be unconscious for eight or nine hours. That's why they sent me home.'

'Poor Sammy. I'm going anyway. I'll see you later.'

'Tessa.' Jed put a hand on her arm. 'There's something you should know before you see her.'

She picked up the pain in his voice and stood still to receive the news.

'She's taken an overdose of painkillers – she had some prescription pills for when it got too much.'

'When . . . when would she have taken them?'

'Within the last few hours,' Jed gulped.

'But, Jed, are they saying she could only have taken that amount deliberately?'

'They're not saying that. But that's obviously what they think from the kind of questions the doctor asked me.'

'Like what?'

He turned away and took a deep breath. 'Like, was she showing signs of depression or insecurity?'

'Oh my God!' Tessa breathed huskily. 'She was depressed all right.'

'Yes,' Jed said, without expression. 'She thought I'd been having an affair with Lucy Thynne.'

'I know. She told me.'

'She even thought I'd stayed with Lucy the night Mike

was killed. Of course, I told her about staying here in your spare room, but I don't think she believed me.'

'Oh, no!' Tessa paled. 'This afternoon, after we left the Serpentine Gallery, she asked if you'd stayed with me that night. She was sounding so paranoid I thought maybe she was thinking you and I had slept together, so I said you hadn't stayed, just to stop her worrying; I said you'd gone to your club.'

'Hell!' Jed swore quietly wringing his hands, slowly rethinking the situation. 'Look – it's not your fault, Tess. Her illness has clouded her judgement. She hasn't been herself for more than a year.'

'I'm to blame, Jed.'

'Tessa, believe me, you're not. It's entirely my fault for not taking her illness seriously enough.' He stared at the vivid Persian rug on the floor until the pattern dissolved into a whirling mass of colour before his eyes. 'I feel so ashamed.'

'Well, it's not too late, thank God. Anyway, I'll see what I can do.'

'But she won't be conscious, Tessa.'

'Then I'll just sit and wait until she is.'

Jed knew it would be a waste of time trying to talk her out of it. The sisters, so different in many ways, were still very close.

He poured himself a large glass of whisky and sat down in one of the big squashy chairs in Tessa's exquisitely furnished drawing-room.

Jed wasn't a regular drinker; soon the alcohol was calming his thoughts, if not his mood. After a while, though, the traumas of the day caught up with him and he fell asleep.

He dreamed not of Sammy, but of Geoffrey Tolhurst and Mike, both telling him to look for George Parker and find out just what had happened – because no one else was going to.

Then, later in his dream, Sammy appeared, lying in her hospital bed, sleeping and silent, and an alarm bell on the wall began to ring until Jed woke and found the phone beside him trilling sharply.

Drowsily, still a little hazy from the Scotch, he picked it up and grunted into it.

'Jed? Jed, is that you?'

Tessa's urgent tone roused him a little more. 'Tess, what is it? Is there any news?'

'Jed, you should come here now, to the hospital.'

'What's happened?' He was completely awake now.

'Sammy needs you.'

Jed's spirits sank. 'Oh, God, is she in trouble?' He stood up, clutching the phone, staring at his own alarmingly dishevelled image in the overmantel mirror. 'I can't drive,' he blurted. 'I think I'm over the limit.'

'Get a cab, then. It'll probably be quicker anyway.'

He stared through the uncurtained windows at the first signs of a damp, distant dawn – the beginning of a day in which he already knew he would have no part. 'All right.' He coughed. 'I'll see you in a few minutes.'

'Please,' Tessa urged, 'as soon as you can.'

Jed put down the phone and stood for a few seconds, thinking what to do.

Should he call for a black cab? It might take some time to come at this hour of the night. So would a minicab. But, so far as he could remember, there were usually taxis plying up and down the King's Road all night.

Resolutely, he let himself out of Tessa's front door, banged it behind him and set off at a brisk walk through the warm drizzle towards the King's Road.

Any cabs that he saw were occupied, and he ended up jogging the half mile to the hospital. When he arrived and asked where he could find his wife, he felt as if he had been running for hours.

The night receptionist made some enquiries; after a moment, a nurse appeared and said she would show him the way. He followed, conscious of the sharp click of his metal-capped heels in the silent corridor.

Tessa emerged from a door and ran to him, throwing her arms around his neck. 'Jed,' she whispered, so huskily she was almost inaudible. 'Jed, I'm so sorry.'

He gently pushed her from him, so he could see her face. The misery in her big, liquid eyes told him what had happened.

'Oh, no! Sammy?' he gasped.

Tessa nodded. 'She's gone – there was nothing they could do to save her. It's so bloody unfair!'

The nurse came up behind Tessa, into Jed's line of vision. 'Would you like to come with me, Mr Havard?'

Jed looked at her dumbly for a moment, then nodded.

Tessa stood back to let him pass and watched him walk into the room where Sammy's body lay.

★ ★ ★

Fifteen minutes later, she drove Jed back to Margaretta Terrace.

Inside the house her tears began to flow. 'Oh, Jed, she was so good and kind and thoughtful – not a bit like me. She really cared about other people. I'm sure that's why she hid the pain she felt until it was all too late.'

Tessa put her head in her hands and her shoulders heaved with the first real tears she had shed since her mother's death.

Jed wanted to join her; wanted the release of his own sorrow. But tears wouldn't come and the dumb misery inside him welled up in his throat, choking him. Why hadn't he stayed with her?

Desperately, he grabbed the remains of the whisky still on a table beside his chair and drained it in one long gulp. As he lowered his glass, his eye was caught by the rearing black horse on the face of the Girard-Perregaux watch. A moment later he was sobbing, his whole body quaking with grief.

In the morning, Jed drove with Tessa back to the hospital where the doctors and the consultant expressed their admiration for Sammy's bravery in putting up with the agony of her disease for so long.

Confused by what he was hearing, Jed made all the arrangements he could for the time being, and was about to leave with Tessa when the senior houseman appeared in the lobby.

'Mr Havard? I wonder if we could have a quick word?'

Jed was tired, but ready to sit and talk all day and night

about his wife and his loss. 'Of course.' He followed the doctor with an apologetic shrug to Tessa.

When it became clear that he wasn't coming back immediately, she declined the offer of a taxi and said she would wait.

It was half an hour before Jed reappeared. When he did, his face was grey and seemed to have shrunk since Tessa had last seen him. She jumped to her feet and ran a few paces towards him. 'Jed, what is it?'

He didn't answer and carried on walking towards the door. Tessa walked beside him, down the steps, along the empty pavement, until they reached his car, fifty yards from the hospital entrance.

'Jed,' she pleaded, 'tell me?'

He stopped and looked at her in the watery sunlight that had come with the morning. 'They're doing an autopsy. There may be a post-mortem.'

'A post-mortem? Why?'

Jed unlocked the car. They both climbed in but he didn't start the engine. 'To make certain of the cause of death. Now they're saying it was the cancer that killed her, not the pills at all. The specialist told me she was absolutely riddled with it.'

'Oh my God!' Tessa said. 'I can hardly bear to think of it, she must have been in such agony.'

Jed sucked in a long painful breath and nodded slowly. 'They said they couldn't understand how she tolerated it, even with those painkillers. And they guessed that's why she'd taken so many yesterday.'

'Oh, Jed. How awful . . .' Tessa gazed at him with her big

green eyes. 'And, do you know . . .' her voice faltered '. . . I feel so ashamed that sometimes – quite often to be honest – I thought she was making a fuss about nothing.'

Jed put his head in his hands. 'Don't tell me, I know. I did too.'

Chapter Thirteen

The second of the two funerals that Jed and Tessa had
arranged inside a fortnight was a more intimate affair than
Mike's. Nevertheless, a handful of racing people turned up
– those who knew Sammy; and those who knew Jed, and
how much he would miss her.

But there was no wake or champagne after this burial
for which permission had been granted once the cause of
Sammy's death from cancer was officially confirmed.
When it was over and the small congregation had dis-
persed, Jed didn't want to go back to an empty Batscombe. He went with Tessa instead to Easerswell, where
they sat, just the two of them, and talked about Sammy
late into the night, until Jed fell asleep on the sofa where
he sat.

When he woke, Tessa had already gone to London for an
early start on the day's filming. She had left a note with an
invitation for him to come and see her any time he needed
to. Jed found himself thinking kinder thoughts about the
sister-in-law he had always considered demanding and self-
centred, and reflected on the irony that tragedy often

granted this sort of fresh insight into a person's true character.

He arrived back at his own farm to find his three grooms were already quietly getting on with their work. They had all come to the funeral the day before and Jed derived some consolation from knowing that they shared his sorrow.

He consoled himself a little by going into Panpipe's box. Murmuring his regrets, he stroked her nose and neck and sucked in the sweet filly scent through his nostrils.

Afterwards he silently joined the others in their tasks, glad of the therapeutic properties of routine. In the afternoon he forced himself to watch the racing, but couldn't raise any interest in it.

He wandered alone through the rooms of the big house, seeing signs of Sammy everywhere, aware of her influence on all sides. Small, subtle touches – pictures, ornaments, flowers, a cluster of plants in the kitchen, the CDs in the rack by the player – all demonstrated the strength of the quiet influence she had had on his life, almost without his noticing. And he ached with loss and guilt that he should have taken for granted so much that she had done for him.

Between eight and nine o'clock, the quiet of the evening was broken by a phone call and the harsh accent of an American at the other end of the line, announcing that he was ringing from the offices of the bloodstock sales in Saratoga.

'Is that Mr Jeremy Havard?'

'Yes.'

'We've been asked to trace ownership of a Northern Baby colt sold here last month by Bullough Hill Farm on

behalf of a Bahamian Corporation called Saxon Bloodstock. Bullough Hill have given us your name as the part
owner. Is that right?'

'I think I may have had a share in a Northern Baby colt
at some point; I handle a lot of horses,' Jed hedged, careful
not to get his hopes up that, at last, perhaps he was going to
see his money. 'But I've got nothing to do with Saxon
Bloodstock. Why do you want to know?'

'The buyer's trainer has filed a complaint. They want to
return the animal.'

Jed felt suddenly sick. 'Oh, really?'

He searched back through his memory of the original
transaction. So far as he could recall, when he and Mike
had bought the in-foal mare, ownership had been transferred directly to Saxon Bloodstock – an off-shore company
Mike had set up in his own name – in anticipation of
bringing her back to Europe. The stud from which they had
bought the animal would be registered as the breeder and
first owner.

'Okay, Mr Havard.' There was a cynical edge to the
American's voice. 'We understood you had been the joint-
owner at one time.'

Jed found himself sweating. 'Well, you were misinformed,
I'm afraid. Has the vendor been paid?' he asked, as if out
of faint curiosity.

'Yeah. We settled with Bullough Hill, and they were
instructed by their client to make payment to a third party,
Mr George Parker, in the UK. We can't get a trace on him.
Do you know him, by any chance?'

Jed's heart stood still for a moment, until he summoned

up enough breath to speak normally. 'I'm sorry, I can't help you. Goodbye.' He held the receiver away from his ear, took a deep breath and put it down.

That night, Jed dreamed of Sammy and woke with his grief undiminished.

In contrast with his usual practice, he lay in bed for an hour or so, wishing he could sleep again, not wanting to face the world.

Eventually he got up and dressed. He was sitting down, trying to read the Sunday papers with Alistair Cooke on the radio, droning in the background, while he struggled with the breakfast he had cooked for himself, when Catherine arrived and invited herself in.

She poured herself a cup of coffee from the pot and sat down opposite him. 'Jed, why don't you take a week or two off? All the mares have foaled, we can look after them, and the vet's only at the other end of his mobile if anything goes wrong.'

Jed knew that she was quite capable of dealing with any problems and the house seemed cold, empty and cheerless without his wife. He looked at his head groom for a few seconds before nodding. 'Of course you can. Thanks, Catherine. I think a week or two away would help and, as it happens, I've got a job to do.'

When she'd gone, the house seemed to echo more and the silence was deeper, as if the place were in mourning with him.

He went out to the yard and busied himself there, to occupy his mind and distract him from thinking about what he had lost, and what he might have done to save his wife.

At the same time, he felt so treacherous at planning to sell Panpipe that he could barely bring himself to look at the filly, though as usual she had whinnied her recognition of him as soon as he had appeared.

As the house and stud were already committed as security against loans from the bank, Sammy's death had made no significant difference to his financial position. Everything her father had left her she had sunk into Batscombe, besides a few thousand pounds in shares. Her cash balance was low, due to the extravagance of the watch she had recently bought him. Though he could have sold it, he couldn't bring himself to part with Sammy's last gift. The proceeds wouldn't have gone far towards dealing with his problems anyway.

For, despite his planned economies in the yard, operating funds were running out. Now that he knew George Parker had evidently received the money from Bullough Hill Farm, finding him became even more of a priority.

And the Saratoga sales company would almost certainly sooner or later be able to confirm that Jed held an interest in the colt, and start asking for their money back. If he ever got his hands on it.

Jed spoke to Tessa on the phone that evening.

She approved of his decision to leave Batscombe for a while. 'I think it's a good idea. Of course the girls will cope without you. In fact, why don't you go down to St Rémy for a week or two – really unwind? It's lovely down there at this time of year.'

'That's tempting, but first I must find out who George Parker is and what exactly happened to Mike.'

'Do you still think there's a connection?'

'Sherlock Holmes was always telling Dr Watson that whenever two unusual things happen in close proximity, one should always look for the connection.'

On his way to see Harry Winter, Jed called in at Lambeth police station to see if there were any new developments in the investigation of Mike's accident. Constable Pullen appeared and invited him into the same small room they'd occupied on his previous visit.

When they were alone it became clear that the policeman had done a little homework. He surprised Jed by offering him formal condolences on the loss of his wife.

He then assured him that there was no fresh information on Mike's death, but if anything else came to light, he would let him know.

Jed thanked him and went back to his car.

The door to Harry Winter's house in Lambeth was opened by a comfortable-looking, grey-haired woman in her late-fifties, who turned out to be Harry's wife.

Once she'd established who Jed was, Mrs Winter seemed pleased that a relation of the famous, albeit deceased, Mickey Powell had come to ask after her husband's health. She showed Jed into the neat little front room, which, apart from a television, was furnished exactly as it might have been fifty years before, complete with flying ducks on the wall above the fireplace.

Mrs Winter left him there and soon Harry himself appeared, a short man in his fifties – though his baldness made him look older. He was wearing a plaid dressing-gown and slippers, one arm supported in a sling.

'Evening, Mr Havard, sir.'

'Hello, Mr Winter. I hope you don't mind my dropping in like this?'

'Lord, no!'

'Well, how are you then?'

'I'll be out and about next week, I should think. The quack says I bruised me innards or something. Nothing too serious, though.'

'I'm glad to hear it. Very bad luck, the whole thing.'

'Bad luck for Mickey Powell. Me – I've got a new Jaguar coming.'

'It was your car, was it?'

'Oh, yes. I always worked for myself, ran my own motor.'

'Companies book you when they need you, do they?'

'That's right. Suits them not to have full-time drivers on the payroll, and I get a better rate per mile, see.'

'I suppose they booked you on the night of the crash?'

'Yes, though it was Mr Powell hisself who rang to say he'd need fetching from South Ken. Why do you want to know about that, guv?'

'It's not important. But can you tell me, when you got to the address in South Ken, what sort of state was Mike in?'

Harry looked puzzled. 'What sort of state?'

'Yes. I mean, was he drunk or anything like that?'

'Lord, no. He came out to the car all spruced up and got

in. He wasn't too talkative on the way, but he certainly wasn't drunk.'

Jed nodded, disguising his scepticism. 'The police say it was just an accident.' Jed watched Harry Winter closely, sensitive to any slight change of expression or demeanour. As with a horse, he knew that these things could reveal a lot. 'I'm not so sure,' he added quietly.

Harry stared at him with his mouth open. 'You mean, it was deliberate? The bloke in the lorry went for us?'

Harry sat down on an old moquette-covered wing chair and unconsciously drew his dressing-gown tighter around him. 'No way!' he said, shaking his head. 'It was an accident all right. I could tell from the way the other bloke was quivering like a jelly after. And anyway, he couldn't have just hung about on the bridge waiting to jump the lights. That'd have been too much of a long shot to be worth the bother.'

Jed sat down opposite him. 'But the accident report said he had been pulled up stationary on the bridge for a few minutes before – looking at his map, trying to find where to go, the driver said.'

'What? On the double red lines? Nobody parks a 38-tonner on a red route.'

'He was French. Maybe he pretended he didn't know what that meant.'

'Look, guv. I don't want to be rude or nothing but I was there, remember. It was a bloody accident. I've never seen anything so bloody accidental in all my life. What happened to Mickey Powell – nobody done it on purpose.'

Jed observed the little man's agitation at the thought of

being mixed up in something more complex than a straight-forward case of human error. 'Okay, Harry. I'm not casting any doubts on your part, but I've reasons of my own for thinking maybe it wasn't an accident, and for the sake of my family, I've got to be certain of what happened.'

'Well, you do what you like, mate, but leave me out of it. I don't want no more bother with it.' Harry stood up and made it clear he wanted Jed and his intimations of murder out of here.

Jed didn't resist. He might need Harry's co-operation later. He thanked him, thought of offering him a tip, thought better of it, and left.

Jed drove away from Harry Winter's dingy street, feeling frustrated and empty.

The only person he felt he could talk to about his problems was Tessa. He rang her at home on his mobile and asked if he could come and see her.

'Of course you can. I told you, you can come and stay here any time you want.'

When he arrived, he found she had made an effort to produce dinner herself.

Once they were sitting at the table, she looked expect-antly at him. 'So, what did you find out today?'

Jed pulled a face. 'Not a lot. The police still think Mike's death was an accident, and seem resigned to the fact that the lorry driver won't be back to face his charge. Still, they say they don't mind my looking into the cause of the crash; they even gave me the address of the lorry driver – which I'm sure they shouldn't have done – and the driver of

Mike's car. I saw him this afternoon.'

Tessa opened her eyes wider. 'What was he like?'

'A sharp little cockney; didn't want to hear any suggestion that the crash might have been caused deliberately. He said the lorry driver was shaking like a leaf after it. But he might have been, mightn't he, even if the whole thing had been planned?'

Tessa was still trying to imagine why anyone would deliberately drive a juggernaut straight into a car, with the intention of murdering them. 'God knows. I can't believe Mike's driver wasn't badly hurt,' she said, recalling the awful television report of the crash.

'He's still laid up, but there doesn't seem to be much wrong with him – some kind of internal bruising and a broken arm.'

'Where do you go from here then?'

'There's a nice little twist to this. You know you suggested I went down to La Fleurie? Well, the driver of the lorry lives literally a few miles from St Rémy, near Tarascon.'

'What an extraordinarily sinister coincidence!'

Jed laughed at her ability to evoke the maximum drama from any set of circumstances. 'It's not particularly sinister. It so happens that this time of year a lot of early exotic vegetables are being hauled up from the South of France to be sold at Nine Elms; the chances of being hit by a lorry from round there are at least as high as being hit by one from Scotland or Wales.'

'Rubbish,' Tessa challenged. 'It's Providence. I suggested you went to St Rémy because I knew it was the right thing for you to do. Now, for an entirely different reason, your steps are being directed there again.'

'Not exactly there.'

'Tarascon is too close for coincidence. I think you should go there at once.'

'Frankly, if I do decide to go to Tarascon, I probably won't have any time to go over to La Fleurie anyway,' Jed said impatiently. 'Mind you, even if I find this lorry driver, I don't suppose I'll achieve much but it's exactly what I need to do to stop myself from brooding about Sammy. You know how I feel about that.'

Later, lying awake and staring at the ceiling in Tessa's spare bedroom, he remembered the night of Mike's accident, and wished that Sammy had believed him when he had told her he had stayed alone, here in this room.

And then, in the depths of the night, he came to an abrupt decision; tomorrow, first thing, he'd head for Le Shuttle and Tarascon.

Powering his Range Rover down the Autoroute du Soleil towards the warm spring weather of Provence, Jed conceded that Tessa and Catherine had both been right about his getting away.

The decisions and actions he'd taken over the preceding twenty-four hours were already beginning to dull the overpowering ache that had suffused him since Sammy's death. At the back of his mind was an inescapable awareness that this trip was a waste of time, a wild-goose chase. But here, in another country, he was removed from the immediate impact of irretrievable loss; and, displacing the pain, the search for the truth about the accident and George Parker had become an obsession.

He followed the Rhône south, and left the autoroute as the great river approached its broad, marshy delta. Driving across the flatlands of the floodplain towards Tarascon, he opened his window wide to let in the smells of the burgeoning vegetation. He had never seen the greenness of Provence in spring, and just filling his lungs with the warm, scented air acted on him like a tonic.

Two days later, Jed was parking his car outside Tessa's house in London. He let himself into the house with the keys she had given him and went up to the spare room where he undressed before going to the bathroom to shower.

He stood limply while the hot water sluiced over him, hoping it would somehow purge the feelings of guilt which had returned so strongly since he'd come back from France. But he was conscious that his trip had achieved nothing – in practical terms, or towards easing the pain.

He had just finished drying himself when Tessa arrived back at the house. She found him walking across the landing with only a towel wrapped around his waist.

'Hello, Jed. When did you get back?'

'Half an hour ago.'

'What happened?'

'Just let me dress and I'll come down and tell you all about it.'

While he was still putting on some clothes, he phoned Batscombe and spoke to Catherine. Once he'd satisfied himself that all was well on the stud and his head groom was coping, he told her where he could be reached for the next day or so.

Tessa had a bottle of Chablis open and wrapped in an ice-sleeve by the time Jed walked downstairs and into her drawing-room. She poured him a glass and handed it to him. The evening sun shafting through the french windows glinted seductively through the pale gold liquid, and Jed took a short, appreciative mouthful.

'Well?' Tessa asked impatiently. 'What did you find out?'

He shrugged his shoulders sheepishly. 'Frankly, I feel a bit of a fool. I met the owners of the lorry, and they thought I was part of an English conspiracy against the free-trade of produce within the EC. I found the driver's mother; she wept when she told me of the horrors her boy had endured in a London jail and said it would take him years to get over the accident.'

Tessa reached out and touched his hand with hers. 'Poor Jed. I do understand how much this thing matters to you.'

He knew she didn't have any idea how important it was for him to find George Parker, from a financial point of view, but was glad she now seemed to be supporting the idea of his search.

'Anyway, as soon as I've found out a little more about what Mike was up to in the weeks before his death, I'm going over to the States.'

They talked until late, united by the loss of the two people closest to them. That night, Jed slept soundly for the first time since Sammy's death.

It was a fine morning in the peaceful Chelsea backwater, and the sun was already showing through the curtains of the spare room when Jed awoke. From the open window, a light breeze gently flapped the Provençal cotton.

He got out of bed feeling refreshed and more able to cope, though it was still only a fortnight since Sammy had died.

He walked over to the window and drew one curtain back a little to let in a few more rays of sunshine. His eye was caught by two men walking slowly down the far side of the street. There was nothing conspicuously odd about them; one – the younger – wore a dark double-breasted business suit, and the other, a pair of fawn trousers and a light cotton jacket; but something about them just wasn't right.

They were ambling as if they might have been walking a dog, but there was no dog and at that time of morning most people would have been hurrying to work – to the tube or to hail a cab in the King's Road.

Jed dismissed his instant suspicion. He dressed, shaved and walked down through the silent house, taking care not to wake Tessa. He began to potter about in the kitchen with the aim of getting himself some breakfast, but that morning the process seemed too much like hard work.

Decisively, he walked back up to the hall. From the hooks on the wall, he took down Mike's old buckskin jacket which Tessa had kept. He shrugged himself into it, then fetched his wallet from his room and stuffed it into the inside pocket of the jacket. When he left the house, he closed the door quietly behind him and strolled up to the King's Road where he remembered there was an old-fashioned café which still served a good, big English breakfast.

He bought a paper on the way and went into the café. The place was already humming with activity – orders being bellowed back to the kitchen and builders laughing huskily at each other's accounts of the previous night's activities.

While he was waiting for his food, Jed tried to read his paper among the busy comings and goings of the place. But the air was smoky and hot and after a while, when his over-sized breakfast arrived, he heaved off the buckskin jacket and hooked it over the back of his chair.

Despite second thoughts about the meal when he was finally confronted with it, he ploughed into the sausages, bacon and eggs, and followed it up with two large mugs of coffee while he tried to plan his next move.

At about half-past eight, feeling better for the meal, he reached behind his back for the jacket.

It wasn't there.

He stood up and looked around the café, annoyed that he had been robbed so easily. The other customers he spoke to claimed they'd seen nothing, until he reached the woman at the till.

'Did you see anyone take it out?' he asked, without much hope. 'It was an Indian buckskin, with a lot of tassels.'

'And a bison on the back?'

'That's it!' Jed nodded vigorously.

'I saw a bloke walk out in it – maybe five minutes ago.'

'Great! Thanks.' He ran for the door.

'Hey, what about paying for your breakfast?' the woman

shrieked after him, but he was already outside the door, trying to decide which way to go.

He ran down the street, peering up and down side roads and lanes for any sign of Mike's jacket.

After seventy yards, in a narrow alley which connected two quiet residential streets, he saw a small, excited group of people standing by something on the ground. Amidst the hubbub, he heard a man shouting for the police, while a woman's voice shrieked for an ambulance. He was going to pass by, anxious to carry on looking for the stolen jacket, when he caught a glimpse of it. Cowering inside it, the focal point of the small crowd, lay a man, groaning and clutching at his legs.

Jed pushed his way through. 'What happened?'

'The bloke's in a bad way,' a man beside him grunted. 'Two guys jumped on him, dragged him up here and slashed his knees.'

'Muggers?'

'I didn't see them – just heard them say he'd got to pay up. Something like that.'

'When was this?'

'A few minutes ago.'

Jed had a sudden thought. 'What were they wearing?'

'I've no idea.'

The man on the ground was swearing loudly in pain.

Apart from Mike's jacket, he was a scruffy individual in grimy jeans, unshaven, with a dirt-encrusted neck. Jed could see a dark pool of blood forming on the pavement.

'It's all right,' Jed's neighbour said. 'Someone's called an ambulance.'

Jed knelt down and reached inside the jacket for his wallet.

'Oi! What do you think you're doing?'

Jed looked up at the man beside him. 'Getting my money back. This is *my* wallet.'

Having checked that his money was still inside, he pulled the jacket from the thief's back and went to the café to pay for his breakfast.

As he walked back to Margaretta Terrace, he tried to work out what had happened, and why. Some sixth sense made him feel that the beating had been intended for him.

By the time he walked back into Tessa's house, she was up, wearing a long, soft towelling robe with her hair in a turban. She was in the kitchen, drinking espresso while she talked through the day's tasks with her maid.

'Hello, Cowboy.' She laughed at the jacket. 'What got you out of bed so early?'

'It was a lovely morning,' he replied, 'and I felt like a walk and breakfast with the paper at a greasy spoon.'

He'd decided not to alarm her by telling her about the strange incident near the King's Road and his own theories about it, or about the two, possibly entirely innocent men who'd been hanging about the street at seven o'clock that morning.

'So,' Tessa asked, 'what are you going to do now?'

'I'm not sure,' said Jed evasively.

'You're going to go on looking, aren't you?'

He nodded. 'Yes I've got to. Partly as a means of dealing with Sammy's death. A distraction, if you like.'

'I understand, though God knows you weren't in any way

to blame for it.' Tessa was sitting opposite him, gazing into his eyes.

He turned his head. She stood up and busied herself making more coffee. 'Is that why you're going to the States?'

'Yes, mainly, though . . .' He hesitated for a moment. 'Tessa, I haven't told you but Mike sort of . . .' Jed sighed '. . . owed me some money before he died, and to be brutally frank, I need it.'

'Jed, I don't believe it! If you need money, I'll lend you some.'

'Don't be ridiculous, Tess.' He shook his head with a dismissive smile.

'You're so bloody honourable and upright sometimes, you're like a character out of Froissart. Anyway, where would you look in the States?'

'Do you happen to know if he was working with anyone in particular here in England?'

Tessa shook her head. 'Only the obvious people you'd know about, and . . .' She paused. 'Come to think of it, there was someone he always used to keep in touch with from his flapping days who used to help out in a menial sort of way when Mike needed him. He was at the funeral. Ev Thomas – you know him – he should be worth a try.'

Chapter Fourteen

The Monmouth & Borders Racehorse Owners' Association were holding one of their irregular, ad hoc meetings in a small field beside the River Usk.

After a string of half-understood phone calls and a visit to a small farm in the hills outside Brecon, Jed hoped that he had tracked down Evan Thomas at the flapping races.

When he drove into the broad meadow lying in a sweeping curve of the quick, clear river above Abergavenny, it was fast filling with battered horse-boxes, muddied pick-ups and long-serving Land-Rovers. The sun was already dipping towards the curving hills on the far side of the valley, lighting the fresh-budded oaks and alders which lined the river bank.

The organiser's office – an old caravan past its touring days – was propped precariously on a small bank overlooking the oval circuit of white posts. A battered chair on a flat-bed trailer was the judges' box, around which a crowd of stout owners and skinny jockeys milled while the first race was organised.

A long way from the rigid restrictions imposed by the

Jockey Club, these owners liked to race their animals under the basic conditions and scanty rules that the flapping tracks offered. A cheaply copied programme billed the event as 'Pony and Galloway races'.

Jed parked his Range Rover and wandered over to watch the runners being unloaded and tacked up, struck by the supreme fitness and condition in which they had been produced.

Some of these horses, he knew, lived in corrugated sheds in the back yards of terraced houses clinging to the steep valley sides of old mining villages. Despite these humble surroundings, no expense would be spared in lavishing everything that was necessary to keep an animal in the sort of peak condition that would have matched a runner at Royal Ascot.

The jockeys were not in such obviously good condition: the sweepings from a few of the mainstream flat yards; lads who had never made it as far as apprentice; sometimes real jockeys who had overstepped the mark and been terminally warned off by the Jockey Club stewards. Hard little men with cynical eyes and bad teeth, they'd had the ignominy of seeing their early dreams of stardom snuffed out by the harsh realities and supreme physical demands of top-level racing.

Some – a few – still rode for the love of it; most rode for the fee, paltry as it was, and the chance to influence the outcome of a race to their own advantage.

Evan Thomas did it for love as well as money. He stood out from the rest of his colleagues for his open, good-humoured face, and the compassion with which he rode his horses. Evan could have been one of the top dozen jockeys of his generation, had it not been for his one foolish indiscretion.

But he'd never been allowed back and now, in his mid-thirties, indulged his love of horses as part-time trainer and jockey to a family of wealthy Welsh butchers who were in flapping for the sport, not just the opportunities to defraud the bookies.

Jed soon spotted Evan, but he hung back from the activity and watched from a distance as the horses were led down to the track for the first race.

A water meadow was a favourite setting for a flapping track – a broad flat space in the loop of a river and draining well. The course by the Usk, defined only by the white posts, had no running rails; the experienced jockeys soon got to know where the sheep tracks, tractor ruts and rabbit holes were to be avoided.

It was, like all rustic flapping courses, temporary and without any permanent structure. The following day, only the turf cut up on the bends would remain as evidence of the event. There was a closeness and intimacy to the races run there which contrasted with the stuffy formality of the grand historic tracks, and despite their unruliness flapping races offered a refreshing chance to get back to the romantic basics of horse-racing.

Jed, an aficionado of jump racing, had always enjoyed the rough and ready flapping tracks which reminded him of the tiny community race meetings he used to go to with his uncle in Killarney when he was a boy.

He watched Evan win two of his races, and noticed the

barely controlled chagrin of two Cardiff bookies who had obviously been told to expect a different result.

Jed walked over to Evan where he had dismounted and greeted him.

'Well done, Ev.'

Evan acknowledged him with a smile, his whip clenched between his teeth as he ran his irons tidily into their leathers.

'Where's the weighing-room?' Jed asked with professional curiosity.

Evan laughed and took the whip from his mouth. 'There's a set of bathroom scales in the old caravan there, though it wouldn't know the difference between Willie Carson and Billy Bunter.'

Evan's family came from the upper Wye valley and his accent, though stamped with a Welsh cadence, was less pronounced than those of the owners and jockeys from the valleys and, like Mike's, held a hint of the English West Country.

'Have you got another ride?' Jed asked.

'No. There's no more horses going to run straight today.' Evan grinned.

'It looks as though those boys over there are already upset enough.' Jed nodded at the disgruntled bookies.

Evan gave him a knowing wink. 'Aye, we had a bit of a tickle on him,' he chortled. 'I must admit he won under rules a couple of weeks ago.'

Jed's eyes widened. 'What's his real name then?'

'Ah, that'd be telling, wouldn't it?'

They laughed, and Jed thought that even if the animal resumed its former identity and ran on official courses the next week, no harm had been done by its running in a flapper, beyond a couple of bookies losing money for once.

'Can I get you a drink somewhere?' he asked.

'You can get cans at the burger trailer.'

'I meant, I'd like a quick chat, a bit privately.'

'Which way are you going after?'

'Up to Beulah.'

Evan looked at him in surprise but didn't comment.

'Fine,' he said. 'I've a couple of things to sort out but I can meet you in an hour at the Bear in Crickhowell.'

Jed enjoyed the peaceful mellow comfort of the bar of the old staging inn and didn't mind that Evan turned up late.

'Sorry,' he said. 'Took longer than I thought.'

'What have you been doing, then?' Jed asked, interested in the workings of Evan's strange brand of racing.

'As a matter of fact, I've been taking my daughter to Brownies. She found she'd forgotten her cap and I had to go back for it.'

Jed laughed at the innocence of it. He suddenly noticed that Evan was looking at him awkwardly, evidently embarrassed by something. 'Jed, I'm sorry, I should have mentioned earlier,' he said. 'I was really cut up to read about your wife. I met her once or twice. I thought she was wonderful.'

'Yes, she was. I'm glad you thought so too.'

Neither of them spoke for a few moments until, to break the silence, Jed asked, 'Now, what would you like to drink?'

'Bitter, please.'

He went up to the bar to order their drinks and carried

them back to the table in the corner.

'Anyway,' Evan said as Jed placed a pint in front of him, 'I suppose you want to talk about Mike?'

'I'm afraid we didn't get much of a chance at the funeral, did we?'

'There was a lot of people there,' Evan said thoughtfully. 'A few important men. They won't be at my wake, that's for sure.'

'Mike was a big part of National Hunt racing for a long time,' Jed commented, wondering if Evan resented this.

'Sure. He deserved to be; he was a beautiful rider. D'you know, I first saw him race, getting on for thirty years ago – he can't have been more than nine – up on a track above Llandodd. Full of rabbit holes, it was, with corners sharp as a fiddler's elbow. Bloody hell, man, he'd go round that track on two wheels!'

Jed laughed. 'I wish I'd seen him riding then.'

'Anyway, that's it, isn't it? We'll never see him again now, will we?' said Evan, becoming suddenly morose. 'He was a bit of a chancer, but I really miss him. You know what he loved – money, and taking risks. If the two overlapped, so much the better.'

'Did you see much of him in the last few years?'

'A bit.'

'Was that . . . for business?'

Evan looked at Jed and grinned. 'Usually, though sometimes we'd take off, just the two of us, and try to catch a few trout and have a couple of drinks up in Rhayader. He and I've been mates since we was nippers. I've rode in hundreds of flappers with him before he went off to Prichard's and I went to Newmarket. Then I got warned off, but whenever there was a job needed doing, Mike always gave me first chance to make a few bob.'

'Doing what?'

'In the last few years, travelling horses for him usually. You'll have seen me at the sales a few times.'

Jed nodded. He recalled seeing Evan, without realising he was working for Mike.

'You mean, horses he'd bought or sold?'

'Yes.'

'Where? Here in England?'

'We're in Wales now,' Evan reminded him lightly. 'But I used to take horses over to the States sometimes. He used to send quite a few over there – if they had American blood in them. I took one over for him three or four weeks ago, and half a dozen others before that.'

'What was the last one?' Jed asked, puzzled.

'Wasn't a bad little colt – bit scrawny but would have made up all right. He bought it from Henry Danvers at Long Crendon.'

'That one?' Jed pulled a face. 'He told me he was going to sell it as a lady's hunter.'

'Well, I think it went for a fair bit of money. I mean, like, it had the breeding.'

'Maybe Mike's feelings about it were right then. Who bought it?'

'Some film producer, I think.'

Jed closed his eyes and winced. 'Oh, God!'

'What's wrong with that?' Evan asked.

'If it's the same film producer I'm thinking of, Mike

sold him another colt – a two year old of which I owned half.'

'So?'

'That wasn't worth ten per cent of what he paid for it either. Mike was up to something; somebody paid way too much for those horses.' Jed thought of the phone call he'd had the previous weekend. 'Whoever they are, they aren't going to be happy when they find out. At least Mike put our colt into an offshore company.'

'Saxon Bloodstock?' Evan asked.

'Yes, why?'

'They'll know that was him.'

Evan sounded so certain, Jed shivered as a sharp chill rippled through him. But he didn't want to tell Evan about the call from Saratoga. 'Even so, there's no way it can be traced to me,' he said, partly to reassure himself. 'I wish to hell he hadn't done it, though.'

'I can't understand it,' Evan said. 'I didn't think he'd been doing too bad. He had a couple of right results last year. Mind you, come to think of it, he had a few problems recently – punters knocking horses back on the guarantees. He'd been paying a lot for foals, too. And some of the older horses he bought, he never should have; he even passed a few on to me.'

'What – to go flapping?'

Evan grinned. 'He rode 'em hisself a few times.'

'You're kidding!' Jed smiled at the audacity. 'He must have been crazy.'

'He didn't often, and he only did it for the *craic*, as the paddies would say.'

'But he'd never have ridden on a real track again if he'd been caught.'

Evan shrugged. 'Mike loved a risk. He told me once it was like having sex for him, though you'd have thought, you know, with that beautiful wife . . .' Evan's views on the complexity of Mike's marriage to Tessa petered out.

Jed thought about Tessa and Mike, too, and how, maybe, it had been a long time since they'd had a full, married life together. Bizarrely, that probably explained Mike's continued obsession with getting his ex-wife back into bed, right up to the evening he died.

But Jed wanted to push his conversation with Evan in a different direction.

'Do you think maybe he earned all the money to buy that bloodstock from somewhere else, and shipping all those horses to the States was just a way of laundering it?'

'You mean – do I think he was pulling horses to order for any of the bookies?'

'I mean, did he have any other source of income, other than legitimate riding and dealing?'

'He never pulled a horse, I can tell you that,' Evan said with a fierce loyalty that surprised and convinced Jed. 'He knew that was a one-way ticket to nowhere. He gave me terrible stick for getting into trouble the way I did, and he was dead right. And I don't think he was up to anything else. I mean, he didn't make a bad living from riding straight; I'm not saying he didn't have the odd bet, too, mind – I done them for him myself sometimes – but he always bet on himself, when he knew a horse had come right, or if the trainer had lined one up, like.'

Jed held up one hand apologetically. 'Listen, Evan, I hope to God you're right, but he's left some strange loose ends hanging around and I need to tie them up. He was married to my sister-in-law for quite a long time.'

'Didn't do him much good though, did it, being married to a film star?'

'They were happy enough for a while.'

'I suppose so. He still fancied her, you know,' Evan said. 'He told me the other day he wished he hadn't blown it with her. We talked about how hard it is for a man to change, even when he knows it's his only chance. He used to say she was the only woman he could ever trust.'

'Really?' Jed asked doubtfully.

'Oh, yes. He said if he was ever in real trouble, she'd be the first person he'd turn to.'

'I'm not sure what sort of reception he'd have got, though.'

'He always said when the chips were down, she'd be on his side.'

'From what I can gather, she didn't give him a great deal of encouragement the last time she saw him.'

'I'm only telling you what he once told me,' Evan said, angry at Jed's scepticism.

He shrugged; didn't see any point in taking it further.

'Do you want the other half then, Ev?'

'No, thanks.' Evan stood up to make his point. Though the jockey's stature let him down, Jed recognised the gesture with good grace.

'Okay, calm down. He was my friend too, you know. I'm just trying to clear a few things up, and Mike wasn't a saint, let's face it. The fact is, I don't think he was killed by accident. He'd changed his will just a few weeks before, left everything to a guy in the States none of us had ever heard of.'

Evan gasped and sat down again. 'Who the hell was that?'

Jed carefully watched the other man's reaction as he said, 'A man called George Parker.'

Evan gave no sign of recognising the name. 'Who's he?'

'He lives in West Virginia. You don't know him from your trips to the States, then?'

Evan shook his head. 'Never heard of him. Is he in racing?'

'I don't know.'

'He'll have to come over here, won't he, to see the solicitors and that?'

'He may. He's told them he's coming, but he doesn't have to. It could all be done by correspondence.'

'But you think he's tied in with Mike being killed?' The little Welshman gazed at Jed with wide eyes.

'I think it's more than possible.'

'What are you going to do?'

'I thought I'd go and see Mike's mother first.'

'You'd be wasting your time. She won't tell you anything. They say she's round the bend. I saw her at the funeral. She's known me for thirty years, on and off, but she looked straight through me.'

'I'm not expecting much,' Jed admitted. 'Now, will you have the other half?'

Evan nodded, depressed by the thought that his oldest

friend may have been murdered. He was hurt, too, that Mike had never mentioned to him the man to whom he'd left the bulk of his estate.

An hour later, burning with frustration, Jed was walking back down a steep, bracken-covered hill through the growing gloom to his car. He felt like a fox-hound presented with a series of scent lines only to find they kept fading.

Although he'd found Megan's house, there had been no sign of her, and this trip to Wales had drawn an almost total blank. He drove down to the village and parked outside the only pub, where he went into a dark, gloomy bar and ordered a beer.

A dozen old men, most of them in cloth caps, regarded him with silent curiosity. He nodded to the group in general and murmured, 'Evening.'

Some returned the greeting, acknowledging that he had at least made the effort.

Jed sat down on a battered old leathercloth bench beside a wizened man of about eighty. 'I've just been up to look for Megan Powell.'

This evoked some interest.

'Oh, ah?' the old man beside him said.

'But she didn't seem to be there.'

'She probably was, but she doesn't like to see people. What did you want to see her for?' the old man couldn't resist asking.

'I was a friend of her son's.'

'The jockey,' the old man announced.

'That's right,' Jed said. 'Maybe you heard? Very sadly, he

died in a car crash a few weeks ago.'

Most of the men nodded; this was the sort of conversation they enjoyed.

'Right little tearaway, he were,' the man next to Jed growled.

'Did you know him, then?'

'His dad were from here. Quiet, like, kep hisself to hisself. Megan – she was allus a bit queer. But that boy . . .' The old man shook his head. 'He was too damn' clever by half.'

'He was a bloody good rider, mind,' one of the others joined in. 'I won a fair few quid on him when he rode the gallopers.'

'Not so much as you lost on him, though,' another of his companions jeered.

'I'm interested in finding an old friend of his,' Jed said. 'George Parker.'

This evoked not a flicker of recognition. 'George Parker?' he tried again.

'Never heard of him,' one of the men said to a general shaking of heads. 'He had a mate, though – a flapping jockey now, Evan Thomas.'

'Yes,' Jed said with disappointment. 'I know Ev.'

'He'd know this Parker, if he was a friend of Mickey's. But then, I don't reckon Mickey kept many friends from the old days, married to that woman on the telly.'

'Tessa Langton,' another of the men supplied.

Jed didn't think it would help to tell them Tessa was his sister-in-law, or that, until the day before, he'd been staying in her house in London.

He bought them pints all round, and a half for himself,

before getting back into the car and heading for Gloucestershire.

It was an hour before he was clear of the Welsh hills and could make a connection on his mobile.

He dialled Tessa's number and waited impatiently until he was answered by a machine. He left a message for her to get back to him urgently, and reviewed his position as he carried on driving through the empty roads of Herefordshire.

Later, as he was leaving the primeval humps of the Malvern Hills behind him, Tessa returned his call.

'How did you get on?'

'Useless.'

She sighed. 'Oh, God. What are you going to do?'

'I'm heading back to Batscombe right now.'

'Jed, do you feel like doing me a big favour tomorrow evening?'

'If I can.'

'There's the first British showing of *Tequila Sunset* at Leicester Square Odeon. Sort of a mini-première. Would you mind coming with me?'

'Okay,' he said. 'If you want me to. I might even enjoy it.'

After he'd finished speaking to Tessa, Jed couldn't rid himself of a vision of the injured man who'd stolen his jacket. He picked up the phone to ring Catherine.

'Why should anyone be lurking around to see you?' she asked from her tiny flat above the stable block at Batscombe.

'I'll tell you later. But could you take your dogs for a

stroll around the garden and the paddocks? They'll pick up anyone.'

Catherine laughed. Her dogs were notoriously sharp. 'Sure. I'll ring you in twenty minutes or so and let you know if they've found anyone who shouldn't be there.'

'Great, and leave the dogs out for a while afterwards.'

'Okay. I should know from their barking whether it's a man or a fox.'

When Catherine called him back and told him that, apart from an old badger, she and the dogs had met nothing, Jed decided it was safe to carry on. He was less than twenty minutes away from home now and realised he wasn't looking forward to the loneliness of sleeping in the bed he had shared with Sammy for so long; found himself suddenly overwhelmed by a surge of grief as he covered the last few miles.

Jed drove up to his front gates and stopped the car. Despite Catherine's 'all clear', the thought of the vicious attack his surrogate had taken that morning made him uneasy. He drove on and pulled up outside a neighbour's roadside barn, a little further on.

The last rays of the sun had faded an hour before and the half moon wasn't due to rise for another hour. In the dim light of the summer stars, Jed quietly let himself out of the car and locked it.

He stood and listened for any sounds above the gentle breeze. The harsh, high-pitched roar of a big motorbike, two miles away in the next valley, burst through the night and across the hills. When it had faded, a tawny owl perched in the ancient beech wood on the other side of the road called loudly to his mate, and Jed set off with a silent tread, back up the road towards his own gates.

Fifty yards before he reached the heavy stone gateposts that marked the entrance to his property, he crossed the verge and climbed over a stile, on to a public footpath on the far side. The little-used right of way crossed one of his outer paddocks, passing a few isolated parkland oaks.

Careful not to make any detectable sound, he clambered over the next stile into a small coppice wood filled in with a mass of overgrown rhododendron.

Pushing his way through thick branches overhanging the path, he carried on through the bushes, veering off the public path towards the lawns which surrounded two sides of his handsome Georgian home.

Just as he reached the edge of the lawn, a single dark shape appeared from the side of the house.

Chapter Fifteen

Bernie Capella's new residence was built where an albatross might have chosen to nest: on a broad ledge, fifty feet deep, cut like a step into the side of a cliff, six hundred feet above the crashing, splintering surf of the Pacific Ocean.

Between California's Highway One and the infinite blue, the house was invisible from anywhere except the ocean. It was approached through a narrow slit, thirty feet high and little more than two cars' width, blasted through the naked rock to the ledge.

A fine, sculpted stone balustrade ran the full length of the ledge. Between this decorative barrier and the house itself had been laid a terrace of white marble, in which was set a glittering, aquamarine swimming pool. At one end of the pool, a Grecian-style temple, whose roof was supported by four perfect, empty-eyed caryatids, served as a changing-room, sauna, games room, bar, and Bernie's office.

Bernie was sitting outside his temple, beneath a wide white umbrella, about to eat lunch with two unsubtly bikinied women whose combined ages and weights matched his own, and a much older man, with thick, straight white hair and a face composed entirely of wrinkles.

Bernie filled half a tall glass with local rosé wine for his male guest, and topped it up with extra fizzy mineral water. He did the same for himself and was lifting the glass to take his first gulp when the phone on a table beside him rang.

He picked it up. 'Yeah?'

'Hello, Mr C. The driver wants to know a take-off time from LAX this afternoon.'

'Pilot, Ricky. A guy who drives a plane is a pilot. Why does he want to know now?'

'He says the air traffic people need to book him in.'

'Okay. Tell him I have to be in London midday local time tomorrow, and let me know what time we gotta go.'

'Okay, Mr Capella. And you said to tell you when Doug Bellamy gets a fix on Powell's partner.'

'Remind me – who's Doug Bellamy?'

'He's the guy in London. He was recommended. Bobby Silver's with him.'

'Tell Bobby to call me.'

Capella put down the phone. He shook his big head and drew back his lips in an expression of distaste that was sometimes – with unfortunate results – taken as a smile.

'Jesus, I wish I'd never let Tessa Langton talk me into seeing that no-good husband of hers. It was a helluva lot easier when I was doing skin movies – you paid the babes the money; they took their clothes off and made noises – never did the dirty on you. They'd never of dared to.'

None of his lunch guests made any comment until the old man spoke in a croaky whisper. 'Tessa Langton's a good-looking broad. Too much class for you, Bernie.'

'Thanks a lot, Uncle Bruno. And, frankly, I doubt it. She must like playing the rough end of the field or why would she wind up with a two-bit jockey who has to defraud honest citizens to make a living?'

'Bernie, come on. You been defrauding honest citizens for years.'

Bernie ignored his uncle. 'He must be dumb as an ox with a tumour to think he could stiff me, with not just one, but two freaking rejects. And he never even levelled with the trainer – *that's* how dumb he is! How was I ever going to know they'd both have failed a speed test for pulling a God-damned hearse? If the trainer would of told me they had some normal kinda problem – like people tell me these horses have all the time – I probably woulda believed him.' Capella shook his head in frank amazement that anyone could be so criminally naive. 'Just for thinking I'm that dumb he deserves what he got.'

'But, Bernie,' Uncle Bruno said, 'all the trainer has to do is arrange for the horses to break a leg and the insurance will pay up.'

'No. That isn't going to happen. You see, the reason Mike Powell never levelled with Robert Newton, who was supposed to train these turkeys – you're not going to believe this – is because Robert Newton thinks he's holier than God. He wouldn't be party to lying about the horses, and he wouldn't consider knocking off a horse for the sake of a miserable half-million-dollar claim.'

'But, Bernie,' one of the women said in a bored monotone, 'if the guy who sold you the horses is dead, who has the money now?'

255

'That's what Bobby Silver's checking out. I paid the sales company, the sales company paid some little ranch that entered the horses for a phoney corporation registered in the Bahamas. I don't know where the money went after that, but some guy called George Parker is involved. And one of these animals was originally sold here in the US to Mike Powell and a partner – Jed Havard, his brother-in-law. And Jed Havard is still alive. For the time being.'

The phone beside him rang again.

Bernie picked it up and barked, 'Hello!'

He listened carefully for a few moments. 'Okay. But don't screw up this time . . . deal with it, Bobby, that's all. Just do it!'

Jed stood quite still, feeling exposed and afraid, in the shadowy darkness. His heart thumped loudly as he watched the large frame of an intruder inching stealthily around his house, shining a small torch in each window.

He was terrified to move in case he was spotted. Even with a head start, he doubted that he'd make it to Catherine's door without being caught. He thought of the thief who had stolen his jacket, lying in the gutter with blood pouring from his body.

He had to get away.

Slowly, and without taking his eyes from the beam of light flicking back and forth in the distance, he dropped to his knees and edged backwards towards the shelter of the trees. When he was just a few feet from the cover of a small stone wall, he turned to find his bearings. Then he heard a movement behind him.

His heart leapt in terror as a large figure rushed menacingly towards him. Jed threw up his arms to protect himself but the force of the man's foot caught his jaw and sent him sprawling. Before he'd regained his balance another blow thumped into his back, just to the right of his kidneys. The force of the kick knocked the air from his lungs.

Suddenly the panic of not being able to breathe was greater than his fear of his attacker. Jed was desperate to bring his knees up to his chest – something from his riding days that he knew would help – but a big hand pulled him roughly on to his back, and he suffered the weight of the man pinning him to the ground.

'So, where's the money?' The accent was American.

Jed became aware of another voice, this time from a cockney who was blinding him with torchlight. 'We've got the right one this time.'

Beneath the weight of the American, Jed's breathing was slow to return. 'I haven't got your money,' he wheezed.

For a moment there was silence. Jed was aware that the angle of the light had changed, and then a feeling of terror gripped him as his legs were wrenched apart. He summoned every ounce of his strength to fight the two men but they were much too powerful.

A blinding pain exploded into his body as his testicles took the full impact of another kick. He lay trembling with sweat as the pain came and went, before receding to a dull, heavy ache.

'This is only for starters, sunshine. Mr Capella doesn't like being ripped off by anyone, and when it's an asshole like *you*, he hates it. Where's the money?'

The revelation that Bernie Capella was responsible for sending these two thugs was half expected.

'George Parker has the money.'

The American gave a grunt of laughter and slapped Jed hard across the face, his ring cutting a nick in Jed's cheek.

'But *you're* George Parker, we know that.'

'If I'm George Parker,' Jed gasped, 'then why am I in debt and looking for him? Give me time and I'll find him *and* your money.'

Jed was desperate. He'd have contemplated anything to be free. 'Get Mr Capella on the phone,' he spluttered. 'I'll explain everything. If he wants his money back, I can help.'

The American looked up at his partner. 'What do you think?'

'I say we beat the crap out of him.'

The American stared at Jed, weighing up his options. 'Nah. He's a frightened piece of shit. If he knew anything, he'd be spilling it out. Get Bernie on the phone.'

Ricky Gradzinski, twenty-five, dark and lithe as a stoat, sat opposite his boss. His elbows rested on a broad maple-wood table. He glanced out of the window, up at the navy blue depths of the sky, from thirty-five thousand feet. Dropping his eyes and craning his neck a little, he saw that far beneath the twenty-seat Lear jet, the sun had turned the Atlantic into a vast saucer of shimmering, blue-tinged mercury.

For all his native savvy, Ricky was excited; this was the first time he'd travelled to England with Mr Capella. He guessed the boss was sizing him up, wanted to see how he'd cope in a foreign land. At least, thought Ricky, they speak the same language.

The telephone tucked into his breast pocket bleated at him. He glanced across the table and pulled it out.

'Hello?'

'There's a call for Mr Capella,' the co-pilot told him.

'I'll take it.'

After a click and a few seconds' fizzing on the line, he heard a familiar voice. 'Hey, Ricky? How're you doin'?'

'Fine, Bobby. We just flew over the Pole.'

'So, don't jump now. Listen, I'm with Doug Bellamy. We've found the guy – the jockey's partner.'

Ricky shook his head trying to follow. 'Yeah, and?'

There was a moment of silence, just long enough to convey a hint of tension.

'The guy,' Bobby Silver laughed, 'is with me now, and I think he ought to talk to Mr Capella.'

He indicated by the lightness of his manner that he was fully in control of this meeting.

Ricky Gradzinski handed the phone across the table to his boss.

'He wants to talk to me?' Bernie growled.

Ricky nodded.

Capella put the phone to his ear. 'Yeah?'

'Hello,' said a nasal English voice. 'Mr Capella?'

'Yeah.'

'This is Jed Havard. I'm Tessa Langton's brother-in-law.'

'So?'

'So, why have you sent these men to my property?'

259

Silver grunted a warning. Jed ignored it.

'Didn't they tell you?' asked Bernie, unruffled. 'They're looking for the guys who sold me the duds that little jerk who used to be Tessa's husband bought for me. They say you owned one of 'em. Now I paid a pile of money for those animals and I don't like people trying to cheat me. Especially when they die before I can deal with 'em.'

'I've had no money, Mr Capella. And what Mike Powell did had nothing to do with me.'

There was a moment's silence in the jet, still slicing its way through the stratosphere.

'Listen – I think you're a liar. Put me back to my guy.'

Jed handed the phone to the American, who took it with a suspicious grimace. Jed waited and listened while the man gave a couple of surly grunts.

'I don't know, Mr Capella. I haven't seen anybody else . . . If you say so.'

Silver clicked off the phone and looked at Jed as he put it back in his pocket.

'You're a lucky guy – for now. But Mr Capella wants to meet you at the *Tequila Sunset* première tomorrow night, and if you're not there we'll be back, looking for you. Not just to talk.'

Jed listened to them go, wondering what he was going to say to Bernie Capella tomorrow. It seemed almost beyond belief that Mike could have been so stupid or so desperate as to try to con anyone as dangerous as Capella.

In the morning, after a few hours' painful and troubled sleep, Jed wrote a note to Catherine and slipped it through the letter-box in her front door, where it was met with clamorous barking.

He drove to London and booked into the Turf Club. He wanted a neutral base in London for a few days while he prepared the next stage of his search for George Parker, his money and the truth about Mike.

Once he was installed, he rang Tessa.

'Hello?' she answered guardedly.

'It's Jed.'

'Oh, good! Are you okay?'

'I'm fine. Are we still on for tonight?'

'Yes, of course. But Jed – some people came prowling around here last night, just after I'd spoken to you on the phone.'

'In Chelsea?'

'No. I'm at Easerswell; I've had my calls rerouted. I'm working on location at Blenheim today so I thought I'd drive from here.'

Jed didn't want to start telling her over the phone about his own experiences, nor about his conversation with her producer – not until he saw her face to face. 'Who do you think it was?'

'I've no idea. It could have been anyone, but I suppose they were something to do with Mike. I was so terrified, I called the police. They came but they didn't find anyone.'

Chapter Sixteen

Late on Saturday afternoon, Jed went back to his club. He swapped his jeans and sweater for black tie and dinner jacket and went round to Tessa's house.

'What on earth have you been doing?' she exclaimed as soon as she saw his face.

Jed explained what had happened the previous evening while Tessa listened in disbelief. She still couldn't take in what she'd heard as they set off in a limousine half an hour later to Leicester Square.

On the way, Jed asked her about Bernie Capella, so that he'd know what to expect when he met him. He realised he and Bernie each wanted to find out what had happened to Mike as much as the other. But he wondered if the film producer knew any more about George Parker.

As it turned out Jed didn't get to see Bernie until after the film.

As the credits rolled, Tessa asked him what he'd thought of it and he realised that he'd barely taken in the story about an American writer, his fondness for tequila and passion for illiterate young Mexican women.

'I'm afraid I couldn't really concentrate,' he said truthfully. 'But you looked fantastic – never better.'

Tessa acknowledged the compliment with a grin. 'The make-up artists know their job,' she muttered. 'But it was your view on the acting I wanted to hear.'

Bernie Capella looked as if he wanted to eat Tessa when they finally came face to face with him at the party in a private room at the cinema. It was hard to decipher the message in the glances he shot at Jed every so often. Jed had warned Tessa to behave as though nothing had happened.

She took the initiative. Seeing the Englishman who had directed the film standing a few yards away, she lightly touched Capella's hairy wrist. 'Bernie, I've just got to talk to Nick. I haven't seen him since we finished shooting.'

Capella made a face that suggested he couldn't understand why anyone should want to talk to the director. 'Whatever.' He shrugged.

Jed stood where he was, and waited.

After a moment the heavy Italian-American turned his whole torso, and with it his gaze, from Tessa back to Jed. 'So, Jed,' he accented the name as if he were doing him a favour by remembering it, 'how do you think the beautiful Tessa's going to make out, now her husband's no longer with us?'

Jed shrugged his shoulders. 'She'd been divorced from Mike three months before he died. I suppose she was already used to being without him.'

'It's one thing to divorce a guy; another thing to bury

him. I got a lot of ex-wives who'll be very miserable when I go.'

That seemed so unlikely that Jed couldn't think of a suitable reply. He nodded vaguely.

'Still . . .' Capella went on, now studying him intently '. . . a cheating bastard like Mike is better off outa the way, don't you agree?'

Jed wondered for a horrified second if maybe Capella was responsible for Mike's crash after all. But he dismissed the idea of retribution being exacted before the money had been repaid.

'It might make recovering the money rather complicated. Perhaps you'd better consider writing it off,' he suggested.

'Mr Havard,' Bernie Capella said in a low voice, still staring hard into Jed's eyes, 'I've never written off a debt in my life. That's why people don't owe me. The money I paid Mike is still around. There wasn't time for him to spend it before he died. If I get to hear any of it's found its way to you, just remember what I'm telling you. You'll be sorry you were ever born.'

Capella swivelled his stocky body at the hips and moved off with two acolytes in tow. Jed stared after him, in no doubt as to the meaning of the threat.

Later, back at her house, Tessa offered Jed a drink before quizzing him about his meeting with Bernie.

'So – what did he say?' she asked with concern.

'What do you know about him, Tessa?'

'He's a perfectly normal Hollywood gangster.'

'Are many of them Italian?'

'Wherever there are big bucks, there are Italian-Americans.'

'Which is a euphemism for "Mafia"?'

'Certainly not! The Mayor of New York is an Italian-American.'

'But *is* Bernie Capella connected to the Mafia?'

'God knows. I don't know how you tell. It's not as though they do funny handshakes like the Freemasons. All I know is that you don't want to be on the wrong side of him, and if you want my advice, if you ever do get the money, give it straight back.'

'I don't know where to begin.'

'Jed, maybe this George Parker was a complete invention of Mike's, ready and waiting as a bolt hole for when all these shady deals caught up with him. Then the crash happens, Mike dies, that triggers whatever arrangements he'd made and buggers them all up.'

'You're forgetting that Tolhurst said he'd already been in touch with Parker.'

'Maybe he wasn't telling the truth – lawyers don't always. Anyway, you told me he specifically said they wouldn't release anything until they'd established Parker's identity. Who knows what's waiting back in the States?'

'Look, Tess, it's a nice idea, but I'm sure there *is* a George Parker, and one day soon he's going to get his hands on a pile of money – some of it mine. He's welcome to his legacy but if I'm to save Batscombe, I need my share from the colt. I can't afford to let this drop.'

Jed thought about ringing the police as he drove down to

Batscombe the following morning. Several times he'd been tempted to pick up the phone and talk to them, but finally convinced himself that until he had a line on George Parker, he didn't have enough of a lead to offer.

Jed checked the horses with Catherine and sorted out the few clothes he'd need for the States. There was just enough in his current account to keep the stud going for a week or two, and he'd managed to get a cheap return flight to Kentucky on a credit card he seldom used, and some cash for getting around there – at least for a few days.

He phoned Henry Danvers and asked him how much Mike had paid for the colt he'd sent to the States. The answer – five thousand pounds – didn't come as too much of a surprise. Jed was on the point of leaving the house when the phone rang.

He picked it up, irritated by the bad timing. 'Hello?'

'Hi, it's Tessa.'

'I was just on my way out.' He immediately regretted his curtness. 'But it doesn't matter.'

'It won't take long anyway. I just wanted to tell you I've decided to go ahead with a memorial service for Mike.'

Jed winced. 'Are you sure? I can't help thinking you're being just a little too sentimental about this. I mean, you had just divorced him.'

'Maybe, but I feel responsible for him now. Besides, quite honestly, if I don't organise it, no one else will.'

Jed gazed out of the window at the stately cedars on the lawn and the long sweep of drive down to the stone wall that fronted the road. 'I don't suppose it'll do any harm,' he sighed.

Having spent the night at his club in London, Jed walked

next morning from the Mall to the street in South Kensington where Tessa said she had dropped Mike on the evening he was killed. The bruises on his face had died down and he felt much better.

As he walked, he turned over everything he and Tessa had discussed, late into Saturday night, and tried to reconstruct what exactly had happened on the evening of the crash.

Tessa had dropped Mike just before eight. Fifteen minutes later, Harry Winter had collected him and, according to the driver, Mike had seemed well-groomed and sober.

So, in that short space of time, he had managed to change, sober up and set off for the South Bank studio. Given the condition he'd been in before Jed had left Sandown, and Tessa's description of him when he came to her house earlier, Jed thought it impossible Mike could have done all that without help or, at least, encouragement – most probably from a girlfriend, as Tessa seemed to think.

He stood outside the address she had given him and looked up at the opulent, white stucco building. He climbed four shallow stone steps and studied the intercom beside the front door.

The building appeared to be split into three large apartments – presumably expensive to buy or to rent. The entry buttons were labelled only with the numbers of the apartments, not the names of the occupants.

Jed pressed the bottom one, marked 'Resident Caretaker'.

A small man – an Arab, Jed guessed – dressed in an open-necked black shirt and faintly grimy dark suit made it clear he could say nothing about the current residents until Jed produced a ten-pound note.

'Most people staying here Arab people.'

It was possible Mike had Arab friends, Jed thought, though unlikely. 'No Europeans?' he asked.

The caretaker nodded. 'Well, there was one American man.'

'What was his name?'

The caretaker thought for a moment, wondering if this information might be worth another ten pounds, until he decided that this one would be on him. 'Mr Parker,' he said clearly.

Jed could hardly believe what he'd heard, but tried to control his excitement. Parker, after all, was not an unusual name.

But he'd come expecting to find a woman. Tessa had told Jed, with an obvious trace of jealousy, that she'd guessed Mike had a girlfriend. Jed hadn't been so sure, but tracing George Parker so easily, if indeed he was the man he was looking for, had been way beyond his expectations.

'What did he look like?' Jed enquired.

The caretaker screwed up his face in a bid to show Jed he was giving value for money. 'Medium height, middle-aged, short brown hair, glasses – like so.' With his index finger he described a pronounced square around his right eye, then dropped his hands to show he had finished.

The description would have fitted a sizeable percentage of the male population.

Jed sighed and persevered. Another ten-pound note elicited the address of Persepolis Property Holdings which owned the building. Their offices were a few hundred yards away in Harrington Gardens.

Jed almost ran there and found a middle-aged English secretary earnestly rattling a PC keyboard. She told him politely but firmly that she couldn't give out any information about tenants or former tenants without authority.

But Jed was now so tantalisingly close to a hard lead on George Parker, he could hardly think rationally. For a moment he considered leaping over the woman's painstakingly tidy desk and shaking the information out of her, when a man walked into the office. From the secretary's reaction, Jed guessed this was her boss.

He was short, dark and Levantine, with dancing brown eyes and an accent to match. 'Good morning, Mr Havard. What can we do for you?'

The secretary glanced at Jed, surprised to find he was known to her employer. 'I'm sorry, Mr Shapur, I didn't realise you knew this gentleman.'

'Mr Havard rode a winner for me once, a long time ago, Mrs Walters. A moderate beast called Snow Board.'

Jed didn't remember the man from among the hundreds of owners he'd met, usually for just a few moments, in a racecourse paddock. Normally he was concentrating hard on what his trainer was saying.

'I am Ehsan Shapur. How can I help you?'

Now Jed remembered the man's horse – an ungenuine grey chaser who liked to go just fast enough to keep warm, but no more.

'I was given your address by the caretaker at 63 Sumner Place,' he said.

'You want to rent an apartment there?' Shapur looked surprised.

'No. I wanted to get in touch with someone who was a tenant there until recently.'

Ehsan Shapur invited further enquiry with an eloquent gesture of his hands.

'An American . . .' Jed noticed the man visibly relax '. . . called George Parker.'

Shapur turned to the secretary. 'Mrs Walters, can you see what we have?'

'Yes, of course, Mr Shapur.' She smiled at Jed. 'I won't be a minute.'

She left the office by the door opposite the entrance. Ehsan Shapur waved Jed to a sofa set between two large potted palm trees in glazed Persian urns. He sat down.

'May I offer you coffee?'

'Yes, please.'

Shapur walked to the door through which the secretary had disappeared and gave a crisp order in a Middle-Eastern language Jed didn't recognise. He came back and sat in an easy chair opposite Jed.

'I read that you are breeding now?'

'I've a dozen or so mares,' Jed confirmed. 'Have you still an interest in any horses?'

'One or two, but they are no good.'

A dark timid woman came in with a tray containing a tall silver coffee pot and two demi-tasses. She set it down on a low table and Shapur filled the two cups with thick, black oriental coffee.

'So,' he said, 'why are you looking for this American gentleman?'

'Well, umm . . .' Jed faked reticence while he tried to

271

concoct a plausible-sounding reason. 'You know how it is when you've something to sell. He'd been down to see a colt of ours, and seemed very interested.' Jed was busking now, but he knew he was dealing with a trader. 'Frankly, I wanted to see if I could get him to close the deal before he went back to the States.'

'But now you find he's gone and you have no other address for him?'

'That's right.' Jed took his cue, and a sip of thick, bitter coffee.

'And deals must be done.' Shapur grinned back at him. 'Ah, here is Mrs Walters. Did you find anything for our friend?'

'No forwarding address here in England, but I have an address in America that was on the gentleman's driving licence.' She handed Jed a slip of paper on which she had written in neat copperplate. 'I see Mr Parker was a mining engineer,' she added.

Shapur raised his eyebrows. 'A wealthy one if he was interested in buying one of Mr Havard's colts.'

'It wasn't a very expensive one,' Jed said quickly.

'Sometimes they can be the hardest to sell,' Shapur said generously. 'Anyway, I'm glad we have been able to help you.'

Once he had left Persepolis Property and could think clearly enough to make a plan, Jed went into a shop opposite South Kensington tube station to buy himself a roomy rucksack which he took back to the club to pack.

When he was ready, he set off for Heathrow, dropping in at Margaretta Terrace en route. Tessa was out. Jed let himself in and wrote her a note to say where he'd gone, that he'd be away for a few days and would ring her. He propped it by the phone after using it to check that his bucket-shop flight was scheduled to leave on time.

At four o'clock in the afternoon, local time, Jed pulled his rucksack from the overhead locker on the Allegheny Airlines flight from New York to Blue Grass Field, Lexington, and walked off the plane into a warm, spring day.

With no bloodstock sales on, the small airport was today the domain of local people in business suits or jeans. For the most part robust country types, they looked very different from the inhabitants of Chelsea, although Jed didn't feel out of place among them, wearing Mike's old buckskin jacket.

He had rung Jim Halliday from New York and his friend was there to meet him.

'So, what brings you back?' he asked as they drove away from the airport.

'Mike, in a word.'

Jim picked up the implication in his voice and glanced at him. 'Left you with some problems, did he?'

'You could say that.'

'I'd heard a rumour that Mike had found a rich patsy.' Jim nodded knowingly.

'Did you know that someone was Bernie Capella?'

Jim smiled. 'Yes, secrets don't keep long in the bloodstock world. What a guy!'

'What a bloody fool,' growled Jed. 'The man's looking for his money back and I haven't got it.'

273

'Why not? It doesn't usually take long to come through.'

'That's why I'm here. When Mike was killed, it turned out he'd left everything to someone from over here – West Virginia.'

'Who was that?'

'A George Parker. Ever heard of him?'

Jim Halliday searched his memory for a moment. 'Nope. Don't know him. Why did Mike leave it all to him?'

'I haven't a clue. None of us had even heard of the guy. He was in London earlier this year for a while, and evidently Mike saw something of him then, though I only found that out this morning. Technically, this man will have access to Mike's accounts and assets here, such as they are, and that includes the proceeds from the sale of our colt.'

'And I guess your Mr Capella would like to get his hands on that.'

'I get the impression Mr Capella is more concerned about saving his reputation for mercilessness than he is about the money.'

Jim looked thoughtful. 'A matter of honour, eh? Lucky for Mike he's dead.'

Chapter Seventeen

After a sleepless night in the Hallidays' big ranch house, Jed thanked them and set off in the small VW he had hired to drive the hundred and twenty miles to Huntington, West Virginia.

He arrived there at midday, bought a map and swiftly pin-pointed George Parker's address. Twenty minutes later, he was heading south out of Huntington up the winding valley of the Guyandotte River towards Orange Creek, a small mining town, according to the local gazetteer, with a population of five thousand.

A few enquiries led him to the address he'd been given by the woman in the Persepolis Property office.

On the outskirts of town, it was a plain, clapboard house, standing in a half-acre plot. The garden obviously hadn't been touched in weeks, and the whole place had an air of having been unlived in for a while.

Jed parked his car, got out and walked up to the house. His hammering on the door produced no response and, cautiously, he made his way all round the house. He didn't know what he'd been expecting George Parker's home to be like, but he hadn't expected this impoverished, rundown dwelling.

'Mining engineer', as entered in the Persepolis Property records, was his only clue to the man's background. And seeing this house in what he assumed was George Parker's home town, any connection with Mike seemed even more unlikely.

He was peering through a front window when a voice behind him croaked, 'He ain't there, mister.'

Jed turned and saw an old man with white hair and no teeth, dressed in faded blue dungarees and a yellow checked shirt. He was leaning on a broom handle in front of the tiny, single-storey house opposite.

'Any idea where he is?' Jed asked.

The old man shook his head. 'He's gone, three months back.'

'George Parker?'

'Yeah. Who d'you think?'

'Does anyone know where?'

'I dunno.'

'I need to get hold of him – urgently.'

'And a few others besides. You from England?'

'Yes. Did you know he'd gone to England?'

'Nope, but you sound like you're English.'

'I've got to find out what's happened to him,' Jed persevered. 'Can you tell me where he worked, or what he did?'

'Not for sure. He came from this town – his dad was a mine-worker – but he hasn't been back here much. 'Specially not since he walked out on Dianne Clayton.'

Jed scented a lead. 'Was she his girlfriend?'

The old man nodded. 'Sure was.'

'Is she still here?'

'Sure is.'

'Where could I find her?'

'Maybe in town. Her daddy left her his mine and real estate. The mining corporation office is in Main Street, side of the bank.'

Jed thanked the man and quickly got back into his car. He found a place to park in the sleepy town centre and identified an old office building with the words 'Orange Creek Mining Corporation' painted on the front window.

As he walked towards it, a woman carrying a pile of books and two brown paper shopping bags walked out of the main door of the building and across the road to a small European car.

Some instinct told Jed that she was the person he wanted to see. There was an obviously unmarried look about her, and she stood out among the stocky, badly dressed local women. She wasn't particularly good-looking, maybe in her mid-thirties, but she had gleaming dark hair and an impressive body. He had a nagging feeling he had seen her once before, but where and when was impossible to pinpoint.

Jed walked up to her. 'Hello?' he said tentatively.

She was trying to unlock the car without letting go of the bags and books.

'Excuse me?'

'Can I give you a hand?'

She glanced up at him for a second from nervous dark brown eyes. She was expensively and tastefully dressed. But for that shy, uncertain manner, she could have been a New York executive.

'Okay.'

Jed stepped forward. He took both bags and rested them on the bonnet of the car before putting his hands firmly to top and bottom of the stack of books, releasing them from between her chin and forearm.

She gasped with relief, and smiled. 'Thank you so much.' She unlocked her car and opened the hatchback, taking the books and bags from Jed and dropping them in the boot.

'Are you Miss Clayton?' he asked.

'Sure, I'm Dianne Clayton.'

'Jed Havard.' He held out a hand. 'From England.'

'You don't say?' she laughed, shaking his hand a little uncertainly.

Jed smiled back. 'I wanted to talk to you about George Parker.'

Dianne Clayton stopped halfway through pulling down the hatchback. The door carried on moving slowly under its own momentum until it clicked shut as she turned to face Jed, hurt and anxiety in her eyes. 'George? What's happened to him?'

'Could we talk?'

She glanced at her car. 'Where?'

'I don't know. My car? Yours? A coffee-shop?'

She considered for a moment. 'All right. There's a place around the block,' she said, and set off at a swift pace.

As he tried to keep up with her, Jed thought about Dianne Clayton. She didn't look like a small-town girl; she didn't seem to belong among these simple people. And her reaction to George Parker's name confirmed the old man's statement that she'd been upset by his disappearance.

When they reached what turned out to be a small bar fitted out like a log cabin, they sat in a dark corner and Jed ordered from a heavy-breasted waitress.

Once they both had a large mug of surprisingly good coffee in front of them, Dianne smiled at him. 'So, you're a friend of George's?'

'No. I've never met him.'

Dianne's face fell. Jed went on swiftly: 'I only found out he existed a couple of weeks ago. I also know he was staying in London until quite recently. Yesterday morning I went round to a big apartment he'd been using in the middle of London. He'd left just the week before, but the property company he rented it from were able to give me an address here.'

'And you've just come all the way from London, to look for him?' the woman asked, sounding alarmed.

'Yes.'

'Why do you want to find him so badly?'

'I'm not sure. He got involved with a friend of mine – a man, that is – and . . .' Jed stopped himself. 'Look, I'll tell you what I know, if you could just tell me when he left, and why?'

'Why?' She gave an ironic smile. 'That's a helluva question.'

'Would you mind telling me about him, Miss Clayton? It seems we're both interested in knowing what he's been doing and where he is now.'

'Call me Dianne. I'm not an old maid yet.'

279

Jed grinned. 'Sure.'

'George and I, we were doing real well, I thought. We neither of us had ever got it together before with people we found truly compatible – or so he said – and when we did, I thought it was a miracle. He's one of the reasons I'm still out here in Deliverance country, this cultural wilderness . . .' She waved one hand vaguely. 'I only came back to Orange Creek when my father died.

'Of course, I knew the place, I'd spent a lot of time here as a kid, though we always had a place in New York, too. But my great-grandfather opened two or three of the big mines up the valley – all worked out now but they made him a pretty big fortune. Though I'm a city girl at heart, I always had a kind of nostalgic attachment to the place. I knew dealing with everything would take a while and used it as an excuse to take time out from Washington.'

'What were you doing there?' Jed asked, curiously.

'I'd been working in the State Department, which I mostly liked, though God knows it could be frustrating. When I got here I heard they needed someone to teach English to the ninth and tenth grades at Orange Creek High School. I was qualified, and for some reason took the job.' She shrugged. 'Frankly, I didn't expect it to last long, but there was still work to do with the property I own here. I was going to refurbish, sell it all, and leave this place behind for good. Anyway, I started at school, and soon after that I found George.' She sighed. 'A perfect man in so many ways – or so I thought. I suppose I should have been suspicious of the fact he hadn't been snapped up years before. But there he was: good-looking, smart, gentle, creative.' She sighed again. 'Sophisticated, too – at least by West Virginia standards. Of course, he wasn't rich; he said he'd lost everything in a mine down in Tennessee. I'm pretty sure now that's not true but it didn't matter to me because I've got more than enough. Of course, that turned out to be the trouble, but then, so far as I could see, he had everything I needed in a man. I'm afraid I don't have a whole lot to show for it now, besides my broken pride.'

Jed didn't find it hard to sympathise. It was harder to understand why George Parker had been prepared to abandon this warm, generous woman.

'Did he tell you he was going?'

Dianne looked back at him, recognising his sympathy and grateful for it. 'Look, Jed, I can see you're all right. If you want to talk about this some more, why don't you come up to my place? I've got a couple of dogs that'll be waiting for their dinner.'

'I'd be glad to,' he answered.

She stood up decisively. 'Okay. Where's your car?'

'Just across the road from where you're parked.'

'Fine. I'll drive out and you follow. It's only a few miles.'

Jed paid, and they walked back to the place where he had first spoken to her. She gave him a last nervous smile and let herself into her sedan. Jed walked across to his, and followed her out of town on the road back towards Huntington.

After a mile on the main road, she turned left across the River Guyandotte, now leaping and gushing down a steep-sided ravine, and took a country road through some oak woods into the hills.

Jed followed her for two or three miles of switch-backs until she turned off between a pair of tall stone gateposts which he guessed marked the boundary of a substantial property.

The drive wound round a wooded bend and ended in a large rectangle of weed-filled gravel in front of a handsomely proportioned, nineteenth-century stone mansion.

The woman drew up and got out of her car. Two big German shepherds bounded out from behind the building, with loud barks that turned to whimpers of pleasure the moment they saw her.

She shooed them away as Jed parked and climbed out of the VW.

'Welcome to Orange Mountain,' she said, watching him appraise the house. 'My dad left this place to me. I came back from DC to get rid of it, and, two years later, I'm still here.'

Jed turned and gazed at the spectacular view across the valley to the rolling ridges of the high mountains in the east. The scent of the pines, the gurgle of a brook in a gully and the haunting calls of the birds in the forest all lent this place a sense of deep tranquillity and distance from the harshness of the real world. 'It's beautiful,' he said. 'I can see why you stayed.'

'George said he loved it too, but he left anyway,' said Dianne flatly. 'Come on in, and I'll make you some more coffee.'

Jed helped to carry her books and bags into the house. Inside, she led him to a comfortable, old-fashioned kitchen which offered another spectacular view up the valley. The dogs trotted along with them, filling the place with their shaggy black and fawn pelts and waving tails. Jed sat down and instinctively made a fuss of them as he might have done with any of the dogs at Batscombe.

Dianne made the coffee while they talked more about George. When it was ready, she sat at the table opposite Jed.

He smiled encouragingly at her. 'You were going to tell me why he left?'

'Yeah.' She nodded ruefully. 'Of course, I didn't know then he was leaving for good, though I should have guessed. Now I know why he went – it was my own fault. I thought it wasn't good for him to be using my money all the time, and told him I wouldn't lend him any more until he'd started making it for himself. Some time back in January, I picked him up at Lexington off a flight from New York. He said he'd been to set up a deal and, driving back here, started saying he really wanted to go to London to follow it up – something he'd gotten into in New York, I thought.

'I was pleased! He was too darn' smart to be sitting around in a dead-end place like this and I could see his self-esteem was at rock-bottom. So I lent him the ten thousand dollars he said he needed for expenses and a few days later drove him to the airport. He took a plane to England, via Atlanta.' She got up and started to busy herself with feeding the two snuffling dogs. 'I never saw him again.'

'Or your ten thousand dollars?'

'Which turned into twenty,' Dianne said, shame-faced. 'He called a few times and wrote some beautiful letters, saying how much he missed me and how he wanted to come back as soon as he could. But he also said he needed just a little more money to set up his deal. After that . . .' she sighed '. . . I've heard nothing from him.'

'Don't you have an address for him – where you sent the money?'

'Yeah, sure. The Berkeley Hotel, London. But he left almost straight after that, even though he wrote me from there a few more times. When I wanted to talk to him, I rang the hotel and they said he'd been gone a long time and they had no forwarding address.'

'And that made you suspicious?'

Dianne nodded ruefully. 'Mostly it was that, but he'd said he had some family business to look after, too.'

'Family business?' Jed asked in surprise. 'What did he tell you about that?'

'Nothing much. In fact – nothing. He said he couldn't yet. He was all mysterious about it, but excited, too. It was kinda strange. I mean, he had no family to speak of here, except Carol. Or not so far as I knew.'

'Who's Carol?'

'She's his half-sister. She's kind of retarded – not exactly a dummy but like a big kid.'

'Where does she live?'

'Here – in town, by herself. She works for the logging company. Apart from that she doesn't have much to do with other folks.'

'What about George's parents?'

'His mom died when he was very young – five or six. His pop remarried and his step-mom took George over completely. George told me he never knew much about his real mother or her family.'

'What did his father do?'

'He came back from the military just about when George was born, I think. He was a miner; worked all over. They couldn't seem to settle for a while, not till he married the second time. Then he fetched up here, working for my father. And George was sort of a prodigy – one of the success stories of Orange Creek High. He went on to college in Charleston but about then his dad was killed in a rock-fall in the mine. George came back to bury him, then just walked away. He must have worked abroad a dozen or more years before he came back here.'

'What did he do?'

'All sorts, but basically he was a geologist, he said – a mining engineer. He went off prospecting for a while, maybe six or seven years in Oregon, then Colombia, mining gold. I don't know what happened there but he got into some kind of trouble.'

'What kind of trouble?'

'Some dispute over rights, he said. I guess it must have gotten pretty heavy because just before he went to London, a Latino guy turned up here asking for him. People in town had told this guy he'd find George here. I forgot to mention it for a couple of days, but when I did and described the guy, George looked nervous . . . That's when I realised there was a problem, though he tried to tell me there wasn't. Anyway, he left for London the next day.'

'You think the appearance of this South American might have encouraged him to go?'

'He already planned to, but I'm sure that made him keener. I knew better than to ask him, of course. I guessed he'd only lie to me and I didn't want that.'

'What brought him back here from Colombia in the first place?'

'I guess the hassles he was having there, but also someone back here had told him about a mine in Tennessee that had more going for it than people thought. George told me he'd come back to try and take it over. It went wrong, I don't know why. He must have been dumb or cheated in some way, but he'd already been back in the mountains a couple of years when I met him again.'

'You knew him before he went away?'

'Not really *knew*. Not then. When he was a kid I'd see him around and notice him; he was good-looking even then.'

'Why did he come back here to Orange Creek?'

'When I asked him, he said because it was home.'

'When he went off on this London trip, how long did he say he'd be gone?'

'Why?'

'I don't know. I'm just trying to make sense of some other things that have happened in England.'

'Well, when he went, it was only going to be for a week or so.'

'So when did you last see him?'

'Ten or eleven weeks ago, I guess.'

'Has he been back at all?'

'If he has, I haven't seen him. Someone in the office said they had – in Huntington a couple of weeks back; they weren't sure. But I don't think he'd come back to Huntington and not come here. I went down to his house and one of his neighbours who's always out messing about in his yard all day said no one had been there except Carol to pick up some things the other week.'

'Have you asked Carol about him?'

'She just said she hadn't seen him, but she reckoned he'd be back soon.' Dianne stood up, gathered the coffee things and put them in a big old sink. 'But even if she hasn't seen him, I think he's very likely called her. It may be he's an opportunistic bastard, but he was always pretty concerned for her. Anyway, that's the way it is – I've told you all I know. How about you?'

'Okay. But I warn you, I don't know where this is going.' Jed stood up and walked across the room so that he could take in the panorama beyond the kitchen window. 'My sister-in-law is a well-known actress in England – Tessa Langton.'

'Tessa Langton? She's made movies too. She's in Nick Steilman's new picture – *Tequila Sunset*. She's really famous!'

'That's her. I saw the British première with her last week. Until a few months ago she was married to a man called Michael Powell, a British jump jockey – he rode over fences, they don't do it much here in the States. I'd known Mike for years and introduced him to my wife's sister – Tessa. I never thought they'd get married, though I suppose they were a good match. Sadly, it all ended last year in a messy divorce.

'Then, in the perverse way these things happen, Mike suddenly said he wanted to get back together with her and started turning up at her house all the time. Last month, he called on her at home just before he was due to appear on a

TV show. Tessa saw what sort of state he was in and, partly to do him a favour, probably to get rid of him, too, dropped him at an address in London where he said he was going to shower and change. Then he was picked up by a chauffeured car to take him to the studio. But on the way there, he was killed in a really horrendous road smash.'

Jed took a deep breath and closed his eyes to the magnificent mountain scenery in front of him as he vividly recalled Tessa's pale face after she'd identified Mike in the mortuary.

'It was only after we'd buried him, that we found Mike had left around three-quarters of a million pounds from a life insurance policy to George Parker.'

Dianne gasped. 'Michael Powell left George all that? But why?'

'We thought it was strange, too,' Jed said. 'No one who knew Mike had even heard of George Parker until recently. And nobody had seen him. All we knew about him was that he lived in the States. Then we remembered the place in London where Tessa had dropped Mike off the night he died. We assumed the flat belonged to a girlfriend, but I went there only to find that George Parker had been living there until recently. And that's why I'm here.' He turned to look at Dianne, who had just finished drying the coffee cups.

'Why didn't you look for him in England first?'

'I had nothing to go on – no leads at all. There were no clues in the papers Mike left in his study. This was my only point of reference; I had to come here.'

Dianne sat down at the table. 'Wait a minute . . .' She

glanced at Jed with a look of sudden enlightenment. 'Maybe there *is* a connection, with Tessa Langton and your friend Michael Powell.' She leaped to her feet. 'Don't go away!'

She left the room hurriedly and Jed heard her running up the stairs. After a moment's silence, she came rushing down and into the kitchen, triumphantly brandishing a copy of *Hello!*

Jed looked at her in surprise.

'George brought this English magazine back with him from New York. I was flicking through it out of curiosity when I found he'd left an envelope clipped to this page.' She had flipped open the magazine to a section with photographs of various social events in and around Los Angeles, mostly featuring movie people.

Jed skimmed through the dozen or so shots until his eyes were brought up short by a good, clear paparazzi snap of Tessa leaving a restaurant 'with her husband, jockey Michael Powell, from whom she has just announced that she is getting a divorce'.

Jed read the caption twice and looked at the date of the publication. 'Okay.' He glanced up at Dianne. 'That's a picture of my sister-in-law and Mike. Why should George have marked it?'

'Look in the envelope.'

Jed picked up the creased, white envelope that had marked the page and slid out a photograph.

He studied it for a moment, fascinated. 'Who is this?'

'That's George,' Dianne said. 'He always said he thought his real mom had come from Wales.'

'The one who died when he was a kid?'

'That's right,' Dianne said triumphantly. 'Maybe that was the family matter he was talking about.'

Jed looked at her and nodded. He started to pace back and forth across the floor as he spoke, trying to put together the pieces of the story he had gleaned so far. 'I wish I could tell you why, but Mike's death has unearthed a few nasty skeletons. Now, I'm not saying George was involved, but I have to be sure. Do you think, for instance, he might have had anything to do with buying and selling horses?'

'Horses?' Dianne shrugged her shoulders doubtfully. 'If you'd asked me before he disappeared I'd have said no, it's way out of his field, but now I'm not so sure. There's a lot of horse-dealing not far from here though, in Kentucky.'

'Yes, I know. Mike and I sometimes came over to Lexington for the sales. I stayed near there last night; I was there in January, too. We used to do a few deals – not so many recently – but jointly we owned a colt which Mike sold last month for a great deal of money. I still haven't had my share of it.'

'Because Mike left everything to George?' Dianne looked at him with a wry smile.

'Yeah, and I want to find him because even if he doesn't have it, he might be in a position to get his hands on it and let me have my share. My claim's very straightforward.'

'I can see now why you want to find him. I wish I could help, but frankly I've a feeling I won't be seeing George again.' She looked resigned to the fact that she'd been duped and dropped. 'Maybe you should try Carol.'

'But you said she wouldn't tell you anything?'

'Maybe she'll tell you.'

'Okay. How do I get to her place?'

Dianne seemed reluctant to let Jed go. He could see that she had been deriving comfort from just talking about George. But she gave him directions, wished him luck and watched while he negotiated the potholes in the long, winding drive.

He waved to her, and zig-zagged down the valley side, back towards the town.

Jed arrived at the address Dianne had given him and found a small, simple lot house, fronting on to a dusty side street. Dianne had told him it had been George's father's, left to Carol when Henry Parker had died. He tapped a rattling glass pane in the front door.

After ten minutes he gave up and went back to his car. He sat in it for a while trying to decide what to do next. Now that he'd found a definite connection between Mike and George Parker, he felt more confident of tracking down the American and he didn't want to let the scent fade.

But he knew there was nothing else he could do for the moment. Reluctantly he went back into town and booked into a motel. From there, he rang Tessa and told her what progress he'd made.

She begged him to be careful. 'It's not just Bernie. From what you've said, this guy George Parker doesn't sound too savoury either and if he's like most people I know, he won't give up any money unless he has to.'

Jed went to bed feeling he was beginning to understand

this man who had suddenly impacted so forcefully on his life. Clearly George was a man of charm, capable of exerting considerable influence, especially over anyone not completely secure in themselves – Dianne, for instance, or Mike. And yet, despite his obvious selfishness, Dianne hadn't wanted to condemn him completely.

It wasn't until late in the afternoon of the following day that Jed finally got to see Carol Parker. After a series of inconclusive enquiries among people in the town, reluctant to talk about one of their own to a stranger, he went back in the early evening for the fourth time. The door was opened at last by a pale, ethereally beautiful woman, perhaps in her thirties.

As soon as Jed saw Carol he was struck by her air of otherworldliness. She didn't look surprised to see a strange man on her doorstep but nor did she look interested.

Having opened the door to him, she said nothing, just waited for him to speak.

'Hello. My name's Jed Havard, from England. Are you Carol Parker?'

The woman gave a slight nod.

'I wanted to talk to you about George.'

She gave no sign that the name meant anything to her, but opened the door wider so Jed could come into the house and showed him into a small front room, filled with cheap furniture and a large television.

'D'you want coffee?' she asked.

Jed had had enough coffee to keep him going all night, but he nodded. 'Yes, please.'

Carol came back into the room with a small teacup overflowing coffee into its saucer and put it down on a chipboard side table. Jed picked it up, took a sip and tried to look as if he were enjoying it.

'Dianne Clayton gave me your address.'

'Oh, yeah?'

'She was friendly with George, wasn't she?'

'She tried to take him from me.'

Carol spoke with the slow accent of the mountain people.

'But she didn't succeed, did she? He upped and went. Did he tell you where?'

Carol shook her head.

'Did you see him, when he came back?'

She didn't react at all. Jed took this for an affirmative. 'Did he say what he'd been doing?'

'He said he'd be back, and he ain't been. And he's always done what he says he's going to – always.'

'Has he been in touch at all? You know, phoned or written?'

She stared at him; for a moment, Jed had the impression she hadn't understood a word he'd said, until she gave a slow nod.

'He sent me some money.'

Jed's pulse quickened. 'Money? How much?'

'Plenty.'

He had to control his impatience. 'How much is plenty? Ten thousand – twenty?'

'Five thousand dollars he sent me. He always said he'd look after me. But he didn't say when he'd come home.'

'Well, I'm sure he will do soon.'

'That's what I told the other guy.'

'What other guy?'

'He was here waiting when I got back from work today. Said he needed to see my brother real bad. Said he had something for George.'

'Where was he from, this man?'

She shrugged her shoulders at the irrelevance of the question.

'Was he American?'

'I didn't ask.'

'Well, could he have been Latin-American, say Colombian or something like that?'

'Maybe. He came once before, when George was still in town – some months back. He seemed real angry then; I sent him up to Dianne's. But when he came today he seemed like a nice, regular guy to me.'

'Did he say he'd be back?'

'Yeah.'

'Shit!'

'There's no need for cussing.'

'I'm sorry. It's just that I'd like to have seen him too. Let me know if he comes back. I'm staying at the motel. Here's the number.'

Jed wrote it down for her, gulped down the rest of the coffee, made grateful noises and forced a friendly smile as he left.

He drove away wondering at the strange world George Parker had led him to: a forlorn backwoods town in these remote mountains, coal-mining in terminal decline and logging unsustainable; the sad, lonely heiress in her mansion on the mountainside; the half-witted, faded sister in her tumbledown house.

Extracting more information from Carol wouldn't be easy, and the quality of that information would be doubtful. But he didn't doubt the existence of her earlier caller.

Chapter Eighteen

Jed drove slowly back down Main Street, thinking that if he was looking for entertainment, he'd be out of luck in this gloomy place. He stopped and got out to buy a beer in a small bar where half a dozen rednecks gazed at the stranger disdainfully. Jed bought a paper and drove back to his motel, wondering why on earth he'd come here; wishing he was back at home, with Sammy; wishing he didn't have to sell Panpipe on his return.

On the way, he decided he should tell Dianne about the money George had sent, and it occurred to him to ask if he could copy her photograph of George.

When he was back in his room, he looked up her phone number and dialled it. It was just nine-thirty; he hoped he hadn't gone out for the evening.

Dianne answered sleepily. 'Hello?'

'Hello, it's Jed Havard. I was up at your house yesterday.'

'Of course, I remember.'

'I wondered if I could come out and see you again?'

'Did you find out anything from Carol, then?'

'Yes, a little.'

'Come on up then. If you want a bed for the night, I've ten spare rooms I can put you in.'

He thought quickly. 'Great, I'd like that.'

Jed paid his motel bill, heaved his rucksack on to his shoulder and carried it out to his small rented car. In the steady drizzle which was still falling, he unlocked the car, got in and drove out through the puddles of the motel car-park.

Thirty feet away, sitting low down in an inconspicuous Chevrolet sedan, Luis Corozal watched the Englishman's progress, and allowed him to drive on to the highway before following him out.

Luis knew the man was looking for George Parker – he had heard the local guys say so. If you were small and Hispanic, like Luis, and stood around dressed shabbily with your eyes cast humbly to the floor, it was amazing how careless people were about what they said.

But Luis knew that this Englishman had played no part in what George had done to him.

He had known George Parker for ten years, ever since they had been prospecting partners in a small Colombian mine. That project had failed, like the next half-dozen they'd started. Sure, they'd put a little short-term money into their pockets, but when there was none left, George had said goodbye and returned to the States. Luis didn't have that option – he was Colombian, and he had five children.

Despite ten years of friendship, he never heard another word from his former partner, until, earlier that year, George had reappeared. Full of laughter and ideas, just like before, he had persuaded Luis to use disreputable family contacts, and every penny he possessed, to buy three kilos of best Medellin cocaine.

George had acted as mule. With the deadly powder packed into condoms and concealed within himself, he had travelled on a regular flight direct to New York, looking every inch a convincingly sober mining engineer.

Luis had followed a day later. George had met him, as arranged, and discreetly handed over a paper-wrapped package before melting away into the crowds at Grand Central Station.

It was only later, in his dingy hotel room as he tore away the brown paper wrapper, that Luis discovered George had kept most of the money for himself. And he had no idea where his partner lived now. He knew, though, that at one time George had lived in Orange Creek, West Virginia. And he knew that anyone who betrayed the trust Luis had placed in them was going to need to run a lot further than that to escape his vengeance.

When Jed reached the mansion on Orange Mountain half an hour after calling from the motel, Dianne seemed as glad to see him as she had sounded on the phone. She took him through to the kitchen where they had talked the previous afternoon.

There was a lap-top computer on the table with books and notes scattered around, suggesting that she had been working on some kind of text.

'I thought you might have been out,' Jed said.

'In the evening? Here?' She shook her head disdainfully.

'Oh, no. Not since George left. There's no one else round here I could spend a whole evening with,' she said bleakly.

Jed looked at her – apparently so self-contained and intelligent, but still vulnerable.

'What are you doing?' he asked, nodding at the computer.

Self-consciously she shuffled the notes and books into a stack – Jed guessed to hide them. 'Working on a novel,' she mumbled, colouring.

'A novel? Tell me about it.'

'Uh-huh.' She shook her head. 'There's still too much work to do on it. Do you want a drink?' she asked, to deflect his curiosity.

'Yes, please, a glass of wine?' Jed wondered if anyone drank wine in the heart of Appalachia.

'Sure,' Dianne said, and took a bottle of good Californian Cabernet from a cupboard. She opened it and filled two glasses. 'So, how did you make out?'

'I went to see Carol, like you said. She told me she hadn't seen George since he first went to London, but she also said he'd sent her some money.'

'How much?' Dianne asked immediately, just as he had done.

'Only five thousand – but it seems to have meant a lot to Carol.'

'I wonder where that came from? He must have had plenty to spare.'

'She also told me someone else had been round earlier, looking for him.'

'Jesus! Not again? Was it the Colombian guy?'

'Sounded like it. She said he'd been there before, a few months back, about when you said.'

'I wonder if it was definitely the same guy? He might just have been from a firm of loan hustlers.'

'Why do you say that?'

'I didn't tell you yesterday, but I had another visitor about two weeks ago – said he was from some kind of loan outfit George owed money to. I wasn't too surprised. I guess by then I realised he had serious problems with money.'

'I should warn you, there'll soon be *another* party after him. I've already had a couple of visits from people determined to be repaid for the useless colts Mike sold their boss for the thick end of a million dollars. They may well discover George has the money now.'

'Was Mike Powell a crook, then?'

'Not quite. Verging on it, towards the end. He'd got himself into serious debt.'

'So what's your connection with this deal?'

'Unfortunately, one of the dud horses he sold this guy was the one I half owned but was never paid for.'

'Like you were telling me yesterday?'

'Exactly. I think Mike must have been on a spree, using the reputation he'd built up to sell horses over here to a few mugs who are now very unhappy about what they bought. One of them was a film producer Tessa introduced him to, who's found out I part owned the animal and assumes I was involved in the scam.'

'When did all this happen?'

'Mike came over to Saratoga for the sales last month;

that's when he sold this bad colt to Bernie Capella, by acting as his buying agent.'

'Is that the movie producer?'

'Yes.'

'Uh-huh.' Dianne nodded sympathetically. 'So, you've been dragged into all this by Mike Powell, who's dead. You've been threatened by Capella's men, but you still want your money?'

'Only to give it back. Though, God knows, I could do with it in the bank. Business hasn't been too easy this last year. But there's more to finding George than just the money.' Jed hesitated a moment. 'I told you, Mike was my brother-in-law. He was also an old friend. The thing is,' he weighed his words, 'I don't believe the crash Mike died in was definitely an accident.'

Dianne's eyes widened. 'My God! You think he was murdered?' She put down her glass to walk across the room and stare out into the starless night. After a moment, she turned back. 'Are you saying, that because he left everything to George, it was George who did it?'

Jed sighed and shook his head as convincingly as he could. 'No. I don't know who it was. But I do know that George Parker fits in somewhere. Maybe innocently – because Mike made him his heir.' Jed could see her distress. 'Besides,' he admitted, 'I'm the only person who thinks it may not have been an accident. The police think I'm barking up the wrong tree.'

After a few moments, Jed gave Dianne a long look. 'Will you be glad to see George again, if he does come back?'

Dianne shook her head. 'He's never coming back here,

I'd be fooling myself to think otherwise. He'd have come by now if he planned to. He must know there are these people looking for him – the Colombian, and maybe Capella's guys. Mike must have told George about his deals with the horses – it sounds like they spent a lot of time together in England.'

'Yeah.' Jed nodded. 'I think they were getting on very well. Two of a kind, by the sound of it.'

'There's something else about George I didn't tell you. I guess it has nothing to do with your friend Mike but I think . . .' She stopped, took a deep breath and looked Jed straight in the eye. 'I *know* George had gotten involved with some cocaine dealers. I guess he made the connection when he was working in Colombia, and I blame myself partly. I think after I first said I was going to stop funding him, he went off and did a run. The guy that came here looking for him told me as much, but he was no Mafia boss, and it wasn't such a big deal. It seems George didn't deliver as much as he should have.'

'But where did the money go?'

'I don't know, Jed. I don't know if it was gambling or what, but he managed to spend it all,' Dianne added bleakly.

The British Airways 747 lifted its stubby nose. Eighteen fat tyres left the runway as the plump fuselage thrust steeply into the blue sky above JFK.

Jed sat back, not unhappy to be leaving American soil after the gloom of Orange Creek. At least he'd made some progress.

He'd uncovered a lot of new information to flesh out the character of the mysterious George Parker. He was leaving the States not because he was scared, but because he and Dianne had come to the conclusion that George was probably still in England. Everything – Capella, the Colombian, and anyone else to whom he owed money – made it a safer place for George, and the right one for Jed to carry on searching.

He had also been prompted to come back by the prospect of seeing Panpipe run in her next race at Newbury the following Saturday, which would perhaps be his last as her owner.

When his plane had landed at Heathrow, Jed drove back to Gloucestershire. Heading away from London, he tried to contact Tessa and tracked her down at Easerswell.

'Jed, where are you?'

'On the M40, passing Oxford.'

'Thank God you're back! Please, can you come and see me on the way?'

'I'll be round tomorrow, I promise.'

'Jed, I'm not being melodramatic, but I *must* know what's been happening.'

He relented and took the small detour to her house on his way home.

When she saw him, Tessa ran to give him a hug.

'I'm so glad you're back!'

'Why, what's going on?'

'I've had people here again today. I didn't know if I should call the police.'

'To do with Mike?'

'Yes, and this Parker person. Did you find him?'

'No, but I've a horrible feeling there may be more than one group of people out there with axes to grind besides Capella.'

Tessa shook her head. 'I suppose it would have been expecting too much for Mike just to go quietly. Anyway,' she said resignedly, 'I'm still going ahead with the memorial service next Monday. There's hardly any racing and a lot of people want to come.'

'Where is it, Stow?'

'Yes. It's quite convenient, except for the Newmarket people.'

'It'll only be a month since he died. Isn't that rather soon?'

'Not if all the people who say they're coming turn up. There's not much arranging to do. I've booked the vicar and half a dozen other people who are going to talk about him, and we're playing the last half-mile's commentary of his Gold Cup.'

'That should bring tears to a few bookies' eyes.'

'You don't think I should do this, do you?'

'No, but it's up to you.'

For a short while at Batscombe the next morning, Jed could almost have believed that all the drama and loss of the past few weeks had been no more than a bad dream.

He sat with Catherine in the kitchen, as he had a few hundred times before, and talked about the mares, the foals, and Panpipe, whom she had seen working the day before.

Catherine was able to report that the filly had galloped better than ever, and had been whinnying for her breakfast. Normally she was a fussy eater who needed to be tempted.

The illusion of peaceful normality was wrecked by the arrival of the postman, and a letter from the bank, noting that subsequent to the death of Mrs Havard and the provisions of her will, the property at Batscombe could no longer be accepted as adequate security against the substantial overdraft Jed had been operating. They would like him to make immediate arrangements to reduce the balance.

He read the letter twice, to be sure he'd understood the bad tidings correctly, before handing it to Catherine. 'Look what the bastards want to do,' he murmured.

Catherine read the letter carefully. She understood it but didn't quite know what to say.

'What if Panpipe wins tomorrow . . .'

'If Panpipe wins, that'll be terrific, but it won't be enough.'

He didn't have the heart to tell Catherine that they probably wouldn't have the filly for much longer. Even if he found George Parker and the money, he wouldn't be able to keep it. He'd probably have to take Capella's colt back, and it clearly wasn't worth much more than meat money.

When Catherine had gone back to the yard, he went into his office, and dialled the number of Andy Nation, a bloodstock agent in Newmarket and a longtime friend, who'd left a message for Jed to ring.

'Hello, Andy. Jed Havard.'

'Jed! How are you? I've been trying to get hold of you.

I've got some great news. I've had a good offer for your filly . . .'

Jed listened to the details with growing sadness. It was, as Andy had said, a sizeable offer, and he knew he couldn't turn it down. He replaced the phone with mixed feelings. A week from now, Panpipe would be leaving. Only one other would miss her more than him and Catherine, and that was Bella. He just hoped she wouldn't pine too much.

The next day – two days before Mike's memorial service – Panpipe ran the third big race of her career, and won it by six lengths.

As Catherine had predicted, for Jed it was the one moment of supreme pleasure in an otherwise bleak period. The filly had made her mark in her first season. He had bred her. It was a tragedy that he had to sell his best horse, but he had no choice. It was either that or go under.

But for a few brief hours after the victory, he was able to push aside some of the apprehension and pain that had filled his life since Mike and Sammy had died.

He and Nick watched Garry O'Driscoll walk the filly off the track towards the winner's enclosure.

'Mike wouldn't have given her a better ride,' Nick remarked.

'Nor a worse one,' Jed put in quickly.

Nick laughed. 'You're right.'

'He had his good points, you know Nick.' Jed could almost convince himself that these qualities had outweighed Mike's manifest faults.

'Don't worry,' said the trainer. 'I'll be there on Monday, and not just for the party.'

Looking at the congregation packing the pews and leaning forward self-consciously in unfamiliar attitudes of worship as the vicar prayed for the repose of Michael Powell's soul, Tessa tried to guess how many of them *had* come just for the party.

And she expected a few more who hadn't the stomach or patience for a church service to turn up afterwards at Easerswell, expecting a celebration worthy of a man of Mike's lavish tastes.

There was good champagne as well as laughter and a surprising fund of goodwill towards Mike at his second wake.

Headed by a brace of Jockey Club stewards, the racing world had turned out in force to honour the memory of the popular jockey. It was a much bigger, more exuberant occasion than the funeral. A large marquee, which Tessa had miraculously summoned up inside a week, was erected in the May sunshine and two hundred people spilled from it over the lush spring lawns of Easerswell.

A general invitation to the reception had been issued on Tessa's behalf at the end of the church service, though she knew personally most of the guests filling the marquee.

Evan Thomas, sad but irrepressible, saw Jed and sidled up to him.

'How's it going? Did you find this bloke Parker?'

Jed put up a finger to warn Ev not to talk about it there, and shook his head.

'I can't discuss it now, but I will when I've found him and got my money. And you'll have to help me sell the colt again,' he added with a rueful smile.

Evan agreed, and went off to talk to a few old colleagues from his Newmarket days.

When he'd gone, Jed found Lucy Thynne standing in front of him.

'Hello,' she said tentatively. 'Look, Jed, I haven't had a chance to tell you myself how sorry I was about Sammy . . .'

He nodded. 'I know. Thanks. But let me get you another drink,' he offered, trying to steer their conversation on to easier ground.

'Oh, yes, please. More champagne would be great.'

Jed took a glass from a passing waiter.

She raised it to him. 'Here's to Panpipe, by the way. She ran an incredible race on Saturday. You could almost enter her in a flat race now.'

Jed laughed. He'd had the same thought himself. 'You may be right, but sadly, I've had an offer for her.'

Lucy stared at him, open-mouthed. 'You've got to be joking?'

'I'm afraid not.'

'Oh my God! But why?'

'It's a lot of money.'

'But, Jed, she's so special!'

He sighed. 'Do you think I don't know that?'

Lucy was going to answer, but stopped short and looked embarrassed. 'Oh, God. I'm sorry, Jed. You've obviously got your reasons. Dad will be disappointed, though,' she went on, 'seeing she was out of a mare he'd bred.'

'He'll still see her winning, whoever owns her.'

'Yes, but he'd rather she stayed with you, I'm sure. He has a lot of respect for you, buying that mare when you had so little money. He likes people with confidence.'

'Well, there it is,' Jed said, never having felt less confident in his life. 'They always say the first offer's the best, and business is business.'

Lucy shook her head. 'You know you don't mean that. Horses like Panpipe come along once in a blue moon.'

After a while, with a tinge of regret, he left Lucy talking to other friends who had drifted up and wandered around the marquee, trying to spend a few minutes individually with everyone he knew, until he reached Tessa.

'Brilliant show as usual, Tess. You've managed to achieve the perfect balance between mourning and celebration.'

'I always knew I should have directed rather than performed,' she said with a quick, grateful smile.

'At least it doesn't seem to have upset you too much,' Jed observed.

'Oh, I miss him all right,' Tessa replied brusquely. 'Dear old Mike. I don't think he really deserved all this, but then I think you do these things for the people who are left behind; they so like to believe they won't be forgotten too quickly either, when they go.'

Jed raised an eyebrow at her cynicism. 'I'll never forget Sammy.'

She put one hand on his arm. 'I'm sorry. I know that. Sammy didn't need a show like this though, did she?'

Jed agreed, and changed the conversation, as he felt himself about to cry.

'What are you doing over the next few weeks?' he asked.

'I'm going down to La Fleurie. I've finished the current series and don't start another film for two months.'

'Good idea. I might come down and join you for a bit. But I've got a couple more mares to foal first and I still want to find out what Mike's will was all about, and at least clear my own name from any involvement.'

'Yes, I suppose the last thing you want when you're a breeder are rumours flying round that you've been tucking people up.'

'And the second last thing I want,' Jed said quietly, out of the side of his mouth, 'is a gang of marauding heavies with a bloodlust and big wages wandering around looking to beat me up again! The sooner I can find George Parker the better.'

'Do you still think he's involved?'

Chapter Nineteen

The next morning, Jed drove across the valley from Batscombe to Easerswell where the marquee was already a whale of billowing white canvas as it was lowered by half a dozen men. Within half an hour, the only evidence of the previous day's function was a patch of slightly flattened grass on the lawn, and a stack of empty champagne bottles in boxes by the garage.

Tessa was unexpectedly practical for an actress, and an efficient delegator. She seemed quite happy that all the arrangements for clearing up were in safe hands. When she had inherited the house from Mike, she'd found that she'd also inherited the services of Dora, his faithful and long-suffering cleaner, who thanks to increased and regular wage packets was busy demonstrating that no particle of dust or spot of grease would be allowed to persist while Tessa was in France.

Jed had promised to drive Tessa to Heathrow, to see her on to the flight to Marseilles. He carried her bags to the Range Rover while she said goodbye to Dora.

Once they were on the way, Tessa leaned back and let her

whole body relax in the knowledge that time was hers and hers alone for the next month.

'I can tell you, Jed, now it's come to it, I really need this holiday.' She sighed pleasurably. 'Just loafing around, reading, eating and drinking, with no one to hinder or pester me – what bliss!'

Jed looked at her with a grin. 'Do you think you'll last long without a man to bolster your ego?'

'Naturally there'll be a few men around to entertain me – gays or has-beens mostly. Which suits me fine for the moment.'

'Are you really missing Mike then?' Jed glanced at her for a reaction. 'I only ask because you didn't seem too distressed yesterday.'

She looked back at him levelly. 'That's because there were a lot of people there saying very nice things about him. It brought back all the good memories,' she added dreamily. 'I think if he'd come back at that moment, I'd have welcomed him with open arms.'

Jed smiled. 'I don't want to sound like an insensitive, callous cynic, but perhaps you're only saying that because you know it's not possible.'

'You *are* an insensitive, callous cynic!'

'And you're an actress.'

They talked about Tessa and Mike in the early days, both consciously avoiding any reference to his troublesome legacies. It was only as Jed turned the Range Rover on to the airport spur off the M4 that he mentioned his own problems.

'I'm going to have to go up to Beulah again to see if I can find Megan,' he said.

'Why?'

'I'm sure she knows more about George Parker.'

'Well, best of luck,' Tessa said with surprising sharpness. 'But if you get anything from the old crone, I'll be amazed. Why don't you just leave it, Jed?'

'Tessa, for God's sake, I've got to settle this business with Bernie Capella. I've been bloody lucky to have got away with it so far, but he's not going to let up. He may be all sweetness and light to you while your film's a success, but he's serious about this money and you know it.'

'Look, I'm not going to make any apologies for Bernie. He didn't become a movie producer to make people happy. But I'm sure he wouldn't do any real damage. I mean, if he killed someone then he'd never get his money, would he?'

'I got the impression he was more interested in making the grand gesture, *pour encourager les autres*. For some reason, criminals seem to be very concerned about losing face.'

'Look, Jed, I'll ring him. Tell him I know you never had any of the money.'

Jed looked momentarily hopeful. 'But will he believe you?' he said gloomily.

'Of course he will.'

Jed was sure he wouldn't, but didn't tell Tessa and returned their conversation to less contentious areas.

Later, he watched her affectionately as she went from the VIP lounge to join her flight. She had been a close sister to Sammy, with whom she had shared her childhood dreams and teenage hopes. However different they were, there was still a small part of Sammy which lived on in her sister, and Jed was deeply thankful for it.

★ ★ ★

Tessa walked from beneath the shade of a tall eucalyptus tree into a wall of heat that wrapped around her body and made it tingle with sexual energy. She couldn't help it; the heat always did it to her.

That was one of the dangers of Provence in early summer. She would always associate the heat, the musky smells and the chitter of cicadas with the most memorable moments of physical love she had known.

It was here, seven years before, that she and Mike had spent their honeymoon – a month of sheer sybaritic and sensual pleasure she had never forgotten. It was then, too, that she had set out to stimulate Mike's native intelligence into a new perception of beauty and the great painters who had been so inspired by the magical light and shifting colours of the Provençal countryside around them.

It was an attempt in which she had come frustratingly close to success, though as soon as he was back in the hard competitive world of racing, Mike had quickly reverted to his earlier philistinism. In the last few years of their marriage, she had watched him become steadily more dismissive of her own tastes and values.

And yet she knew that lurking not far below the surface of the hard-drinking risk-taker there was a man with a real capacity to savour the more subtle joys of life.

Walking across the lawn of coarse Mediterranean grass in her bare feet, with a creaking wicker basket under her arm, she wondered if she was simply comforting herself with this memory of the man she had married; she couldn't escape the idea that since the crash, she had wished a hundred times that she could have another opportunity to uncover his secret soul.

She unpegged a cluster of bone-dry clothes from a line stretched between two trees in the full glare of the sun and carried them back into La Fleurie.

She yawned, basking in the sounds and smells she loved; happy, for the most part, to be here alone. She had soon slotted back into a routine of total relaxation that suited her well. She dumped the clothes on a sideboard for the maid to iron, topped up her coffee and started to map out her day. It was already after noon, but she wasn't due at lunch until two.

A rich old novelist had invited her to eat with him and a pair of interior decorators – three witty men, two of them gay, who always made her laugh. After that, the decorators were coming back to La Fleurie to look at the *salon* which hadn't been touched since her father had bought the house twenty-five years before.

In the evening, she planned to drive to Aix with an old friend – a scruffy English musician – to watch him play with a jazz trio from Chicago.

She nodded with satisfaction. Just the kind of day she liked. The heat had made her yearn for the past, but back within the cool of the thick earth walls, self-control returned.

First, she would drive the two miles into St Rémy and buy a couple of little cotton skirts – the sort that would float freely off her hips, and keep the trumpeter on his toes.

She parked her hire car in the main square of the old town and sauntered over to a *presse* to buy an English paper before she started shopping. She sat at a table outside a small café in the main *place* and flipped through *The Times* over a cup of coffee, glad not to be recognised and pestered for autographs as she always was in England.

Looking up to take another mouthful of strong, sweet coffee, she gazed around the square until her eyes were stopped dead by the sight of a man on the far side – a man who was instantly familiar yet different in a way which temporarily prevented recognition.

She closed her eyes to focus her memory.

When she opened them, he had gone.

She swept the whole square again with her eyes but he was nowhere to be seen. She watched the doorways of the other bars and shops, hoping he might reappear from one of them. But after ten minutes there was still no sign of him.

Annoyed with herself for having been so slow off the mark, she folded up her paper and walked to the Provençal print shop on the corner.

She kept her eyes open for the man for the rest of the morning, and for the rest of the day his face flashed into her head and an idea nagged her until she was practically certain of his identity though she could hardly believe she hadn't immediately recognised him.

Jed's plans to set off early to see Megan Powell in Wales the morning after Tessa had left for France were thwarted by an unwelcome phone call.

Andy Nation phoned to say that he had received the money for Panpipe, and was sending a horse-box to collect her that afternoon.

Jed was feeling bleakly alone now that Tessa had gone, but put a brave face on the depression that enveloped him and went out to the yard to break the bad news to Catherine and the other grooms.

Almost as soon as the fawn-grey horse-box had rolled under the clock-tower arch into the yard, Panpipe and Bella seemed to know something was up.

For the first time in her life, the filly made a fuss about being loaded, and the mare in the next stable kept up an incessant, desperate whinnying.

It was a heart-rending experience. Jed was feeling distinctly shaky when he watched the lorry drive away with Catherine standing wet-eyed beside him.

'Oh, Jed,' she said, 'I wish you hadn't had to let her go. She's going to leave a tremendous gap, and it seems to me we've lost too much already.'

He had never before seen Catherine show such open emotion. He gave her muscular arm a gentle squeeze. 'I know. Somehow, everything seems to have hit us at once. But it was either this or go under.'

The sun was dipping behind the Cambrians as Jed swung the Range Rover off the main road at Beulah. Past tiny chapels and mills, the lane snaked between a steep wooded bank and a bright, prancing tributary of the Wye.

He knew where the faint, barely used track started from the lane, to wind up over a bare, brown hill to Megan Powell's cottage.

The last time he had come up here to see her, a neighbouring farmer who was looking after her stock had turned him back with the information that Megan had walked over the hill for her annual visit to the doctor.

This time, when Jed reached the rutted track, he thought of Mike growing up in a place like this – even more remote thirty years before.

He drove on in the Range Rover as far as he could, and parked it to one side of a gateway, a quarter of a mile up the track. He got out and let himself through a rickety iron gate to trudge the last few hundred yards up the hill on a surface of slate chippings and mud.

Mike had sometimes talked about the cottage which Megan had moved to after his father had died, and how, with her deep fear of bills and debt, she had eschewed a phone line and electricity. The white-washed stone house was, by modern standards, little more than a beast shed – a single-storey dwelling, just two rooms, two windows and a front door.

Although Evan had warned Jed what to expect last time he'd come, he had been horrified by the sheer harshness of the life the old woman must have been leading, and yet, he knew, less than a hundred years ago, everyone on these hillsides had lived like that.

Mike had said his father had left next to nothing for her after forty years of struggling and obstinate failure to claim CAP hill-farming subsidies. Megan had bought the cottage for a few thousand pounds and squeezed a living from what she could grow and the dozen ewes she still kept on the hillside above.

As he approached the flaking blue door in the twilight, Jed wondered if Megan had fully understood Mike's bequest to her, though he recognised that his friend had pitched it deliberately at a level that she could just about cope with without altering her life completely.

As Jed had learned on his previous visit down in the village, Megan had an almost medieval reputation for being a witch. Nobody said quite that, but it seemed that her self-imposed loneliness up in the hills had gradually turned a notoriously old-fashioned woman into an unapproachable eccentric.

As she had no phone, Jed was coming once again without any warning, or any certainty he would even find the old woman there.

He rapped on the weathered blue door, and took a step back.

When Megan opened it, she showed neither surprise nor recognition. Jed could read nothing in the dark blank eyes buried in that prematurely wrinkled face.

'Hello, Mrs Powell,' he said. 'Do you remember me – Jed Havard, an old friend of Mike's?'

The woman didn't speak or move.

'I was at the solicitor's in Cheltenham, remember? And we took you to the station afterwards.'

'I know who you are.'

'I wanted to talk to you – about Michael. May I come in?'

She looked at him for a few seconds before she nodded, and opened the door wider to let him in.

It was dark when Jed came out again on to the bare hillside. Megan closed the door behind him without a word of

321

farewell. Only a faint glimmer from an oil lamp showed through one of the two small windows; Jed stood on the large flagstone in front of the door and shivered. In the hour he had been in the cottage, clouds had swept up from the south-west, blotting out the moonlight. He hadn't brought a torch with him and struggled in the dark to find his way down the shale track through the bracken in the warmly murmuring wind.

The old woman's story had stunned him.

Even after he'd found his way back to the Range Rover, and was powering through the black night with warm air and Elgar blasting from beneath the dashboard, he found it hard to take in what he had learned.

It was the first really mild night of the summer in the Cotswolds.

Jed had the windows of his bedroom wide open and lay awake, listening to the night sounds in the grounds outside. A vixen barked. An owl called. A blackbird woke among the rhododendrons with a frantic 'chit-chit-chit', and Jed was instantly alert.

He got out of bed and padded to the window. Opening the curtain a crack, he surveyed the matt blackness of the gardens in front of the house, and strained his ears for further signs of intrusion.

A cat, a fox, even a badger could have got the blackbird going, but it was unusual, and Jed was still ultra-sensitive to anything that might be considered unusual.

Nothing else happened to justify his wariness, and after a while he went back to bed.

He was almost asleep when an outburst of barking from Catherine's Weimaraners echoed through the gardens from the stable block.

Within seconds, he was on his feet, into a pair of trousers, pulling on a T-shirt and running down the stairs.

He heaved open the back door to hear the dogs still barking madly, almost drowning out the angry shrieks of their owner. 'Freddie! Siggy! Shut *up*, you bloody animals, or you'll wake the whole place.'

Jed walked briskly round to the yard, triggering the floodlights which bathed the whole area in a strong halogen glow. The dogs and their barking had disappeared in the darkness down the drive.

'Sorry, Jed,' Catherine called from the window of her sitting-room above the feed store. 'They let themselves out and probably found a fox or something.'

'Don't worry, Cath. I'd far rather they barked. I'm just going to have a look around.'

Jed carried on through the yard. On the far side, standing in the arched entrance, he stopped and listened to the dogs' progress, already a quarter of a mile away down the hill towards the main gates.

Then he heard a sound which was out of place: the faint click of a car door closing, followed by a couple of turns of a starter motor.

Jed reacted before he was conscious of having made a decision. He ran straight to the barn where his Range Rover and VW Caddy pick-up were housed. He flung open the doors and felt for the spare key to the pick-up in its hiding place under a work bench. Once he'd found it, he jumped in and seconds later was backing it out of the barn.

He reached the top of the drive, turning down it just in time to see a pair of headlights swing through his own main gates, out on to the lane.

He skidded into the ninety-degree turn at the bottom of the drive and shot out into the road. He didn't know for sure which way the strange car had turned, but followed a hunch and swung left, accepting at the same time that the chances of catching anyone with such a lead weren't good.

Half a mile later, he was faced with the fork in the road – and a decision. He chose the route that led to Stow and the nearest main roads.

Two hundred yards further on, he braced himself to take a tight corner and stamped on his brake pedal, just in time to avoid colliding with an overturned Ford hanging halfway into the ditch and partially blocking the road.

He pulled up with his headlights illuminating the scene. Before he had time to get out of his vehicle, the driver clambered from the skewed door of the car, gave a quick, startled gaze into Jed's headlights and ran off down the lane for a few yards before disappearing over a gate in the hedge.

Jed scrambled out of the Caddy and gave chase. He reached the gate, grasped the top rail and swung his leg over it.

He dropped down the other side, and stopped quite still.

In the starlight, a twenty-acre sea of barley rippled in the breeze, and he strained to hear a sound that would pin-point his quarry.

During a full minute which felt like an hour, he heard nothing out of place.

The man who had clambered out of the Ford could have been anywhere.

Then, above the natural sounds of the night, he heard another car approaching fast down the lane, from the direction of Batscombe. He waited for the inevitable heavy braking; it came with an accompaniment of angry hooting.

Jed cursed and ruefully climbed back over the gate. He jogged up the lane and waved at the driver of the car revving behind his.

As Jed pulled over to let the car pass, he resigned himself to the fact that he wasn't going to get anywhere else tonight. He searched the Ford for a clue to the owner but found nothing. Maybe, in the morning, the police would be able to help. He wrote down the number of the car, got back into his pick-up, turned it by the gate and headed for Batscombe.

Next morning he was woken by the phone ringing beside his bed.

It was already eight o'clock.

He picked up the receiver. 'Hello?'

'Is that Jed Havard?'

It was a woman's voice, American. He couldn't place it at once.

'Yes?' he said guardedly, seeing the time. 'Who is it?'

'Dianne Clayton.'

The two words took him straight back to West Virginia and Orange Mountain.

'Dianne?' He looked at his bedside clock. 'What time is it with you?'

'Just after midnight, but I've been worrying for the last

twenty-four hours. Jed, I'm so glad I found you. I had to call. Two things have happened. George was back here . . .'

'Did you see him?'

'No. Sadly, not. I know he won't be back for me. A friend of mine saw him in Huntington a couple of days back, but he never came to Orange Creek. I spoke to Carol who said he'd called her to say he was going back to Europe. Did you find him?'

'No, not yet. I don't know where to look.'

'Huh! I don't know if I care. But *you* should know that the South American guy who came looking for George before, came back again to Orange Creek, asking around. He came to my house. He said George had cheated his family out of everything they owned, but more importantly, managed to get his eldest daughter pregnant. This guy's been hunting him all over the States.'

'Did you tell him where George was now?'

'No, of course not, but Carol was fooled by him and thought he was a friend of George's. She told him George had gone back to England. I think she gave him your name and – ' her voice faded, as if she were holding the phone away from her mouth '– your address, too.'

He felt a sudden chill run through him. 'I think he's already been here,' he said, as calmly as he could.

'It's not you he wants,' Dianne said hurriedly. 'It's George, of course. But he went on and on, and said he'd seen you in Orange Creek, heard you'd been up here looking for George. Poor Carol – she was on her own; she just wanted him to go.'

'It's okay, I understand. Don't worry.' Jed paused and took a deep breath. 'And thanks for letting me know.'

As soon as he'd put down the phone, Jed picked it up again to ring the police in Stow.

When he got through to a central exchange, he passed on the information about the crashed Ford, explaining that he had seen the driver leave the scene of the accident.

He rang off feeling he hadn't generated much interest in the event and, to satisfy his own curiosity, went out, climbed into the Range Rover and drove the two miles to where he'd found the crash.

There was nothing left of it, beyond a set of faint skid marks, some churned up verge and a hole in the hedge. He walked up to the gate to see if there were any signs in daylight of the route the driver had taken.

There was a clear set of footprints along the headland to the left, between the crop and the hedge. Jed followed the trail for two hundred yards until he was sure there were no return tracks.

Back in his car, he picked up his mobile and rang the police again.

This time, he was put through to someone who seemed interested to hear from him.

'I'm glad you called back, Mr Havard. We've got a bit of a problem with this one. The vehicle's been recovered, but there's no trace of the driver, and I understand you saw him?'

'Yes, but only for a second or two.'

'You didn't exchange any words with him?'

'No.'

'The car-hire people rented this car to a South American gentleman – a Luis Corozal, from Medellin, Colombia. Was there anything to suggest this might have been the man you saw?'

Jed took a deep breath. 'It's quite possible, but I'm not sure.' He then went on to explain why he'd followed the car in the first place.

'You weren't in any way connected or involved with the accident?'

'No. Not at all.'

'We need to know why the driver didn't stay with the vehicle or report the incident. And, of course, the hire company need to hear from him in order to process their insurance claim.'

'I'm afraid I can't help you. Sorry.'

Once Jed had put the phone down, he drove back to the stable yard. As therapy, he went through the motions of checking the horses. But, despite his own reassurances, he couldn't push from his mind the thought that the intruder was out there, that Bernie Capella still wasn't satisfied, and the extraordinary tale Megan had told him about Mike's relationship with George Parker.

The second morning after she'd arrived in France, Tessa went into St Rémy again, telling herself she had more shopping to do. But first, she sat in the square drinking coffee in the hope that she would see the bearded man again and clear up the puzzle he had created.

But there was no further sign of him. She asked several of the waiters in the café where she usually sat and in others on the square if they'd served or seen a man of his description, but no one had.

By now, Tessa was becoming almost obsessed with her need to find him. She wished she'd had just that extra few seconds to confirm his identity as soon as she'd seen him looking at her across the busy square.

She finished her shopping and was driving away from the centre of the town when she saw him again.

She stabbed her right foot down on the brake pedal. An old corrugated Citroën van squealed to a stop inches from her rear bumper, but when the van driver leaped out to complain, Tessa dismissed him with a dazzling smile and a humble apology. She waved him on round her car and ran up the alley where the man had disappeared.

She saw him, walking briskly away from her.

'Hello?' Even as she ran, she winced at the sound of her own voice echoing thinly up the high, narrow gap between the buildings.

But the man gave no sign of having heard her and a moment later turned out of the end of the alley and disappeared.

Tessa reached the end, panting, and leaned on the rough corner stones of the building while she got her breath back and scanned the street ahead.

Triumphantly, she caught a glimpse of his back disappearing into the gloom of a small bar below a cheap hotel on the far side of the road.

Breathing more steadily now, she walked briskly across and went straight in. Her eyes took a moment to adjust to the gloom before she saw him, already sitting at a table in the corner.

She walked towards him. 'Hello,' she said again, more calmly this time.

He looked up. A slow, lazy smile spread across his handsome face, and Tessa realised he'd known all along she'd been following him. 'I suppose you want a drink?' he said.

Tessa didn't answer. She pulled back a chair, sat down opposite him and reached over to remove the dark glasses he was still wearing.

'Don't you think it's about time you told me what's going on?'

Chapter Twenty

The day after Dianne had rung with the news about Luis Corozal, Jed woke feeling frustrated. He had no idea what to do next. He couldn't think where else to look for George Parker, and as for the Colombian, he couldn't deal with him either until he had found him.

Sitting in his office later that morning, he accepted that he would simply have to wait for something to happen.

Resigned to doing nothing, he went out to the yard and tacked up a mare who needed a little gentle exercise, trying to forget his troubles for an hour in the warm, humming air of the wooded Windrush Valley at the bottom of his farm.

He arrived back at the stables and was unsaddling the mare when Catherine called out from her office.

'Jed! It's Lucy Thynne on the phone.'

His hand, unbuckling the throat lash on the mare's bridle, faltered for a moment. Even the thought of Lucy unsettled him. He still ached with pain at the loss of Sammy, but couldn't pretend that talking to Lucy didn't exhilarate him.

He went into Cath's office and nervously picked up the phone.

'Hello?'

'Jed? It's Lucy. How's it going?'

Jed tried to make light of his problems, but Lucy could sense his dejection.

'Well, listen, I've got some news that might cheer you up.'

'What's that?' he asked, trying to believe that something could.

'I've bought a horse to ride in the amateur riders' flat race at Newmarket on the thirty-first.'

'Is that a good idea?' Jed asked, with some surprise.

Lucy laughed. 'I may not have raced for a couple of years, but I've been riding out most days and I'm perfectly fit.'

'Sorry,' he said. 'I didn't mean to sound rude.'

'The thing is,' she went on, 'I want it to be a complete surprise for Dad, and wondered if I could keep it at your place until then?'

'How much will I need to do? It's just that I'm fairly busy at present.'

'You can do as little or as much as you wish. You did a brilliant job with Panpipe.'

Jed took a deep breath; he hated having to let anyone down.

'Well . . .' he started.

'Jed, please! I know you've got other things on your mind, but I thought you might like to be involved.'

He came to a sudden decision. 'All right,' he said. 'Drop it off here. I may have to go away for a couple of days, but

I'll make sure it gets looked after all right. What's it called?'

'Risque Lady. I bought it in Ireland yesterday.'

Jed searched his memory for the horse, but couldn't locate it. 'What's it done?'

'I'll tell you all about it when I come over with it on Monday, okay?'

'Oh, fine,' he said with a spontaneous smile.

He put the phone down, knowing he was looking forward to seeing Lucy and that she was right – he would enjoy having a runner at Newmarket.

The lads from Nick Thornton-Jones' stables usually drank in the back bar of the White Horse. They didn't have any difficulty accepting Luis Corozal's story when he came in at lunchtime, the day after his visit to Batscombe; it wasn't unheard of, or even unusual, for men from other parts of the racing world to turn up at the pub, hoping they might find a job. The swarthy little man with the lilting, slightly American accent told them he was Mexican, called Miguel Sanchez, and that he'd worked in a big yard near Gulfstream Park racetrack in Florida.

Luis didn't know a lot about racehorses, just enough to bluff his way into the conversation, but he was a quick, intelligent man. He had studied for his mining degree at UCLA, and spoke English well.

He soon discovered all he needed to know about Jed and his brother-in-law, Mike Powell; several of the people in the pub had been to Mike's memorial service a few days before.

Luis followed up the information in some racing reference books he found in a bookshop in Stow. And as soon as he saw a photograph of the late Mike Powell, he began to see a connection between Jed, Mike, and George Parker.

He knew that his next task was to find Tessa Langton. The assistant in the bookshop told him proudly that she lived in the house she'd shared with Mike at Easerswell, not far from Stow.

Nor was it far from Batscombe, Luis thought happily, as he studied a map of the area.

His trip to Batscombe had ended in disaster. Luis had cursed himself afterwards, not just for renting the car in his own name, but also for crashing it so easily, then letting himself be seen by Jed when he'd chased him. But he'd guessed he wouldn't have long before someone caught up with him. He'd abandoned the car, hoping that by the time the police had established its hirer's name, he'd have done what he'd come to do and would already be out of Britain.

Being careful not to draw any attention to himself, he'd walked to Stow and stolen a 125cc motorbike.

Now, since leaving the hire car in the ditch, Luis had taken just twelve hours to find his way to Tessa Langton's house. But Easerswell was thoroughly locked up and alarmed. He didn't even consider trying to get in, anxious as he was to find Tessa or anything that could tell him where she had gone.

A few enquiries at the cottages down the lane from Easerswell took Luis to the council house of Tessa's cleaner, Dora, where he was rewarded with the information that her employer was having 'a bit of a break, down at her place in France'. Dora wrote down the address in St Rémy for him on a blank betting slip, once he'd assured her of his need to write to her.

Early the next day, Luis set off for London. He found a pub in Wandsworth, whose name he had been given by contacts in New York. After several searching questions from the landlord's brother, he was sent on to a man who agreed to trade in his bike for a well-worn .45 automatic pistol and some ammunition.

Luis took a cab back into central London, aiming for one of the big railway terminals where in his experience he would be likely to find cheap hotels, shops and travel agents.

In a guest house in Victoria, he planned his next move. He had bought the gun in London because he doubted his ability to carry off the transaction in French.

He looked at his options and made up his mind to take the train direct to Paris from Waterloo, in case the police had traced the hire car to him, and that triggered some kind of response at an airport when he showed his passport; it was in his own name, and it was too late to buy a substitute. He didn't know if any security checks were regularly made on the train itself or at the terminals, but decided he wasn't going to expose himself to additional risk by carrying the gun with him.

He concealed the weapon in his room and went out into the busy Friday afternoon streets with a mental list of what he needed. When he got back to the guest house, he wrapped the gun in oil-cloth and unwrapped a gift hamper he'd bought from a big food store. He took out a large

Dundee cake, scooped out the middle from underneath and buried the gun in it, before returning the cake to its metal tin, and parcelling up the whole hamper. He took the package out with him and went into the first travel agent he came to. Here he checked the names and addresses of hotels in St Rémy, and booked a room in the name of Miguel Sanchez. At the post office next door, he express-mailed the parcel to himself at the hotel in Provence.

Tessa watched the last of her guests leave La Fleurie after the kind of Sunday lunch she always loved. The weather had been perfect and obliged them with a light breeze; the bougainvillaea was beginning to bloom with crimson bracts; her guests had been in sparkling form and the chef she had borrowed from the Swiss banker who lived further up the hill had earned every one of the two thousand francs she'd paid him.

Tessa poured herself a fresh glass of the local rosé and carried it outside. She sat in a large wicker chair in the shade of a verandah which stretched the length of the western side of the house. It was seven-thirty, and beyond the drooping branches of the eucalyptus tree, the Mediterranean sun was already sinking towards the jagged crest of Les Alpilles.

She gave a hopeful sigh. She didn't want anything to interfere with a new and utterly unexpected period of happiness this new man had brought into her life, but she knew that if she was to avoid a tragic end to it, she would need to plan, patiently and well. Just then, though, she felt anything but patient.

She also knew that, in another couple of days, she would have to summon up the courage to ring Jed.

★ ★ ★

In England, the following Monday while Jed was shaving, he watched from his bathroom window as a horse-box trundled up the drive with Lucy's new horse on board. He went down to his office and carried on with what he was doing, deciding to wait until Lucy herself had arrived before going out to inspect her buy. He heard the thump of the lorry ramp hitting the ground followed by a continuous screaming of horses.

Two minutes later, he heard Catherine opening the back door and clattering through the kitchen corridor.

'Jed!' she shouted before she'd reached his office.

'What's happened?' he asked apprehensively. 'What's the problem?'

'She's back! Come and see for yourself.'

Jed shrugged his shoulders and followed her into the yard, across to the largest, most favoured box between the feed store and Bella.

Catherine unbolted the door and went in, beckoning Jed to come too.

He walked in to the scent of fresh straw and found a handsome, bay horse, already quite at home, picking at a hay rack.

He had been expecting to see Lucy's new horse, but found himself staring at Panpipe instead. He looked at Catherine who nodded again with big, excited eyes.

'Panpipe!' Jed gasped. 'What the hell's going on?'

'The transport guy said it was definitely the horse sent by Lucy Thynne.'

'Did he have a passport for her?'

'No. He said Lucy was bringing all the paperwork.'

Jed shook his head in wonder. 'Bloody hell!' He grinned. 'Well, whatever's going on, it's great to have her back. But how long for, I wonder?'

Catherine cocked an ear at the sound of a car racing up the drive. 'That's probably Lucy now.'

Jed walked out of the stable feeling as if a limb he'd lost had suddenly, miraculously been restored, and went out under the arch to greet his new owner.

Lucy shot up to the top of the drive in her small silver Peugeot and squealed to a halt in front of him. She turned off the engine and sprang out of the car, leaving it where it had stopped. She looked eagerly at Jed and read his expression.

'Hi. I see my horse has arrived safely?'

'How do you know?'

'It doesn't exactly take a mind reader.'

'Okay,' he said. 'But you told me you were sending a horse called Risque Lady, and we appear to have been sent Panpipe.'

'I know, but I changed my mind, if that's okay by you?'

'When did you buy her?'

'I didn't. Dad bought her.'

'Ah.' Suddenly, it all made sense. 'I suppose you told him I was selling her?'

'As a matter of fact, he'd already heard. Andy Nation likes to earn his five per cent the easy way.'

Jed laughed at his own naivety. 'Oh, well, who can blame him? I never even thought of asking your father. The truth is, I simply didn't want to have to go through the business of selling her myself. Anyway, it's great to have her back here. Do you still want to ride her on Saturday?'

'Of course. I entered her this morning.'

Jed nodded. 'Okay. I don't see why she shouldn't go all right for you. She always works well with girls.' They were walking under the arch into the yard, and Panpipe had her head over the door of her box. 'My mare's chuffed to bits to have her back,' laughed Jed. 'But how long have we got her for?'

'You'll have to ask Dad. In the meantime, we'll see how she goes on Saturday.'

They discussed a training schedule for the next five days before Jed and Lucy went to his office to phone for the entries for the race. Jed found videotapes with some of the other runners, and played them to see how they performed.

'I think you ought to do some fast work on her yourself, at least once before Saturday.'

'Sure. Suits me. When?'

'As soon as possible, I'd say. Tomorrow? Eight o'clock at Nick's?'

'Fine.'

'Where will you stay?'

Lucy didn't answer for a moment. 'No problem. I've got an old friend in Stow. He'll give me a bed for the night.'

'I hope that's all he gives you,' Jed said, almost before he knew it, and regretted it at once.

She glanced at him, quizzically.

'I know I can't stay here.'

He nodded. 'Better not.'

'But can I take you out to lunch – now you're my new trainer?'

'I'll take you.'

At lunch, in a busy Italian restaurant in Cheltenham, they talked enthusiastically about Panpipe and her prospects on the flat.

The mutual attraction they'd experienced over dinner in Lexington six months earlier was still there, but neither made mention of it.

Lying alone in his bed that night, Jed thought with a warm glow of his day, and how he had no reason for guilt or self-recrimination. For the first time in weeks, he slept well and woke, if not happy, at least contented and looking forward to the morning's gallop.

He had surprised Nick the evening before by phoning to say that Panpipe was back at Batscombe and racing at Newmarket that weekend. He'd arranged to use Nick's gallops and drove the filly over to Fencote himself. When he arrived, Lucy was there. He didn't want to admit the adrenalin rush brought on by the sight of her, ready and waiting in her jodhpurs, attributing it instead to his excitement at the thought of working his favourite filly once more.

In the evening, Jed went into his office and dialled the number of La Fleurie.

'Hi, Tess. How are you?'

As soon as she heard his voice, Tessa knew it spelled the end of the idyllic few days she had just spent.

'I'm absolutely fine, I've been having a wonderful time.' She told him about the lunch parties; the days spent exploring the courtly citadel of Les Baux and the elegant Roman ruins of Glanum and Orange; the dinners at the Baumanière and other illustrious restaurants of the region; shopping in Aix and swimming in the dappled pool at La Fleurie. But she failed to mention that it had all been in the company of the man she had met in St Rémy.

'It sounds as though you've been having a fantastic time.' There was a faint note of reproach in Jed's voice. 'I had assumed no news was good news.'

Desperately, Tessa tried to believe that, just possibly, this last magical week might be extended, even made to last indefinitely. 'Yes and no,' she said. 'There is news, but it's good.'

'Oh?' Jed was surprised. 'I'm glad to hear it. What is it?'

'George Parker's here.'

There was a few seconds' silence before Jed spoke. 'Where? In France?' The softness of his voice didn't disguise his shock.

'Right here – in St Rémy. He was in this house two hours ago.'

'Good God! When did he appear?'

'Last week. Someone told him I'd come here, and he thought this would be the best place for us to meet.' Tessa took a deep breath. 'And he's been utterly fantastic.'

'Fantastic?' Jed's stomach was churning with doubt and confusion. 'What do you mean "fantastic"?'

A tremor in his voice made Tessa feel momentarily guilty. 'I mean . . . he's told me all about Mike, and what he did for him in the few months before he died, and why.'

'I see,' Jed said, still trying to absorb this extraordinary twist in events. 'What did he do – and why?'

'He's Mike's cousin! That's how Megan knew who he was, remember? She had a sister.'

'I know,' Jed broke in. 'Gwynneth.'

'You knew?' Tessa gasped. 'I never did – in all the time I was married to Mike. In fact, I don't even think he knew until George told him. But anyway, this sister, Gwynneth, was George's mother.' She waited for Jed's reaction.

'Is that all he told you?' Jed asked flatly.

'Yes,' Tessa answered sharply. 'He'd never been to England before, but came over, found Mike in a bit of a mess, and decided to help him out. Mike told him all about the horse deals and everything.'

Jed decided this wasn't the right moment to tell Tessa exactly what Megan had told him.

'If he says he's Mike's cousin, can he prove it?'

'He doesn't have to. It's obvious.'

'Tessa, I'm worried.'

'Don't be!' she said, with a hint of panic. 'I'm quite safe – I promise.'

'But, Tess, I've been looking for this man for weeks and I've found out a lot about him – and I can tell you, he's not to be trusted. Not at all. He's an out-and-out crook. I'm certain when he came over to London in the first place and found Mike, he realised he could take advantage of him; he used the fact that they were related to rip Mike off in some way, and ended up nearly driving him over the brink.'

'Jed, I promise, there is a perfectly good explanation.'

Jed heard the conviction in Tessa's voice. George had obviously done a thorough job of convincing her of his good intentions. 'Tessa, don't forget, somehow he made Mike change his will in his favour – in England, and I bet you'll find in the States too. And I have to tell you, whatever else he is, or says he is, George Parker is also a drug runner.'

'What!' Tessa's surprise was obviously genuine.

'It's true. His girlfriend in West Virginia told me. And there's a Colombian guy he ripped off out looking for him right now. He even turned up here, for God's sake. If he discovers where George is now, he'll be after him there – and that could put you in danger too.'

'I don't see how. And, frankly, I just don't believe this tale about dealing drugs; probably just the ex-girlfriend dishing out sour grapes. Jed, I appreciate what you're saying, but I need a few days more with him, okay? Please, Jed?'

He gave a long sigh, loud enough for her to hear. 'All right, Tess, if you're sure. But be careful.'

When Jed put the phone down, he felt shattered.

Suddenly, in a complete turnaround, after weeks of seeing George as the fugitive villain, Tessa had let herself be convinced by him and apparently accepted him totally – more than accepted him, by the sound of it. Worse still, despite what Jed had just told her, it seemed she was determined not to lose him.

Jed had promised her he wouldn't come to France until she'd spoken to him again, but he couldn't wait. He picked up the phone and with his next call booked a seat on the morning flight to Marseilles.

★ ★ ★

Jed hired a car from the airport and drove through the afternoon sun to St Rémy.

When he reached the town, he didn't drive straight to La Fleurie but parked his car on the road which ran south, a few hundred yards from the bottom of the narrow, shady track that wound uphill to serve the half-dozen or so large villas there.

Hugging the deep shadows beneath the trees that lined the lane, Jed set off on foot towards Tessa's villa, a mile or so up the quiet lane.

He wasn't sure why he felt she shouldn't have anything to do with this American stranger, who was, it seemed, already so intimately connected with them all. He had thought of nothing else for the last eighteen hours, and had had to consider the possibility that this man might not be the complete monster who had lived in his own imagination for the last few weeks. He was also excited at the prospect of retrieving his money. Even if most of it would find its way to Bernie Capella.

Jed sniffed the air and strode out, admitting to himself that whatever happened, he was going to enjoy the sheer drama of arriving at Tessa's, completely unexpected. It was possible, of course, that she wouldn't be there. But he hadn't wanted to scare George away by announcing his arrival beforehand and he was prepared to take his chances. At worst, if she was out, he could sit and wait and surprise her when she did return.

Since there were so few houses served by the lane, few pedestrians or other vehicles used it. Most of the comings and goings Jed guessed were by gardeners and other domestic staff, who greeted him cheerily enough, assuming, because he was on foot, that he must be one of them.

Fifty yards before he reached the high, wrought-iron double gates that gave on to the grounds of La Fleurie, he stepped round a man kneeling next to a motorbike at the side of the road, wielding spanners and pliers with sporadic curses at the engine.

He carried on and a few moments later was pressing the bell-push set in the stone gatepost, below an iron-work sign announcing 'La Fleurie'.

When he heard the remote-controlled lock click, he pushed the right-hand gate and walked through, remembering from previous visits to push it back behind him.

He strolled down the drive, wondering how Tessa would react, while appreciatively sniffing the herb-scented air. He wished he were here on less disturbing business; he would have enjoyed a few weeks' idleness in Provence.

When he came round the bend, in full sight of the house, he saw that the front door stood open as it often did when the house was occupied, to encourage a fresh breeze to flow through it.

Tessa emerged from the gloom of the interior and stood waiting in the wide porch, amid a vivid red sea of potted flowers.

She struck a tolerant pose, waiting for Jed to reach her before she spoke.

'Well?' she asked, as if his abrupt arrival was quite expected. 'Don't you trust your sister-in-law to make a sound judgement of a man?'

'How many people make sound judgements when their emotions are involved?'

'Oh, well.' She dismissed this with a shrug. 'As you're here, you may as well come in.' She waved him into her house and he followed her through the cool interior and the scent of old wood and pot-pourri.

She made the cup of tea Jed asked for and they sat on the verandah overlooking the back garden and the mountainside beyond. Tessa languidly draped one leg over the side of her chair and rested the other on a lichen-coated wooden table.

Jed had known her long enough to recognise this display of indifference as a heavy disguise for nervousness.

'It's great to see you, Tess, but where is he?'

'What made you think you'd find him here at the house?'

'Your tone on the phone yesterday.'

'You promised you wouldn't come until I rang.'

'I'm sorry, but I had to. You must have known?'

'Yes, I suppose I did.'

Now that Jed was here talking to Tessa in the flesh, his former assumptions were less solid than when they'd spoken on the phone. The light here, and the heat that made the mountains seem to quiver, lent an air of unreality to everything he saw or heard. But he took a reassuring gulp of tea.

'Have you slept with him?'

'I don't think I have to answer that, do I?'

Jed grunted. 'Maybe not to me, but you might have to tell the police.'

'Don't be ridiculous!' Tessa snapped.

Jed took a quick sideways glance at her. 'Listen, don't forget that Mike was killed in a crash just a month after he'd changed his will in favour of George. Now George turns up here, looking for you. If you're telling me that doesn't point the finger at him . . .'

'Okay, it doesn't look good, but that's an awful long way from being able to prove anything definitive. And it's only you who thinks it wasn't an accident, anyway.'

'Well, I'm looking forward to meeting him. Is he due back soon?'

The tension between Tessa and Jed hadn't eased much by the time they heard a car draw up at the gate a few minutes later.

'That must be him,' Tessa said.

'I'll go and let him in.'

'No need, he's got a zapper.'

'Already?'

'I lent him mine.'

Jed got to his feet. 'I'm going to go and introduce myself.'

'No, Jed,' Tessa said quickly, swinging her leg from the table. 'Wait, please.'

He gave her an enquiring look. 'Why?'

'It wouldn't be fair to surprise him.'

Jed ignored her pleas and walked away from her, along the verandah and round the side of the house.

She wanted to run after him and block his way, pleading like a heroine in a silent movie. But she sat still and watched him go.

Jed rounded the side of the house, to be presented with a view of the drive and garden.

He saw Tessa's rented BMW moving slowly and hung back, partially hidden by the luxuriant vegetation. He watched while the driver parked.

Jed saw a man of around his own height, wearing a lemon yellow shirt and loose navy chinos. He had dark hair, a short black beard, and wore Ray-Ban glasses.

The man started to walk towards the house with a light, leisurely stride. There was something strangely familiar about the way he moved; something which seemed to confirm what Megan had told Jed the week before, high on her windswept hillside.

He stepped out on to the stone path that led along the front of the house towards the front door. The man saw him, stopped, and almost took a step back.

Jed spotted the movements – which registered surprise and recognition.

'Hi,' the bearded man said, in an unfamiliar American accent. 'You're Jed, aren't you?'

'Yes. I take it you're George?'

The man nodded, and visibly relaxed as he extended a hand.

After a moment's hesitation, Jed shook it and noted again how uncannily similar the man's gestures were to his dead cousin's. 'I'm glad I've found you at last,' he said. 'I've been halfway across the world looking for you.'

'Tessa told me.'

They were at the front door now. Jed stood back deferentially, allowing the other to enter first. They walked through the house in silence, until they reached Tessa standing in the gloom of the *salon*, whose french windows gave on to the verandah.

'You've met, then,' she said anxiously. 'Great! Let's all have a drink.' She turned to Jed. 'I know you want to sit down and fire off questions but we might as well be civilised about it, don't you think?'

'Of course.' Jed nodded. 'Anyway, I'm sure George understands why I must.'

Tessa fetched glasses and a bottle of champagne from a chiller in the *salon* and carried them outside. 'Let's go and sit under the eucalyptus,' she said brightly and, without waiting for an answer, led them to a fine old wrought-iron table and chairs which had been placed many years before in the natural shade of the tree, but with a clear view of the mountainside to the south.

She filled the glasses as if they were celebrating some achievement or rite of passage in their lives. 'It's great that we're all here,' she said with a vivacity which even delivered with all her skill, somehow failed to convince.

The two men had not exchanged a word since entering the house. Jed picked up his glass and took a slow sip. He looked at the other two in turn.

'Before I say anything else, I should tell you what Megan Powell had to say when I went to see her recently. I don't think she's ever told anyone else what happened in the summer of 1958 – June the twenty-first to be precise.

'She was pregnant and went into labour. She was in a cottage on the family farm, five miles from where she now lives. She'd been looking after the sheep herself because

Ivor, her husband, was away doing his National Service. But she wasn't entirely alone. Her younger sister, Gwynneth had come to stay with her. Gwynneth had run away from home the year before, and ended up living with an American soldier called Henry Parker. But just then, Henry was away from the barracks in Norfolk, on a tour of duty in West Berlin.'

'You're talking about my dad, right?'

'I'm coming to that,' Jed said, and saw the other man grow tense. 'It was particularly poignant that the sisters were together at that moment,' he went on. 'Gwynneth had just been to see the family doctor in Builth Wells. After an examination he'd told her it was unlikely that she'd ever conceive.

'This was really bad news for Gwynneth who was convinced Henry wouldn't marry her if he knew. But all the same, according to Megan, she threw herself into helping with preparations for the baby, which was pretty important, given that Megan was having the child at home, there was no phone and they were at least half an hour from the nearest doctor.

'Because Megan wasn't sure when the baby was conceived, she didn't know exactly when it was due. As a result, she went into labour much sooner than she'd expected. There certainly wasn't time to get the doctor. But at least Gwynneth was there to help. They'd both done their share of lambing all their lives and thought they knew what to do . . .'

'Jed, where exactly is this going?' The anxiety in the strange American voice was temporarily drowned by the high-pitched buzz of a small motorcycle blasting up the lane.

As the sound dwindled, Jed took a deep breath. 'Where was I now? Oh, yes, Megan was about to give birth – which she did, to a handsome bouncing boy.'

'Michael?' Tessa asked.

'Yes, and that was all fine.' Jed paused to look at his audience, to make sure they didn't misunderstand what they were about to hear. 'But then, she found that she had a second baby waiting to be born.'

'What!' Tessa gasped. 'She was carrying twins without realising it?'

'In those days before scans and things, it wasn't unusual. Anyway, the second baby followed ten minutes later, and it was another handsome, bouncing boy. They looked at the two little brothers,' Jed paused to let the idea settle, 'and Megan decided that the second son was a sort of bonus from God – a gift to her barren sister.' Jed took a deep breath. 'Gwynneth was almost overwhelmed by the offer of a son, but she accepted.'

He left the words hanging in the air.

The man opposite him jerked forward in his seat.

'Jesus!' he whispered. 'Are you telling me George was my twin brother?'

The words were uttered in a voice Jed had known for twenty years – the unmistakable Welsh cadence to which Mike always reverted when taken by surprise.

Chapter Twenty-One

For several long seconds, the cicadas croaked more loudly and the eucalyptus leaves above them seemed to hiss as they absorbed the impact of Mike's words.

Jed looked at Tessa who was gazing with dismay at the man beside her.

'Oh, Mike,' she sighed, then spoke to Jed without looking at him. 'I suppose it was too much to hope.' Steadily, she turned to face him.

Jed leaned across the table, and lifted the glasses from the still, bearded face opposite him. 'Mike?' he whispered, looking into familiar bright blue eyes. He glanced back at Tessa and knew the answer to his question before he'd asked it. 'You knew, didn't you?'

She nodded slowly.

Mike turned to her and shook his head. 'But you didn't know George and I were brothers, did you?'

'No,' she declared with a dramatic gesture of her hands. 'But you told me you and George were very similar, so does it really surprise you?'

Mike breathed in deeply and gazed at the distant

mountains. 'God, I don't know! I mean, I knew we were alike but – brothers? Twins!'

'You must have known you were exceptionally alike,' Jed said, 'or how could he have gone to the television studios in your place? I take it that's what happened?'

'Yes, it is.'

'I just don't know what to make of you,' said Jed, still too shocked to take it in. 'I mean, we identified him as you!'

'Actually, Jed, if you remember, it was *I* who identified the body,' Tessa said calmly. 'And no one was going to contradict me.'

'Look, Mike, just start at the beginning and tell me exactly what happened?'

Mike sat back and took a sip of his champagne before clearing his throat.

'Well, you know what a state I was in that evening – I was already drunk when I left Sandown. Not surprising, really – I'd lost half a million quid the week before, then I'd bought those colts for Bernie Capella for close on a million bucks – from myself!'

'And me,' Jed interrupted quietly. 'And I haven't had the money, so Bernie's after me, too.'

'I'll sort that, Jed, I promise. But at the time I must have been crazy. I knew Bernie would go mad when he found out, but I didn't care – I was desperate; in so deep, it was uncharted territory for me.' Mike shrugged. He picked up his glass of champagne again, looked at it, and put it down untasted. 'Then I went to see Tess.' He glanced at her with deep affection. Tessa was looking back at him, a tenderness in her eyes Jed hadn't seen for ten years.

He was almost shocked by the change, but beginning to see how it had been brought about.

'Look, Tessa's heard most of this,' Mike said, turning back to her. 'Shall I tell Jed about it all later?'

'No. He should hear it now. I'll go and sort out dinner.'

She stood, topped up Jed's glass and strode back across the lawn to the house. Mike followed her with his eyes.

Jed glanced at him without speaking. He got to his feet and followed Tessa into the house. He stopped when he reached the french windows and glanced back. Mike hadn't moved; he appeared resigned to the fact that his fate was in their hands.

Jed found Tessa in the kitchen, pretending to busy herself with a chunk of veal.

'Now, hold on,' he said. 'We've got an impossible situation here.'

'I had noticed, Jed.'

'Well, we can't just pretend it'll go away. If the police ever get on to it, God knows what he'll be done for, and we're both involved.'

'We've always been involved in Mike's life, you know that. And there's no way we're bringing the police into it.'

'We may not have a choice,' Jed said. 'But if we're not involving them, we'll have to deal with this ourselves.'

'Jed,' Tessa said with quiet firmness, 'why do we have to do anything?'

He looked at her sharply. 'Bloody hell, Tess! We've got to do something – there's Bernie champing at the bit, and this Colombian guy dead eager to get even. If Mike just carries on being George, he'll end up dead. And what about you,

Tess? What do you want?' he asked. 'To live a complete lie?'

'Okay, Jed, okay. Of course I realise this cocaine merchant George stitched up could reappear at any moment and I don't know what the hell we'll do about that, but you can't expect Mike just to go back to being Mike – I mean, it's not really an option, is it? And as for living a lie – how many people do you think present their true selves to the world? Mike's changed, I know it. He simply isn't the same man who walked out of my house drunk that night.'

'But, Tessa . . .' Jed shook his head, trying to understand how she had arrived at this position. 'He screwed Bernie Capella and got me beaten up as a result.'

'I know, Jed, I know,' she pleaded. 'But I'm sure he'll put it right.'

'I'll believe that when I see it! He's had a month or so to sort things out already.'

'He didn't know that Bernie had rumbled him. He'd ducked right out of sight while the dust settled.'

'Well, it's still stirred up as hell from where I'm standing,' Jed said bluntly, and sighed. 'Listen, I'm going to go and talk to him. I need to know what he thought he was going to achieve. If George's death was an accident pure and simple, as everyone seems to think, then it wasn't Mike's fault, and nothing we can do will bring George back.'

'Whom neither of us knew anyway,' Tessa added.

'All right, but he died doing Mike a favour. I don't know – it's hard to judge what Mike's moral position is.'

'He's in the clear, morally, if you ask me. The money he's got is his own . . .'

'Apart from Bernie's, and the fact that the rest was from

an insurance policy against his own death!'

'I suppose that *would* interest the police.'

'It would interest the insurance company, who would insist that the police got involved.'

'But immoral? I mean, he didn't plan the crash; he just took advantage of it once it had happened.'

'Letting the world believe he'd died? Driving home to change his will? I suppose there aren't any rules for this situation.' Jed sighed. 'I'll have to talk to him, and take it from there.'

Tessa nodded. 'Okay, but don't do anything hasty, please. And remember how it must be for him – and me.'

'So when did Tessa realise it wasn't you who'd been killed?' Jed asked his friend patiently.

'Well, as you know, on the night of the crash, she took away my car keys and gave me a lift to George's place. When I got to the flat, he was waiting, all spruced up and ready for anything. He talked me out of going on live television; knew I'd get into trouble and make a fool of myself. So I told him to go in my place. He wandered off and came back dressed up in the dinner jacket I'd brought with me. I gave him my cuff-links, and the invitation, of course. Anyway, the car came then, I wished him luck and he went. It wasn't as if he went pretending to be me. I mean, we were similar but not identical.'

Mike stopped and looked around him, acknowledging the utter bizarreness of his story, as if challenging the birds which chirruped in the bushes behind him to call him a liar. While, on the mountainside just across the

357

valley, a motorbike spluttered to a halt and magnified the silence that followed.

'This is the strange part,' he went on. 'When I turned on the telly to watch the show, I couldn't see him anywhere, so I thought he must have got cold feet. I was feeling lousy so I forced myself to drink about five pints of water until I nearly threw up, and all the time I'd left the telly on. I was still watching it later when they announced I'd been killed.'

Mike grunted in disbelief. 'I couldn't believe it. That really sobered me up. Of course, I knew at once it was George who'd died, and to begin with was stunned. You see, George had been a real mate, and I still think that – even though I know what he did to me now. But in a strange way, once he'd gone, it was as if he'd never existed – as if he'd never been more than a dream. After all, I'd never set eyes on him four months ago, never knew I had a cousin – let alone a twin brother.

'Then slowly, bit by bit, as it sank in what had happened, I realised that here was the answer to all my problems. Even Bernie Capella wouldn't bother to chase a dead man, and I had insurance policies to pay off my loans to the bank. Plus, on top of that, there was a huge pay-out coming on a life policy I'd taken out years ago. I felt I'd earned it – God knows they'd made me pay premiums way over the odds because of my job.

'As I sat there sobering up, trying not to cry, I realised you rarely get a chance like this – to wipe the slate clean, become a new person.' Mike gave a philosophical chuckle. 'I decided to take mine.'

He leaned back in the cast-iron chair, so that he was out of the shade, and the sun glinted off the unfamiliar, black beard.

'You've been a lucky bastard,' Jed said as he stood up, stretching a little and walking out from beneath the tree. He gazed across the valley, and saw the sun glint off something on the empty hillside.

'Come on, let's take a walk. This is going to take some getting used to.'

Mike nodded and joined him. Jed knew there was a small gate at the top of the garden, between two thick clumps of pampas grass. They let themselves out and started slowly up the hill behind La Fleurie. A breeze rippled past them as they threaded their way among the stately old trees of an abandoned olive grove.

Luis Corozal thrust his hired motorbike beneath some low ground cover.

Crouching down behind a cluster of scrub oaks, he crept down to the valley floor. He crossed the dry gully there and scrambled up the far side until he found himself in view of his target, fifty yards away. He sank back behind a screen of scrubby thorn and opened up a small webbing rucksack and pulled out the automatic Colt he had bought in London and the box of .45 calibre cartridges. They had both arrived for him that morning, two days after he had checked into the small hotel room in St Rémy. He loaded the gun and, dropping on his stomach, crept cautiously from behind his cover.

George Parker may have grown a straggly black beard,

but the disguise did not fool him.

He watched the two men – Parker and the one who had hounded him off the farm near Stow – slowly walk up the hillside through the olive grove, engrossed in conversation.

They were making their way closer to him with every step, until Parker stopped and sat down under a tree. The Englishman joined him, and Luis cursed as they were obscured by intervening bushes and a tumbledown stone wall.

He took the opportunity while he was out of sight to wriggle closer, ignoring the tugging, tearing thorns and spines of arid vegetation, until he was no more than thirty yards from his quarry. But still he couldn't take a shot – not at an obscured target, with only a handgun, at this distance.

And then, after what seemed like an hour, Parker stood up and ambled out into the sunlight, to sit on the crumbling wall.

Luis took his time; his two years in the Colombian army hadn't taught him much, but he had learned that you can only be sure of a good shot if you don't hurry it. And at last, after months of trailing his prey halfway across the world, he had him in his sights. Parker was about to pay his dues.

It would earn Luis nothing, but justice would have been done to him and his family.

As Mike and Jed left the more formal surroundings of La Fleurie's garden and struck out on to the hillside, Jed found, as he had hoped, that the change of scene to this ancient empty landscape prompted Mike to explain.

He cleared his throat. 'Tessa told me you thought the crash wasn't an accident.'

'Did it never occur to you that it may not have been?'

'No. Not at all. There was no way anyone could have planned what happened that night – not with more than the lousiest chance of it working.'

'I suppose that's obvious now I know the truth, but at the time I was convinced George Parker had done it, knowing he'd collect on your will.'

Mike laughed. 'He wouldn't have known about the will because I hadn't even made it by then.'

'I see.' Jed nodded. 'Tolhurst, your lawyer seemed a little surprised by it too. How did you arrange it?'

'Well, once I'd made up my mind what I was going to do, I had to get back to Easerswell as soon as possible. The trouble was, my car was still parked in Tessa's street, and she had the key.' Mike turned to Jed with a sardonic grin. 'So I had to decide there and then if I could bring her in on it. I mean, I knew how much Tessa always liked a melodrama, and took a punt on her not being able to resist the idea, especially as I was almost stone cold sober by then and absolutely clear about what I had to do.' He gave a short laugh. 'And, thank God, she went for it! Once she was over the shock of seeing me on her doorstep when she'd just been told I was dead, she threw herself into the part.'

'So you'd already been to Margaretta Terrace before I turned up?'

'I was still there when you arrived, and when you and she went off to identify my body.

'I'd told Tessa what to expect. She knew she'd find

somebody who looked quite like me.'

'What was he really like – this twin of yours?'

Mike sat down on a comfortably rounded, exposed root of the mighty barren olive beneath which they were standing. He shook his head mournfully. 'A con man. I couldn't believe it when I first discovered how he'd ripped me off. I'd trusted him like a brother, you see, without knowing he was my twin.'

Jed sat down beside Mike, but could barely hear the whispered words.

'For God's sake,' Mike went on in his normal voice, 'he *was* my brother – my own twin. I can't believe what he tried to do to me.'

Jed sensed a huge relief in Mike at being able to talk about it all.

'I'm sure he never knew you were brothers. No one ever did, except your mother and Gwynneth – and she wouldn't have told him. How did he say he found you?'

Mike was looking at the ground, making a pattern in the dusty earth with the heel of his boot. He glanced up bleakly and gazed at the craggy peaks of the mountains rising on the south side of the narrow valley.

'When he first came, he said he'd seen my name and picture in the racing pages. But later, after he'd been over in England a month or so and we'd become good mates – or so I thought – he told me it was you who'd triggered the whole thing.'

'Me?' Jed grunted in astonishment. 'What the hell did I have to do with it?'

'You saw him – at Blue Grass Field, that time when you

went over for the sales in January. You thought he was me, and called over to him. He wasn't too sure who it was, so he ignored you – but he heard you all right, and saw you. He realised you'd mistaken him for me, but didn't think about it too much then. His girlfriend had come to pick him up.'

'Good God! That was George Parker? And Dianne – I knew I'd seen her before.'

'Yeah.' Mike nodded. 'And it was just after that he saw a piece in *Hello!* and a picture of me and Tessa. He told me he'd always had a vague memory of things his mother had told him, before she died. He was only five then, but always remembered she'd said they had relatives in the UK called Powell. I suppose it looked to him like a good inside chance to con some money out of a rich, successful jockey.

'Of course, when he first came over, he gave me some story about how he'd heard about me in England, but he admitted to me later it was the *Hello!* shot that really got him started. When he realised how skint I was, he talked me into a deal to save myself . . .' Mike gave a short, bitter laugh. 'He got me to hock the house to raise the money for it. When I "died", I was damn' glad they'd made me take out a separate life policy to cover the loan so Tessa could have the place without any bother.'

'But he wasn't the only one guilty of opportunism, was he?' Jed said slowly.

'Listen, Jed, I don't know what's going to happen now – it's all up to you really.' Mike looked at him remorsefully. 'And I'm sorry for the trouble you've had over Bernie, and the other guy who was after George. I promise I didn't want anything to happen to you. I was so close to getting where I wanted, though I suppose I always half-knew you'd find out sooner or later.'

'But what made you think you could go on conning people for ever? Making them believe you weren't Mike?'

He sighed and shook his head. 'In a way, I *am* someone else, both inside and out. You know, while George was around, I learned a lot about the different ways a personality can be projected; and I realised I could put all the bad stuff behind me, and I vowed to be a better person from then on.'

Jed was finding the new Mike hard to believe. 'Okay, but tell me what you did after Tessa and I went to the mortuary?'

Mike looked at him with a faint smile. 'It was the strangest feeling – seeing you go off like that to identify me – but I knew there'd be no problem. I was quickly getting used to the idea and there was no way I was going to back out. For a start, there was this currency deal that had gone wrong. George had sucked me into buying millions of Japanese yen. I thought I'd sorted it when I sold those colts to Bernie Capella. But then I heard that his boys were on to it and Bernie wasn't amused – he was threatening to kill me if I didn't give his money back.

'I didn't believe it, and anyway I hadn't got the money. After he'd told me just to get on and buy the horses, I hardly thought he'd notice if they weren't exactly Shergar. I mean, there's thousands of people every day buying very expensive racehorses which never perform – look at that colt the Arabs bought. Thirteen million bucks and never saw a racetrack, for God's sake! And those two I sold

Bernie weren't badly bred . . .'

'What are you talking about, Mike? They were a couple of yaks. You were lucky to find a trainer prepared to take them into his yard at any price.'

'All right,' he conceded. 'Bernie's been after you, I know, and you haven't had the cash yet. I'll make sure he gets his money back. The trouble is the money from the sales went into my special account in the Bahamas, and it'll take a bit of time for me, as George, to get my hands on it.'

'But what have you been living on if George was broke and the lawyers haven't released your inheritance?'

'There's what you might call a nice irony to that. Of course, as George Parker, I had access to all his accounts . . .'

'And what was in them?' Jed pressed.

'So far as I could tell, most of the money I'd given him to pay for the yen. He told me I wasn't a big enough player to do it under my own name and that I'd have to do it through his account. So I made out my cheques to him – and I saw from his bank statements that he'd just hung on to the money himself. I guess he knew the yen was going to tumble and sent me phoney letters from the bank telling me my margin money had all been used up.' Mike shook his head indignantly. 'If the yen hadn't collapsed I suppose he'd have just disappeared with my money anyway.'

'You didn't already know he had, before he was killed, did you?'

'No, of course not. But like I said – when he was, it looked like a perfect way out. I was really sobered up by the time you and Tess left, so I put on George's big glasses and brushed my hair forward, the way he did. I went out, found my car and drove down to Easerswell. I wrote a back-dated will and left it in the desk for the lawyers to find. Of course, when I found most of my money for the forex deal still in George's account, I didn't have to be in too much of a hurry to get my hands on what I'd left to him.'

Jed stood up, juggling the bizarre truth and the emotions in his head, while he tried to make up his mind what he should do next.

The only people who knew that the man in front of him was Mike Powell – not George Parker – were himself, Mike, and Tessa.

He still could not really believe that Tessa wanted Mike back now. He was doubtful, too, that she would, or could, keep the truth to herself for the rest of her life. Besides, Jed had to ask himself, was it right that Mike should go free? Did he deserve it?

Mike sensed his dilemma and smiled uncertainly as he pulled a cigar from his pocket. He put it between his teeth and struck a match to light it, sucking in a long draught of aromatic smoke. He stood up, like Jed, to stretch his legs and walked out from under the tree into the bright sunlight to sit on the remains of a low stone wall which had once enclosed the olive grove. He smoked silently for a few moments before turning to look at Jed.

'Well?' he asked impatiently, trying to read his friend's expression. 'Who are you going with back to La Fleurie? Mike Powell or George Parker?'

Jed sighed and leaned back against the thick, flaking trunk of the old olive.

Slowly, a wide smile spread across Mike's face and Jed found his own lips twitching in reply.

A shot echoed around the narrow valley.

They froze for the microsecond before Mike's body, hit in the abdomen, jerked and spun like a demented puppet and crashed over the wall on to some scrubby bushes beyond.

Jed watched – bewildered – seeing it all at quarter speed until the dust and silence had settled.

Heedless of where or why the shot had been fired, he ran towards Mike and scrambled through fallen stones to his bloody body lying draped across a thorn tree. Profound silence followed, broken by sporadic harsh cicada trills and the rustle of olive leaves in the hot breeze.

Jed gulped for breath, dusty air rasping his throat. He gazed, horrified, at the circle of blood on Mike's back, spreading steadily over the pale yellow shirt, then gagged and looked away.

Through the shimmering air, above the chittering of the crickets, the sound of a police siren reached him.

He wondered vaguely why they had come so soon. But he had another, more pressing problem.

The silence was shattered again – by a second shot.

Luis had squeezed the trigger slowly and with deliberation. The report echoed in front and behind, reaching him for the third time after his target had jolted into the air and over the stone wall, while Luis watched, fascinated, satisfied as the first spurt of blood was loosed from the man's chest.

And he fired again, at the Englishman.

This time, he missed. He didn't know why, but he knew he didn't have a second chance. He didn't mind. The Englishman's death would only have been a bonus – a loose end tied up.

While the shots still echoed, and his targets dealt with their pain and confusion, he heard the sirens. He got to his feet, hunched low and raced down the hill, across the dry river bed and up the far side until he reached his motorbike. He was quivering with excitement. His pulse began to race until he thought it would burst. He heaved his bike from the bushes and drove it wildly down the rocky track to the valley floor.

Jed dived for cover behind the stone wall seconds after the bullet had passed. He stared at the point where it had struck the ground – a small plume of dust still floated three yards from where he lay – listening to the siren, and the sound of a motorbike, kicked into life a little way across the valley.

'Jed . . .'

The harsh, breathless whisper made Jed spring to his feet. He clambered quickly back to his friend. 'Mike!' he gasped. 'Thank God!'

'Jed, for Christ's sake, the police mustn't find me . . .' His voice trailed off doubtfully.

'No, they mustn't,' Jed said slowly as the siren drew closer.

He guessed he had a couple of minutes. He bent forward and lifted Mike from under his arms, and heaved him round, draping him like a bulky stole over one shoulder, and carrying him back through the irregular pattern of olive trees, until the weight and the heat were too much and he had to stop.

Jed deposited Mike against the bole of a tree where he propped him as straight as he could. But Mike slouched sideways at forty-five degrees. He opened his eyes; his mouth tightened in pain. Blood seeped unchecked through the fabric of his ragged shirt. A moan escaped his white lips.

Jed stood, watched and listened to the siren. The police car was coming by the road from St Rémy to Les Baux; it should have turned off to the left by now, into the narrow dusty lane up to La Fleurie.

But the pitch of the wailing ebbed and with a surge of relief Jed realised it was receding. For a few seconds, he stood and breathed deeply to release the tension that racked his body while the dwindling sound was overwhelmed by silence once more.

'Jed?' There was more depth to Mike's voice this time, and he lay with his eyes closed, breathing gently now.

'How is it, Mike?'

'Not good.'

'The police have gone; they weren't coming for us.'

'That's great.' Mike gave a short grunt of laughter. The pain it triggered made him wince. 'But if I don't get to a hospital soon, I'm going to die,' he said simply.

Jed looked at the familiar blue eyes and the new black beard.

'Jed, I'm so sorry,' Mike whispered. 'I wish I hadn't

started all this.' He groaned again. 'But I wanted Tessa back so badly . . .' He took a deep breath and slowly turned his head. 'I don't want to die.'

Jed looked at him and shook his head slowly.

'I think I'd better get you to hospital. If George Parker dies, Tessa will never forgive me.'

Chapter Twenty-Two

'What's he like then, this new boyfriend of Tessa's?' Lucy asked, studying Jed's profile. He was driving the Range Rover, skirting Cambridge on the way to Newmarket.

'Oddly enough he rather reminds me of Mike, except he's much gentler and infinitely more charming,' Jed said after due consideration.

'Well, it's great that Tessa's found a man. I'm really looking forward to meeting him.'

'I very much doubt we'll be seeing much of them. Tessa's decided she's going to base herself in Provence and Mauritius from now on. She's selling Easerswell, and probably her place in London too.'

'I suppose she wants to be domiciled off-shore and not pay any tax,' Lucy observed drily.

'You're such a cynic,' Jed chided her. 'I don't think it's that. Anyway,' he said, quickly changing the subject, 'only two hours to go and you'll be jumping up on Panpipe. How're you feeling?'

'What do you think?'

'Sorry you had breakfast?'

She laughed. 'Mostly. I just hope I can hold her.'

'I don't think that'll be a problem; the race won't be run very subtly – more "go like hell" than waiting tactics. Just sit against her and let her find her own pace.'

Lucy grinned broadly at the prospect. 'I feel like I'm going in for my first gymkhana.' She put a hand on his shoulder and squeezed, so that he felt it through the cotton jacket he was wearing. 'I'm only sorry she won't be running in your colours this time.'

'I don't mind,' Jed said. 'So long as she runs well.'

'Are things still pretty sticky on the stud?'

'I think I can weather it.'

He didn't disclose the immense relief he'd felt at the removal of the threat posed by Bernie Capella's wounded pride. Mike had produced the money for Jed to return to him, the colts were to be sold in America without reserve at the next suitable sale.

When they reached the racecourse at Newmarket, as soon as Jed had parked the Range Rover, Lucy leaned over, planted a quick kiss on his left cheek and rushed off to take her kit bag to the changing room.

Jed gathered up his binoculars and followed more slowly. He noticed that he had parked beside a small car, identical to the one he'd found in the ditch the night he'd chased the intruder from Batscombe. Inevitably, he thought of Luis Corozal.

For the few days after Mike had been hit, he and Jed had lived with the possibility that the Colombian might have realised Mike hadn't been killed. But there had been no sign of him, and they concluded that from Corozal's perspective,

George Parker had been shot and retribution extracted. Jed had left Mike in hospital in St Rémy certain that they'd seen the last of the Colombian.

Jed strolled on round to the stables to see Panpipe. As soon as he saw the filly, he knew she was in season. He could always tell from the slight change in her attitude. It must have come on overnight. She had been her normal, ebullient self when she'd left Batscombe the previous evening.

His immediate reaction was to withdraw her from the race. Running would do her no harm, but she simply wouldn't concentrate and give of her best.

Then he remembered, she wasn't his to withdraw.

And besides, there was Lucy to think of.

Cath, who had come with Panpipe, came into the stable and stood beside him.

'She's . . .'

'Yes,' Jed cut in, 'I know.' He shrugged his shoulders. 'It's too bad, but Lucy'll still get a good run out of her.'

'Are you going to tell her?'

'And give her a ready-made excuse? No way!'

Catherine grinned. 'She's a good sort, Lucy is, and a fair rider.'

Jed smiled to himself. This was serious praise.

Most of the spectators were surprised that the race was so hard fought, but only the most competitive female jockeys would submit themselves to the rigorous training required to put in a halfway competent performance in this very public event.

There were a lot of points to be scored, and a lot of work was put in to persuade trainers to let some of their best horses run.

Panpipe was on top form, Jed knew, and he didn't doubt that Lucy was fit enough.

But Jed knew before they went down that they were outclassed by two animals who had run in listed races.

That didn't stop him hoping and praying right up to the line, when Panpipe and Lucy were the third to cross it.

Jed carried on watching Lucy through his binoculars as she eased the filly back to a trot, leaning forward to pummel her neck as if she'd just won the Oaks.

He was pleased for her, but couldn't deny a sudden surge of regret that he'd lost this, the best of all the horses he had ever bred himself.

For despite the handicap of being excitable and in season, the horse had run a dazzling race – as good as her top performance, and carrying a stone and a half in dead, lead weight to compensate for Lucy's diminutive frame.

'Good,' Jed heard Geoffrey Thynne mutter.

Lucy's father was beside him in the stand, lowering his glasses. 'That filly'll win again on the flat, with a real pilot on her.'

Jed laughed. 'I thought Lucy rode brilliantly.'

'And so she did, for an amateur. Sorry you don't get any of the owner's prize money.'

'Oh, well,' Jed said. 'I'll live.'

In the winners' enclosure, Jed watched with trepidation as

Lucy approached. He saw her slide off her horse's back as if in slow motion. He knew that in a few moments, she would fling her arms around him, and hug him and kiss him; he knew that wouldn't be unpleasant; but he was unsure all the same.

He closed his eyes and thought of Sammy, gentle and thoughtful, sitting on his hospital bed after a fall, softly stroking his brow.

He thought of earlier times in their marriage, when they had made love with such tenderness in the meadows down by the Windrush at Batscombe.

And suddenly, Lucy's special scent was in his nostrils, and he felt her hands caress his neck as she slid her arms behind his head, and stretched up to kiss him on the lips.

Kindly, tenderly, patiently, she didn't allow her lips to linger; almost before they had touched his, she withdrew them and curved them into a gleeful smile. 'Oh, Jed, thank you so much!'

'Don't thank me, thank Panpipe,' he laughed.

'I already have.' Lucy grinned. 'I almost got a reprimand for beating her, I was patting her so hard when we came back in.'

She took her hands from behind his neck and stood back to give him a cryptic look. 'I hear she's going to be half yours again.'

'What?'

Geoffrey Thynne was beside them now, having relinquished the filly to Catherine. 'Yes,' he said. 'I've told Weatherbys to mark you down for a half share in the horse, to run in your colours from now on.'

Until he felt his own jaw almost fall from its socket, Jed had never really believed it could happen. For a moment, he stood with his mouth open, until, abruptly realising what he must look like, he snapped it shut and tried to think of some words of thanks.

'But . . . er . . . er . . .' he jabbered. 'But Geoffrey . . .'

'You sold her too cheap, and despite public opinion, I'm an honest man. Besides, Lucy insisted, and I still haven't worked out a way to resist her. I doubt that you will, in time.'